New and re[vised]
of an outstanding literary ✏ **W9-BDL-690**

THE BOOK OF MAMIE
Winner of the 1988 AWP Novel Award

Praise for
Duff Brenna

THE BOOK OF MAMIE

"There is much to be admired in Duff Brenna's ambitious first novel. A work of varied textures and unusual richness, it has an energy that catches hold from the very first sentence...A risky, graceful book." —*New York Times Book Review*

"*The Book of Mamie* is of epic proportions—a great big novel, filled with mystery, humor, power, kindness and wonder...Brenna writes consciously in the American tradition, invoking Mark Twain's *Hucklberry Finn* in both the voice and the story. There are echoes as well of Melville's *Moby Dick* and Willa Cather's *My Antonia*, along with a hint of Flannery O'Connor. The allusions work, and Brenna is in good company with the great literary voices to whom he pays homage...It is as radiant and welcome as first novels get." —*San Francisco Chronicle*

"While this work may be a modern-day *Tom Sawyer*, it is also a *Pilgrim's Progress* that surveys each experience for knowledge, truth and some distinction between right and wrong...The nonstop action pulls the reader from one escapade to another through a book peopled with eccentric characters and suffused with Barthian surrealism...In short, the story is deceptive in its complexity. On one level it can be read as a lusty, action-filled romp. But it deserves a second reading to mine the riches that were missed the first time around." —*San Diego Union*

"Big, courageous, and it *sprawls*...If you relish the idea of curling up in your favorite chair and being carried away by a strong tide of marvelous words spoken by unforgettable characters telling a great, galumphing story, *The Book of Mamie* is for you. Duff Brenna is an American treasure." —*The Bloomsbury Review*

"*The Book of Mamie* is a mix of growing-up story and American folktale, its narrator reminiscent of Huck Finn in his wily innocence. Mamie herself is a finely exaggerated Paul Bunyan figure, stronger than any man or woman and superior in her insouciance as well." —Toby Olson

"John Beaver is truly a force of evil, a father to bring daytime nightmares to a child's mind; the kind of man who skins a mink alive and listens to it scream, who has the physical power of any 10 men and brings down upon those around him chaos, violent death and suffering. Mamie has grown up under this monster, both literally and figuratively." — *Small Press Review*

THE HOLY BOOK OF THE BEARD

"Duff Brenna is emerging as a formidable literary presence...The sheer energy and humanity of *The Holy Book of the Beard*...leave the reader eagerly awaiting Brenna's next act." —*Milwaukee Journal Sentinel*

"Loaded with all the ingredients of an underground classic, engrossing and uproarious, it is nearly impossible to put down...More important, though, Mr. Brenna writes with an honesty and vigor that makes his characters and his vision matter." —*New York Times*

TOO COOL

Too Cool is an unfaltering, unflinching, piercing look into a tormented youthful heart; it is finely modulated both in style and moral tone and provokes a hard-won sort of compassion at the end."—*New York Times*

Brenna has created a poignant portrait of an antisocial youth bent on violence and self destruction... Pacing his narrative with the suspense of a thriller, Brenna writes grippingly and with uncanny insight into the mind and heart.. — *Publishers Weekly*

...a rich, original ride.— *San Francisco Chronicle*

THE ALTAR OF THE BODY

""The Altar of the Body" is a moving meditation on the dissipation of youth and our raw need for intimacy and love. —*New York Times*

Brenna's examination of the obsession with youth and looks demonstrates how easy it is to choose the appearance rather than the reality of health and success. Grounded in reality, the novel brings George, Mikey, Joy, and Livia to life in every passionate detail. —*Booklist*

"Crystal-clear writing...Brenna sees his larger-than-life creations with an unflinching eye, but also with measures of love." —*The Washington Post*

"Duff Brenna is a master at capturing the helplessness of humans, particularly humans with 'tough' written all over them." —*Los Angeles Times*

"An artfully written, evil and eerie novel...Magnificent." —*Chicago Tribune*

The Book of Mamie

Other Books by Duff Brenna

The Holy Book of the Beard
Too Cool
Altar of the Body
The Willow Man

THE BOOK OF
mamie

A novel by

Duff Brenna

WORDCRAFT OF OREGON LLC

2006

What follows is a work of the imagination. Without exception, every character and event is fictitious. Any resemblence to persons or events, living or dead, is entirely coincidental.

Wordcraft of Oregon, LLC
David Memmott, Editor/Publisher
P.O. Box 3235
La Grande, OR 97850
www.wordcraftoforegon.com

Cover Design by Kristin Johnson, redbat design.
Cover art based on original oil paintings by Alice Maud Guldbrandsen and digitally collaged by David Memmott in Adobe Photoshop 6.0.

Printed in the United States of America on acid-free paper
by McNaughton & Gunn.

For Nancy Rae

Introduction

It is no wonder that Duff Brenna's *The Book of Mamie* was lavished with rave reviews all over America when it appeared in 1989—east to west, north to south, in virtually every major and many minor newspapers.

It is no wonder that *The Book of Mamie* won the coveted, national Best Novel Award of the Associated Writing Programs (AWP).

And no wonder that its readers find it a gateway to a New World, vast and exciting.

The wonder is that it was allowed to go out of print after its second edition sold out and while people were still buying it.

The wonder is that it has remained out of print for fifteen years.

For *The Book of Mamie* is, itself, a wonder.

Anyone who ever dreamed that Mark Twain might be reincarnated to tell us an American story of our times can have his wish fulfilled right here. Any American woman who ever snorted skepticism at Paul Bunyan, thinking, It's the women who were the giants, who had the real muscle—well, Mamie is your girl. As her narrator, Christian Peter Foggy, puts it, "If Orphan Annie and Paul Bunyan had had a daughter, I figured something like Mamie would be the consequence. Mamie Bunyan... Tinkerbell with a gland problem..." *Uberfraulein.* First Saint of the Church of Mamie.

Or anyone who wishes old Steinbeck could have given us one more of his best or who has read through all of Dickens and yearned that he might come back as an American, or that a new American Dostoevski might appear with a heartlands, tall-tale sense of humor—here they are, ladies and gents, reborn in a guy who has lived the life: dairy farmer, juvenile delinquent, paratrooper, gantry operator, truckdriver and award-winning professor of literature, all in one.

Duff Brenna *is* American literature, and all our great writers inform his heart and his talent, though he is quite himself as well. He could make a dyed-in-the-wool New York City boy like myself yearn for the midwest and swear it truly is the real heart of the heart of our country.

The Book of Mamie makes you remember what a great novel is, a wild exciting read, a book that opens your eyes with wonder, that every twenty pages or so makes you jump up and walk a circle on the rug just to cool down enough to keep going. This is not art about art or the vague posturings of a writer reaching for a lacey metaphor; this is a great big, awe-inspiring, wonder-inspired story about American people in the heartlands.

Here you'll find characters who step off the page into your life—or grab you from your easy chair and drag you into theirs: the fire-breathing John Beaver who would scare the proverbials off a brass monkey; old Jacob Foggy, the malapropic half-wise patriarch with his foggy wisdom; Kritch'n Foggy desperate to understand so he can teach that understanding, pummeled by jealous brothers and face to face with a moral choice that sets him on a merry chase from hell; and of course, Mamie Beaver herself, a benevolent pagan goddess innocent, idiot savant, who fishes with her nipples for bait and crackles with electricity.

The paradise of the American wilderness is born again here—fruit and game, rivers and green shelters, wild onions, roots and berries, streams and lakes full of fish. Here is an original American picaresque road show, complete with giants and mad preachers, creaky out-back diner philosophers who hypnotize you with the truth and steal your money, crotchety railway men and sumo-sized ne'er do-well seekers of Art who weep at a drop of blood, rifle-mad killer farmers, hunter taxidermists crazy as Norman Bates, good country people and bad country people and all manner of people, farmers who practice a religion based on Shakespeare, a whole town of Mamieites worshipping Melville and Shakespeare in conflict with the Christers, Church of J.C. vs Church of Hoomanity, suffering Catholics who worship pain, broken-backed workers felled by Hurry UpMoney, and an aging hot mama who thinks everyone is trying to peek up her dress—not to mention a cow named Jewel who'll steal your heart and a golden lab named Emma so real you long to scratch her ears and you'd swear you really saw her dance beneath the moon in a snowy field... There are book burnings, sex and violence, incest and murder, fear and joy and the thunder of God, and heroes more innocent than rogues pounding along on their feet of clay, a cast of characters who would make Dickens and Twain sit up and salute: John and Mamie Beaver, Kiss of Death Cody, Mongoose Jim, Charlie Friendly the barman, Phoebe Bumpus, two-tonned Don Shepard, Teddy Snowdy, Robbie Peevey, railroad Amoss, thick-necked Bob Thorn, Blind Venus the hoochy-coochy carnie girl, Anna and Soren Gulbrenson and their feisty little Pekingnese riding herd on them all, and all the Foggy's—Jacob and his sons, Christian, Cash, Cush, Calvin, Calah and Cutham and their sister, Mary Magdalene...

Brenna knows the people and he knows the land, knows how it's been used and abused, he knows the machines and the scams used to work it, knows the animals and the plants and trees and fields, knows about harvest and silage, harrowing and plantings, he knows how the color of paint on a farmhouse will respond to the change of seasons, and he knows what people do and have done, and he tells us everything he knows and has learned and shows us his America in a language uniquely American, beautiful as the summer sky over a wild wood lake, soddy as the earth, snowy as a deep-winter pine forest, tender as fresh alfalfa in a cow's maw, exciting as a car chase on a country road...

Anyone who has read the great American writers—the ones with strong blood beating in their veins, Twain and Faulkner and Steinbeck, Melville and Whitman and London and Sinclair Lewis, all of them—will hear their spirit humming again in these pages, fueling Brenna on. And those who have *not* read them will discover a glimpse of them in the spirit of this *new* great American writer, Duff Brenna.

Praise to David Memmott and his Wordcraft of Oregon press

for putting this American classic back within the reach of people hungering for a great read.

Enter this novel, ladies and gents, and prepare to laugh and to weep, to chuckle, gasp and pause to think. Prepare to meet America. More: prepare to be amazed!

Dr. Thomas E. Kennedy,
Farleigh Dickenson University, *The Literary Review*
Copenhagen, Denmark, 2006

Do I contradict myself?
Very well then I contradict myself,
(I am large, I contain multitudes.)

—Walt Whitman, "Song of Myself"

Drowd'n Man

Mamie Beaver, she had to come from the moon. Or maybe even the stars. One star, big and fat and fiery. First one at night, star light, star bright. It just seemed that way, seemed natural—more natural that that she was John Beaver's daughter. Except that she had his size, she didn't look a thing like him. They were opposites. They were like two forces of nature, two winds coming from opposite directions, two mountains breeding landslides, two oceans battling it out, making storms like the Atlantic and the Pacific dueling at Cape Horn.

Mamie Beaver, head like a proud pumpkin, a froggish ear-to-ear smile. Retarded Mamie Beaver? Brain of a five-year-old? Quiet and slow-moving body, with arms held straight down, fingers rigid, like Frankenstein's monster. She was a farmer's daughter, and she was his mule. Her strength was legend throughout northern Wisconsin. Her father would loan her out for harvest work, and it was said she earned him enough in season so that he didn't have to keep but a pig and a steer and a dozen milk cows, together with his garden, and that was enough for the two of them to live at Bulls-Knoll independent of the world.

We were farmers too, but there were nine of us altogether, with Mama and Pa and six boys and one girl, so we never had any cause to hire Mamie. She was just GIRL, the myth-legend kind, like the Amazons or Wonder Woman. We'd heard stories about her all our lives, and Pa used those stories to put us in our place once in a while, especially if we whined about something he wanted us to do, like putting up bales—a thousand bales in the field, each one weighing fifty to sixty pounds—and having to get them in because rain was expected overnight. "Oh," he'd say, "don't trouble your puny selves. Mamie'll be by soon and show you how it's done." None of us could stand the thought—a balloon-headed Beaver coming to add notches to her reputation at our expense— the hay always got up without Mamie.

Back in the days near the end of 1949, she had hopped aboard the school bus each morning and rode with us to Cloverland. They put her in first grade with me. I had just turned six and she was already ten or eleven years old, looking like fifteen or twenty. There was some law forcing John Beaver to give her another try at schooling. He had pulled her out of school when her mama died, but now he had no choice but to let her go again. She was a flop right away, though. I mean she couldn't even learn her ABCs.

In any case, for the few weeks that Mamie went to school, she and I became friends. I did my best to teach her something, sitting with her in the back of the bus and writing the ABCs over and over on her tablet, while she watched, fascinated, a trickle of drool running from her mouth sometimes. Which I would wipe off using her sleeve or her collar. But then she would forget. And down it would come, a watery thread. Chin glistening and her slow voice stammering, "A-yay . . . Bee-yce . . . Cee-yee . . ." And that's as far as she would get, and sometimes in frustration I smacked the tablet over her head and called her stupid, stupid, stupid. She always smiled and nodded when I called her stupid. Yeah, she understood; she got that part.

At school we called her Horsy and rode about saddled to her hips, yelling for her to giddy up. She liked it. She would neigh and cry, "Hippa-weee!" and snort and race across the schoolyard, clicking her tongue against the roof of her mouth, making the clippety sound of a galloping horse. There was no wearing her out. We stood in line, elbowing to get a turn at her. But other than at recess, everyone pretty much ignored her, including the teachers, except when they would watch us spurring her and get so excited they would holler, "Haw, Mamie, haw!" and look as though they would ride her themselves.

Then one morning, as the bus was climbing the Bulls-Knoll

road, someone yelled for us to look-see. We all jammed our noses against the windows to see Mamie racing down the Beaver driveway, her arms flailing the air like penguin wings, trying to get the bus to stop. And running behind her, waving for the bus to go on was John Beaver. He managed to tackle her before she reached the mailbox, and the last we saw he was sitting on top of her, rapping his knuckles on her head and yelling something we couldn't hear.

I missed her a lot at first, but then she just faded from my thoughts the way things do, to be brought out for a second or two whenever Pa mentioned her, or when we heard some story of her bending horseshoes or throwing a steer or throwing hay bales around like they were basketballs.

Ten years passed before I saw her again. She had run away from John Beaver. It was a surprise to everyone because none of us thought she would ever be smart enough to figure out that running away from him was exactly what she needed to do. One Sunday near noon, I was at the Brule, leaning against a log, my line and bobber in the water, having no luck and not minding at all. Warm June sat on my chest, and everywhere round about was the scent of pine and slow water. Trees guarded me on both sides of the river. I felt safe and glued to life and the land, like something immortal—one of the Elect. I had decided to become a teacher when I grew up, and I had until milking time to dream of how successful and famous I would be, so mind-penetrating an intellect that no one could resist learning from me. I would always know the right things to say to reach the most stubborn or slow-witted minds, and I would know so much about everything in the world that no one could ask a question to stump me. So my fame would spread far and wide, across the country and around to the far sides of China. Statues would be erected in my honor. Biographies would be written about my humble beginnings and my rise to greatness and my unbelievable genius. And schools throughout every state would fight for the right to be called CHRISTIAN PETER FOGGY SCHOOL. My portrait would hang in the entrance halls. Mothers would point to my picture and tell their children how grand I was, and how they prayed that their own little ones would follow in my footsteps. "Remember humble Christian Foggy," the mothers would say whenever the children refused to study. Even my own mother would tell at the interviews that she'd never dreamed I was so special. But Pa would say he knew, because Pa knows everything. Ah, it was wonderful to me on the bank of the Brule that day to be almost sixteen and to have such a large future stretching in front of me.

Then, in the midst of my dreaming, there she was, sudden as an earthquake, lumbering toward me and blotting out the sun. The same though slightly altered Mamie Beaver—taller, broader, with bosoms, large ones, like fists in boxing gloves. Her nose was the same, full of freckles out to her ears, and her nostrils, wide as thumbtips, quivered as she breathed. A wide, thin mouth with upturned corners, like a jack-o'-lantern with big horse-style teeth; flat eyes, like an astonished fish; the same moon-round face with its cap of Orphan Annie hair. Mamie Beaver, the runaway. John Beaver was so furious to have her back he had offered a thirty-dollar reward.

She squatted in front of me. Dollar signs danced in front of my eyes. Thirty bucks for her! She stared at me, solemn as a bluegill. I stared back. For a time it was a standoff. Then she looked away and started searching through the brush and grass around her. She found a wild onion and pulled it up, rubbed it on her pants, and ate it. "Um um um," she said, and she pulled another onion up and handed it to me. I brushed it on my jeans and ate it. "Um um um," I said back to her. And I said, "You probably can't remember me, huh? Been near ten years since I seen you."

Her mouth and chin worked away at what she wanted to tell me, moving up and down and side to side like rubber turned loose in a ticklish wind, trying to clamp down on the words and form them into syllables that would fall out just right. Finally she managed to stammer, "Yaay, I mmmm-member." I asked her what my name was.

And she said, "Kritch'n," and poked my chest.

"That's good," I said. I was amazed she knew me after so many years, and I told her she was smarter than people thought she was.

"Smma-art," she replied, grinning, tapping her forehead.

"And do you know your ABCs yet?"

She nodded her head like she was pounding nails with it. "Yaay!" she told me.

"Well, let me hear them," I told her.

Her chin went up. She looked at the sky as if the letters were printed there, and she started out, "Aaa-yay, bee-yee, cee-yee." Then she stopped and sucked her finger. Her eyes studied the trees or birds or the empty spot where *d* was supposed to be.

Finally she reached across without looking at me and took up my arm, giving it a squeeze. "B-b-bony," she said. I was bony all right, meatless angles from head to foot, but I didn't appreciate her reminding me.

"Yeah? Well, you're fat as a cow!" I told her.

She leaped up like she was spring-loaded and cried out, "Hippa-weee!" and pointed to her back. I remembered the playground, the riding her up and down. I climbed into the saddle of her hips and wrapped my fingers in her fiery red hair. "Haw!" I yelled, and off she flew down the shoreline, a hundred yards or so and back again, clicking her tongue, neighing and snorting. She was panting a little and had lathered around her lips, but there had been no quit in her. Beneath me had been that same sure power I had felt before. I swatted her bottom and told her she was a treasure.

"Yaay!" she said, nodding in agreement. Then taking me up in her arms, she smashed me spread-eagled and breathless against her in a killing hug.

"You're killin me," I croaked.

"I f-fix him f-fish!" she cried.

She let me drop and ran to my line, pulling it from the water and unpinning the bobber, stripping the salmon eggs off the hook. And from her pocket she produced a piece of Velveeta cheese. Then she pulled up another wild onion, chewed it, spit the juice over the cheese and molded it around the hook. It looked like a pale orange pearl. She gave a short cast and let the line drift under in the current.

In less than five minutes she caught two fat trout. Which I am not partial to. Trout can be gamy sometimes. Upriver with the fish, following a path through the woods we went, until we came to a meadow surrounded by trees and layered with dandelions and timothy, the dandelions blooming, creating yellow diadems woven through pale green hair. And some had gone to seed, the seed drifting fairy-like through the moist air, and insects flew up sizzling. There was a woody, grassy aroma, thick in the warm sun, exhaling peace and the quiet breathing of neighboring pine.

Tucked in a corner at the edge of some trees was an old cabin. Fresh red clay chinking shone between some of the logs. The rest of the chinking had gone pallid gray with age. A small window next to the door had no glass in it but was covered in waxed paper tacked to the frame. The door itself was held in place by leather hinges. Outside was a log bench. A small garden area had been cleared a few yards away from the shade.

We went inside, where I saw an old table and a wired-together chair. Pine boughs and a blanket piled in one corner showed where Mamie slept. There was a shelf with salt and pepper and flour and other things on it. Out from the wall in front of the shelf was a small, potbellied stove, in which she started a fire. While the fire got hot, she scraped the scales off the fish, salt and peppered and floured them. In a skillet she fried bacon and in the bacon grease she fried the floured fish. She sprinkled wild onion over the fish and, lastly, she smothered everything in dandelion greens. We ate together right out of the pan, a bite for her, a bite for me. I told her that even if she didn't know her ABCs, she sure knew how to cook a mess of tasty trout. Most definitely.

Afterwards I sat on the bench outside and watched her wander among the dandelions, picking one here, one there, picking them according to her fancy, which, watching her, I figured had no rhyme or reason but a rhythm sure enough, like the rhythm of a cow or a deer grazing. In the wild, with the meadow and the sun and the flowers, and the river shushing nearby, and the odor of fried fish and bacon hanging in the air like a lazy dew, Mamie blended in as well as anything born to be there. Mamie of the earth and the forest, the river and the meadow, like an agile bear, a graceful antelope, a prancing mare high on character. I knew it would be a shame to send her back to John Beaver. But thirty dollars . . . it was a lot of money in 1959.

When she came back, arms full of yellow flowers and green-garnishing timothy, I asked her if she knew her pa was looking for her. She set the bouquet in my lap and screwed up her eyes, cocking her head to one side in a heavy think.

"John Beaver," I said, prompting her. "You remember your pa?"

Curling her upper lip so her big front teeth sliced the air she said, "I nnn-know'm."

"Well, he's looking for you."

"W-w-where?" she asked, eyes rolling back and forth.

"Here and there, high and low. He worries about you."

"Naw," she answered. Then she whinnied, lips rolling in a dribbly, dobbin-kind of display. She looked so funny I had to laugh at her. We had ourselves a fit of giggling in each other's faces. Then suddenly she broke it off and asked me if I liked her pa.

"*Your* pa?" I didn't know anybody who much liked John Beaver. She rapped the top of her head and said, "Ouch!"

I knew what she meant. It was no secret that he beat her. But her being retarded, I guess no one thought it necessary to do anything about it. But there she was in front of me, showing me that she knew he treated her badly and telling me *ouch it hurt*. She wasn't just a mule after all, not that it would make it okay to beat her even if she were. Mules have feelings too.

I recalled a time one winter when I had been running my trap lines along trails I had known since I was five years old and my brother Calvin showed me how to set traps. I had been at it for so many years that I thought the trails belonged to me, so it was a shock one day to find out that someone was stealing my catch. I got up extra early one morning and set out, determined to find out what was going on.

Light was seeping over the horizon when I arrived at the spot of my first snare. In the snow were boot marks, and I could see where a rabbit had been flicking its hind legs against the pull of the twine. But it was gone and the trail led north. It was at the next spot that I found my thief. I heard a sound that made my blood freeze - the sound of something in hard pain, a sound like nails screeching across a blackboard, high and horrible and pitiful.

Through the naked trees I could see an inky shadow swaying and humming, arms busy with the thing that screeched at each flick of the knife. A mink was hung between two saplings. A wire hook through its nose was holding its head tied to a branch above, and its front and back legs were spread wide, like it was caught midway doing jumping jacks. John Beaver was skinning it alive. I hid myself and watched. I wanted to help the mink, but I was no match for John Beaver no way. Me and my five brothers would not have been a match for him—throw in Pa too. I was terrified simple and frozen to the spot and praying to God that Beaver wouldn't notice me.

When he finally had the pelt off, he rubbed it in the snow and threw it over his shoulder, together with the rabbit pelt, and away he strolled, humming and happy as a preacher on Easter morning. I crept forward and found the bare, bloody mink was still alive. I cut its throat and took off running home. And I set no more traps that winter. Actually, I've set no traps since. It's been three or four years, I guess.

Nope, I didn't like John Beaver any more than Mamie did herself or anyone else I knew. And I admitted to her how I felt, and I asked her what she would do if he found her. She studied it a moment, her eyes closing in a serious think. Then she slipped her hands together sideways, like cymbals clashing, and told me, "Mmmm-Mamie run like hell!" I nodded in agreement with her. She took the flowers off my lap, and turning away, she arranged them in her hair, a dandelion here, a dandelion there—like fluffy buttons, like yellow polka dots. When she finished, she looked over her shoulder at me, shy but flirty, smiling invitingly.

"Aren't you so pretty?" I said.

She ducked away and whinnied and started running a zigzag course across the meadow. I got up and chased her. The dandelion seeds rose thickly around us, like exhaled memories of snow. All the yellow and green and the buttery sun and the silvery seeds made the meadow seem like a land of dreams, everything giddy and full of a joy I couldn't name.

I followed her all the way to the river and watched as she slipped out of her overalls and shirt and turned towards me.

"Kritch'n n-naked!" she said.

"Ey? What?"

Her hands flew and my clothes were off in seconds and then she picked me up, like I was no more than a beach ball and threw me in the water. It was cold and I yelped and she cried out, "Drowd'n man!" and jumped in to save me. She soon had me on the shore again, but before I could even catch my breath, I was back in the water and she was yelling, "Drowd'n man!"

After the third toss I decided I better just relax and let her have her way. For half an hour, I'd say we played drowning man. Really, it was a lot of fun. Usually, when I played it with my brothers, I would end up drowning half the time. But Mamie didn't let me drown once. I was proud of her, and when I finally was let to stay on shore in the warm sun I told her she was wonderful strong, and I'd never forget feeling like the hands of God were whooshing me out of the water. We lay naked drying off, the river at our feet all sparkly like it was made of melted diamonds, the meadow unseen on the other side of the trees, but still sending an occasional dandelion seed over us, a tiny whirling ballerina.

I thought about what I was doing, lying alongside a naked girl, and I knew it was something I would not dream of doing with any others that I knew, not even Mary Magdalen, my sister; but with Mamie it seemed to be just the right thing. She was almost like one of my brothers, except her arms were bigger, and she was taller, and she had those things called boobs. As a matter of fact, she was better than my brothers. She was calmer for one thing, and a hell of a lot nicer. She didn't pick on me like they did, smack me around, beat me up. She didn't laugh and let me drown.

I dozed a bit, and when I woke she was curled on her side, head resting on her arm, staring at me with a small smile on her face. I asked her what she thought she was doing and she said, "Sss-savin you f-from Inians."

"I bet you would," I told her.

She caressed my hair and said, "Sneezeweed."

"Yours is curled carrots," I said. "Hey, can you really say the ABCs?"

"Aaa-yay, bee-yee!" she yelled. Then stopped and gave me her pumpkin frog grin.

"Well hell," I said. "Look here, Mamie. You can get this. I know you can."

I turned over and wrote the ABCs in the sand. Then went from letter to letter with her, having her repeat each one. She did all right that way. I told her I was going to be a great teacher someday and that I would teach her to read and write. She nodded solemnly, aware that I was saying some very important stuff. I wrote the word *dandelion* in the sand and told her it was her first word to learn, *dandelion*. I took her hand and made her write it over and over. After several tries, she did it, sort of, but some of the letters were backwards or upside down.

"Now look, this won't do," I told her. "This is stupid."

"Stuuu-pid," she replied, rapping her head.

Which made me feel bad. "Naw, Mamie," I said, "I'm the one who's stupid. Let's try this. Let's sing the ABCs." And that's what I did. I sang from A to Z. I did it twice. And the second time she joined in with me and did it perfectly.

"Do it again!" I said.

And she did it again and her voice sounded sort of like mine, at least to my ears it did.

"Now if you could just write the letters down, you would be on your way in no time to being a reader. Try it, Mamie. Look at the letters, then turn away and write them down A to Z. C'mon, girl, let me see you writing as you sing. Go on, sing it. ABC—"

She bent low over the letters in the sand, staring at them with all her might, as if through sheer will power, she might unlock their secrets. A moment later she turned away and with her finger wrote ABC. And stopped.

"What is this?" I said. "How can you sing the letters and not write them? I don't get it, Mamie girl."

Again she tried and again she gave up. Only this time she raised her head toward the skies and sang the letters rhythmically at the top of her voice, "Aaa, Bee, Cee, Dee, Eee —" and so on and so forth. I listened to her singing the twenty-six letter alphabet over and over and over. Even when I shook her shoulder and told her to quit, she wouldn't stop. She was into it and what I said didn't matter. So I got dressed and left her there, naked and preoccupied, serenading the earth all the way downstream to where Lake Superior at last captures the Brule.

At least she knew the letters in her head, I told myself, even if she couldn't write them down, nor write *dandelion* or anything else, not even her name.

Far, far away walking homeward I could still hear her, a haunting echo, like spirits in the trees happily singing the ABCs.

I'm a Dirty Ratter

I was late for milking. The old man was standing at the entrance to the barn, hands on hips, staring at me like Jehovah eying a lowdown Canaanite.

"I–I fell asleep," I told him.

"You been asleep since you was born," he said. "Five o'clock! We milk at five o'clock."

"Yessir."

"Five!"

"Yessir, Pa."

He showed me his watch. "You know what time it is? It's six-thirty. We done the milking, boy. Done your share. You hear what I'm saying?"

I bowed my head, shuffled my feet.

He pointed his crooked finger at me and said, "You see what I got here to work with, Deity? You see what Jacob Foggy has to put up with? You see this little ulcer-maker, this torment of my philosophizing heart, this sleeper-by-the-Brule, this dreamer-in-the-sand, this bare bodkin rotting up stinking Denmark?" His finger had once been broken in an apple press. It looked like a gnarled twig. He kept shaking it at me. "I don't want to hear anything from you about sleeping in them woods," he said. "I don't want to hear any fairy tales about fishing and sunning. I was fifteen once. I know the tricks. All I want you to do is get your bony ass in the barn and turn them cows out and clean them milkers by yourself. And get it done before supper! You savvy, boy?"

"Yessir, Pa."

"You're gonna be late for your funeral."

"Yessir."

"I'm giving you thirty minutes. No dragging ass."

"I'll get it done, Pa."

"You keep us waiting supper, I'll clobber you. You understand my poetry?"

He caught me as I tried to slide by into the milkhouse, cuffing me a light one on the back of the head like he always does to punctuate what he says. It didn't hurt. He never hit any of us hard. But I said, "Ouch!" anyway to let him know he was getting his point across.

"No excuses," he said. "No sleeping and dreaming when we got milking to do. We got a farm to run. We got to pull the load like a family, or we'll end up like Fortinbras squatting on a postage stamp. Ain't no glory in making war on Poland, boy. You savvy?"

"Yessir," I told him, but I had no idea what he meant. He quoted his own version of Shakespeare and you just had to roll with it. Nod your head, say yessir, whatever you say, sir.

Up the drive and into the house he went, while I turned the cows out and cleaned the milkers. I knew I was a Jobian trial to him, but I also knew my brothers were harder on his nerves than me. They were always scheming behind his back, saying how they were going to get him someday for making them work like dogs, like he was some Pharaoh or Simon Legree and we were his slaves. They were going to go out and conquer the world and throw him on his ear when he came begging. They might talk about how tough they were, but they shut up soon enough when he came around putting his Old Testament eyes all over them. He would sometimes stare at my brothers with a snaky grin, like he knew what trash they were thinking. And he'd wink at me like we understood each other and what the rest of them thought about things didn't much matter. So I always felt special to the old man, and when he got mad at me, I didn't mind too much. Took it in stride, like most everything else the farm handed out.

I got to the table in time for the blessing. My sister and Mama crossed themselves, like Catholics do, but the rest of us being what Pa called deists just sat with our heads bowed over our plates. He quoted one of his favorite verses: "A wise son maketh a glad father, but a foolish son is the heaviness of his mother." I saw he had his eyes on me. His voice rumbled across the table, like wind ruffling a sheet of tin. He went on a mile about finding purpose and wisdom in doing one's duties to one's family and telling the truth because beauty is truth and truth is beauty and the bread of sincerity is truth and great is truth it shall prevail for it is the lamp that keeps us all from darkness where we would dwell with fanatics and the spiritually unevolved. His prolonged version of grace was wearing me down, and I knew my brothers would be after me because it was my fault they had to sit and listen so long before Pa would let us eat. But at last he ran out of inspiration and we said amen.

While I was eating, I was thinking about how I could get back on his good side, and I wondered if I ought to tell him about Mamie—get his mind off my transgressions and on to her. But then again, I thought he might get madder because I didn't bring her back or because I didn't speak up sooner, so someone could go get her. Also, contrary to telling on her was the memory of how she fit so fine where she was, doing what she seemed meant to do. How for all her size she romped so beautifully, like a deep-chested elk galloping mightily in the meadow, a glory to the sight of anyone who cared for nature. But then again, there was that thirty dollars to think about, and of course, doing what the old man would call a Samaritan righteous thing.

So while I was soaking up the last spot of gravy on my plate with the last bite of bread, I threw out as nonchalantly as I could that I had happened onto Mamie Beaver at the Brule. Everyone stopped eating and stared at me. Mama touched my arm to stop me from swirling the bread. She took my chin in her hand and looked at me seriously—which surprised me because she hardly ever touched me or my brothers. She was usually kind of quiet and hardly seemed to do much thinking about anything except praying Rosary with Mary Magdalen and weeping over the sins of the world. She could turn those waterworks on like a gate-valve faucet. But mainly Mama was just there every day, moving steadily, doing her work, and once in a while saying something about her arthritis or her sciatic nerve, which pained the left side of her lower back and leg. Seemed like the only fun she ever had was when she brushed and braided my sister's hair. The two of them might spend an hour or more trying on different styles, a French braid now, a helmet poof, a curtain down to her wingbones, a curled thing they called the Foggy Pollyanna, and a swept-back look that accentuated her eyes and forehead. You could tell it was fun for them. Mary Magdalen sitting in a chair, chewing gum and talking up a twister, while Mama would play and brush and get creative and tell Mary Magdalen her hair shined brighter than sunshine on September wheat, and sometimes they would sing, and that would stop us in our tracks; and like hypnotized cows we would gather round and listen.

So Mama took my chin and leaned close to me and asked me what was that I had said about Mamie Beaver. I repeated that I had seen Mamie, and I added that she was fine, and Mama shook her head and tears welled in her eyes and she sadly said, "Living in those dark woods, that poor imbecile thing." And she looked at Pa and told him he would have to do something. Her voice had a kind of whine in it, so he wouldn't think she was trying to give him orders.

I told her Mamie wasn't a poor imbecile thing at all. "She's got a cabin with a stove and a comfy bed and she catches fish and pulls up dandelions to eat and wild onions and all kinds of stuff. You should see her, she looks great."

Big brother Calvin had to get his two cents in just then, saying, "What do you mean she's got a cabin, boy? She burgle somebody's cabin, ey?"

"Mamie's no goddang burglar, Calvin!"

"Hey, hey!" Pa said, pointing that apple press finger again. "Son, you're walking on egg shells today. You better show some respect at the table and catch that running-off mouth of yours and make it behave. No *goddangin*, you hear me?"

"Yessir," I answered. I knew better than to say god-anything in front of Mama. Cuss words were for outside the house, where Pa himself hardly held back. But in the house in front of Mama cussing was a quick way of getting smacked and given extra chores. I went on to calmly mention that Calvin shouldn't call Mamie a burglar. She was just doing what she had to do to survive. I told everybody how she had fixed up that old cabin off on the east side of the Brule, where the old, wild timothy field was. Nobody owned that cabin or that land. The cabin was run down and had been built by some trapper when there were still beavers and muskrats in the streams feeding the Brule.

"It still ain't her property," said Calvin.

Mary Magdalen scoffed at him. "Oh, what you think she should do, you phony hypocrite, live in a tree?"

"*Ain't*," crooned Mama. "Calvin, you know better than to say ain't."

Pa tapped Calvin's shoulder. "I told you till I'm blue in the face, only lowlife hicks say ain't. It's not in the dictionary."

"Yeah," said Mary Magdalen, "that's you all right, Calvin. A lowlife hick. Manure for brains."

"Shut up," said Calvin.

"You shut up," said Mary Magdalen.

"Shut up."

"Shut up."

"That's enough!" said Pa.

"Mary Magdalen, don't say shut up to your brother," soothed Mama.

"Oh, he makes me sick, Mama. He ought to clean off his own doorstep before he calls Mamie a burglar and such. Big jerk."

"I didn't say she was a burglar. I just asked a simple question," said Calvin.

She stuck her tongue out at him. He stuck his tongue out at her. Cash took up Mary Magdalen's side, both of them sticking their tongues out at Calvin. Calvin was scowling like a gargoyle, while Cash told how Calvin stole the Hank Snow record at Zimmerman's Five and Dime. "I saw the dirty devil steal it," Cash declared righteously.

"Ten years ago, or maybe five. I saw him too," added Cutham.

"It was just last year!" I shouted. "Cutham, you're a moron."

"Don't call me no moron."

"Moron."

"Pa!"

"Shut up all of you!" commanded Pa. He was looking at Calvin. "You steal from Zimmerman?"

"I never!"

"You did!" we all shouted.

We were pointing at him and he was blushing. It was funny seeing big Calvin with his ears glowing, his lips trembling. He was denying his thievery for all he was worth and darting desperate looks at the old man, who was taking deep breaths, puffing himself up as we went to yelling, "Thief! Thief! Thief!"

And finally the old man bellowed, "Shut the hell up all of you!"

"Now, Jacob," murmured Mama, "remember about your vein."

Pa had once broke something in his throat so that he spit blood for a few days. He broke it yelling at Almer Tubman for letting the rope go slack when Pa was castrating Almer's bull and the bull kicked Pa in the leg and the gut, a one-two punch. Pa later termed what he said to Almer as "righteous cursing." Talk about cussing! It was the granddaddy of cussing that's what it was.

"You let me worry about my vein, Ruth," he told her in a tight, throaty voice. She pulled her head in and looked down at her plate, but I could see a faint smile on her mouth.

And Pa was tapping the table as if driving home each one of his words. "May the steely-eyed Deity who's got his eye on the dead sparrow have mercy on any child of mine I find out to be a lowlife thief. That child of mine might as well give his soul to the Deity cause I'll have his assss."

Mama gasped and shook her head and crossed herself as she always did whenever Pa lowered his voice like that and pronounced his favorite soul-and-ass intentions, adding his patented little hiss at the end and clutching his fist like he held it, the ass in question, and was going to crush it.

"I never, Papa," said Calvin feebly. "Honest, I never." And he looked round the table at all of us and his eyes were pleading and he said, "Don't get me in trouble, guys. Tell Papa the truth. Please!"

"You getting this boy in trouble, Cash," said Pa, wiggling his crooked finger at Cash. Then going on to Cutham, "You getting this boy in trouble, Cutham?"

Cash and Cutham sank back and tucked their heads in the way Mama did. Mary Magdalen looked at Calvin, who was looking pitifully like he was going to cry, and she said it wasn't Calvin who stole the Hank Snow record. It was Ramsey Brown, that city trash boy. "He stole it and gave it to Calvin. I saw him do it and I was so shocked I couldn't say a word. And then on the way home Calvin sat on the darned record and broke it."

"That's the truth, Papa," said Calvin, laughing nervously. "I'm such a clod I sat on the dumb thing and broke it, ha ha."

"Ramsey Brown stole it," Cash agreed. "He was sweet on Mary Magdalen and tried to give it to her, but she wouldn't take it. I was there. I saw it all."

"Ramsey Brown is body scum," declared our sister. She was scraping gravy with her fingernail, running it round the edge of her plate.

And Papa said, "Ramsey Brown gives you a stolen record, Calvin, and you sit on it and break it?"

"That's the truth, so help me, Papa."

"At least one of you boys, or you Mary Magdalen, should have turned him in. I'm ashamed of you all. But you see what happened? The stolen goods got broken. What do you call that? You call that instant judgment from the Deity for taking something from the hands of a thief. There's more in heaven and earth than Horatio can figure out, let me tell you."

"The Lord works his ways," added Mama.

"I never liked that Ramsey Brown anyway," said Calvin.

"You keep away from him," said Pa.

Everyone's head was nodding up and down. Bad Ramsey Brown versus the good Foggy boys and their perfect sister. "Now, Christian," said Pa, "what's this Mamie Beaver business all about anyway? What's going on with her?"

I told him everything that had happened, except the naked swimming. Pa was interested in her learning to sing her ABCs. "That gal has a memory," he said. "I seen it in action myself one time when she was making out like she was Charlie Chaplin in the movies, doing all his walk and things with a stick and a hat. This was when Mary was still alive. And there was another time when she had taken Mamie to some other movie and when they got home she heard Mamie talking in her room. And according to Mary, retarded Mamie was quoting the whole darn movie from beginning to end."

"I remember that," said Mama. "Mary told us that story when she was here that day for something. What was it?"

"I don't know," said Pa, "but what I know is retarded or not that gal has bursts of memory that can't be explained. Science should do a study of her."

"She's a good mimic too," said Mama.

"Yeah, she is."

"John Beaver's got a thirty-dollar reward out for her," said Calvin.

"I know," said Pa. "But that don't mean Christian would get it. I wouldn't trust that ornery son of a farmer any farther than I could throw him. Which wouldn't be far. He's got to weigh two-eighty at least. John is stronger than any northerner I've ever known. Broke a man's back in a wrestling match at a carnival. I seen him do it. Squeezed the poor fella up in a bear hug and snap! You could hear them vertebraes cracking."

"What's thirty dollars these days anyhow?" said Mary Magdalen.

"Thirty dollars is thirty more than I got," I told her.

"I don't care. I wouldn't give that John Beaver the satisfaction of catching her. Not for a hundred dollars."

"A hundred dollars?" said Calvin.

"Not a thousand dollars. Not a million." Mary Magdalen's stubborn chin was thrust forward like she was daring someone to try and sock her.

"Geez, I would," said Calvin.

"It ain't the money we should be thinking about," said Pa.

"*Isn't*," whispered Mama, her eyes showing she was happy to have caught him again.

"Ruth, I'm talkin here!" He looked at me sharply. "And you shouldn't be thinkin of rattin on her for thirty dollars. Thirty pieces of silver."

"Amen," said Mama and Mary Magdalen simultaneously.

"What is at question here," continued Pa, "is our Samaritan duty. John Beaver, rotten soul that he is, is still her father and memory-bursts or no, she's still bats in the belfry. You understand what I'm saying? She needs someone to look after her. At least John does that much. Everyone knows he's awful proud of how hard she works, how strong she is."

"Proud of her like you're proud of the Farmall because it can pull five bottoms in clay," said Mary Magdalen. She was pushing her luck with Pa.

"Let me tell you something, Miss Smarty Pants. Any tractor that pulls five in clay is a tractor to be proud of, and any daughter who can out-pull any five men you can name is also something to be proud of. At least he cares that much for her. He'd never let her starve. He's a rough booger but that's his daughter out there in them woods all alone, and we got to do what our deistic or Catholic consciences dictate."

"But he beats her, Papa." Mary Magdalen's stubborn chin was quivering.

"God knows what else," said Mama.

"Beats her, pinches her, works her like a dobbin, and probably puts a halter on her and rides her like his hobbyhorse!"

"She's strong enough," said Calvin sniggering.

"Not funny," Pa told him.

I was ready to forget the money and leave her alone. But ultimately the old man decided there was more to it than money. "Mamie Beaver's just a child out there, and we won't abandon her to the elements," he said. "Woods are full of bears and full of traps. What if she should get caught in one and eaten by the other? You want that on your conscience, Yorick? It's going to be the winter of discontent in a few months. How's she going to live a healthy life, I'd like to know? How's she going to get enough to eat when the snow comes and the wind blows? If she don't die of starvation, she'll freeze to death. That slow-witted ole thing ain't—isn't—equipped to survive. She's got less brains than King Lear's Fool. who says to let go of a wheel when it runs downhill and go to bed at noon. You see what I'm saying? She's been lucky so far, but it won't last. Ask King Lear about luck. Beaver might abuse the old beefer now and then, but she's still better off with him. I mean imagine having a gal like that around—why, she'd try the patience of Horatio himself, who would say, 'Put this bout aside for now, my, lord.' Because he knows that warm in winter and fed year round is what's best for a Mamie Beaver in this merciless world. The ole girl goes home tomorrow, Christian."

"Yessir, Pa."

Mama and Mary Magdalen made the same gesture, a kind of fluttering of their heads, stray strands of hair waving at the beams coming through the window from the setting sun, reminding me of those dandelion ballerinas at the Brule. The old man had spoken. There was nothing more to say.

I went outside and got a gunnysack from the granary and went out to my pickle patch. I figured as long as I was going to have to ride with John Beaver in the morning, I might as well take along a hundred pounds of cucumbers and get five cents a pound at the pickle factory on the way. As I was kneeling and studying the cucumbers for the finger-sized ones the buyers like so much, my five brothers came up and surrounded me. They were looking for trouble.

"You oughta know to be home on time for the milking, boy," said Calvin.

"I did my share," I said. "And Pa already cuffed me, so there's no need for your stupid two-cents worth of nothing, Calvin."

His mouth hung open like a large-mouthed bass. He gulped air and said, "Oh, yeah, cuffed you like this." He gave Calah a light rub on top of his head. "He never hits you nothin, Christian."

"You're his goddamn pet!" said Cush.

"His pet!" agreed Cutham.

"I never been Pa's pet," whined Cash.

"All five of you turds make me want to throw up," I told them.

"Oh yeah?" Calvin snarled. "Well, listen up, Christian. You're the turd, see. Every time you screw up the old man gets on us, and we're sick of it."

"The old man gets on you for you, not cause of nothing I do."

"Not cause of nothing I do," said Cutham.

"Not cause of nothing I do," said Cush.

"You a parrot, Cush?" I said. "Just because you're Cutham's twin doesn't mean you have to say everything he says."

"Shut up!"

"Screw you."

"Duh, *you're* the parrot."

"Duh."

"Duh!" the twins shouted.

I told them they looked like cretins. They did, it's true. Both had big wet lower lips always hanging and glistening like lips on chimps. My other brothers were just barely more tolerable to look at. I was thankful to the Deity that he had given me a spoonful more of brains and no hanging lip gathering curds of spit.

"We gonna take this kinda crap from a runt like him?" said Cutham.

"Runt like him," said Cush.

And then their voices came all over me: "You better watch it!" "You the cretin, Christian." "You the parrot." "You parrot everything Pa says." "He thinks he's so damn smart and you think you're so damn smart, but neither one of you is."

"Pa is smarter than all you put together and so am I," I told them.

"Duh!" they answered.

In the middle of all the duhs and grumblings, Calvin switched to another subject. "What you and big boobs do all day out in them woods?" he asked, his lips twisting like a wet worm around a hook.

"Get your ugly face out of the toilet, Calvin!"

"Mamie show you how?"

"Ick!" I cried.

He laughed at me. I threw a cucumber at him and hit him in the chest.

"Threatening me with body harm!" he shrieked. Reaching down he grabbed a dirt clod. Then they all reached down.

"Stone the bastard," said Cutham.

"Stone the bastard," said Cush.

"You throw those at me and this time I'm telling," I told them.

"Yeah, fork you, Christian!"

Calvin raised his arm. "You gonna tell us what you and Mamie done in them woods?"

"Tell us," said Cash, "or we'll clod you to death."

"Come on, Christian, tell us," pleaded Calah. "Did you do it? Did you, huh?"

"None of any of your goddamn business!"

"That's the last insult I'm taking from you," said Calvin, and he let fly and the clod hit my knee, exploding in a puff. I leaped to my feet and headed across the pickle patch out to the pasture, dirt clods disintegrating all around me. I gave the race my hunkered-down, foot-flying best, but I could hear them gaining on me, especially Calah, who had a pair of thighs on him like Hercules. I might have done better had my stomach not been so heavy with supper, the gravy boiling inside. Calah caught me by the hair and yelled, "Gotcha, buttface," as he whirled me around. Without meaning to, I threw up on him.

He jumped back. "Look at this shit!"

"Jesus, Christian, no fair!"

"Fuckin Christian, man, he fights like a girl."

"Kick his ass. Get him! Get him!"

They got me. Someone had me in a headlock, someone had me in a half nelson, someone was trying to pull my hair out, someone was trying to make me lick my vomit off the grass. I heard Calvin saying if I would give the dirty details of what Mamie and I did they would let me go.

"Tell you shit, you assholes!" I told them.

They worked me over pretty good, until they got tired and no one could think of any more names to call me. And I told them that, yeah, eat your hearts out because Mamie and I swam naked together in the Brule and played Drowning Man and she saved me easily every time I yelled. And I told them that they were all pussies compared to Mamie.

"Pussies," breathed Calvin. "I love that word. You must've been naked body to naked body when she saved you."

"That's right."

"Ooo, how did it feel?"

"Stupid question. It felt like a naked body."

"But those big boobs, Jesus she must have had them all over you. What did that feel like?"

"About the same as Cutham's blubber belly."

"Naw!"

"Yeah!"

"No way!"

"Well, maybe a little more solid."

Cush grabbed a handful of Cutham's belly and said, "Mamie's boobs." And they all got hysterical. Even Cutham laughed for a second. Then he and Cush started wrestling.

"You touch it?" asked Calvin.

"Touch what?"

""Oh sure, like you don't know. Her *pussy*, man."

"Get lost."

Calvin laughed at the sky and cried, "He touched it! He touched it!" And then he was dancing in circles and yelling that I touched it. Cutham and Cush looked up from the grass and said, "Touched what?" Cash was pulling my nose and saying I was too young to appreciate the knock of opportunity. Calah pounded his big thighs and said that that was where women felt the power.

"Women love for a man to have thighs like mine," he said. There was giggling and rolling of eyes. Tongues hanging out.

And I said, "Jesus Christ, let me out of here!"

They let me go and I went back to the pickle patch. The old man was there. He said, "Work it out with your brothers?"

"Those jerks," I said.

He dusted me off. And then he said, "John Beaver will be by at five to pick you up. So looks like you'll get out of chores again and have to settle up with the boys again. Every day they get more like your ma's family, like them oddball brothers of hers."

I offered to do the night-milking by myself. He said there wasn't any need for it, that what I was doing was a legitimate excuse to miss a milking. Then while I squatted and picked cucumbers, Pa said:

"You're feeling low about what you're doing to Mamie. I can tell you're feeling yourself a real ratter."

"Yeah," I said.

The sky was getting dark blue above the old man's head, and I saw a faint star open its eye. I made a wish that I would wake up in the morning and take John Beaver to the Brule and Mamie would be long gone.

"When you're ratting on Mamie, it's bound to feel bad in your heart, son. Bound to. I mean it's only natural. I'd feel it too, if I was giving her away like you. Yeah, you know because of you she's going to get caught and probably get her ass whipped." Pa sighed and shook his head and looked at me like he couldn't believe I could be such a dirty rat. "Makes you feel rotten in Denmark for sure," he continued, "and Horatio's philosophy don't help you none. Yep it's a hell of a thing your doing, son. Let me see if I can't make you feel better about it."

Squatting over those cucumbers while he talked, I felt long of claw and tooth, a varmint tugging at the vines, a thing of twitchy nose and whiskers. I wanted to spit myself out.

Pa had lit his pipe and was puffing hard to get himself up a good cloud. The air smelled of hay, tobacco and cucumbers and dirt. "But, though you feel like a lowlife shit, let me tell you something. It's one of them mixed truths of high principle that Shakespeare likes to tell about. You know, to be or not to be, and all like that. I've read him cover to cover and practically wore out that Oxford book, and I'll tell you he knew as much as the Bible about it. Take comfort that men back in the days of swords and battleaxes were going through a set of principles that pulled them back and forth like two men on a tug-of-war. You see what I'm saying? Listen, you're doing something that's got a hair's fineness for moral weight. The Deity looks down and sees you trying to figure it out. He looks to see which side you're going to put the hair on. Should you be the Good Samaritan? Pour oil and wine on her wounds and bring her out of the wilderness?"

He puffed and puffed, getting a grip on the pipe and his words, settling into them, satisfied. "That's you, son, the Good Samaritan—the one who showed mercy—your brother's keeper fighting the contrary side of conscience slipping the rat style to you. To be or not to be. Moment of truth. Emerson might say to you, 'Doubt not, O Christian, but persist. Ever the winds blow, ever the grass grows, and ever are men and women atoms of the wind and the grass and each other.' 'Look for me under your boot soles.' Or is that Whitman? Yeah, Whitman. But you are Mamie's keeper because you're your own keeper. Pay attention now," he ordered. "Ignorance wants to make its own laws—anarchy, nihilism. It's awake and full of tricks—making you think you're a rat doing wrong instead of right, ah, hmm, yes. Ignorance." His face was foggy with lavender smoke. It was some god speaking from a cloud. "Awake and full of tricks. What shall I do to inherit the Deity's respect? Get smart. Be a thinker. Figure out the truth. I'm giving it to you free of charge. Mamie is in you and you in Mamie, and both of you are limbs of the organ of life and the organ is the Over-Soul, the Deity under your feet and over your head and in every breath. And if you allow him, he'll guide you to the truthful, righteous thing to do. He'll have his bond, and he will burrow the truth into your ignorant heart."

Pa waved the cloud away from his head. "Mercy is to Mamie Beaver whatever you do with her tomorrow morning. Don't give it another thought. Just act on those holy instincts I know you got. Have I ever steered you wrong? Gather these cucumbers while you may, my son. It's all piling up points in the Deity's omnivorous heart."

A Moment of Truth

John Beaver showed early just as my brothers and Pa were headed to the barn for chores. My brothers' eyes slashed over me like razors. I was getting out of chores twice in a row—unheard of—and they would make me pay. Pinches and punches and dirt clods, hammerlocks and hair pulling were in my future. I was already sick of the day and wanted it over with, wanted the nighttime quiet of my bed after the lights were out and the house was cooling and creaking. The escape into sleep, where I could forget all the crummy human doings that I was involved in. But capturing Mamie had to be done first. No getting out of it. It was my duty.

I heaved my sack of cucumbers on top of some rope curled in the back of Beaver's Dodge pickup and climbed in next to him. The cab was filled with his massive bulk, and I scrunched in the corner as much as I could. I didn't want to touch any part of him.

"Where to, Foggy?" His voice was raspy, coming from some wet spot deep in his throat. He was eyeing me in the gunmetal morning light, his face boxy and gray-shadowed. There was a lump of tobacco puffing out his left cheek. The breath of wet Redman and splow and armpit and hot clutch stuck like tiny thorns in my throat. I whispered hoarsely that he should head for the Brule, where it ran under highway 2.

"Good boy," he said, ruffling my hair. I rolled the window down and inhaled the homey scent of barnyard flower. I didn't want to leave it. The clutch engaged and the old Dodge shuddered as if it didn't want to go either.

On the way to the river, John Beaver kept pumping me for information about Mamie. I did my best to answer politely, but it got harder and harder with the questions he asked. First it was just how she was and what she looked like, had she lost weight and did she have much to say? Then he said, "How can that big dummy know nuff to get along so good out there, Foggy? How you figure that? What's her secret, ey?"

"I think she's smarter than we know," I told him. "She can sing her ABCs now. I taught her how to do it and she caught on like that." I snapped my fingers. "She still can't write nothing, but she's got a good memory."

"Smarter than we know? Neh," he said. He spit juice on the floorboard between his legs. Adding to a puddle that was already there, dark and slimy as an oil leak. "Maybe someone smart has been sportin for her, ey?" He poked me in the ribs with a finger that felt hard as a wooden dowel. I rubbed my ribs and knew I would have a bruise there. "Yeah, maybe someone been hep'n hisself to some moose meat. I mean it's just a little thought that's been occurrin to me since your old man called me last night." Again he spit between his legs. "Ey?" he kept saying, twisting his head towards me. "Ey?" Grinning tobacco stained teeth. His ammonia breath made my eyes water. I felt acid melting my insides, nauseating me.

"Not me, Mr. Beaver," I managed to say. "Not me. Nosir."

"Ey? Course not, course not. That good little Christian Fluppy wouldn't think of such a lowlife, mean ole thing. Some would, though. Some would take a'vantage of that lunkhead. But not you, not ole Fluppy Puppy. Some would, though, uh-huh, some would just for the fun of it. Know what I mean? She wouldn't know what you were up to. She'd think you was playin a game, just sportin her. You been sportin my Mamie, Fluggy Muggy?"

"Nosir, honest. Not me."

"Good. Glad to hear it. Good Fluggyboy like you, no way, no how." He flicked my ear with his fingernail. It stung like a spider had bit me. "Come on over here," he said, reaching out and grabbing a hunk of my hair.

"Yeow!" I hollered. "Let go! Lemme go, goddamn it!"

"Shet yer face, you little pile of crap!" He pulled my head round like it was attached to a balloon string, giving me a hell of a shaking.

"Pleeease sir, p-pleeease s-sir," I stammered. My voice got high as a girl in a chorus reaching for high C's. "I'll shut my face, sir," I shrieked.

"Damn right you will, Fuzzybutt. Now, tell me the truth, when did you hear bout my givin out with a reward, ey?"

"I don't know, sir. Maybe a week ago. Don't know."

"A week ago?"

"Yessir. Thirty dollars everybody's saying."

"Greedy little pecker poker. Maybe you heard it yestiday."

"Nosir, before yesterday."

"But maybe yestiday and you decided she wasn't worth givin up no thirty bucks, ey? I got yer number, pecker poker."

My mind was off-track. I didn't know what to make of what he was saying.

"You know," he said. "You know what I'm talking bout, boogie-woogie. You the one kept Mamie out there so you could play house. And she done some things for you, Foggybottom, heh? Didn't she? Mamie knows how. Oh, don't she ever!" He shook my head again. I thought the roots of my hair were coming out and I'd have a bald patch right in the front and have to comb my hair forward to hide it.

"Yeow!" I kept crying. He shook harder still, and I couldn't stand it. It seemed better to let him have his way. So I said he was right. "Yessir, you're right, sir."

"Uh-huh," he answered, satisfied. "That's what I thought, that's what I fuck'n knowed. Nasty little pecker poker."

He let go of my hair and I tried to rub the roots back in. Jesus, it felt on fire.

He was talking, saying, "Ain't nobody put one over on this badass Beaver yet. I seen right through 'em, goddammit, don't I though? I know what makes 'em tick. You pimply pecker pokers is all the same—full of sap! Nasty-sticky-icky that makes you tick. And Mamie's easy. You wanted her to yourself for a while. Ain't it so?"

"Yessir."

"Best not to be lyin to the Beaver, Foffybuns."

"Yessir."

"You and Mamie, right? Keepin her in the woods, ey?"

"Me and Mamie, yessir."

His hand swept backward across my mouth. I tasted blood and was too stunned to yell or even to feel anything for a moment. Then my front teeth started aching and my lips pounded like my heart had leaped inside them. It was all I could do to keep from weeping. I was in pain and terrified. John Beaver was as much a horror as that naked mink had said he was. I wanted my Pa and my brothers. I wanted Calah to hammerlock the sonofabitch and Calvin to pull his hair and Cush and Cutham to stomp him, pinch him, rub his face in the slimy tobacco juice between his feet. But even as I thought it, I wondered if twice ten of them put together were any match for someone so huge, so thick and wildly ape-built. One of those gorilla silverbacks you see in zoos.

"That's a promise of what you deserve for all that sticky sap of yers!" he said. Brown spittle flew from his mouth, raining on the windshield and dashboard and the backs of his hands. For a moment he was quiet, and then his voice came at me low and slyly. "She do the no-rain dance for you?" he asked, coaxing me with his elbow.

"No-rain?"

"You playin dumb again, Foggywoggy? You tellin me you don't know what her no-rain is? You don't wanna tell me that, son. She done it for you, didn't she?"

"Yes, the no-rain dance."

"I woulda give ten toots to see that. Nasty plowboy plowing," he said. He was breathing hard through his nose, his nostrils flaring and "Heh, heh, heh" sounding like hiccups coming from his mouth.

We drove slowly, the truck rattling over the bumpy road coming at last to the highway. Where we turned east and passed the factory at Blueberry that would have bought my cucumbers. But I wasn't about to ask John Beaver to stop. I was in no mood to do anything but point the way and keep my mouth shut. Let him collect Mamie and take me home. I was sick at heart that I was leading him to her, but it seemed there was nothing else I could do.

"Heh heh heh, I got the goods on you, Fluffybum," he said. "You a little poontang monster! Heh heh heh, got the goods on the poontang monster. I bet yer sayin to yerself, 'Fuck that reward money, I want my mama.' Is that what yer sayin, Fuzzynuts?"

"Yessir."

"You juss tell ole upright Jacob that you couldn't take no reward for hep'n a worried-sick papa get his baby girl back home safe and sound. A good neighbor juss wouldn't wanna take rewards for something noble like that. Now would he?"

"Nosir."

"Gotta keep a step ahead in this life, Fluggybunny."

When we came to the overgrown path going north toward where Mamie was hiding in the cabin, Beaver pulled the pickup over to the highway shoulder. He wanted to know how far in we had to go. When I told him it wasn't more than a hundred yards he said it would be a nice little hike, a commune with nature. We got out and crossed the highway. I led the way into the woods. By the time we arrived at the ridge overlooking Mamie's valley, the sun was a hand above the horizon. The dew was rising. The air was damp. Peaceful bees and dragonflies looking like chips of stained glass were going places already. As I walked in front of Beaver, a monarch landed on my arm. A big one with black-veined wings spreading out to catch the sun. John Beaver tried to catch it, but I waved my arm and it got away.

"Pretty, ain't it?" he said, as it fluttered over our heads.

Pretty? I took a long look at Beaver as he watched the butterfly, but I couldn't figure out how the word *pretty* could come out of such a mouth. I pointed the way, and he followed me down the path through the last of the pines shielding the cabin. We came out on Mamie's meadow. A flock of crows shot up from the field clucking a warning. My mother would have crossed herself and called it an omen. It felt like one all right—those black-feathered bodies climbing the air and circling and cawing. I knew in my bones that something terrible was coming.

John Beaver pushed his way in front of me and took out a Buck knife. Unfolded it, the blade four or five inches long. There was nothing left to do but pray, so I crossed myself and asked God to make Mamie vanish. Then I noticed there was no smoke spewing from the stovepipe, and I started thinking that maybe my prayer had been answered long before we got there. Maybe Mamie wasn't home!

"Ha!" blurted out of me. I slapped my hand over my mouth. Beaver turned round and gave me a shove that set me on my can. He put his finger to his lips. When he lumbered towards the cabin, I saw the blade in his hand catching sunrays, flashing like a mirror. My mouth was working with the need to tell her - *Run Mamie, run!* But I was too scared to yell it. In my mind's eye I saw John Beaver whirling around and coming for me, splitting me open from my chops to my navel. It was my moment of truth and I was failing it.

When he got up close, he peeked in the window. I heard a scream and saw John Beaver backing up, his legs tangling in firewood, tripping him. He made a snarling noise as he fell. Despite my fear, the look of him bowling over made me nearly hysterical. I was laughing and slapping my thigh and pointing at him. And then came Mamie storming out of the cabin, running for her life. Her orange hair looked like a ball of flame streaking across the meadow, her big legs winging effortlessly, hardly seeming to touch the ground.

"Go, Mamie, go!" I cried in admiration. A thoroughbred couldn't have run more gracefully, more powerfully. Mamie was beauty in motion.

Beaver was up and after her. He didn't leap and wind-breeze like she did. His way was to tear through the flowers and grass. He had a kind of relentless power, a bull hurtling along that nothing but both barrels of a shotgun could stop. The two of them, father and daughter, ran in a wide circle, edge to edge round the meadow, Mamie hardly touching the tops of the timothy; Beaver a juggernaut pulverizing the roots. When they got far away they resembled two children having a good time, playing tag, grinning and cavorting. But as they came round the circle closing in on me, I could see that Mamie's grin was the grin of terror. Beaver looked like a panting werewolf preparing to shred her.

She might have run him to ground had she just kept smooth grass under her, but on one of her leaps she came down on something that threw her off balance, and over she went in a somersault, arms and leg flailing like a decapitated goose. Beaver was on her before she stopped fluttering. He grabbed her, flipped her over on her stomach and sat on her butt. He rubbed her face in the grass. He was gasping and spitting Redman, a reddish rain falling around her.

"Gotcha," he gasped. "Gotcha."

Mamie lay limp as death.

"I ought to skin you alive," he said. "Runnin out on me who fed your fat ass all yer goddamn ungrateful life!" He jerked her head back and showed her the knife. "You think I won't?" he said. And then he sawed off a handful of hair. "I'll cut it all off, that's what I'll do, like them baldy whores in World War Two sleepin with the enemy. You and that Foggy pecker poker." He cut off another fistful and threw it into the air. The hair a sparkling ghostflame carrying with the wind. Above us, the crows kept circling.

Mamie didn't react. She was spread-eagled and letting him cut her hair, pinch her, rap the knife hilt on her head, whatever. She did nothing and said not a word. I had seen this sort of thing when I would trap a woodchuck sometimes and it would lie there all depressed and waiting to die. A wild thing with no chance to survive and just wanting to end it. It made John Beaver madder that he couldn't make Mamie react. He growled and snarled, huffing and puffing and spraying the air with drops of tobacco. Putting the blade on the back of her neck, he swore he was going to scalp her first, then skin her, then tack her hide to the side of the barn to let it dry in the sun. He wiped the blade on his pants back and forth, whetting it, warming it up.

I can't say if he would have scalped her or not. But the sight of him wiping that blade back and forth like that, and of Mamie limp and helpless and already dead with no will to fight him, then him touching her skin once more with the blade and slicing just slightly, so the faintest trail of blood followed along—and then hearing Mamie screech. That was it. That was all I could stand. Something snapped in my head. I grabbed a split of firewood and laid it as hard as I could across the back of John Beaver's head. He lifted his hands to the spot and turned to look at me.

"What!" he yelled, half-rising. "Conspiracy! You double-crossing motherfucker!"

So I hit him again. "Cocksucker!" he called me. And then his legs gave out and he toppled over. He lay there gurgling Redman, blood dripping from the top of his head onto a pillow of dandelions, turning the yellow petals red. The knife lay beside him, the blade dull in the shade of his belly.

I stood above him, gawking and trembling at my handiwork. I was amazed at myself, amazed and terrified and somewhat proud. I couldn't figure out where it had come from—the nerve to smack him on the head like that. And down he had gone on the second swing, so he was mortal after all, no harder to kill than a breeder bull in heat if you use the right instrument.

And I said aloud to his bleeding head, "A two-pound hammer between Ferdinand's eyes wouldn't have dropped him so easy as I've dropped you! So ha! Two swings and you're out! Instead of coming after me like a nightmare should. Not you, no sir, John Beaver, fuck you, you mean bastard. Nice and neat now, snoring Redman deep in your throat, and I hope your lungs drown in the filthy stuff!" One of his eyes was a bit propped open, looking as dull as a pinto bean. It was my bony arm that had dropped him! "I'm bad! Don't fuck with me," I said, shaking the piece of wood at him.

Mamie picked herself up and stood next to me and she said, "K-k-kilt him, Kritch'n. Good for y-you."

"No, no, he's still breathing," I told her.

She wiped the blood from the back of her neck and looked at her hand. Then she kicked him. He groaned. She kicked him again.

He blinked. His eyes rolling into focus. He looked at us and said, "Ehhh?" He raised himself up on one elbow. He saw the club in my hand. "Ehhh? You hit me with that, Fartbottom?"

"Sorry, Mr. Beaver, but—"

"You gonna be more than sorry. I'll put you in jail for this. Assault and battery. Interfering with a father rescuing his daughter from your dirty clutches. I'll see that they send you to reform school, you fuck'n delinquent. And you too, Mamie!" He jerked his head at her and blood spattered on his shirtsleeve. "What's this?" he said. ""I'm . . . I'm—by God I'm bleedin! You made me bleed!"

He sat up and felt all over his head and winced. Blood was trickling down the sides of his face and neck. "Where's my goddamn knife? I'm sure as hell gonna kill some sonsabitches makin me bleed!"

He found the knife and started to rise. I felt the club leave my hand. I saw Mamie raise it and bring it down—*whump!*—across her father's head. Blasted him. Slaughtered him. I knew that no mortal head could stand what she had done to his. He wasn't gurgling now. Nor nothing else. His eyes were fixed and bulging as if she had driven them nearly out of their sockets—startled white balls with B-B-sized pupils, at which Mamie pointed and said, "Boo's eye."

"I—I think he's dead this time," I told her.

"Yaay, Kritch'n."

"I mean really he's dead." I had never seen a dead person before. A hunk of bloody-headed human meat. It was interesting. And it was awful.

Mamie wasn't concerned. She tossed the club in the air and took my hand and led me off to the river. She stuck her head in the water and washed her face and the cut on the back of her neck. I washed too. The water cooling my brain helped me think more clearly about what we had done. And what we had to do.

Mamie picked me up. "Drowd'n man!" she cried.

"No, no! Please, Mamie, not now!"

She lowered me into her arms, cradling me like a baby, looking down into my face, blinking slowly, expecting God knows what. She kissed my forehead. For a second or two it seemed possible that what had happened hadn't. And we could play. We could play drowning man. Or whatever. Catch some fish and cook them and stroll in the sun. The air smelled inviting. Insects bumbled about, birds argued, and flowers stretched in the sun. The evil crows were gone. The river mumbled along like a shy old man. Nothing had changed. Everything had changed. There beneath it all, crushing dandelions, was John Beaver, his neck bending over like a shanked nail. Three criminal bumps on his head, so the autopsy report could name the cause of death. Mamie was a murderer. I was an accessory.

"You got to understand, Mamie. We are in some deep shit now."

"D-d-dip shit."

"We got to get away far from here."

Her voice matched mine now, solemn and low and breathy. "Yaay, Kritch'n."

My mind turned over the sound of the club hitting Beaver. That bone-cracking crunch. I wanted to get away from that sound and this dream-like place where such a sound should never have happened. Our meadow of peace, with its illusions of seeds swirling like fairies in the wind was not coming back. Not ever. It was a meadow of death now, of the police handcuffing me and Mamie and leading us away in chains, while my parents and brothers and sister watched dumbfounded. Christian Peter Foggy getting hauled to prison, locked up, the key thrown away. The force of my fears wouldn't let me stay and face that. A voice inside me said, "Go! Get away! Run for your life!" And that's what I knew me and Mamie had to do. No getting out of it. We were desperados.

Running Away

Mamie followed me out to the highway, where the Dodge was parked. I opened the groaning door and climbed in the cab and saw the key was missing. It was still in Beaver's pocket. We needed that key, but I couldn't make myself go back and touch a dead body. I told Mamie she would have to do it. I told her to get his money too. Off she went at a jog, while I sat on the fender to wait. The whump of wood on Beaver's head still echoed in my ears. I talked to it, told it I was sorry. It was an accident, I said, a little accidental murder happening before I could understand what I was doing – and the difference between just killing a man or putting him to sleep for a while was probably no more than a pound, or maybe even less than an ounce of wood and willpower. Besides, I said, Mamie did it, not me, not Christian Peter Foggy the good boy who was going to grow up and be a teacher. Not him. Someone should send him home to do his chores and get beat up by his stupid brothers. He shouldn't be a part of something so bad as human slaughter. Especially when it wasn't really his fault. He should be left to go home and slip a Surge milker on a cow and stand there in the barn rubbing the cow's udder to relax it, and no such nightmare whump of wood on Beaver's head should ever enter the ears of such a kind, hardworking, harmless farmboy. Convincing myself of my innocence took all my concentration and that is why I didn't see the patrol car pulling up behind the pickup and the cop getting out. It wasn't until the door slammed that I woke up and realized that I was caught.

The cop straightened his gun on his hip and adjusted his smoky-bear hat squarely. "So what's up, partner?" he said. "You broke down? Need a tow?" He was a thin-faced man, with deep crater-like eyes and an O for a mouth. He had tiny pockmark craters covering his nose and cheeks as well. His stomach pushed over his belt, and his narrow shoulders swayed as he walked, like a buoy rocking in water.

"Just waiting on someone," I said. I could hardly talk my mouth was so dry.

The cop patted the pickup like it was a friendly dog. "You got yourself an antique here," he said. "She's seen better days, ey?"

"Yeah, it's pretty old," I answered. My voice shook a little, but he didn't seem to notice.

"What year is it?" he asked.

I shrugged.

He looked at the grill and said, "Must be a thirty-six, I'd say." His O mouth made him look slightly startled. His crater eyes were shaded by the brim of his hat, which made them seem like smudges of ash. "So, you're waiting on somebody," he said. "I thought maybe you broke down."

"Nope, just waiting, sir."

"Yeah, I though you might need a tow."

Nope, my friend went into the woods to, ah . . . you know."

"Oh," he said. "To see a man about a dog."

I grinned and he laughed softly and nodded his head. I liked him then, even if he did have an ugly mouth and an acne-scarred complexion.

"So how's the old girl run?"

"Runs good. Got loose fenders and such, but the engine is strong."

"Yeah, built 'em to last in those days." He petted the Dodge some more. Then said nonchalantly, "So, you from round here, son?"

I told him who I was and where I lived and that I was going to sell my cucumbers up in Iron River, where they give better prices than the factory in Blueberry.

"So you're one of the Foggy boys, huh?" he said. "Hey, I know your dad." He paused and looked around. I knew he wanted to wait and see who was going to come out of the woods. "So, how is your dad?"

I said everything was fine with Pa, the same as ever.

"You know, I haven't seen him in probably ten years. He used to come in and shoot the breeze at the feed store. Before it went bankrupt and closed down. I remember him pretty well. Say, does he still quote Shakespeare? Everything was 'rotten in Denmark' and all that kind of stuff about Horatio knowing heaven and earth. Something like that."

"'There are more things in heaven and earth, Horatio, than are dreamt of in your philosophy.' Yeah, Pa still says it all the time. He can quote reams of Willie S. all day if he wants to."

"Willie S? Oh, I remember, yeah, he used to call him Willie S." And he said, "So are you a chip off the old block? Do you read Shakespeare?"

"I like stories about animals. Someday I'll write about cows."

"You want to write about cows?"

"Nobody writes about them. Cows are more interesting than people think."

"God, you're Jacob Foggy's son all right. Listen, I'll tell you what, I was raised on a dairy farm over by Turtle Lake, and I'll tell you what, I've never come on anything dumber than cows. Except maybe some hunters I've know who don't know a cow from a doe. But no, I'll tell you, nothing much can touch a cow for plain stupidity. I've seen cows that would let you beat them to death before they would step across a sixteen-inch manure gutter, and I've seen some that would leap over that same gutter like an antelope, when all they had to do was take one small step across. In fact, I've seen them do dumber things than that. I've—"

"But geez, you got to understand their thinking," I interrupted. "You got to be able to think like they do, and then they don't seem so dumb. You know, they get confused easy. If you ask them to step across a sixteen-inch gutter, especially if it's the first time, they got to decide if they can maneuver that big belly and those four knobby legs all at once and not have some part fall in the gutter causing a thousand pounds of trouble and grief. Things look different to cows than they do to humans. Why should they trust us to get them across? Half the time we're petting them, half the time we're smacking them and cussing them out. If I was a cow, I sure wouldn't trust a human. Would you? Every cow knows that someday you're going to do something bad to her, shoot her or send her to Packerland. Every cow knows the truth in her bones. Heck, to them maybe Packerland is just across that sixteen-inch gutter, know what I mean?"

The cop was smiling at me. His teeth didn't look real. Too perfect. Too plastic. "Jacob Foggy written all over you," he said.

"We got a cow at home," I told him. "Her name is Sugar. And you know what? I'm never going to ship her – never in this life. She's mine, and she did sixteen thousand pounds in her first lactation. She's just like a pet dog, following me around and wanting me to pet her all the time. I've told her I'd never ship her. I've been there, to that slaughterhouse. That place would turn your heart to concrete if you stayed inside it very long. I bet if everybody had to see those cows smelling blood and slobbering on the floor because they're so scared, we'd all be vegetarians."

"You a vegetarian?" he asked. I had to admit I wasn't, though I wanted to be, but it was hard to be eating meat all your life and then just stop. "I'll tell you what," he said. "You can show us all the slaughterhouses in the world and all the cows smelling blood and slobbering on the floor, and you can show us that guy with the explosive rod rapping those cows between the eyes, and you can show us the cows falling dead and getting hauled up by their heels and gutted and skinned and shipped off in trucks. And you know what? We'll still eat 'em. It's nothing. Hell, I'm a cop, and I've seen enough to know that if it wasn't for the law keeping us from each other's throats, we'd kill and eat each other. It's real thin, son, this notion called civilization. You grow up and become a cop and you find that out real soon. Anybody could be a killer. You could be a killer. You know what I'm saying? But look here, son, I wish you and Sugar luck. I hope you never have to ship her, but soft-hearted farmers, you know how they end up?"

"How?"

"They end up as shovel-jockeys."

"I don't care. I won't ever ship her," I said.

"You're a good boy. You got a good heart." He patted my

shoulder and gave it a friendly squeeze.

It was right then that I heard Mamie. She was pounding up the path like a T-Rex after a gopher.

The cop turned to look at her. My ears felt on fire. I could see that she had blood on her forehead. She waved when she saw me. I jumped off the fender and ran to meet her. I yelled, "Mamie, what happened to your head? You fall down?"

At the edge of the trees, I grabbed her and whispered, "Stop!"

"I g-g-got it," she said shoving the key at me.

I took the key. "Cop, cop, cop," I whispered. "You got Beaver's blood on you."

"I g-g-got his dollars too." She shoved a wad of bills at me. I stuffed them in my pocket, while I had her bend down so I could examine her forehead.

"It's nothing bad," I said, swiping a tiny cut above her eyebrow with the jagged edge of the key.

She squinted in pain, whispering, "Oooch."

I led her back to the pickup and the cop asked what happened.

"She walked into a branch," I explained. "She's a little clumsy sometimes."

"I've done it myself," he said. "When I was a boy I was out cutting wood and walked right into the end of a dead branch. It was like walking into a spear. It knocked me cold and wrecked my mouth so bad I had to have my teeth pulled and my lips sewed back on. I got scar tissue all round my mouth from so many surgeries trying to fix it. Yeah, I know what a stupid branch can do. Come on, let's clean that up."

We went to his car. He took out a first-aid kit and cleaned Mamie's cut with some cotton and a squirt of Bactine. As he reached up to fasten a bandaid on her, he said, "My god, you're a hell of a size. What are you, six-two, six-three? What do you weigh?"

Mamie shrugged her shoulders.

"I bet she could whip both our butts," he said, chuckling.

"She's a hard worker," I said. "You should see her out in the field. She moves beautiful out in the field."

"I bet she does," he said. "I'll tell you what, I like the way she looks. I don't go for these skinny girls, all these wannabe models looking like a bunch of scarecrows. Be like hugging a sack of bones. She's different. Look at these fine shoulders here. I mean, this is a man's shirt she's wearing and it can hardly contain her muscles from ripping through. This woman has done some work in her life. Hey, I pity any stupid cow that kicks her!"

"Yeah, nobody messes with Mamie," I said.

We laughed about that and both of us were patting Mamie's big shoulders, while she gave us her best froglike grin.

At last the cop said he had to get along, but he hoped to see us around and he wanted me to tell my dad hello from Ken Maydwell. He got in his car and pulled back onto the pavement. Gunning the engine he laid some scratch and gave us a whoop of his siren. We waved him down the road.

When he was out of sight, we hurried into the pickup and took off. I turned us in the opposite direction, drove a few miles before going north on O up to highway 13. Which I took east for a while, before getting off onto some dirt roads, zigzagging around, just driving I didn't know where. And then the radiator boiled over and we had to stop to let the engine cool. The truck sat on an uphill, bordered on both sides by alders and pine and white birch.

As we sat there, the radiator steaming, the engine ticking and the stale odor of John Beaver hanging like an infection in the air, I started wondering what on earth I was doing. I closed my eyes and said to myself, "This must be a dream. How could this happen to me?" When I opened my eyes, Mamie was hovering inches away, her eyes beaming with a blue, electrifying light that was hypnotic. Her hair had been wind-handled and stood out around her head like shiny copper, a kind of wiry pot scrubber you might say with two chunks tin snipped. If Orphan Annie and Paul Bunyan had had a daughter, I figured something like Mamie would be the consequence.

"Mamie Bunyan," I said.

Her mouth was working like it was on rubber hinges. "La-la-la," she stammered.

"Say it slow," I told her.

She pointed to me, then to herself.

"Yeah, you and me, Mamie. You and me. But what're we gonna do now? You got any ideas?"

She pounded the dashboard, which rattled and yelped with each blow. A lightning crack ran up the windshield. "G-g-g-!" she hollered. "G-go!"

I turned the engine over until the battery ran down. Then I coasted backward and tried to pop-start it, but when I let the clutch in something snapped underneath and the shift lever flew into neutral and wouldn't go back into gear. While I was trying to force the lever, grinding the gears, the pickup was still rolling backward. It rolled off the gravel and into a ditch. Mamie's side lifted and hung in the air for a second before settling over. The pickup rested softly on its left side. Mamie fell on me and the sound our heads made coming together reminded me of the whump of Beaver's head. I saw white dots floating in front of my eyes. Mamie was giggling. She was slobbering on my cheek and saying, "La-la-la," her mouth working on my cheekbone the way a snake's mouth works on an egg. Finally she brought forth her version of the word *love*. Mamie lufed me.

"Yeah, okay," I said. "But would you mind getting the hell off me? I can hardly breathe."

My head was throbbing. Mamie was crushing me and slobbering on me and la-la-la-ing me and I had had about all I could stand. And also it occurred to me that the pickup was on its side and that gas was probably leaking onto the hot manifold, which could start a fire and fry us both. I imagined for a second that I heard a fire whooshing to life, but it was just Mamie's heavy breathing.

Loving me too much, she began digging her fingers into my ribs, the sore ones that Beaver had poked earlier that morning.

"Mamie, you're driving me crazy," I told her. And then I told her to knock off the bullshit and get her fat ass off me and get out of the truck before the whole thing blew up.

She looked solemnly at me and asked if I was scared. "K-keer'd Kritch'n, keer'd?" Her voice was tender.

"Damn right I'm scared," I answered.

Standing up, she popped open the door above us and jumped out like her boots were springloaded. Then she reached back in, grabbed me by the ankle and lifted me out as if I were hardly more than a marshmallow. She lowered me softly to the ground and then jumped down beside me. She had to hug me half to death for a few seconds.

"Oh, dammit all," I told her, "this is no game, Mamie. I'm not your boyfriend, so just stop slobbering on me and get a grip. You got to get it through your thick skull that we are in very bad trouble. They put kids like us in prison and throw away the key. You understand my poetics, Mamie? Huh? We are in way over our heads."

"Shush," she said, soothingly. "Shush, shush. I la-luf you."

I turned away in disgust and limped into the woods. She followed along and took my hand and led me about fifty yards in through the trees, until we came to a giant fir with its lower branches hanging tent-like to the ground. We crawled underneath into a sort of teepee suffused with a soft gray light. The place felt restful. I lay down on a bed of needles and held my head. Which was still throbbing. Like maybe I had a concussion. Or worse, I was having a stroke.

And I said to myself, I said, *You're going to have to ditch this Mamie before she kills you. You'll never be able to stand her. Tinkerbell with a gland problem. Jesus.* She was still stuttering and stammering about loving me, singing it like she sang her ABCs, and she put my head in her lap and rubbed my temples softly. I moaned when she kissed my mouth and my eyes and both my cheeks and my aching head.

"Ah God, can't you leave me alone?" I said.

I dozed and woke all day and finally my headache eased. As evening came I drifted into sleep and had a nightmare: John Beaver was sitting on my chest, hitting me with the butt of his knife and saying, "Skin you, Fuggy, skin you, Fuggy and hang yer hide on the barn." It took a million stars to wish on to make him quit. Cool air was on my face when I woke up. It was dark and the smell of pine was thick. My head was clear as a summer day made for haying, and I was hungry and thirsty, with no idea where I was going to find food in these woods. No weapons, no traps. We would need to find a stream of water, or a clean lake if we were lucky. Where was the Brule? Back there somewhere - where I used to have a home-life and very few worries. That was just yesterday morning. When I was simply Christian Peter Foggy. Before John Beaver and Mamie forced me to make a decision that had changed everything. For the rest of my life? For her, this girl I hardly knew? She held me spoon-fashion against her, a leg and an arm wrapped over me. The rise and fall of her chest against my back was like the surge of a river.

The No-rain Dance

Opening my eyes I saw fir needles spreading like giant fans over me. The tree exhaled a heavy piney smell. The woods were alive with singing birds and the murmur of wind through the tips of trees. I lay curled into myself, just listening and absorbing. And then—

It all came rushing back to me, the ride with Beaver, the sneaking up on Mamie, the scream, the chase, the fall, the orange-red hair flashing in the sun, the blade slicing her freckly neck. Which made me smash John Beaver's head. And the rest of the images flying by at light speed, and here I was beneath a sheltering tree and Mamie was—

Mamie was where? I sat up. Next to me was my sack of cucumbers and the long piece of rope that had been curled in the bed of the pickup. "Mamie?" I called softly. "Mamie, where are you?" The birds stopped singing. The sound of an engine roaring and the clattering of something metal troubled the air. I left the shelter of the fir and headed toward the road. And the sounds got louder, the clatter of machinery moving and a human voice shouting, "Let's turn her by hand!"

Answered with, "That blasted gear again, Tony! Listen to the sonofabitch rattle!"

There was a noise like gear-grooves kicking a crowbar. And the Tony voice said, "Let's just turn her over by hand, Red. Come on, she's almost there. We can do it. Come on, you guys, give a shove."

I crawled within sight of what was happening. There were four men, two of them in overalls and baseball caps. The other two were uniformed Highway Patrol. One was Ken Maydwell. He was staring into the trees, hands on his hips, O mouth stretched like a silent howl. The other men were waving to him and saying, "Let's do her, Ken." He walked over and took a hold of the pickup and all together the men rocked it and said, "One! Two! Three! Heave!" They bullied the pickup over onto its tires. It exhaled leaves and dirt from underneath, then was steady. The driver's side was rumpled but not too badly.

"I told you we could do it," said the one called Tony. He thumped his chest like a gorilla.

The one named Red pulled out a cigarette and lit it. "Let's get the cable working," he said. "I don't want to push this hunk of junk up to the road."

They went to work on the tow truck's cable and finally got the gears meshed and were able to pull the Dodge back onto the road. Ken reached inside the glove box and pulled out a slip of paper and said, "It's John Beaver's all right. Here's the registration."

Red was pointing at the tire tracks that led to the ditch. "Looks like they rolled backwards, then went over. What the hell you suppose they were doing? Playing grabass?"

"I think they're not going to come back and tell us," said Ken. "They're out there somewhere." He pointed almost exactly to where I was hiding.

"A hundred miles of forest," said Tony. "You ain't gonna find em, unless you get some dogs."

"Maybe they'll come back on their own," Red said.

"Come back on their own?" said Ken. "Would you come back if John Beaver was waiting for you? Hell no!"

"Naw, me neither," said Red.

"I might just be a dumb cop suckered by those kids, but I ain't crazy. They better hope we find them first because if Beaver does, he'll tear them apart."

"I never seen a guy so fucking mad," said Ken's partner. "Especially one with a concussion."

"He was foaming at the mouth," said Ken. "I'll tell you what, that bastard should never have lived through what they did to his head. You and me would be dead as doornails."

"Head hard as an oak stump," said the other cop.

All four men chuckled at the oak stump comment. Then Ken said, "You see he's got an X on his crown now, Frank? All those black stitches. Did you see that?"

"X marks the spot," said Frank. "Yeah, I seen it. And he kept saying he's a-gonna kill that kid, a-gonna kill that kid. That Christian Foggy he said had the face of an angel but the mind of a demon from hell, haw haw haw!"

"Yeah, such a clean-cut boy," said Ken wistfully. "I just never figured—"

"We'll be after that Beaver for murder one day soon. Mark my words," Frank said. "That little fucker is in major boo-coo trouble. He'll never be able to come back here."

"But it don't compute, Frank. This kid I'm telling you had the softest heart. Real tender when he talked about cows going to Packerland for slaughter. Practically had tears in his eyes. I'm saying Beaver must have done something pretty bad to make a boy like that pick up a club and clobber him."

"What did he call him, a little baby-faced poontang monster?"

"I thought I'd fall on the floor. It was funny how he said it, and then saying, 'Who'd ever thunk a baby-faced punk like him could down a Beaver,' that was funny too."

"Brave little shitbird."

"Had to be. You see Beaver's arms, Frank?"

"A pair of boa constrictors."

"Crush that boy like aluminum foil."

"God help that kid if that bastard finds him before we do."

"Yeah, God help him."

I was trembling head to toe. My mouth felt like a dustbin. I could hardly breathe. John Beaver wasn't dead after all. I wasn't an accessory to murder, but that didn't make me feel any better. John Beaver was after me, coming to kill me, coming to crush me in those boa constrictor arms. I was as worse off as ever. Maybe worser. John Beaver or jail. Assault with a deadly weapon. Attempted murder. Grand theft auto. Mug shot. Fingerprints. Articles in the news about vicious Baby-Face Foggy. What was it Ken said? "Such a clean-cut boy." I wondered how I looked now, dirty and scruffy, a hunted, haunted look in my eyes, fear and maybe even madness written all over my face. Was I crazy? I felt like maybe I might be. Else how could I be creeping through the forest on my hands and knees with my mind full of vicious thoughts wishing John Beaver was dead of a fractured skull? Buried like those Nazis in World War II tried to bury their sins. Whatever it took, just so that ogre couldn't be coming after me. I mean why me? For crying out loud, all I wanted was to go home and mind my own business. I wanted my cows and the farm back, my mother and my father. Even my ornery brothers and Mary Magdalen. I wanted eggs and potatoes for breakfast. I wanted fishing at the Brule and going back to school when summer was over. I wanted God to stop the sun like he did for Joshua at Jericho and then add one more miracle to that. Put the sun in reverse and make time go back to the moment just before Mamie showed up on the shore and caught those fish and fed me and romped through the meadow - all those antics attracting my admiration. To hell with it. To hell with her. She had earthquaked my life to pieces, crumbled it all to hell. I hated her!

Behind me I heard Tony yelling to watch out! The tow truck engine was revving and gears were grinding and Tony shouting, "It's no go! Look out!"

I saw the raised front of the pickup flopping down on the road and the cable flying from the reel. The other three men were trying to hold the truck back, but it was no good. They were being dragged along with it. Red tripped and fell and tumbled. Frank fell too. Ken let go and shouted, "Fuck you!" And the truck went rolling like a boulder down to the bottom of the ditch again.

Tony was still grinding the gears on the back of the tow truck and when the pickup rolled over he hollered, "Oh, shit, fellas!" Then he started laughing and slapping his knee.

"Goddamn you!" Red yelled. He had tumbled all the way to the bottom of the ditch just like the pickup.

Tony was giggling and apologizing to Red. "Oh, Red, man, I'm fucking sorry, tee-hee-hee!"

"Oh, God, my fucking back!" Red said.

Bursts of laughter came from Frank as well. And then he said he was sorry. "But you looked so funny going ass over teakettle like that!" Then Ken started laughing too and all of them were pointing at Red, who was telling everybody to shut the fuck up and fuck off! I was chuckling myself and caught up in what was happening, and didn't hear Mamie coming up behind me.

"W-whoa, Kritch'n," she murmured. Which just about gave me a heart attack. Her finger pointed at the mess in the ditch and she whispered, "How f-funny."

"Let's get out of here," I said. I headed back through the trees with her behind me. We came to the fir and crawled under into the steeple-like feel of it.

"Where you been?" I said. "I been looking all over for you."

She dug in the gunnysack and handed me a cucumber. "I f-find a p-place to g-go," she said. "A p-pond and hmmm-huckleberries."

I bit into the cucumber and it was bitter. "They're all too young," I said. "They'll all be bitter."

Mamie sat cross-legged, munching hers and smiling. I bit into another one and it was bitter too. I threw it away. She was eating cucumber number two like it was an ice cream Bonbon. "Don't you got no taste buds?" I said.

"T-t-tastes l-like w-watermelon rind," she said.

"Like hell it does," I said. "Well, you ain't human, anyway. You from another planet, that's all I know for sure."

Far off, we could hear the tow truck hauling the pickup out of the ditch again. And at last we could hear everybody driving away. Then in a little while the birds picked up where they left off and the trees were full of song and Mamie was making moves on me. More of that la-la-ing and hugging. I threw her arms off and told her to leave me alone.

"Anybody ever tell you you're crazy?" I asked.

"Uh-huh," she said.

"Yeah? Well, you are. But look here dammit, Mamie, what the hell do you want to do?"

With her hands she cleared a place in the needles. Then she took my hand and pressed a finger in the dirt and sang, "Aaa, bee, cee, dee—"

"You want me to teach you to write? I'll teach you to write. Here, write this." I wrote *H-O-M-E* with my finger. She pondered the word. "It says home, Mamie. I wanna go home."

She pointed to me and pointed to herself and said, "Home."

"All right whatever you say," I said.

In an instant she was yanking me from beneath the boughs and towing me through the woods, dodging trees and brush, Mamie neighing and shouting "Hippa-weee!" and moving with that natural grace that no human being I had ever known could imitate. For probably half a mile we ran, leaping ferns and swishing here and there through sudden grasses and bushes, until we came to a clearing and a large pond. Mamie stopped at the shore and held her arms out wide, embracing the sky like an Indian embracing the Great Spirit.

"Home!" she hollered.

It was pretty nice all right. The water clean. The bottom sandy. Trees in a horseshoe shape surrounding the three far sides of the pond, while behind us were sandy patches and grass and farther back vines full of huckleberries, blue, purple and black. A breeze tickled the leaves of the vines, making them wiggle like thin tongues. The huckleberries glowing in sunny clusters looked mouthwatering. Mamie pointed at a rabbit-run coming out of some brush down to the water. "Bunbuns," she said.

"How we gonna catch em?" I asked her.

From her farmeralls she pulled Beaver's buck knife, a coil of shoestring rawhide, a leather sling, and a fistful of kitchen matches. She shook her treasures at me. I could see the possibilities. But for the moment the berries would do. I started stripping off handfuls of fruit, cramming them into my mouth. After a few minutes of pigging I slowed down and got more picky. The darkest berries were the sweetest. I popped them into my mouth and savored the squish of juice over my tongue and down my throat. My palms turned blue-black. The syrup made my lips sticky. It was huckleberry heaven. I ate like I had found manna in the wilderness. Ambrosia. The tree of life. It took me a long time to get satisfied, but getting my belly full changed my attitude.

I told Mamie, "Shoot, this ain't half-bad. We got Beaver's

money and we can hike out and find a store and buy some supplies, see? And we can catch rabbits and fish, pull up wild onions, eat roots and berries, sleep and wake when we want to, lay in the sun, swim in the pond all we like. We'll make the best of what we got. You and me, Mamie. Me and you. No brothers, no Pa to tell me what to do. And especially no John Beaver. Thank God for small favors."

When I finally turned around to see how she was reacting to my speech, I found Mamie naked and up to her waist in water. She was bending forward just enough so her nipples were getting wet. She was fishing - her face a study in concentration, like she had switched her brain to automatic instinct, so it could instantly decide when it would be best to make a move. Her eyes stared at the water as curious bluegill came to nibble at her nipples and fingers. She kept so still she seemed to be one of those statues a long-ago Greek might have carved. Except for that wild-reddish, hacked-up hair flirting with the wind. I thought about how solid she looked, and for all her manly size she was actually beautiful, rounded and firm and feminine, only the smallest roll of fat over her abdomen.

The juice on my lips and hands had dried to a tar-like texture. I wanted to wash it off, but I didn't dare go near the water and scare the fish. So I squatted next to the vines, rested my chin on my knees and waited.

By the time Mamie finally threw the first fish on the shore I was half asleep. I saw the fish flying toward me, hitting the sand and flopping all over. I hurried to catch it. The surface of the water broke again soon after, a bubbly wave releasing another fat bluegill. I caught it too and tapped its head with the butt of Beaver's knife. I sliced the two bellies and cleaned them out. Before I was done another fish landed at my feet. Then another a few minutes later. Mamie was in her stride. She had her timing down. Within an hour or so, we had a fire built and a dozen fish to fry, each one not much more than a mouthful. We draped them on green sticks through the gills and gave them five minutes over the flame. They were smoky flavored and so tender they just sighed away in our mouths. And they did the job. Between the bluegill and the huckleberries we got full enough to settle back on our elbows and relax and enjoy the warmth of the day, the slip-slip sound of the water.

"Now this is living," I said. "This is the good life, don't you think?"

Mamie sat beside me, smacking her shiny lips, licking her fingers and burping profoundly. Round the nipples of her breasts were reddish nips where the fish had come to feed. I asked her if they hurt. She shook her head no and told me that the fish gave tiny pinches, but we gave them back big bites for that. She opened and closed her mouth to show me how we gobbled up the fish. She laughed happily and sprayed fish bits in my face.

"You sure are a heathen," I said. "Close your mouth. Ain't you got no manners?"

"Nup," she said, and to prove it she broke wind.

I lifted my leg and gave her a good one right back. We both laughed like a couple of drunks rolling on our backs, howling. Farts are always funny when you're a kid. After a while we sobered up, and then I asked Mamie how it was she knew to angle for fish that way with her nipples and fingers.

She cocked her head in a heavy think. Then said, "Smmma-art," tapping her head.

"Damn smart," I said. "I'd never thought of it in a million years."

She told me in her stammering way that huckleberry leaf makes good tea, that fireweed tastes like asparagus and dandelions are better than spinach. She said you catch frogs with your shirt as a net, but you only eat the legs. Slingers are for picking birds off limbs, and snares are for bunnies that hop down the bunny trail to get water at night.

Later I gave her another writing lesson. I wrote her name and told her to follow each letter one at a time right below where I had written it. She tried, but still the letters were all crooked and the E was backwards. I couldn't figure it out. I rocked back on my heels and told her to keep trying. She looked like some bulky animal come out of the water to scratch and grub in the sand. She was what the caveman might have been so long ago – heavy bones, heavy muscles, thick neck, thin mouth clamped tight as an oyster, and a roundish, moonish face with a forehead climbing out of darkness, growing broad and shiny the same as her eyes so wondrous large, like the eyes of an alert owl watching a mouse scurrying. I was wishing she were smarter in book-ways that she could learn from me. But inside her brain there must have been a missing gear that wouldn't let her see alphabet letters clearly. In any case she had proved she was fairly smart about some things, and, in fact, smarter than me when it came to nature in the raw and a little thing called survival. I was the pupil in those particulars; she was the teacher.

I took a nap and when I woke the sun was west, it's bottom edge touching the tips of the trees. Mamie was several feet downshore, still scrawling her name. I stood up and looked at dozens of jagged MAMIEs lined up in a row at the water's edge. The wind had strengthened and was sending waves ashore that had rubbed out a MAMIE here and there. The sky was clouding over south of us, cumulus clouds tumbling our way. The smell of woods and water was heavy with moisture in my mouth and nose – sure signs of coming rain. I called to Mamie, telling her we had to get back to our tree because a storm was coming. She looked up at me, her eyes peculiar - sort of narrow and puzzled. Like she didn't quite know who in the world I was or what I was talking about.

"It's me," I said. "What's the matter with you? What you looking at me so funny for? Are you sick?"

She rose up tall, wide-shouldered, naked, her bush a tangled, reddish nest. Her knees were covered with damp sand. Her eyes blinked slowly. The wind played with her hair, whipping it into licks of flame. Her mouth drooped. Spit had hardened on her lower lip in ridges white as chalk. I swallowed nervously and thought, *God, what a creature! What a scary thing it is.*

"Gonna rain," I told her. "Rain's coming, see?"

She stared. Eyes burrowing into mine violently. It looked almost like she hated me.

"We best get back to the tree," I said. "Mamie, what you doing? You're looking sort of nutty, you know? You're foaming at the mouth, Mamie. Hey, wake up! You're scaring me!"

She started singing, "Hiya, hiya, hiya." Her body swaying, her big feet pounding the sand, like an Indian doing one of those dances they do. Snake dance. Buffalo dance. Rain dance. I heard invisible drums beating in the background. "Hiya, hiya," and then she added "No-rain, no-rain, no-rain." Her voice was mannish, not a trace of stammer, chanting evenly the same way she did her ABCs—"Hiya no-rain, hiya no-rain."

I was skittish, but also fascinated. I watched her lift one leg, then the other faster and faster, her feet pounding the damp sand in time to the beat of hiya no-rain, hiya no-rain. Big breasts bouncing. Solid thighs corded with blood-gorged muscle. She held the knife over her head pointing it towards the sky, before tossing it high, the twirling blade reflecting slices of light, like a star winking on and off. When it came down, she timed it perfectly, catching the hilt in her hand. And all the while singing, "Hiya no-rain, hiya no-rain."

Next, she turned in circles, stomping her legs harder and harder, circling my way. I watched her coming and tried to read her face as it whirled round and round, but I saw nothing there to give me any confidence. I wondered if she was having some kind of seizure, some kind of fit. Or maybe she had finally gone totally off her rocker and was going to cut my throat.

Fuwump, fuwump, fuwump! said her feet coming closer and closer—*fuwump! fuwump!* I felt paralyzed. *Christian, you are going to die,* I told myself. Soon she was close enough that I could smell her - her body musky, dampish, cowish. I tried to wave her away, but she was over me hovering - a human horror. Maybe she needed some pill, one of those anti-psycho medications that kept crazy people calm. Maybe that was how John Beaver kept her under control. What did I know? I knew nothing really about her. And I had no idea how I was supposed to act. I went with my instincts and shucked my clothes off to be naked like she was, and I started moving my legs like hers up and down and I joined her in the hiya no-rain song. Her face came within inches of my own. Her breath blew bluegill fragrance into my mouth as she sang the hiya no-rain faster and louder and faster. And faster. Jesus! We were dancing frantically, our feet thumping the sand, packing it and making footprints running back and forth from the shore to the water and back again, and all the time shouting hiya no-rain at each other. I mean what do you do when a nut acts nutty like that? Best to act nutty yourself. Otherwise you might be insulting her. Otherwise she might see you as the enemy.

It went on and on, Mamie's face glowing with an inner fire. Her skin the color of wet pink bubblegum. Her eyes like twin pilot lights. Her mouth drawn back so far that the corners nearly touched the lobes of her ears (hiya no-rain). I was looking at a pink-faced frog. A grinning pink-faced frog whose tongue was going to whip out and zap me like a witless fly. She jabbed the knife up and up. I was sweating buckets, gasping for air, my legs heavier and heavier, so I could hardly lift them. I couldn't sing hiya no-rain anymore. My chest burned. The knife kept poking the air above my head. And all out of puff, I finally collapsed, whispering, "Don't" to Mamie as she came for me, her legs parting as she straddled my waist, her bottom grinding me into the sand. Her head came at mine like a club and then she was kissing me, sucking my life away. I felt sick to my stomach, on the verge of vomiting. That frog mouth on mine, that tongue probing inside, tickling the back of my throat. I was smothering. So this is how we die. It comes out of nowhere and in seconds we are gone. Her hips were working over my hips, a wetness sliding up and down. Without wanting to I got an erection and Mamie slipped it inside her. Back and forth, up and down she moved.

Ungluing her lips from mine she murmured, "Hiya no-rain, Kritch'n," slowing the pace, moving her hips in time to the rhythm of her song. Then she was singing louder, shouting and moving her hips faster and faster in a bucking bronco motion. The knife went over her head again. I closed my eyes and heard the sound of the blade slicing the sand beside my ear. Mamie shuddered and cried out like she was in pain, but when I opened my eyes I saw that she was smiling frog-like again. She brushed my cheek with the back of her hand.

"Hiya," she said.

"Are you killing me?" I asked.

She got off of me and grabbed my hand. "Drowd'n man," she said, dragging me to the water and throwing me in. The shock of the water woke me up. I felt as if the whole no-rain thing had been a dream - a wet dream that is. She hadn't really done what I dreamt she had. Not a chance. I let her toss me around and rescue me a few times, until finally she dragged me back to shore and stretched herself beside me in the sand. The warm wind dried us. The sun was down. A hazy blue twilight filled the air. The clouds had tumbled farther south. The stormy mood was gone.

"You made the rain go away," I said.

She fingered her belly.

"The rain's in there?" I said.

She cupped herself. Then raised her fingers to my nose. I smelled musty rain. I stood up and said, "Mamie, wake me up. I think I'm dreaming."

She slapped me on the ass and laughed hugely, the sound echoing over the water. Which is where I ran to get away from her. Next thing I knew she was after me, coming on like a tornado, shouting, "Drowd'n man!"

Nightmare Beaver

One day we searched the shore on the other side of the pond and we found an old campsite. Half buried in the sand and ashes were a rusted grill and a big tin pot with a hole in the bottom about the size of a nickel. We also found some rusty tin cans, their jagged lids peeled back for handles. We cleaned them up and used them to drink from and for boiling huckleberry leaf tea. The hole in the pot we plugged with clay and baked it in the fire. The grill was useful to fry fish and squirrel and rabbit or whatever else we caught. A nice, fat pheasant one time.

Our snares worked pretty well. But unfortunately we caught a skunk one day. We would have let it go, but it wouldn't let us come near, overpowering us by fouling up the air so bad we had to run back to the pond and jump in the water. All day we could smell skunk lingering like microscopic drops of acid hovering near us. For four or five days after the poor thing died, we could still smell it when the breeze shifted our way.

After we got a routine going, we were able to make up all kinds of recipes, not just fried fish and huckleberries. Our favorite was a soup of dandelion greens and wild onions with red squirrel or rabbit. Squirrels were nearly as plentiful as bluegill perch, and Mamie was deadly with her sling, whirling it overhead round and round in a blur, the humming of it like a nest of bees, and then fwap! Letting it go and plucking a squirrel off a branch as easy as plucking an apple.

The Wisconsin woods were easy-going and helpful. Even the mosquitoes weren't as bad as usual, so long as we stayed in the shade or close to the smoky campfire or in the water. We of course did get bitten now and then and itched a lot, but we figured out that a coat of mud smeared on our arms and legs and neck did wonders. Some days we would smear mud on each other head to toe. The mud would dry and become a light reddish color. We would go around like that, like those Africans that smear themselves with ochre. At night we always took a bath in the pond water and came out clean. We slept in each other's arms beneath the fir tree on fresh boughs every night.

When we weren't hunting for food or playing in the pond or exploring, we pretended we were in school. I was the teacher and Mamie the pupil. With a little help she could sort of almost write her first name. I would scratch MA in the sand and she would complete it, but often as not the E would be backwards and the M upside down. Then I would write BEA and she would pay close attention to the letters that followed and sometimes even get them right. And yet if I quoted something to her, like *To be or not to be that is the question*, she would zip it back to me without a flaw. Mamie was a great mimic, no doubt about it. I dug out of my head all the poems and the lines of Shakespeare that I knew and she had no trouble memorizing everything she heard. I also sang songs and she would listen once and sing them to me with the same nasal twang that I used in order to sound like a cowboy, like Hank Williams singing *"Your cheating heart will tell on you,"* or Faron Young singing, *"I'm gonna live fast, love hard, die young, and leave a beautiful memory."* I knew all kinds of songs like that and pretty soon, Mamie knew them too, and we would be doing duos and sounding professional. Well, maybe not professional, but not bad, anyway.

One day we were checking our snares and we had caught another rabbit. It was jumping at the end of the noose and trembling. Mamie lifted the rabbit and slipped the noose off its head. It was a cottontail, brown and white, about half-grown. Nose twitching nervously. Eyes wide as quarters.

"Not much more than a baby," I said.

We looked at each other.

"You ha-hungry?" asked Mamie.

"A little bit. Not much."

"Kritch'n eat the b-bunny?"

"Nah, let it go."

And she did. She put the rabbit down and it ran into the underbrush. We stood awhile, Mamie and me staring at the close columns of trees that kept the woods in permanent shades of lavender and shades of gray, and I for one imagined what they would be like in winter ghosted with snow. I asked Mamie what we were going to do when summer was over. She didn't know.

So I decided to do something about our situation. I told Mamie I needed to find a phone and call my parents.

"W-w-why?" she said.

"Because this isn't the Garden of Eden, and my parents need to know I'm okay and also my pa will know what we should do."

Mamie waited at the pond, while I hiked out to the road and followed it to the highway. It wasn't long until I came to a town called Flato. WELCOME TO FLATO said a sign outside a gas station/general store. VACATION IN FLATO – ACCOMODATIONS – WATER HARMONY – FISH! – BOAT – SWIM – HIKE – STAY WITH US AWHILE FOLKS! The letters were faded. The sign leaned like it was about ready to fall. Someone had written graffiti at the bottom. In messy black letters was the sentence, *cuntemplate your navel Budda*. The town itself was hardly more than a wrinkle in the road. Other than the gas station and general store, there was a boarded up café and some cabins for rent. Some boats were down by a lake a few yards away. The door to one of the cabins was open, the curtains drawn back. I could see the silhouette of a man as he backed away from the window. I went into the store. It smelled like mildewed wood. Canned goods with sun-bleached labels sat on several shelves. There were some loaves of Wonder Bread, lots of Twinkies and chocolate cupcakes in a two-pack. Candy bars were piled in an open display case. A refrigerator with a round cooler on top buzzed. One wall was covered with carved wooden signs: HOME SWEET HOME IS WHERE YOU HANG YOUR HAT – LOVE IS A TWO-FOOT MUSKIE – DEATH IS LIFE'S WAY OF TELLING YOU TO SLOW DOWN – A CONTENTED MIND KNOWS PEACE AT ANY AGE – WHERE THE HELL IS FLATO WISCONSIN?

Unlit signs advertised beer and soda. Behind a counter lined with toadstool seats sat a bald man with a long, white beard. The bottom half of the beard rested on the man's chest. He stroked his beard like he was petting a cat. Behind him were a grill and a coffee pot and a case that was supposed to have pies and cakes in it but was empty. I sat on one of the toadstools and asked the man if I could have a hamburger and a cup of coffee. My mouth was watering at the thought. He shook his head at me and frowned and said:

"Got no hamburger meat. Got no buns. Got eggs."

Eggs were fine with me. He lit the grill and scrambled two, put them on a plate and poured me a cup of coffee. I handed him a ten-dollar bill that had belonged to John Beaver. The man stuck it in his pocket and sat down.

"It cost ten dollars?" I said.

"What?"

"I give you a ten."

"You did?"

"Yes sir."

"Okay, you're welcome."

"But—" I didn't know what to do. I picked up my fork and ate the eggs. They tasted like air. The coffee was bitter.

"You got a phone I can use?" I asked the old man.

"Out of order," he told me.

"Where's a phone I can use, do you know?"

"What you want a phone for?"

"Never mind," I said. I looked out the smeary window, wondering where I should go to find a phone. "Sure quiet here," I said.

"Quiet as dust on a door ledge," he replied. He petted his beard and told me that there was no justice in the world, just lots of cutthroats. Fancy places up in Millacs and north of Duluth sucked vacationers out of Wisconsin, so only the oldest of the old-timers came to Flato anymore, and those old farts were dying off. No one had a vision of the way resorts should be, those who didn't like no cluttered-up nature were souls of the long ago past and most of them were dead. And the rest were dying.

"I like it here," I told him. "It's peaceful."

"So is a cave," he said. "Lots of time to sit and think. All the time in the world to ask yourself who you are and what you're doing in this backwater. Time to wonder about how smart you've been chasing rainbows all your life. Time to wonder if maybe less appetite and more spirit would have given you a better sense of proportion. Your juices dry up and your body gets wrinkled and dull, so all you've got left is your mind – if you've got a mind, I mean. Can't even enjoy a woman anymore. But you make the best of it and say good riddance. Now you can get peaceful inside yourself. Now you can work on the inner light. Be all right if you had no memory of what women looked like naked and what they feel like when you slip them on. Don't let anybody kid you, sonny – old age isn't for sissies. Old age is like being chained in a pit of memory and staring at shadows of yourself on the wall. And nobody comes to see you because you talk too much about nothing. At least they want to think it's nothing, but they'll find out. Nobody but the immature dead get out of getting old. And you know you're talking too much, but you can't help it. You see an ear and you've got to bend it. But nobody comes to listen, because people like you want gadgets. No gadgets here. Just old age and a grumpy old man who won't shut up. Fish don't even bite no more, they're so bored. Had one customer since I opened this summer. He's out there now. All he does is prowl the woods all day. Won't rent a boat, the bastard. Buys beer and potato chips. Ugly mug on him, like a troll under a bridge. Tells me to shut up when I try to talk to him about important things like what I'm telling you. I hate people who won't listen."

I got up and walked around the store. The old man raised his voice. He wanted me to know about solitude, that solitude was tolerable if you didn't think about long legs and big tits. What you had to learn was meditation, to go into a trance for hours and probe the mysteries of life and to come to understand that only a decent set of ethics made life worth the trouble, because the mysteries never talked and nobody ever knew anything but that nobody ever knew nothing.

While he rambled on, I decided to steal some things to take

back to Mamie. I mean what the hell he had stolen my ten dollars. Well, John Beaver's ten dollars. The old man wasn't watching me, so I reached inside the case and fisted as many candy bars as would fit in my pockets. I took Twinkies and cupcakes too and slipped them inside my shirt. When I estimated that I had close to ten dollars worth I stopped. The old man was saying that death would be the best sleep you ever had and maybe you wake up later and talk to your dead friends, so what was there to fear about dying?

His voice followed me as I scooted out the door. I could hear him all the way to the edge of the store and beyond, like the faint buzz of a locust up in a tree. I took out a pack of cupcakes and tore the wrapper off. I stuffed my mouth full of sweet and gooey chocolate cake and frosting, I ate both cupcakes in five seconds and walked along licking my fingers.

"Crazy old coot, ain't he?" said a familiar voice at my shoulder.
I leaned over and threw up.
"Hey, hey, you shouldn't eat so fast, Fluffynuts."
"Please don't kill me," I begged.
"Kill you? Why would I want to kill you?"
"I'm so sorry about everything," I said.
"I know you are. I know you're sorry. Yeah, I been waitin and waitin to hear you say how sorry you are. I been stayin in that mouse hole of a cabin for many a boring day, ever since they found my truck near here. I knew you was still around. I knew you would come out one of these days. I'm so damn smart it scares me, Fluppypuppy. Scares you too, ey?"
"Yessir, Mr. Beaver."
"Yeah, you crushed the side of my truck. I couldn't get the door open, so I had to take it off. But you can't hardly kill a Dodge. She runs pretty ragged though, you know. Yeah, pinched the hole off in the radiator so it hardly leaks none. It's here to get us all home, Foggywoggy. I promise you a free ride in the bed if you want."
"It was an accident," I said. "I'll pay for the damage, I promise, Mr. Beaver."

"Oh, sure, sure, you bet, you bet," he said. He spit a brown gob on my boot and patted my head hard. "I knew you wouldn't be far. What do they call that? Is that called being psycho? This is the only store for miles. You had to come sometime, right?"

"Yessir."

"You always say yessir, you're always polite. I like that about you. Hey, I want to show you something." He took his cap off and bent down so I could see the top of his head. A stitched lump was there, black threads forming an X just like Ken Maydwell had said. "How many times you hit me, Foggydoggy? A hundred times? I've had a touch of amnesia about it."

"Three times, Mr. Beaver."

"Three times. And you with them puny arms. How can a pair of broomsticks like these knock out a bull like me."

"Well, but what if Mamie hit you too?"

"Now that would make some sense. But don't try putting the blame on her. Mamie's trained not to hit her pa. She wouldn't raise a hand to me."

"No sir."

"You juss hit a lucky spot." Putting his cap back on, he ran his thumb in an X over my head. "Right there, X marks the spot. Boom!"

"Please don't kill me, Mr. Beaver." I started to cry. Sniffling into my sleeve and crying like a scared girl. I offered him a twosome of Twinkies. He fingered the tobacco out of his mouth and ripped the cellophane off and stuffed both Twinkies in his mouth.

And then with his mouth full he said, "Don't take on so. I wouldn't hurt yer little Fluffyass for nuttin in the world. You wanna know why? Because you gonna tell me where you stashed my girl." He swallowed and said, "That was good. Ain't you gonna tell me, slimecock? Ain't you?" He took a hold of my hair and yanked it.

"Yessir."

"Just be honest with a fella."

"Yessir, I'll take your there."

"I know you will. You're a good boy. I said over and over that a boy like you would want to help a griefin man to get his lovin dotter. I miss that girl. She's all I got , you know. She's the beginning and the end of me."

"You can have her," I said. "She's too much trouble. I didn't want to leave you out there with your head broke. She made me come away. I'm glad you caught me. I'm glad this thing is over."

"I know you are. Yer homesick, and I are Mamiesick. Go on now, son, let's show the lovin papa the way."

I started off fast, but he caught my shoulder and told me to slow down a mite. He said that since I conked his head, he had been a little unsteady. Had dizzy spells. Yes, he said, I might have killed him, but Beavers are known for having hard heads. He would be moldering in his grave like John Brown right this minute otherwise.

I told him that the whole thing had been a miserable mistake and that Mamie would probably be glad to see him. Which cheered him up. He grinned crookedly and said he thought she was no doubt ready to go home. Home wouldn't look so bad now. Come back to her poor papa that loved her and missed her more than he would miss life if he was dead. She was everything to him since her mama died. Then he told me about Mary Beaver, his wife, and bragged how she could do it all. She milked cows and cleaned the barn, cooked dinner, gave birth to four dead babies and got up and went right back to work after each one. Except when Mamie was born. Mamie was too big and damn near killed her. Mary had to take the whole day off to recover. He told me how she died hauling on a stuck calf that was coming buttfirst to get born. Mary died trying to get the calf out, strained so hard it burst her heart, and Beaver lost the cow and the calf as well. He had hauled them all to the woods, skinned the cow and wrapped Mary in the hide and buried her in 1948 next to the Brule, right in the corner of Foggy land, buried her beneath that big birch tree that used to shade part of the pasture.

And as he told about it, I remembered 1957, when my brothers and I found Mary Beaver. We had pulled her up with the stump of that big birch tree. She was full of roots and worms – Mary Beaver reduced to a pile of bones wrapped in a Holstein hide. I remembered, too, that at the base of the stump he had carved her name and below it carved *GUD WERKER*. We reburied her in the same stump-hole and never put a plow near the site. What she had for company was a winter blanket of snow. Timothy and brome in summer that went to seed in autumn, when leaves blew from across the river and spread dry rainbows over her grave.

Beaver followed within five or six feet of me while he talked about this and that. I led him by the tent-tree where Mamie and I slept. And I wove him through a stand of maples. We were within shouting distance of the pond and the place where we had set our largest snare, thinking maybe a bear might wander by. Or a deer. The trap was tied to a bent poplar, a wide ring of heavy rawhide on the ground covered with leaves. Whatever tripped it would be standing on its head awhile. As we got closer, my mind was whirling like an unbalanced flywheel. I felt wobbly and like I might faint. Beaver was fighting his way along the path through some brush and I stepped lightly around the big snare and said, "Look there, John Beaver, a grouse!"

"Where?" he said, looking up to where I was pointing. Stepping true, his foot caught the snare, the anchor popping and *whoosh!* he was hind-side-to. "Yiiii!" he hollered. His head was going up and down like a yo-yo tapping the earth. I could see the poplar tree was straining to keep him. It was making cracking-creaking sounds. There was no time to waste. As I started to leave, Beaver cried out, "But Foggy, wait! C'mon, Foggy, yer my buddy. Get me out of this. What about the poor papa come for his dotter? I got that reward, Foggy!"

I squatted so I could look him in the eyes. "You really think that I would turn Mamie over to the likes of you?" I told him. "You're dumb as an anvil, Beaver."

Glaring at me he pursed his mouth and spit but missed me. He called me a lying sack a shit and a motherfucker. I kicked him in the stomach, which was a mistake because he grabbed my ankle. I fell on my back and started kicking with my other foot and yelling for Mamie. He grabbed my other foot and held them both, and we stared at each other. It seemed to me that he could eat me if he wanted, start with my toes and stuff me in his mouth like a python gorging down a goat. I was screaming as he grinned wickedly and pulled me toward him.

He had worked his way up to gripping my knees when I felt my armpits getting yanked on. Mamie's face hung over me. It was a tug of war. She was pulling one way, while Beaver pulled the other. The tree was cracking more. Beaver swayed on the rope, stretching it to the breaking point. Mamie dug her heels in and pulled me backward an inch at a time, until the tree broke in half and Beaver hit the ground and the force of the blow freed my legs. I was up and running, following Mamie as she skirted the pond and headed in the direction of the road. Looking over my shoulder I saw him coming on.

His hands were gesturing, making as if he was ripping something apart. Up one hill and down another we ran, whizzing through the trees on a course we had never run before. We came to a ridge that someone had once dynamited for ore. It was now a steep hillside of powdery red earth. There was a pit off to one side and a rutty road leading west. Mamie jumped off the edge and I followed after. We were making little hops going down, the fine dirt burying us up to our ankles each time we landed and bounded kangarooish upward and down some more. At one point I pitched forward headfirst into Mamie. Down we went the rest of the way in a heap of arms and legs. Dust rose around us, clogging our noses and mouths. For a few seconds I was blinded. I couldn't breathe. I felt like my bones were flying through the air like lost spokes from a bicycle wheel.

When we hit bottom and rolled to a stop, we heard John Beaver shouting above us. I cleared my eyes in time to see him coming over the edge – a black giant with arms outstretched against the sky, legs churning like a bowlegged ape as he leaped after us. Then he went over too, belly first, cap flying, his face shoveling the dirt and making a furrow. When he hit bottom he lay for a second moaning. Then he raised his head and looked at us and said, "Come on, guys. Ain't you had enough?" His voice was miserable.

"Booshit!" said Mamie.

"Old pegleg can't catch nobody!" I added.

We took off running backward, watching him as he pulled himself erect and took out a knife, a long pig sticker. He made gestures of gutting us, slicing morsels off our bodies, popping them into his mouth. We left him there, staggering toward us and making those carving gestures. I was convinced it would take more of a limping effort than he had in him to catch us now.

The King of Lake Flato

We were panting our lungs out by the time we reached Flato. Standing in the middle of the paved road turning in circles we didn't know which way to go. Then I remembered about the boats, and I told Mamie to follow me down to the docks. We took the first boat we came to. Mamie took the oars and I pushed off. We rowed toward a jaw of land swooping out in the water, forming a peninsula behind which we could hide. I watched Flato growing smaller, the cabins turning into dollhouses. Until at last I couldn't see the town anymore. Which was when I finally relaxed. I was sure John Beaver hadn't limped fast enough to reach the town in time to see us rowing off over the water.

"I think we made it," I told Mamie. I settled back on my elbows and said, "We ripped him good."

"R-ripped em g-good," she agreed.

"Did you see the way he nose-dived down that hill? Wasn't that funny? He looked like a pig rooting up a pasture."

"P-p-pig in a p-p-poke," she said.

"Pig in a poke making those stupid breathing noises."

"S-s-snuffa chugga chugga."

"That's it. That's what he sounded like all right."

"Hey, what the hell you doing?" someone yelled from the shore.

I saw four guys about my age at the water's edge. They were all naked. We stared at each other for a few seconds. I could hear water lapping the sides of the boat. The oarlocks creaking.

Finally I hollered, "Who're you?"

"Who're you?" one of the boys asked. His tone was aggressive. He was Indian-looking, or maybe Spanish, big cheekbones, black hair hanging to his shoulders. He was thicker than the other boys, muscular arms and shoulders. "So what's your name?" he said.

I told him our names.

"My name's Mike Quart!" he said. "I'm the king of Lake Flato." His voice hit the air like a hammer hitting a fender. It echoed.

As we stared at each other, a bald eagle cut between us, swooping low over the water and catching a fish and flapping majestically away, the fish's tail switching like a broken rudder in the eagle's claws.

"Goddamn, you see that?" said one of the boys.

"Neat as shit!" said another.

"Speared that mother-sucker!" said Mike. "Hey, let's make some spears and go spearfishing. The hell with fishing poles!"

One of the boys asked if we wanted to join them. He was a slim kid with a long, narrow jaw and a mop of blondish hair. "I'm Arty," he said. "C'mon over." He waved his arm.

Mamie turned the boat towards shore and rowed in. Her back was to the boys and it wasn't until she got out of the boat that they saw she was a girl.

"Humping holy shit!" said Mike.

Two of the boys took off for the tents behind them. Mike and the fourth guy jumped into the water. "Why didn't you tell us she was a chick? You seen we was naked!" said Mike.

"She don't care. Shoot, we get naked all the time, right, Mamie?"

"Yaay," she answered. "N-n-naked b-boy. I like'm." Next thing she was shucking off her clothes and diving into the lake. The other two boys came back wearing swimming trunks. They were both as skinny as me, twiggy legs and bony knees. Mamie came out of the water and stared at them.

"Look at her, Arty," said one to the other. "Right out of *Playboy Magazine*."

"Look at them boobs, man," said Arty. "Thems are nice, man. Those nipples could poke your eye out, man."

"You should see the view from back here," said Mike. "She's a goddamn Holstein, man. Moo, moooo."

"M-m-moo," Mamie answered. She was smiling over her

shoulder at Mike.

"You don't wanna push your luck with her," I told him and the others. "Mamie is solid muscle."

"Fuck her," said Mike. "Right, Timmy?"

"Yeah, fuck her," said Timmy. "This guy here is Mike Quart, King of Lake Flato, and he ain't afraid of nobody. He kicks ass, so watch your step, girl."

Timmy was a kind of a squirt with squinty eyes that made him look like something in his head was hurting. He had upturned nostrils and mousy hair. His upper lip was curled as if he smelled something bad.

"Hey, I thought we was gonna spear some fish," said Arty.

"Umgawa," said Mike. "That's Tarzan talk," he said to me. "You know what it means?"

I shrugged.

"It means eat shit and die." He laughed and so did the others.

"Umgawa," said Mamie. "Umgawa, umgawa."

"Hey, you telling Mike to eat shit?" said Timmy. "She's telling you to eat shit, Mike."

"She gives me the creeps," said Mike. "You sure she ain't a man who had one of them operations?" He came out of the water and looked Mamie up and down.

"Don't push her," I said. "She could break you in half."

He looked like he wanted to try her, but then he turned his back and walked toward the camp. "Fuck it," he said. "I'm gonna make a spear."

Two of the boys followed him. Arty came up to me and told me not to push my luck with Mike Quart. "He has a mean temper. Really savage."

"I'm not looking for trouble, Arty." I put my hand on Mamie's shoulder and added, "Mamie, don't stomp that Mike fella unless I say to, okay?"

"Yaay, Kritch'n."

I patted her butt and told her to go catch us some fish for dinner. She went back in the water and dangled for fish. The boys came back with knives lashed to popal poles. They saw Mamie using her breasts and fingers as bait and everyone got quiet and watched. The minutes passed. Then Mike said he was getting bored.

He pushed the kid next to him and said, "Show her how you catch fish with your pecker, Wes."

"Hey, fuck you, man." Wes was about the same size as Mike and looked him in the eye for a second. Then looked away.

"Timmy, get in the boat. Let's fish off-shore," said Mike.

"You betcha, Mike," said Timmy in a suck-up tone of voice.

"I'm gonna search the inlets," said Wes.

I sat down to wait for Mamie's fish. Arty sat next to me

"We'd do better using the fishing poles," he said. "But once Mike gets a hair up his ass, it's better to go along with him."

"I got an older brother like that," I said. I was thinking of Calvin.

"Kick your ass, do he?" said Arty.

"Since I was knee-high to a heifer."

"The thing with Mike is that we know his moods, but we still get in trouble with him. We've all growed up together in Iron River. He's always been the stinker of the outfit, but he'll stick up for you too. I mean, if you're his friend, he'll fight for you. Once these four guys was on me and he jumped right in the middle and kicked major ass. They wanted no more of me with him around." Arty chuckled. "He's mean as shit. But like I say, he can be a hell of a friend when he wants to."

"Mamie isn't mean," I said. "But she could break his back if she wanted."

Arty sized her up. She was still bent over and beckoning the fish to come get a nibble. The deep power of her body from the waist up was obvious. "But Mike would knife her before she could get a hold of him," said Arty. "So just make sure she doesn't mess with him. He's quick with that knife of his."

I told him it wasn't Mamie's way to mess with anybody. She was mostly gentle and not too bright and never hurt no one. Unless he made her.

"She's retarded, ain't she," said Arty.

"Maybe she is. I don't know. Sometimes she seems to be retarded, but there's more to her than meets the eye. I have to admit I haven't figured her out yet myself. She's been full of surprises."

He wanted to know about us. Where did we live? Who were our folks and all?

I told him we were just drifting.

"No kidding?" His eyes were bright with interest, but I didn't think I should tell him anymore about us. He looked trustworthy all right – eyes that looked honest, not veiled, not seeming to hide anything – but I didn't want to take any chances. Not with John Beaver still out there somewhere and maybe offering another reward for our capture. Arty went on talking, signaling with his words that he was on to me about being simply a drifter. He told me that he had run away from home one time, and it had been pretty rough and scary. He had gotten as far as Ashland and was starving and freezing to death, and he slept in a church and froze the whole night long, but he didn't want to go home anyway to a stepfather who would bash his head and make him pay just for being alive. A cop grabbed Arty the next morning in a railroad yard waiting for a freight. Arty's mom picked him up at the police station and asked him why he ran away and he blurted it all out to her, how the stepfather beat him when she wasn't around and that's why he had so many black eyes and split lips, not from fighting kids at school like he always told her, but because of the beatings he took at home. That was the end of the stepfather. Arty's mother threw him out and divorced him.

"What a neat mother," I said.

"Yeah, she is. More mothers need to have them kind of balls. Like Mike's mom, she takes such shit from his dad you wouldn't believe it. He beats her when he's drunk. He beats all his kids. There's six of them.

I told Arty more about Mamie then. I told him that her father beat her as well, and not only that, but even worse things.

"Does he screw her?" he asked.

I nodded my head, though it was mostly just an educated guess. She had never actually said that he screwed her. I was just putting two and two together. I told Arty I was rescuing her and that there was no way to ever go back to Cloverland, not with John Beaver waiting there like a hungry wolf. Arty called me a goddamn hero. He said that Mamie and I could hide out at the lake the rest of the summer and he would bring us food and we could use his tent. And if John Beaver showed up, all of us would jump him and throw him in the lake. We would drown that son of a bitch.

"But Mike might not want us to stay here," I said. "He doesn't like Mamie and I don't think he's too fond of me either."

"Yeah, you're right," said Arty.

We were watching Mike trying to spear a fish while standing in the boat. The spear was poised over the water. He was saying over and over, "Come on, you fuck'n fish, come on, you fuck'n fish."

"I think we can get around him," said Arty. "Mike isn't too quick on the uptake, if you know what I mean. He's easy to manipulate if you just give him a few strokes. Know what I mean? Just let him be the boss of everything. Don't challenge him. Don't ever stare him in the eyes. He's like a German shepherd when you stare him in the eyes. He takes it as a challenge. You see how Wes went eye to eye with him? Only Wes can do that. Wes ain't scared of him like we are. The thing is, you don't want him centering on you. If he centers on you, it's better to humph around and fake like you're mad at yourself or something like that. Call yourself stupid. He'll agree with you and maybe not pick a fight. That's what Timmy does all the time. Mike will say, 'Timmy, you're a snot-faced little bastard prick.' And Timmy will laugh it off and say that he is definitely a snot-faced little bastard prick. You notice that big strawberry on Timmy's ass? It's a birthmark. Mike makes fun of it – tells him no girl is ever gonna want to fuck him with such an ugly ass. Timmy says he knows it, and that's why he's such a jerk-off artist. He's got a twin sister, Long-lips Karen, and she's got a birthmark too. Hers goes from the side of her neck clear down to her left tit. Mike says that Timmy rubbed his ass on her in the womb and ruined her tit. Timmy just agrees with him. That's how a guy that puny manages to get along. Who's to blame him? Mike could smash him to smithers if he wanted."

Mike stabbed the water and missed whatever was swimming by. "Fuck!" he screamed. Then he turned around and kicked Timmy and told him to be still. "Quit rocking the boat, you fucker!"

"Sorry, Mike," said Timmy.

"Goddammit, don't move!"

"I won't."

"You better not."

Arty told me that Mike might mess with everybody else, but not with Wes anymore. He and Wes had a fist fight once and it ended up a draw. The fight was over Karen's raspberry birthmark. Wes stuck up for her and said that the birthmark wasn't her fault and Mike was an asshole for bringing it up all the time. And Mike fired back that Wes was sucking her birthmark and making it worse.

"And maybe he was," said Arty. "I think they've had something going for a long time. They don't let on, but you can see it when they're around each other. The way they look, you know? But, shit, it was one of the best fights I ever seen," said Arty. "Neither one would give in until they were both so exhausted they couldn't raise their arms no more. It was blood everywhere. Now if that had been me I would have punched Mike as hard as I could and then when he punched me I would have pretended he knocked me out. That would have ended it. Think about it if he comes centering on you. Just go down and it will be over. He might even throw water on your face and help you up. Once he's conquered you, he don't hold a grudge."

We heard a splash and saw a fish flying off Mamie's hands. It was a walleye, about a foot long.

"Look at that!" cried Arty, jumping to his feet. "That's the damndest thing I ever saw. Did you see her?"

I grabbed the wally and put it on a string. "There'll be more," I told him.

"That's amazing, man. I'll tell you, I'm impressed as hell."

"How'd she do that?" said Mike.

"You see it?"

"Yeah." Mike was nodding his head up and down slowly, his eyes squinting at Mamie. "Very cool," he said.

Arty knelt close to the water and caught the next fish that came out. It wasn't but half an hour and we had a string of wallys and some trout and a couple of perch. It was enough for all of us.

Mike had given up trying to stab what wouldn't hold still. He threw his spear in the bottom of the boat and rowed in. When he got on shore, he pulled up the string of fish and said, "Let's eat these mother-suckers! Timmy, clean this string."

"Right, Mike."

When we got to camp, Mike got a fire going. We fried the fish in a big black pan. Mike took the first three wallys for himself, but there were plenty and no one starved.

After Mike was finished he told Timmy to take the dirty tin plate to the water and wash it. Which Timmy did right away. "It's women's work. Should have made her do it," said Mike, staring at Mamie. "She's the fuck'n girl. Look at her. Big as a fuck'n moose. You fuck her you better tie a board to your ass."

"Hey, man, come on," said Arty.

"What's your problem Artsy-fartsy?"

"Jesus, man, who wound you up?"

"She thinks she's so fuck'n smart, catching 'em like that."

Mamie gave him her biggest grin. She was frying the last two fish.

"Goofball cunt," he said. And then he said, "Bring 'em over here, I'm still hungry."

Mamie put the fish on a plate and started toward Mike. She glanced at me and sort of tripped (or pretended to trip) and the fish slid off the plate and under her feet, getting all ground up in nothing flat. "W-whoops," she said, looking down. The fish were mush.

"You fuck'n moron!" said Mike.

Mamie started putting the pieces of fish back on the plate. Bending over she broke wind – baa-womm! – in Mike's direction. He started waving at the air. She kept on picking up the pieces and acting like she hadn't notice anything unusual. We all stared at Mike, who was staring straight up Mamie's backside, his slanty eyes wide as they could go, his hand still waving in front of his nose.

"Did she do that on purpose?" he said.

"Guess she told you, Mike," said Arty, laughing loudly.

90

"She sure did," said Wes. He was laughing too. We all were.

Mamie carried the ruined fish to the water and threw them in.

Mike suddenly exploded to his feet, swearing to kill the first faggotface who laughed anymore at him. He grabbed a stick and threw it at Mamie, but it missed her far wide and she didn't seem to notice. She was squatting at the water's edge washing her hands. Mike saw the stick miss her and then he grabbed a trenching tool next to his tent and went after Mamie with it. I hollered for her to watch out. I jumped up and took off after Mike to stop him. He came up behind her and swung for all he was worth, but she did a little side dip and the shovel missed, the force of the swing turning Mike around backwards and then over Mamie's ankle and into the water. Timmy was rushing beside me as Mike sat up and said, "Oh, my fuck'n head. I hit something!" He dug around in the water and brought up a stone the size of a grapefruit. Timmy helped him stand and guided him back to his tent. Mike was tenderly feeling the back of his head and saying, "A real goose egg. Wonder I don't got a fractured skull. Jesus fucking—"

Mamie waited a minute, then went into the woods. In a few minutes she came back with some wild onions. Lifting a coffee cup from the table, she cut up the onions and threw them inside and then pounded them with the blunt end of the Buck knife. She added salt, a dab of water, a bit of dirt and a pinch of flour and pounded some more. She spit in the cup a few times, mixing everything into what was a dirty-looking paste. She kept testing it with her tongue until she was satisfied. Then she bent down behind the moaning Mike and gently covered the lump on his head with the concoction she had made.

"That stings," he said, whining a little.

"Damned if I'd be so nice," said Arty.

"What is that stuff?" asked Wes.

"It's a remedy that takes down swelling," I told him. "Onion and salt kills bacteria and draws moisture. Mud draws too. The flour will harden and make a sort of plaster. My mom makes it all the time on the farm. Lots of farmers do."

"No way is she retarded," said Arty. "Not if she can do

that."

"She's damn sure neat," said Wes. "Like an oak tree is neat. Like the way a cougar moves is neat. Like a fox outfoxing hunters is neat. Know what I mean?" He was staring at Mike and grinning.

Timmy told Mike he would have hit Mamie with a rock, but he couldn't react fast enough.

"You woulda, huh?" said Mike. "You little shit. I don't want you watching my back anymore. Some friend you are."

"I'm your friend," said Timmy.

"Friend, my ass," said Mike. "Get away from me!" He backhanded Timmy across the mouth. Timmy slumped onto his side and curled up.

"Mamie," I said. "Who does this guy remind you of?" I was pointing at Mike.

"Papa," she answered smoothly.

"Like I give a flying fuck," said Mike. Standing up, he took hold of Timmy's arm, pulled him to his feet, marched him down to the water and had him wash his face. "You're lucky I didn't slug you," said Mike. "Probably would have broke your jaw. Maybe even killed you." Mike was staring at his fist, admiring it. Then he started yelling our way, telling us about fights he had been in and how he had nearly killed this one guy and there was this other guy and - boom boom boom, no one was as bad as Mike Quart. And no one but a fool would fool with him either.

"I always get my revenge," he said.

Mike Quart Meets His Match

The next morning I woke up smelling ashes. I had curled myself around the warm stones of the dead fire. I hadn't remembered doing that. It was strange to realize that I had fallen asleep beside Arty's tent, using a blanket he had given me, and had unknowingly crawled to the warmth of the stones surrounding the fire. But time and again I've learned that the body doesn't always need to be conscious to know what it's doing, or at least to know what it wants. Pa told me once that humans live in a world of feeling and that we do things *not* because we are rational beings, but rather because of how we feel at the time. From the time of hitting John Beaver over the head to almost everything I had done afterwards, the truth of what Pa said had become clearer and clearer. As I lay clutching the warm stones I wondered what I would do next without thinking. And I thought about Mamie and wondered if that was how she lived all the time, like an animal always acting on instinct. But then again, maybe I was that way too; maybe every thing that moves is nothing more profound than matter in motion. That's what I was thinking and then I thought: *Well, look here, Christian, you wouldn't be thinking you were matter in motion if matter in motion was all you truly were.* I blinked my eyes and sat up and said aloud, "What did you just say?" And then I said, "Where did all that stuff come from, anyway? And where by the way is Mamie?"

When I finally stood up and went to look for her, I found her already at the lake, a pile of fish flapping around in a little pool she had dug on shore. I thought about what we should do. John Beaver had probably gone up and down the road looking for us, but would have had to give it up by now. I figured it was safe to leave if we wanted to leave. I washed my face and hair in the water. I used my shirt to dry myself. My face felt cool and clean. No Pa-type ramblings were playing with my sensible mind. I felt that I was thinking clearly now.

"One more day and then we go," I told Mamie.

She was concentrating so hard, I didn't think she heard me. It didn't matter. I knew she would do whatever I said.

When I got back to camp, Arty had the fire going again. Everybody was warming up, except Mike, who kept cussing us from inside his tent for waking him. Mamie brought the fish back ready to fry. She put a pot of beans on the fire. There was toasted bread and Kool-Aid. We pitched in with her and got the breakfast made. Mike stayed inside brooding, until he smelled the food and said, "You eating without me, you mothersuckers?" Mamie was sitting on a log, with her foot against the tie-down that held up the spine of Mike's tent. The pressure of Mamie's foot had pushed the stake at an angle. When she lifted her foot the stake flew out and the tent collapsed on top of Mike.

"What the fuck?" he yelled. "I'll kill the mothersucker!" He was punching and kicking at the lumpy canvas and threatening bodily harm to every mothersucker who fucked with him.

Nasty temper so quick, I was thinking. And it occurred to me that I had always thought John Beaver was sort of unique, maybe one of a kind in the world, but Mike changed my mind about that notion. Quarts or Beavers, it's in the blood and maybe something that has come all the way down from the time Cain killed Abel— a sort of pointless rage when observed from certain angles. The sight of the puffing canvas made me think of the cat we had had one time. It liked to play inside a gunnysack. It would crawl in and bat the sack this way and that, just like Mike was doing.

"He looks like a cat in a sack," I said to the others. We all laughed. Which made Mike madder.

"Who's laughing at me?" he shouted.

And Timmy whispered, "Shit, guys, don't get him no madder. You know he'll take it out on me."

So we didn't laugh anymore. And finally Mike worked his way

94

out of the tent and stood in front of us panting and snorting. Mamie handed him a plate of fish and beans. He knocked it out of her hand and said, "You did it, didn't you! You the one!"•

"Uh-huh," she agreed.

"An accident," I said. "Your main stake was in soft ground. Her foot just happened to trip it."

"Accident, my ass," said Mike.

Arty and Wes both chimed in saying they saw it and it was an accident. Mamie didn't mean to collapse the tent.

Mike pulled out his hunting knife and said in a vicious voice, "Somebody better tell this balloon-headed bitch how good I am with this thing." He held the knife up in a shaft of sun angling through the trees. The blade sparkled like a lethal diamond. "Timmy, tell fatso what I did to that fat toad the other day," Mike continued. "You remember that fat toad I stabbed?"

"You stabbed him through the back, Mike."

"That's fuck'n right. How far away was I?"

"Ten feet at least."

"Your ass, I was twenty feet or more."

"Twenty feet, that's right, Mike."

"Yeah, and how did I do it, mothersucker?"

"You threw your knife and got him. You just threw it, man."

"Like this!" said Mike, throwing the knife at the ground in front of Mamie, burying half the blade, the bone handle not even quivering. "You see how fuck'n good I am, lard-ass. I could've put it in your foot. You sure you wanna fuck with me? Find me another toad, I'll show you what I can do with this thing." He pulled the knife from the ground and threw it at a tree. It stuck and this time it quivered. "The King of Lake Flato is a fuck'n knife wizard!" he shouted.

I had to admit he was a knife wizard. His demonstration had made me very afraid for Mamie. What could she do against a knife? It had taken me banging Beaver's head to make him stop cutting the back of her neck. I didn't know if I would get that chance with Mike Quart, and I didn't have a clue how he and Mamie were going to play out the little drama they had going. I only hoped I'd be ready to do the right thing, when the right thing was needed.

After we finished eating, we cleaned up the dishes, and then the guys got their stuff together and said we were going overland to Coffin Lake. Mike said he was going to spear fish the way fish were meant to be speared. We went about a mile around to the far side of the lake and over a ridge and on the other side sat Coffin Lake. It was a creepy-looking oval of water, gray and covered in a low, misty fog. It was maybe two hundred yards across and side to side. There were lots of little pools and inlets. The sun was shining on the fog, giving it a ghostly light. The air was very still and seemed heavy and not too healthy for breathing.

Arty gave me some cheese for bait. Everybody but Mamie and Mike baited up and threw their lines in the water. Mamie sat quiet on the shore and stared into space. Mike tied his knife to a pole again and scoured around the pools taking stabs at fish that kept eluding him. His mood got blacker and blacker.

Within a few minutes, Wes caught a tremendous carp, about three feet long, which most people won't even eat, but they're not so bad. I've had trout that tasted more gamy than carp. Casting again Wes settled back and told us how good it felt to have a fish tugging at his line. The fog was still hovering a foot above the water. It was a narrow band of fog that you could easily see through to the other side of the lake crammed with evergreens.

"Fishing is sacred," Wes said. "Catching a big fish like that says God favors you. That's how it is, you know. If you see fishing in a Christian way like I do. Fishing is what Jesus did, you know. A fisher of men, you know what I mean?"

Arty nodded. And said, "Very deep, Wes."

"Yeah that's what it is, it's a deep feeling. I get it because I believe in the Great Spirit. It's nothing I can prove. It's a *feeling*. But I've seen how people always look up to good fishermen. Take my dad; he's admired because he wins fishing trophies. He caught a state-record wally out of Lake Nabagamon. It was five years ago and that record still stands to this day. He's the one gave me the idea that he who is superior in catching fish is favored by God. If other men see you're favored by God they favor you too, because they know in their hearts that God is a fisher of men."

"So what if you've no luck with fishing?" I asked.

"It's a bad omen," he said. "God's not much on your side."

I felt a little chill in my heart. Like maybe Wes knew something I didn't know about that other world where things were being decided. I looked at Mamie and thought of what I had done to save her. Why would God be mad at me for that? Well, but then she was John Beaver's daughter after all. He owned her, so to speak. I was just this outsider messing with his property. In more ways than one. I ran it all back through my mind and realized I had never been very good at catching fish. Mamie on the other hand didn't even need a line and bait. The fish just came to her like disciples crowding around to serve her.

"I'll tell you something," continued Wes. "Don't laugh, okay? It's like catching a soul. It's like Jesus and Peter on the Galilee bringing up a net full of fish. My dad says that story is a symbol. He says that story predicts all the coming Christians caught in God's net. He says when we eat a fish, we are eating God's body, which is similar to what Catholics do when they take Communion. Ain't that a weird thought?"

"It's deeper than deep," said Arty.

Wes made me think of how my pa would go on and on about some kind of far-out idea, mixing Shakespeare and Emerson and the Bible into a religion of his own terms because, he said, religion was in everything a man did to try to make sense of the world. The whole idea, it seemed, was just to talk your way to the truth, and then to savor it when the feeling hit you that you had found it. I had never found it. The "deep" that Arty meant was a place that my mind had never had the capacity for to go. Brooding on a flat stone next to the shore, I watched Wes catching fish after fish. And Arty and Timmy caught some too. But not me. And not Mike. Mamie could have caught them if she had wanted to, I was sure, but she was content to stare God knows where and let time drift like my bobber on the water.

The sun got high and hot and burned the fog off the lake. The fish quit rising to the bait, so we let our lines go slack and the day was peaceful while it lasted. Then Mike came back carrying his spear like a hunter ready to throw it. His dark face was thrusting out, the cheekbones looked sharp as axe blades, his eyes burned in their sockets.

"Look out," I whispered to the others.

"Christ, he looks like he's gonna eat us raw," said Arty.

As Mike approached he stopped and stared at Timmy's catch squirming listlessly on a string at the water's edge. Mike raised his spear to stab them.

"Hey!" I yelled. "Those are Timmy's!"

Timmy looked at me like I was crazy.

Mike's Mongol eyes shifted to me, and I felt my stomach go queasy. I glanced at Mamie. She was lying back with her forearms folded under her head, staring dreamily at the sky.

"I mean, Timmy caught them," I said weakly.

"So who gives a fuck?" said Mike.

I don't know what would have happened, but just then Timmy started hollering that he had a big one. He had jumped up and was running backwards with his pole and reeling in his line. Up out of the water came a fighting muskie, twisting and flipping all over, trying to rid its mouth of the hook that was steadily forcing it towards the shore. Timmy played it just right and in a minute or so the fish was out of the water and banging around on the stones. And then it ripped the hook out of its mouth somehow and before you could say "Grab it!" the muskie flopped back in the water and vanished.

"Jesus, what a fish!" said Wes.

"Bigger than three foot for sure," said Arty. "Bigger than your carp."

"I ought to smack you for living, Timmy," said Mike.

Timmy's face screwed itself into the makings of a big baby about to cry. He dropped his pole and trudged off to be by himself.

Mike turned to us. "Did you see that? Lost the meanest fish in the whole fuck'n lake! What a punk he is! I ought to smack him for living."

"I wish I'd caught that one," said Wes.

And Mike said, "See, you guys been feeling sorry for the little fart. Now what do you think, huh? You know he puts the wood to his sister, man. You know that, don't you? And worse yet, he loses the meanest fish in the whole fuck'n lake. Am I right about him or what? How can we have a punk like that around?"

"He doesn't put the wood to his sister," said Wes. "You shut up about that shit, Mike."

"Or what are you gonna do?"

"Shut up."

"You shut up."

"You—"

And on it went for a while, both of them telling the other to shut up. Until Arty stepped between them and said that they had been good friends for lots of years and shouldn't let Timmy losing a big fish break that friendship up.

Wes said, "Well, maybe Mike is right. Maybe we shouldn't hang with Timmy anymore. I don't know what to do. I feel bad for him. It ain't because I'm stuck on Karen either. I mean, Jesus, you know, his old man shot himself. We got to cut him and his sister some slack for that."

"Ah, fuck em," said Mike. "The guy's a loser."

"But his father—"

"He was a loser too."

"It wasn't his fault, Mike. The guy had a brain tumor."

"He was a punk just like Timmy. Nobody liked him." He shook his spear in the direction Timmy had gone. "I ought to smack him for living," he repeated.

"Timmy's dad was no punk," said Wes. "It takes some guts to shoot yourself because you've got a brain tumor."

"Well, maybe," said Mike.

"Don't you think it's time to go?" I asked.

We gathered up the fish and equipment and started back to the ridge. A minute or so later Timmy was standing in front of us with a banded black and yellow snake in his hand. "I caught it," he said. "It tried to get away, but I grabbed its tail. It whirled round and tried to bite me, but I'm so fast I caught its head. See?" The snake's head poked out from between Timmy's thumb and forefinger. Its tongue was testing the air. Its pellet eyes were full of murder.

"Fuck'n cool as shit, man," said Mike. The snake had wrapped its body around Timmy's wrist. It looked like a bracelet for an Egyptian princess. Mike crooned to it, telling it, "You're cool as shit, man."

"You want it, Mike?" asked Timmy. "You want it, you can have it."

"Shit yes, I want it. Give it to me."

Mike unwound the snake and took hold of its middle and reached with his other hand to grab the head. But Timmy let go too soon, and the head darted out and bit Mike's cheek and then his lower lip.

"Eeeefuck!" he screamed, throwing the snake into the air. It whirled above us like a wavy stick, fell in some undergrowth and was gone. Mike was holding his lip for Arty to see and saying, "Can you suck out the venom?"

"Fuck that, man," said Arty. "Don't you know nothing?"

"I feel faint," said Mike.

"Black on yellow, kill a fellow!" shrieked Timmy. And then he laughed hysterically and pointed at Mike. "That was a coral snake. You're gonna die!"

Mike slumped down and held his head. "Oh my God," he whimpered. "Black on yellow kill a fellow!" He started making a noise in his throat, a sort of gurgling that was sad to hear.

"Neh," said Wes. "It's red on yellow kill a fellow. – not black on yellow."

"Wes is right," said Arty. "You're okay, Mike."

Mike recovered quickly. The color came back into his face and he exploded. Leaping up he yelled, "Fuck you, Timmy! I'll kill you, you bastard! You almost give me a heart attack! By God I'll show you black on yellow!" He slugged him in the stomach. Timmy fell like a rock. He lay on his back with the wind knocked out of him. We watched him struggle for air for a few seconds. Then he was breathing again, more or less gasping out that he hadn't known it was red on yellow kill a fellow. He had always thought it was black on yellow.

"Shut up, you little mothersucker! I'll punch you again." Mike was petting his swollen lip. "I'll probably get a disease from this thing. Snakes give people gang-green, you know. If I have to have my lip cut off, I'm killing you, Timmy. That's a promise."

Mamie reached down and lifted Timmy up and led him back to the water. She washed his face. Then took his hand and brought him back to us. We started off for camp again. We were carrying the fish and our equipment. Mamie had a fishing pole over her shoulder. She still hung onto Timmy's hand. It was pretty steep going back up the ridge. The dirt on the hill was a little loose and it was easy to slip. But Mamie went upwards towing Timmy like she was a mule hauling a clumsy plow. She reached two-thirds of the way before the rest of us were even at the halfway mark.

It was then that I stopped and looked up and saw something tiny flashing in the light, darting here and there like a silver fly. I saw that it was the hook from the pole Mamie was carrying. The hook and the line had come loose and were waving in the air, jerking up and down with each step Mamie took. It was fascinating to watch the hook darting around and the line growing longer and longer, until the hook was floating above Mike Quart, who was crawling on all fours to get up the crumbling slope. I watched the hook float over him. Then saw it drop ever so lightly, gently onto his shirt. Above me Mamie was still pounding up the hill, and as she stepped forward, the pole stepped with her and the line jerked and the hook set itself in Mike's back.

The same "Eeeefuck!" came out of him as when the snake had bit him. He straightened up and whirled around, his hands trying to reach the hook in his back and pull it out. But the more he tried the more he whirled and the more he became entangled in the line, until he was wrapped up like a feast for a spider. He lost his footing and went headfirst back down the hill, tumbling, rolling, shrieking bloody murder all the way to the bottom.

"Fuck'n Mike, look at him!" said Arty.

We were all laughing, although we probably shouldn't have. I mean, Mike could easily have broken his neck and we could have been laughing at a dead kid. But that didn't happen. He was bam bam bam all the way down like a runaway log and then he was lying there in a cloud of dust and we could hear him moaning.

"Poor Mike," said Timmy, grinning at Mamie.

"Poor Mike," she said back to him.

"Check it out," said Wes, "am I crazy or is that foot going the wrong way?"

"You're not crazy," said Arty.

And back down the hill we all went, where we found poor Mike in pretty bad shape. We cut the line off of him and pulled the hook out of his back and turned him over. His eyes fastened onto Mamie. "K-k-keep her away from me!" he cried. He was white with pain. It was a bad break he had. The shinbone was sticking through the muscle, the foot hung at a crazy angle, the wound from the hook was seeping blood, the snakebite had turned his lip into a giant purple grape.

We had to get him up the hill and back to the camp and Arty's car. We carried him at first, each of us boys taking a limb and digging our feet into the hill, but we kept sliding back and jerking him around and he was shrieking again and again in pain.

"This is no good, we're gonna kill him," I said.

"Let's go get help," Arty said.

Mamie said, "Nup, nup." She handed me the pole in her hand and motioned that we should stand Mike up. Which we did as she bent down and took him over her shoulder like a sack of potatoes. Up the hill she went with the rest of us scrambling behind her. It wasn't ten minutes before we were back in camp. Five minutes more we got to Arty's 49 Chevy and put Mike in the back seat. The other boys got in and the engine started. As the car backed up and turned to go, Mike, who was leaning his head out the window, opened his eyes and looked at Mamie and suddenly his face went wild—

"Fuck you!" he screamed. "F-fuck'n cow!" And then softer he said, "What did I ever do to you that you done this to me?"

They drove away, and Mamie and I went back to camp and rested for a while.

Later on, I told her we were going to grow gills if we didn't stop eating so much fish, but we fried a few anyway and ate the rest of the beans and bread.

While we were eating I asked Mamie if she had thought it all through and planned what happened to Mike Quart, or was it all an accident, just one of those freak things? She chewed her food and stared at me with those huge round, innocent eyes.

"P-poor Mike," she finally said.

"You feel bad for him?"

"I f-feel b-bad for him, Kritch'n."

That night we slept on sleeping bags next to each other under the stars. One star was especially bright and I told Mamie that maybe it was Venus, big, fat and fiery shining down on us from out of the dark universe.

"Star light, star bright," I sang. "I wish I may I wish I might have the wish I wish tonight." And then I told her I couldn't tell her the wish or it wouldn't come true. (The wish was that John Beaver would be killed dead by lightning and Mamie and I could go home.)

Mamie propped herself up on her elbow and sang her ABCs, all the while staring at me, as if looking for my approval. And the light in her eyes was full of feeling. And the light in her eyes felt like a blessing falling on me.

Dragon Fire

We were hitchhiking when this guy in an old, beetle-shaped Nash stopped for us. He stared out the window for a moment, not talking, just sort of sizing us up. He had bulging eyes with heavy lids and girlish lashes. He had a blond beard and blond hair so blond it was nearly white. His hair fell partially over his face and to his shoulders like a monk's cowl. He made me think of pictures of Jesus, where Jesus is pointing sadly to his bleeding heart.

"Runaways, runaways," he said in a thick, syrupy voice. "I can spot runaways a mile away. What's the story, children?" The tone of his voice pulled me toward him. I liked listening to the sound, syrupy and deeply musical, like he might be an opera singer. A baritone. I told him we weren't runaways, that we were orphans heading for Ashland, for the farms hiring hay buckers. He smiled slyly and nodded his head. "Sure, sure," he said, "whatever you say."

"It's the truth," I answered.

Still nodding and slyly smiling he said, "I travel the byways of Minnesota and Wisconsin, up and down them, day after day, doing what I can to get the message across. We've lost touch with the Father. We've lost touch with the love. We hate our children because we've lost touch with our souls. You are evidence of it - poor, young throwaways, tomorrow's trash in America."

I told him we weren't runaways, nor throwaways, but he insisted we were, and we weren't to worry - he would die painfully of the bubonic plague before he would betray us. "Thirty-times-thirty pieces of silver wouldn't drag your secret from me, brother and sister. Nay, I travel the byways to rescue whoever I can because

Armageddon is coming. We live in the end times. The prophecies are being fulfilled. The final battle with the anti-Christ is on the cusp. Titanic forces are at work to destroy the world, but they won't succeed. When Christ sweeps the anti-Christ aside with his mighty arm, the rapture will come and all true believers will be saved. Hallelujah."

While he was talking, his long-fingered hand was sweeping the air like he was gathering in the true believers, the saved.

"Me and Mamie believe in God," I said.

"I know you do," he replied. And then in a matter-of-fact way he asked me if I knew how to drive a car.

"Every farmer's son knows how to drive," I said. "I learned when I was ten."

"Yes, of course, but can you drive this dying miracle?"

He got out and ran his hand over the roof. I stepped back and looked at the entire Nash. The fenders were full of rust holes and dents. The bumpers were rusty too with here and there a hint of chrome. ROLLING GLORY was painted across the trunk, and there were two bumper stickers as well. One said THE WORLD ENDS TOMORROW, and the other said JESUS IS COMING AND BOY IS HE PISSED. The engine was idling roughly, little puffs of charcoal smoke shot from the exhaust pipe. I told him I was pretty sure I could drive it, that I had driven a Dodge pickup that was worse.

"Then let's go. We got work to do," he said.

He climbed into the back and I got behind the wheel. Mamie rode shotgun. I put the car into first gear and eased my foot off the clutch. The clutch was slipping badly and the smell of hydraulic fluid hung inside the car. The gas gauge said empty; the temperature gauge said hot. The engine shuddered like it was hitting on only five cylinders. But the dying miracle moved forward and we were on our way to somewhere east of where we were.

Above the chatter of the car itself I heard, "I'm Robbie Peevy. I'm on a mission from Jesus to save the town of Temple, where I was born thirty-two years ago and where I first heard the call. Those who are true believers in my divinity are gathered in Temple right now, waiting for me to do something dramatic. I won't disappoint them. Dramatic is my middle name." He winked at me in the mirror.

Then he said he had figured out that if I kept the car moving at forty-five miles an hour, we would be in Temple in two hours. I wasn't to go over forty-five, however.

"It's the breakup barrier for the likes of this sore-footed beasty," he said, pounding the car's ceiling. "Above forty-five its life breath is sucked away and its body starts to disintegrate; rust shatters and falls like red snowflakes, leaving us riding a bent frame, butts tanned in asphalt, terror in our hearts, and no triumph in Temple." Patting my head gently, he asked if I understood what he was saying. I told him I wouldn't go over forty-five.

"Bless you, my child," he said.

I said I wasn't a child, I was almost sixteen, my name was Christian, and next to me was Mamie.

"Well then, Christian and Mamie, howdy!"

"Howdy!" Mamie answered.

He leaned over the seat and looked closely at her. Then he said, "What a big one you are! A real leviathan!"

Mamie shook her head in agreement.

"Jesus has done it again," said Robbie. "Worked a mysterious purpose for me this day. I can *feel* it, yes, Lord. A boy named Christian climbs in my car with an angel-faced leviathan beside him. What could be clearer than that? It's no accident, I'll tell you truly. There are no accidents in this life. Our lives have all been a rehearsal for this glorious meeting on the road to Temple. I can *feel* it! Yes, Lord." And then Robbie burst into song, singing, "A *migh-ty for-tress is our God—*

When the song was over I told him that we needed gas and water for the car.

"Not to worry, my son."

"Gas says empty. Water gauge says hot."

"Faith cures a nervous disposition. We ride on the breath of Jeee-sus! Besides, those gauges don't work no how."

Glancing at Mamie, I saw she was bending close to Robbie's golden hair, which was hanging partially over the front seat. Her lips were puckered and she was blowing air and making the hair shiver.

"It all falls into place," said Robbie. "My faith is rewarded with a sign." He put one of his hands on my shoulder and the other one on Mamie's shoulder. "I can *feel* it. I can *feel* it." And then he added, "Keep it under forty-five, Christian. Look how close you're getting. Feel this dying miracle vibrating? She's talking to you, son, saying you're getting close to the disintegration barrier. Pay attention, son. Pay attention to her voice."

He burst into song again. This time singing—"*I got Chris-tian and Mamie go-ing my way; I got tri-umph in Temple today; but go forty-five, o-o-o forty-orty-five, I say; old beee-easty canna take no mo-ore; we'll be fa-alling through the flo-or; yahoo, yeah, yeah yo, ain't it so, Joe-o-o?*"

He patted our backs and laughed. His laughter was low and heavy like the beat of a bass drum. We laughed too and he said, "Does that mean you like my improv song?"

"Real good," I told him.

"You know what?" he continued. "I once knew a holy man who was slain by demons. Oh yes, I'm talking now! Telling you the story, children. Listen to me, listen to me good. This holy man he had the gift of healing. God told him the future and gave him the gift to heal the sick. He saw demons causing diseases, and he used his power to cast those demons out. Just like Jesus, I'm saying. But then one day he tells me, he says, 'Robbie, my son, they're ganging up and plotting against me. I won't last long. But I want you to remember that I forecasted my own death. I'll die on a certain appointed day. Tell it to the believers. They'll take comfort in it.' He said he wasn't afraid. No, he wasn't worried. That's what it means when Jesus puts the finger on you. You never know fear afterwards. The promise of the resurrection keeps a perfect niche in heaven always in front of your eyes. Glory! All glory to God! I've been promised it too. Like Elijah, I'm going up on a whirlwind a straight shot to the balcony. That holy man he did die on the appointed day just as he said he would. Death came for him in a mysterious way. Very mysterious, very mysterious. He was out for a little ride on his motorcycle, riding along in a place he had been a thousand times before. I'm saying he knew it like the back of his hand. The pavement was as dry as Ezekiel's bones in the valley of dry bones. No traffic neither. No sudden wind. Everything perfect, but the holy man – he crashed and burned just the same. The demons ganged up on him obviously. But Jesus rescued his soul and carried it to heaven where it sits at the right hand of God. Oh howdy, howdy!"

"How—" echoed Mamie.

"Demons, darling. Demons did it. Demons shut his medicine down the way they do. That's how they are." He paused, taking deep breaths and staring hard into Mamie's face. And he said, "But you know what? They'd have a tough time with you. You'd give them back hell I can tell." He looked at me. "Christian," he said, "tell me the truth. Is this girl as strong as she looks?"

"Probably stronger," I said.

"And maybe just slightly dense?"

"Slightly, yeah. She can't read or write."

"*Jesus loves her, this I know, for the Bible tells me so!* Holy Fools! He loves them!" Robbie turned around and looked out the rear window. "But watch out, there might be demons who hate her. Could be, I'm saying, they could be on her trail. Wake me up if you think you see them closing in. I've got a hex and a prayer that will ward them off."

With those last words Robbie flopped down on the seat, and in a few seconds I heard him snoring. I drove on toward Temple, keeping it slow, forty-five. The woods were thick going by, looking endless and heavy with varieties of green, and shading the road and standing stiffly beside us. I wasn't worried about nothing. The car kept hiccupping along and belching black smoke now and then, but truth is I felt a holy man was lying in the back seat, and those demons nor nothing else could bother me. Robbie had said we were riding on the breath of Jesus. What could be better or more comforting than that?

Mamie put her head back and fell asleep too. Which left me with my mind wandering over what Robbie had said about the holy man and the demons. I asked myself how did they do it? Did they jump in front of the motorcycle? Did they crawl up his leg and grab the handlebars? Did they leap onto his back and put their hands over his eyes? Maybe they threw a rock at him. Maybe they wormed their way inside him and exploded his brain. How do demons do the things they do? Make pigs run over cliffs and such as that? How can they do anything at all if the Deity prefigures everything and decides the way it should be? He knows when the sparrow is going to fall and he lets it fall. He knows the plan of the demon and lets it be. Does that make him a conniver with evil? God can't be a conniver. The holy man was doing his work, just like Job had been doing what God wanted, but both got abandoned to the demons. I was giving myself a headache trying to figure it out. God. Demons. Jesus. Demons. Satan. Lucifer. God. Jesus. The Holy Bible written by—

I had talked to Mama about it one time. She being a Catholic believer in all sorts of devils and saints. And I asked her how she could excuse God for not sticking up for Job. "Job must have had some sin in him," she said. "He was proud. He thought he was special. He needed a little humbling. We all need humbling from time to time." That wasn't the way I had read it. The way I had read it, God said to Satan, "See Job? He's the best fellow on Earth I know. Sic him!" Satan kills Job's sons and daughters and takes everything away. Job is real depressed about it and asks God what the hell is going on, Big Guy? And God thunders at him like a bully, like it's Job's fault that Satan murdered his children and his life is one red-hot boil. God let Satan break God's own law – thou shalt not kill. And then he thinks he'll be generous and give Job some new sons and daughters? Better ones, maybe? Seems like Job comes off looking more holy than God. Pa always called the Old Testament God a mighty warlord with the moral sense of a bumblebee in a hothouse filled with flowers. Pa said that the Bible is a record of man slowly making God human, making him the Deity. But still in all, I couldn't help thinking that the holy man on the motorcycle didn't get any more protection from demons than Job. And neither would this fellow Robbie Peevy in the back seat, and, of course, neither would innocent, slightly dense Mamie or me. Now I had talked myself right out of feeling like I was riding on the breath of Jesus. The comfort was gone and I was nervous and feeling depressed and scared.

The *why* of suffering and death was bothering me. The holy man doing for God and getting a kick in the teeth for all his trouble – what did it mean? I wondered if maybe I just hadn't been around long enough to see there was a great wisdom at work – none so blind as those who will not see, that sort of thing. Maybe it all clears up with age. Maybe. Maybe not. Maybe if you read enough you don't have to wait to get old before you know something about God. Maybe the secrets are in books that guys like Socrates and Shakespeare and Emerson wrote. Or maybe a fellow should go lose himself in the woods or on a mountain and dream his way to the truth. Not eat for three days, like the Indians did when they wanted to talk with the Great Spirit. Or maybe a fellow should pray the Rosary and read the Bible every living day and then – bingo! All the answers rush in. But who has the answers? Where did he or she get them? How does a person know that what they know is the Truth? And why didn't Jesus answer when Pilate asked him straight out, "What is truth?" That would have been a perfect time to give an answer that we could cling to.

My thoughts were picking up steam and going a mile a minute and my headache was getting worse. I said to myself, I am definitely not built for deep thinking. All the thinking was turning into fussing and the fussing was turning into more and more confusion. The confusion made me get mad and cuss under my breath. "Religious mutterings just turns a mind in circles and gives it no satisfaction," I muttered. The whole thing made me a believer in one thing – truth was my mind wouldn't shut up, which was what always happened to my father whose mind meandered constantly, and I was my father's son, and I couldn't run away from being like him, even if I wanted to.

The miles rolled by and one hour became two, and we were closing in on Temple. Down a long, snaky road, we went. There were some sharp curves. I had to use the brakes a lot to keep the car below forty-five. I could smell the brakes, a sharper nostril burning stink than the clutch, and I could feel the brakes starting to slip just like the clutch. I pumped and pumped, but it did less good each time I did it, until finally there was nothing there and the car shot forward like it had hit a patch of grease. We swooped around a thirty-mile curve doing well above disintegration forty-five, the tires yowling like sick dogs, the Nash all but standing on its side, so deep in trouble I could have reached out and petted the pavement as we whisked by.

All the noise woke Robbie and Mamie. Mamie started pounding the dash as if she meant to beat the car into behaving itself. Robbie kept crooning, "Be careful, be careful, be careful . . ." We went into another curve and slid hard off the pavement and into the gravel, little rocks flying like bullets into the trees beside us. The rear of the Nash slipped sideways a little but we somehow made it around the curve and straightened out again on the pavement. And then we got lucky because the down-slope gave way to a rise and we slowed down to about thirty. Then over the top of the rise we saw the city itself, thousands of houses and tall buildings and a water tower that said TEMPLE WISCONSIN.

We were heading downhill again and picking up speed. I shifted the car into second gear and heard something shatter. Then I heard it bellringing on the pavement beneath the car. I knew before I saw it in the mirror that I had dropped the driveshaft. It scooted out the back of the car and rolled awhile behind us. "No driveshaft!" I yelled. "No gears!"

"Eek!" squealed Robbie.

"Eek!" Mamie answered.

We went past the first house, all steep-roofed and white walled, and with picket fences for barriers. The houses were so alike that if you took a picture of one you pretty much took a picture of all. The road had gone level and we were slowly slowing once more. Ahead of us was a two-story brick schoolhouse. A mess of people was in front of the school, people who were *not watching* us bubbling and gurgling toward them like we owned the road. They, the people, were holding picket signs. Some were waving the signs angrily. The car floated down the street straight at them like a dying moth giving its last flutters. I tried to honk the horn, but it didn't honk. I waved my hands for the people to get out of the way. I yelled out the window "Look out! No brakes!" I knew we were going to kill some of them. Then finally someone noticed us and started shouting and running, and others ran too, people scattering left and right. I felt Robbie reaching across my shoulder and grabbing the steering wheel. He jerked it, so that the car bounced over the sidewalk, the marchers peeling away from its sides, some of them falling over each other, looking like bowling pins going down haphazardly. The car ran over a row of short shrubs and came to rest in the middle of the schoolyard's lawn.

"Good one," said Robbie.

"Jesus, I think I'm having a heart attack," I said.

"You're a great driver!" said Robbie. He was patting me on the shoulder.

The people picked themselves up and started gathering around the car. Some of them didn't look at all friendly. Eyes glaring, mouths frowning, lips curling back on vicious teeth. Fists shaking.

"Brakes!" I yelled. "It was the brakes!"

A wide-mouthed woman shoved her face close to the windshield and peered inside and started screaming, "It's Robbie! It's Robbie!"

"Yeah, Lulu, it's me!" he shouted back.

"Thank God you know her," I said.

She turned away shrieking, "It's him! It's him! He's here!"

There was wild cheering from the crowd. Someone yelled out, "He always knew how to make an entrance!" There was more cheering, followed by shouts of "Robbie! Robbie!" A couple of men pulled him from the car and lifted him onto their shoulders. "Robbie! Robbie!" everyone kept hollering, parading him around while he grinned and threw kisses.

"He must be a hero," I told Mamie.

Breathing hard, her eyes wide with excitement, Mamie was bouncing up and down and grinning. Next thing I knew she was out of the car and burrowing through the crowd. Everyone was reaching up to touch Robbie, like sick people reaching for Jesus and asking him to cure them.

A minute or so went by with Robbie on various shoulders being passed around and he couldn't have looked happier. Round and round he went, his sweet, gleaming smile going by like a strobe light. He looked something like what a true believer might see as the Second Coming. I felt as if I was watching one of those mob mentality happenings, and yet I had a big urge to dive in and join the mob myself and jump around shouting "Robbie! Robbie!"

Getting out of the car, I climbed up on the hood, so I could see better. A man in a blue uniform stepped out of the school's front door. A sign above the door said TEMPLE HIGH SCHOOL The man stood on the top step, hands on hips, mouth scowling, and behind him came a second man in uniform and two men in gray suits. Both of them wore glasses and had bald domes with hair on the sides of their heads. The taller of the two cupped his hands around his mouth and started shouting. The two policemen took out their whistles and blew them. The other gray suit started punching the air like it was insulting him. It took a while for the whistles and shouts to get the crowd's attention. The noise died down and the fellow who was making a trumpet of his hands shouted, "What the hell do you think you're doing? This is not the way to get what you want!"

A voice yelled back at him, "We're mad as hell, Vendenberg!"

"You sure are," said Vendenberg. "You're all mad as hatters. What kind of example you think you're setting for the children who go to school here? You're acting like idiots! A mob of idiots!"

"You forced this on us!" someone answered.

"We warned you!" cried another.

"Idiots we are indeed!" said Robbie. "Idiots for Jesus!"

"Hooray, hooray, idiots for Jesus!" came a yell from the crowd.

Across the crowd Robbie and Vendenberg faced each other.

And Vendenberg said, "Robbie Peevy, putting you away obviously didn't do you any good. You're still a raving lunatic!"

"And you're still the devil's pawn," Robbie replied.

People were telling Robbie to give Vendenberg the wrath of God's tongue.

"Lay it on him, Robbie!"

"Vendenberg, ye shall have the rod of my anger, the staff of my fury!"

"Oh please, spare me you're biblical nitwit shit, Robbie."

"We shall tread you down like the mire in the streets!"

"Boo, Vendenberg," people kept shouting. "Hooray for Robbie!"

And Vendenberg was saying, "Robbie Peevy, you need help. You need to be on medication."

"The Lord is my medication," said Robbie. "He is all the medication I need."

"Monster of iniquity!" shouted a woman, who had run up the steps and was in Vendenberg's face. "You had our Robbie committed!"

Vendenberg rolled his eyes and shook his head. "His parents had him committed. You can't just go around setting fires for the Lord and expect people to think you're normal."

"I burn sin!" shrieked Robbie.

"Burning the school was burning sin?"

"That school needed burning, just like yours does. If a school produces sinfully educated children, it must be dealt with harshly. Jesus told me to burn the sinners out and when Jesus gives you a command you better obey." Robbie looked round at the people left and right, his eyes were shiny with tears. "Brethren, am I a lunatic for obeying the command of God?"

"No, you're God's angel!"

And the people chanted, "Angel, angel, angel—"

"Was that a lunatic preaching to you every Sunday in Huckle's barn?"

"Angel, angel, angel—"

"Where would a mere strip of child get the words to prophesy the corruption of your children's minds caused by the sulfur of this pit of hellish so-called modern education?"

"Angel, angel, angel—"

And he did look like an angel up there, his hair and beard flowing bright as cornsilk, all of him sparkling in the sun. As he turned side to side, his blue eyes dripping tears, "Angel, angel," rose like a protective prayer all around him.

Some of the people bounced their signs up and down in time to the chanting. The signs said things like MARCH FOR SANCTIFIED READING; DOWN WITH PORNAGRAPHY; JAMES JOYCE IS THE ANTICHRIST; BURN FALKNER IN HELL;

CATCHER IN THE RYE CORRUPTS; ONLY QUEERS READ DEATH IN VENICE; DARWIN IS THE DEVIL IN DISGUISE; NORMAN MAILER WRITES DOO-DOO! FREUD IS A FOOL; THE ONLY BOOK WE NEED IS THE BIBLE! There were a bunch of them, lots of them warning about some bad book or some filthy writer. Some signs had black drawings of a skull and crossbones, some had pictures of human brains being burned, some had drawings of a library with HERE BE DRAGONS printed on the doors.

Vendenberg was holding his hands up, trying to get the crowd to quiet down. The sheriffs were blowing their whistles. The gray-suited crew-cut guy was shadowboxing the air again, giving it uppercuts. The crowd paid them no mind at all, until finally Robbie pointed like Moses parting the Red Sea and shouted, "Vengeance is mine, Vendenberg! Unbar the door! We're coming in!"

"Like hell you are!" said Vendenberg.

The people stopped chanting angel, angel and took up Robbie's command—"Unbar the door! Unbar the door!" They surged forward like wheat in a windy field. That's when I caught sight of Mamie. She had Robbie on her shoulders. A man from the crowd leaped on the steps and joined Vendenberg's side.

"You can't do this!" he shouted. "You're crazy!"

He was a big fellow, broad and deep like Mamie. He wore a T-shirt advertising Old Style Beer. His face was square, his neck bullish and so short it was hardly a neck at all. "C'mon, people, what're you doing?" he said. "You don't want to do this." He looked at Robbie. "Call it off, dipshit, before I hand you your head."

"And howdy to you, too, Bob Thorn," said Robbie.

"Howdy yourself, Hitler. You still want to burn books, do you?"

"No, don't want to, never wanted to, Thorn. But the choice isn't mine. I get my orders from the Lord."

"Hearing voices again are we?" Bob Thorn pointed toward the sky. He cupped his ear. "What's that? What's that you say? Robbie Peevy is a mindless fanatic?"

"Fanaticism in the name of God is not a vice. Praise his holy name!" Robbie held his arms out like he was on the cross. He shouted to the sky, "I am scorned of all my adversaries, a horror to my neighbors, and an object of dread. I have passed out of mind like one who is dead; I have become a broken vessel. Yea, I hear the whispering of many as they scheme together against me, as they plot to take my life. But I trust in thee, O Lord! Deliver me!"

"Kiss my ass, you brain-ruptured schizo," said Bob Thorn. "Get back in your cloud. Go back to Camelot."

"But they laughed them to scorn and mocked them," said Robbie.

"Oh, shut up." Bob Thorn told the people to take a good look at Robbie. "Look what you got here. This is Robbie Peevy, you know him. He was the boy wonder who was going to lead you to the Promised Land. This is the nut who used to preach in Huckle's barn and tell you he could hear voices in the rafters, remember? This is the guy who got committed, for Christ's sake. The doctors said he had delusions of grandeur and he was a pyromaniac. He was dangerous. Listen here, citizens of Temple, Wisconsin, you've got to be nuts to follow a nut!"

"Each is my people," said Robbie. "The chosen ones. They called me back from Camelot. And God said that I must heed their call. In the name of God, Bob Thorn, stand aside and allow us to enter. We don't want to hurt you or anyone else."

Bob Thorn laughed scornfully. "You don't want to hurt me, huh? Just try it, piss-ant. I'm the linebacker who led Temple to a state title, remember? Most valuable player, that's who I was. And who were you? Milksop little punk picking your nose and preaching against the sins of football. Neh, you don't want to try to get past me. I'll hand you your head, Peevy."

"Behind you is a den of evil, Bob Thorn. You are protecting a den of evil. Every evil under the sun is all laid out in there for the little ones to read and distort their pliable minds. Sick slime and infection dribbling from sick, slimy minds, the likes of Faulkner and Hemingway and . . . and that dirty homasekshul Whitman and—"

"And Salinger!" yelled some woman.

"And Salinger! And Mark Twain in league with the devil. Scum like that dribbling on our little children their pestilence of the soul. All that is ugly and crazy. All that is putrid and foul. All that is of Satan's going to and fro upon the Earth is glorified for the children of God to read and call it life. It's not life! It's death! It's perversion and slaughter! Jesus, save us!"

"The truth will set you free!" cried a voice.

"We're here to save our children!

"You don't know what you're talking about," said Bob Thorn. "The books you got on your signs sit and dry-rot on the shelves. None of the kids I ever knew read them. Not nobody no how. You ever try to read them? Try Faulkner some time, I dare you. It's another language. It might as well be Greek or Swahili for all the sense it makes. Ain't no kid would understand a thing. Am I right, Vendenberg?"

"You never been righter in your life, unfortunately," Vendenberg answered.

A woman raised her fist and called both men liars. "My daughter was made to read *Elmer Gantry* in Mrs. Modeen's shameful class. When I learned what that book was about, I almost died on the spot. Corruption in the church, drunkenness and fornication!"

Other people shouted out names of books their kids brought home from school. Filthy commie works like *Grapes of Wrath* and *Brave New World*. I heard *Anna Karenina*, *Huckleberry Finn*, *The Great Gatsby*, *Guilliver's Travels*, *Madame Bovary*, *Ball-zac* and more. One of the titles I knew pretty well, actually. It was a book we had at home that Mama and Mary Magdalen read all the time. It was called *Making it with Mademoiselle*, a book of dress patterns and such.

"Hey, that's no filthy commie work," I said. But nobody listened. The calling of the titles had stirred the crowd up again and they started yelling for the men to get out of the way—"Unbar the door!"

Robbie leaned down and said something to Mamie and pointed toward the door. She took off like a racehorse out of the gate. Bob Thorn was knocked aside, as were Vendenberg and the others. All of them disappearing in the boil of people following Mamie and Robbie. The door was opened and the crowd rushed in. I followed after them, not to destroy the horrible books in the library, but to find Mamie and get the hell out of town.

When I got inside, I saw her far ahead. Robbie was off her shoulders and running in front. I kept my eyes on Mamie's head, floating above the other heads like a bobber down a stream of water. Through some double doors we went and then we were in the den of sin itself—the library. Pulling myself out of the main flow, I was able to stand on a chair and search for Mamie who had disappeared somewhere in the rows of books. I didn't see her. It was a big library and I had no idea down what row she might be. The people were pouring over the shelves and grabbing everything. Voices cried out titles to Robbie. He was standing on a desk and giving every title the thumbsdown: *Lord Jim* – thumbsdown; *Crime and Punishment* – thumbsdown; *Studs Lonigan* – thumbsdown; *War and Peace, Moby Dick, David Copperfield, The Possessed, Nuts and Seeds* – all of them getting the thumbsdown and being chucked out the windows, where other folks waited to pile them up for burning.

It wasn't long till no one bothered to shout the titles anymore. Everything went. I looked out the window and saw someone pouring kerosene over the books, matches were lit. The books bursting into flame, the pages curling into ashes quickly. The smoke went up as the fire took off and there was a roaring and sparks flying. The smell of smoke filled the library.

I pressed myself against a wall and watched armful after armful of all those words flying through the windows. Robbie turned and saw me. He jumped off the desk and gave me a hug.

"Christian, you hung in there," he said. "Look! We're finally doing it! We are God's will in motion. We are the center of the universe!"

"Help me get to Mamie, Robbie," I told him.

A woman shoved a book in Robbie's face. It was Lulu. Her lips were flecked with foam. A glassy look was in her eyes, "*Samson Agonistes*, Robbie. Is it a holy book?" she asked.

"Neh, Lulu, chuck it!"

"What about the Shakespeare? He's so depressing!"

"Yes, he's the one that said life is a tale told by an idiot full of sound and fury, and then Faulkner used *The Sound and the Fury* as the title of a filthy book. You see how all these things of Satan are connected? Yes, Lulu, chuck the Shakespeare and chuck filthy Faulkner too.

Lulu turned around and shouted down one of the rows, "Chuck all the Shakespeare! And get Faulkner!"

"Get Faulkner! Get Faulkner!" I heard someone echoing.

Samson Agonistes went out the window. And *Paradise Lost*. Robbie bent over and picked up a small book someone had dropped. He handed it to me and told me to throw it on the fire. I checked out the title in my hand. It was *Blithe Spirit*. I slipped the book into my back pocket and went over to the window and watched the fire growing. Book after book flew toward the flames, pages opening and flapping like the wings of helpless birds. The fire was getting so big it was beginning to singe the mulberry bushes that made a barrier between the grass and the building. I could feel the heat on my face, and I was pretty sure that eventually the school would catch on fire. And then I saw a line of police cars arriving, tires squealing and men getting out, men with clubs in their hands.

Mamie appeared from between a row of shelves, books loaded to her chin. She carried them to the window where I was standing. Knocking the books out of her hands, I grabbed her shoulders and shook her.

"Cops!" I cried. "Cops coming to get us!"

"C-cops?" Her eyes were glazed. She didn't seem to know who I was. I slapped her. She tossed her head back and forth and blinked her eyes. Then she was focusing on me, her eyes looking like dawn peeping over a hill.

"Kritch'n," she said softly.

"Cops, Mamie. Gonna lock us up. We got to run."

I took her hand and yanked her towards the door. She followed, but it was like trying to swim upstream because of all the people in the hall fighting to go both ways. Finally I put her in front of me and she made a path for us. When we got outside, I saw Vendenberg standing on the hood of Robbie's car, shouting orders and pointing. He was saying, "Get him! Get her! That one, that one!" The police weren't paying attention to him, but he went on yelling anyway, "Get him! Get her!" The police were grabbing the keepers of the fire and handcuffing them and clubbing some who resisted. Bob Thorn was helping out. He was tackling the ones who were trying to sneak away.

Mamie and I were working our way out between the wall and the mulberry bushes when Bob Thorn spotted us. He came running over, shouting, "Aha! Aha!" He got in front of us and crouched like a wrestler, his arms out, his upper body swaying. "Come out of them bushes, you bastards!" he ordered. When he saw Mamie step out, he said, "You're the one knocked me off them steps!"

"She didn't mean to," I told him.

"Come on," he said to her. "Try it again, come on. Hit me with your best shot, baby!"

Mamie stared at him, her eyes fascinated, her mouth hanging open in a dopey smile. She started imitating his wrestling stance, arms out, body swaying. He dove at her, trying to tackle her legs. Mamie, like a muscled-up cat, leaped in the air and clear over his diving body. He hit hard on his belly. Before he could get up, she grabbed him by the belt and by his neck and hoisted him up to her waist and using her knee catapulted him into one of the bushes. He got all tangled up, his legs and arms thrashing the bush to pieces. Mamie stood in her crouch, waiting for him to try another round. I was pretty sure he was through for the day. I yelled at her, pulled her arm, kicked her butt, but she wanted Bob Thorn again. Finally she went over to the bush, grabbed his legs and pulled him out.

"Whoa! Whoa!" he shouted, covering his face with his arms.

"He's done for, Mamie," I told her. "Giddup now! Haw! Haw!"

She responded and we took off at dead run over the grass and across the street. We galloped away from the school at eye-watering speed, and when I looked back, I saw the cops still cuffing and clubbing people and the fire still burning and smoke rising. We came to the end of the street and headed across a vacant lot. A stand of trees stood in the distance.

Man of the Trains

On the other side of the woods was a road. To the left was the way to downtown Temple. We could see cross-streets and stop signs, rows of buildings. People going places. To the right were some railroad tracks and a train station. That's the direction we took. I had an idea that we would hop a freight and get a ride going south where the big dairy farms were, where we could get jobs milking cows. We crawled between pillars under the station's platform, way in the back where it was cool and the dirt was fine like talcum powder. In the station house above us we could hear someone walking around, stopping to close a door, open a drawer, sit down in a chair, rising again and walking some more. We could see the tracks and the road as well, all the way to town, some houses lining both sides of the street. Traffic going by. But the station itself got quiet. Sort of hauntingly so, until a car roared to a stop near the platform steps and a cop got out in a cloud of dust and yelled, "Hey you! Get out here! Move it! I'm in a hurry!"

I thought he meant us.

But then I heard the feet overhead shuffling. A door opened and a querulous old man's voice said, "Who you think you're talking to like a dog?"

"I'm in a hurry, Mr. Potter!" said the cop.

"I don't give a good gaddamn if you're a doctor on 'mergency call," sassed the man. His tone was shrill. "Doctor on a *'mergency* call," he repeated. "You don't say to me, 'Hey you, get out here.' I don't know any man that's got nuff lead in his ass to give Amoss Potter orders to 'get out here.' You don't give me no orders, you young punk, you sassy face copper. I know who you are, little Ronnie runny-nose. Knowed you since you were shitten in your diapers. I'll tell you what, I been a man of the trains forty-four years, and I been fifteen years here as stationmaster. And I tell you what, I throwed paying customers out the gaddamn door for getting smart-alecky with me. I held up the gaddamn U.S. of A. mail itself cause some punkass engineer thought he had nuff lead in his ass to yell at Amoss Potter. I even told my two-bit, beak-nosed boss to put it where the hand of man don't belong, when he got uppity with me. Nosir, I brook no brass and take no sass from man, woman, child, or morphodite. Don't give a damn if you're rich or poor, old or young, a fat slob or so bony you have to stand up twice to make a shadow. This is my station, *my* station! And nobody tells me a gaddman thing, not nothing, see? And specially nobody tells me to gaddamn get out here on my own platform, and it don't matter none at all if he's a shiny-faced, sassy-assed cop or the gaddamn president of the whole gaddamn country. And look here, let me tell you one more gaddamn thing, youngster—

"Jesus Christ, do you ever shut up!" shouted the cop. "Listen, Amoss, shut the fuck up or I'll arrest you for obstruction of a peace officer in the line of duty!"

There was a second of silence. Then the old man shuffled his feet back the other way and we heard the door close and heard him walk to what I figured was the chair in his office, where he sat down heavily. The cop was ordering him to come back, but he wasn't listening.

A few seconds later, the cop went inside the station house and said in a gentler tone, "Look here, Amoss, we just want you to be on the lookout for any strangers trying to hop a ride out of town. Some communist agitators caused a riot at the high school and tried to burn it down. We caught the ringleader and some of the others, but a few got away and we're trying to track them down. So if you see any strangers acting strange, give us a call, okay?" There was no answer. "Amoss, will you give us a call? Please."

"I might," said Amoss. "If I see something."

"That's all I'm asking. That's all I want. Thank you, sir."

The cop went back to his car and drove away. When it was quiet again, we could hear Amoss say, "Might not, neither. Most likely won't, you sonofabitch. Just try to arrest me for ubstruction. I'll ubstruck your gaddman nose from your gaddamn face, you sorry, sassy, punk sonofabitch. I'll shove that gun of yours down you sissy throat, you butt-sucking blue-belly bastard, and you'll be shittin little toy pistols, you upstart, lowlife, morphodite heathen. Little Ronnie runny-nose. Knew you since your were sucking titty, and you gonna tell me 'Hey you, get out here'? Not fuck'n likely. I'm no dog that you can call me *hey you*. No way."

It went on for quite a time, the old man grumbling and carrying on. But finally he trailed off, though every once in a while he would burst out with "Sonofabitch!" And do some more growling.

After awhile I crawled out and looked in one of the windows. The old man was sleeping. He was leaning back in his chair, feet up on a desk, chin resting on his chest. He wore a striped engineer's cap and overalls. Sewn on the cap was a red and white patch that said AMOSS. He had a face full of deep wrinkles. There were pigment splotches on his cheeks. His nose was reddish and pitted, and his hands twitched as he slept. There were scabs on the backs of both hands as if maybe he scratched them a lot.

I thought he would probably sleep quite a while, so I sat down on the edge of the platform and took out the book that Robbie gave me, the one called *Blithe Spirit*. It was a play by a guy named Noel Coward. I read some of it, but it was mostly boring and I didn't really know what was going on. Flipping through it I came to a place I liked better. Someone named Madame Arcati saying, "Ghostly spectre – ghoul or fiend / Never more be thou convened / Shepherd's Wort and Holy Rite / Banish thee into the night." I said the lines out loud a couple of times just to savor them. Mamie had come out and was watching me with interest. Next thing I knew, she was saying the lines just the way I had. When she finished I told her she had darn good recall for someone who was a semi-retardo.

"Smma-art," she said, tapping her head.

"Yeah, you are," I said "But it's more than that. You've got one of those photographic memories I wish I had. Seems like kind of a waste God give it to you instead of me."

We both perked up at the sound of Amoss inside the station. He was moaning. We peeked in the window and saw him leaning forward in his chair, holding his belly. His face was all screwed up in pain and the moaning getting louder. And then he turned his head and looked at me and Mamie. "Who the hell are you?" he said. "You them agitator commies?"

"No sir."

"What you want then?"

"I heard you sounding sick, sir."

"Christ, yes, I'm sick. If I don't get some milk in me my ulcer is gonna bust. It's happened before. Every time I get upset my ulcer starts a'roaring. I had a punk cop up here awhile ago picking on me. Got this thing all stirred up, the gaddamn bastard." He stood up and shuffled out of the office and came to the door. He looked us up and down, his eyes lingering a long time on Mamie. "What the hell did your mother feed you, gal? You're big as a tree."

"She's Mamie," I said. "I'm Christian."

"I knew a Mamie Eisenhower once," said Amoss. He was searching through his pants pockets and he brought out some change and asked me to go buy him some half and half cream. He pointed down the road and said to just keep walking and I'd come to a Piggly Wiggly. I stepped away from him, not taking the money. I didn't want to go into town and maybe have a cop see me, but I didn't want the old guy to be suffering either. But if I got picked up what would happen to Mamie? Who was more important, him or her? Of course she was. My pa always said that when you don't know what to do, arrange your values in the order you hold them. Mamie came first in that system, so I wasn't going to do anything that would jeopardize her.

Amoss kept rubbing his stomach and staring at the ground. He bent half over and the moaning started up again.

"What we gonna do with him?" I said. "Where do you live, Amoss?"

He pointed and said, "Not far. Just a couple blocks is all. I got milk and some medication there."

"Let's take you home," I said.

"I don't know if I can walk it, son. I wish I could just throw up. Sometimes it helps."

"We'll carry you home," I said. "Mamie, let's carry him home, so he can get his medicine. Okay?"

"Yaay, Kritch'n." With that she swooped him up in her arms, cradling him. He was blinking with surprise, but not fighting it.

"Do you want her to put you down?" I asked.

"Leave her be," he said. "Don't you know who's gaddamn sick around here? I'll be burping blood if you don't get me home. Our house is the first one you see on the right side of the road just past the woods. We're next to the movie house. It ain't far."

"Well, all right," I said, wanting to help but wishing we hadn't come to the station house in the first place. "I guess it's the Samaritan thing to do. Let's go, Mamie."

And we set off, Mamie carrying Amoss along like he was in his second childhood and she was carrying him to bed. He talked the whole way, telling us that he was forty-four years a man of the trains and that if his boss found out how sick he was that would be the end of his job. Men being laid off left and right these days, so we had to keep it quiet, these killer guts of his just-a-churning, but a coat of cream would calm things down and the medication would help dry the ulcer up and this is what happens when you get old, your nerves get bad, you can't handle the stress like you used to, it would have been a good thing not to have stayed a bachelor, times of sickness you need a woman around, like this one here, this Mamie big as the love of God, look at how she is carrying him so gently. And if he could, why, he would marry her in a minute, having her around the house day and night would be dandy.

We came to a shabby house that Amoss said was home. The house was a faded yellowish color with whitish-gray trim. There was a wide wooden porch in front. In the driveway was an ancient Ford, a four-door model A from back around Herbert Hoover's time. A huge, half-dead elm tree took up most of the front yard, shading part of the house and running humpy roots up under the sidewalk so that it was tilted and cracked severely. There was a worn path on the grass next to the sidewalk.

"Follow the path," said Amoss. "You don't want to trip on that stupid walk and toss me, do you? Take me right inside. Open the door, it's okay."

I opened the door and Mamie carried Amoss in and put him in an overstuffed chair. Beside him was an end table with a lamp on it and a book entitled *Latin Quotations At Your Fingertips*. Next to the book was a small bottle of pills, which he opened and shook one into his hand. "I should know better than to go anywhere without these," he said. "But I always been a hard-headed old fart. Can't learn nothing. Would you check the fridge, son, and grab me that cream?"

I went to the refrigerator and found a carton of half and half and gave it to him. He drank it down non-stop. And then cut a pair of huge, gut-bubbling burps that rattled the glass in the windows. He looked at us afterwards and said, "I'll live a bit longer now, I guess. Thank you for helping me. You're good youngins. Not all youngins are. Most aren't, in fact. Amoss Potter thanks you. What else I got in the fridge? Did you take inventory?"

"I found wieners and cheese and lots of beer."

"Can't handle no weenies and beer just yet," he said. "Gimmee some cheese. Cut it up. Get them crackers in the cupboard. Let's all have some. Help yourself to the weenies if you want. Or the beer." Slicing up the cheese I put it on a plate with some crackers. I opened beers for me and Mamie. We sat around a coffee table picking at the food and talking. I told Amoss we were farmhands looking for work.

"Ain't you got no parents somewheres?" he asked.

"We both of us are orphans on our own. Been working farms for years."

"You don't look that old."

"Well, I'm not. Mamie is twenty. I'm near eighteen."

"You look no more than fourteen or fifteen. Orphans, huh? Life is tough on orphans." There was a look in his eyes that said he didn't quite believe me.

"We're good with cows. We know dairy farming pretty darn well."

"Farmers, yeah, that's hard work. Break your back. I was raised on a farm. I know what I'm talking about. Now, this gal here, she looks like she could wrestle a buffalo. But pardon my saying, you just don't look strong enough to pull your own weight on a farm. But whatever you say, it's no mind to me." He was rolling up his sleeves and he stuck one arm out and grabbed one of my arms and compared them. Both arms were skinny. Mine had more muscle definition than his did, but nothing to brag about. Our hands looked a lot alike, wrinkled and rough.

"You got an old man's pair of hands," said Amoss. "Those are farming hands all right. I suppose you're what you say you are, but even if you're not I don't care. It ain't none of my business. You helped me and that's what matters now. Even if you are probably a couple of those agitators little snot-nose was talking about. Hey, I mean it, I don't care a'tall. You're my new buddies."

He told us that we could hang around as long as we wanted. He told us he lived with a guy named Don Shepard, who would welcome us too. Shepard owned the movie house next door and was in the process of renovating it. He was going into business showing classical movies. Shepard, said Amoss, was an expert on movies.

"You'll like him. He's a big, overgrown baby, but kind and gentle and something of a genius. That's what he says anyway, that he's a genius. He reads the dictionary cover to cover and knows big words and likes to use them. Maybe he will hire you to help renovate the theater. Would you be interested in that kind of job?"

I shrugged. "Maybe, I don't know, we'll see," I said. Along one wall of the house was a huge bookshelf crammed with books. "All those are yours?" I asked.

"Naw. Those are Shepard's. His bedroom is stuffed with that many or more. Go ahead take a look, you'll see."

Shepard's room was a mess. It had shelves and a big desk piled high with books. I saw titles like *Great Movies of the Past; Movie Classics from the Past Twenty Years; The great Money-Making Films of All Time*, and so on – dozens of them, with wrinkled covers and with slips of paper marking pages. I opened a book at a marker and saw a picture of a blond man in a black outfit. His name was

Laurence Olivier. Beside the picture in the margin was a note that said - *Open Artlife with this!* The movie was *Hamlet*. I wondered if Pa knew that someone had made a movie of it.

I went back to the living room and saw Mamie holding a book upside down. Amoss jerked his thumb her way and said, "What's she doing? Can't she read?"

"Can't read nor write," I told him. "But she has a super memory. You quote her something and she'll memorize it and quote it back to you. Not that she really knows what she's saying. She'll just say it, but I doubt she knows most the time what the words really mean."

"Hmm, that's strange, that's funny. But whatever - it takes all kinds to make the world go round." Amoss burped again. This time softer. "You know, I'm feeling a mite better. How about you get me one of those beers too? Oh, and there's some Tums on the counter, would you grab those?"

Mamie went on playing with the book, leafing through it, then putting it back on the shelf and grabbing another one and leafing through it too. Like she was speed- reading. Amoss ate a handful of Tums, washing them down with beer. I finished my beer and went for another. When I came back in the room, Mamie was pulling more books off the shelves. She wasn't leafing through them anymore. She had a puzzled look on her face. Or maybe it was an angry look. She was piling up a whole armful of books. Then she headed for the door.

"What's she doing now?" said Amoss.

"Mamie, don't!" I yelled.

She was about to throw the books out the door. She stopped and looked at me. "What did I tell you? Books are good, Mamie. Put them back."

"Kitch'n, s-say it dis," she said.

"Say what?"

"Ghostly spectre - ghoul or fiend. Say it dis, Kritch'n." She looked frustrated. She held the books out to me. She bounced a little on the balls of her feet.

"I can't say them all, Mamie. It would wear me out reading them all to you. It would take years. You've got to learn to do it yourself. There's no other way, so don't give me dirty looks. Put the books back now. They don't belong to you."

She put the books back on the shelves. She kept muttering, "Ghostly spectre – ghoul or fiend–" But I knew she didn't know what it meant. Actually, I didn't know what it meant either. I just liked the way it creeped me out.

Amoss said, "Mamie bring me one of the books you picked. Hell, I'll read it to you, come on. She handed him *Great Expectations* and sat on the floor next to him as he opened the book at random and read: *Keep still, you little devil, or I'll cut your throat!* He was a good reader, but it was stop and go Dickens between burps. Until finally he snapped the book shut and said too much reading boiled the brain. The story was making him nervous and his belly was getting bloated again, filling up with gas. He rocked forward and belched another long, rolling, wet one. Mamie swallowed air and imitated him. He burst out laughing.

And he said, "*Get me some wittles . . . or I'll have your heart and liver out.*"

Open-eyed, freckle-faced, moon-headed Mamie grinned at him and said, "*Get me some wittles . . . or I'll have your heart and liver out.*"

They both laughed like they had never heard anything so funny. Then they started burping at each other. It was a childish game and I wasn't going to get involved. I sat by the open door, leaning on the shelf of books, drinking my beer and listening to Mamie and Amoss thinking they were so funny. It wasn't funny at all. Not unless you think stupid is funny. Actually, I guess it is now and again.

Bleeding Ulcers

I had dozed off and when I woke up, it was dark outside, the door was closed and the lights were on. Amoss looked tiny sitting in a corner of the couch next to a man as huge as a Sumo wrestler. Mamie was sitting comfy on the overstuffed chair. She was drinking a can of Grain Belt beer. There were bent beer cans piled all over the coffee table. The room was filled with the smell of book dander, sweaty bodies and booze and a mildewed foundation.

When Amoss saw I was awake, he waved me over. "Come here, sleepyhead," he said. "Come tell this ton of blubber that Mamie's got perfect recall at will. Did she or did she not quote Dickens right back in my face as good as an actor?"

"Yeah, she did."

"Well, why won't she do it now?"

Mamie looked blurry-eyed. A sloppy smile played over her lips. A low chuckling rose from her throat as she crossed her eyes at me. "I think she's drunk," I said, indicating all the beer cans.

Pointing to the fat man Amoss said, "He said she was a faker, a faker, a faker. I ought to kick his shins. This is Don Shepard, by the way. His parentage is part walrus as you can probably tell."

"I did not mean to imply there was fakery afoot, Amoss," said Shepard in the highfalutin voice of someone educated and superior. "It was merely a teasing tautology repeated for effect, yum yum. To get you riled. You're so easy to rile, you know. But let me say, a face like this could never fake a thing. She's as open as a book. A face as innocent as the innocent moon. As innocent as cherries in June. As innocent as—"

"Glad you think so, because I'm gonna marry her. Don't tell

me I'm too old. I'll wipe the floor with ten of you."

"So this is Christian Foggy," said Shepard, ignoring Amoss and smiling benevolently at me. He stood up and held out a pancake hand. Monstrous tall he was, taller than Mamie and twice as wide. Maybe three times. Four hundred pounds of blubber was my guess and he sort of did look like a walrus. Big mustache and no front teeth, just the dogteeth grinning out of a pinkish hole; heavy cheeks and double chins; eyebrows wiry like the mustache; twinkling eyes in a nest of wrinkles; forehead like a washboard; tangled grayish-brown hair balding in front and all of it needing a comb. He had a nose that resembled a plum, or maybe a purple light bulb screwed into his face. That nose was a wonder. It shined brighter than his very bright cheeks, as if he had used ox-blood shoe polish on it and a buffing rag.

"And you thought Mamie was big, hey?" said Amoss, looking Shepard up and down and wagging his eyebrows at me.

"I'm getting a crick in my neck," I said. Shepard kept my hand buried in his, shaking it like it was a pump handle.

"Disengage the putterings of a mind so futile as the burden of dross Amoss carries in his head," he said to me. "A billion cells buried in a fog of alcohol. He won't remember tomorrow that you were here tonight. I, on the other hand, am a bona fide genius, quick-minded as yum yum pearls of wisdom spouting from the apology of Socrates to the reactionary rabble that sentenced him to death. If there is anything you want to know, just ask me and I will tell you. I can't help it, it's my nature to flavor fomentations for tender minds like yours. And hers." He pointed to Mamie. "Though I think you're right, inebriations have for the moment stolen her wits away. Oh, and thank you for saving Amoss from his ulcer crisis. He's such foolish man, playing out the last sorrows of his time by using alcohol as an all-purpose balm. Let's treat him gently. Let's give him love."

"I got twenty good years in me," said Amoss. "You, on the other hand, is so fat you're gonna crush yourself. One of these nights when you lay down in bed, your blubber will collapse your lungs and you'll sleep permanent from then on."

"Note the tautology: 'you'll sleep permanent from then on,'" said Shepard. "He can't help it. He was born to sneeze twice in a row. It's genetics. It's—"

Amoss overlapped him, saying, "You should hear how loud this man snores. Like sonic booms attacking the ceiling. It's why the timbers are coming loose in this house. It's why the windows rattle when you walk across the floor."

Shepard bent closer to me, his eyes fixed on mine like fat-encased beacons. "Shiny luminescence of such tender years, don't be bothered by anything this decrepit product of Temple's ignorance tells you. He lacks judgment and he lives in the end times of a vast bone-bare intelligence. I, on the other hand, am a lustering, lushly luscious yum yum tower of the best that art has ever offered in a purely artistic man. As you can see, I am stuffed with it." He patted his belly with both hands splayed wide. "Art, I'm saying. An embodiment of all ages of art in one immensely gorgeous ton of flesh, every inch of me as lickable as a strawberry ice cream cone. Don Shepard at your service. You know, I once had eyes like yours, clear as sapphires, compassionate as raindrops on a thirsty flower." He spoke rhythmically, like he was reading poetry, his tongue darting around the words as if tasting them before he let them flow.

"Cut the crap!" said Amoss. "You never had no eyes like that, not even in your dreams, you pied pretender." He raised the beer to his lips, drank noisily, then crushed the can and threw it on the floor and kicked it clattering across the room. "Empty," he grumbled in disgust.

"No more for you," said Shepard. "You're getting obstreperous!"

"Hump a duckfuck!"

"See what I mean?" said Shepard putting his shovel spade of a hand on my shoulder. "Oh, for a homo of the sapient variety who can hold his liquor! I, on the other hand, am the only one who exists of that noble breed, as far as I can tell these days, anyway. I can drink a quart of one-fifty proof splow and never show it. But, ah, anyway, my crystal Christian. Nomenclature on the fragile side!" His forefinger went up like a baton conducting some notes he was going to pull out of thin air. "A crystal! I like it! Crystal Christian. And you may say that I am Shepard, the conductor of the river of the soul, the *anima mundi* collecting streams of art." Patting me gently he added, "Crystal Christian, how well the name fits you, such lovely fragile clarity as you are, my boy. Yes, you make me dream of caressing a long-stemmed glass, yum yum." He bent down and gave me a smacking kiss on my forehead. Startling.

"You makin movements like a gaddam fruitcake, Donny!" Amoss shouted. "Knock it off before you scare this kid half to death. You been drinking too much splow. Stick to beer if you wanna live longer."

Shepard waved him away. "Poof poof, genius has spontaneous love and power and magic that old sourdoughs and whippersnappers cannot understand. It's beyond you and you and you. Not for the rat-a-tat hoi polloi, but for those who live belly to belly in the belly of the gods!"

Turning away he went into the kitchen. He bumped belly first into the counter. Then the stove. Then the refrigerator, grabbing the door handle at the same time and swinging the door open with a bang against the counter. Gathering six beers, three in each hand he brought them back to the couch and dumped them. And said, "My dear old dipsodear likes his beer, but I can't allow him to drink it anymore. You two can have as much as will make you run from sun to sun like savages. I want to watch that. The truth is, I'm a voyeur. Drink your corroded hearts into contentment, dear ones. What else have you got? Keep it up and you'll look like him." He nodded his head toward Amoss, who was eyeing the beers fiercely. "Poor old boy on his bowed legs. Rickets when he was a child, you know. But I love him. I wished he loved me too, but he doesn't. Suffering men whose mothers hated them are incapable of love, you know."

Shepard's voice had changed, gotten softer and moist and shuddery. There were tears running down his cheeks. I couldn't believe it. For several seconds he was actually sobbing.

"What happened?" I asked, looking at Amoss.

"Don't pay it no mind, it'll pass," said Amoss.

Shepard took a hanky out and gave his magnificent nose a good blow.

"He bawls over anything," said Amoss. "Tweak him on the

ass, he'll wail like you shot him. Sit down, jellybelly, take a load off those sixteens before your ankles crumble from the strain."

Shepard sat and the couch dipped under him, the sides of the cushions pulling in and the frame creaking like a rusty hinge. He handed Mamie and me a beer and opened a can for himself. "To our current companions born on a half-shell, Mamie and Crystal Christian." He lifted his can and drank, while Amoss complained that he had been left out. "None for thou, old dipsodear! You must soothe that ulcer before it turns to cancer."

Amoss snatched a can defiantly, opened it, and drank the whole thing non-stop. The burping afterwards was grander than the bellowing of a bull.

"He's determined to disgust us," said Shepard. "Please don't encourage him, Crystal. It is best to ignore these theatrical displays of juvenilia."

"Pompuss ass," hissed Amoss. "Stick your rear in your ear and your prick in your beer. Put a rose up your nose till it glows, hee hee hee." Grabbing another beer, Amoss ripped it open. Grinning, he poured beer over his teeth and down the sides of his face and neck, soaking his shirt collar. His Adam's apple bobbed up and down. And then came the mighty burping again. Rolling thunder.

Shepard's head jerked away at a haughty angle. He stared at me with cozy eyes and asked me if I liked going to the movies. I said I did. And he said he had bought the theater next door and was going to make it the art center of Temple, a kind of art shopping mall. He had been in the process of renovating it for several weeks. Actually six or seven months, but one day it would be finished and become a beacon for art lovers all over Wisconsin. Perhaps even a beacon for the Midwest. Or maybe, who knows? A beacon for America. Even the world. Like the Louvre!

"It will be relevance and purity," he continued. "Great paintings from Eau Claire; great books from defunct libraries; great sculpture from the Black Hills of Dakota and totem poles from British Columbia. I am currently scouring the world for underart, those places of genius that few have discovered along the byways of creation's currents. I have a nose for smelling true art's wholeness, harmony and radiance in underrated places. What you will see when I am finished is a sublimity that no one has even imagined before. This is genius, you see, the world made new, caught in a pristine flavor that few have tasted, yum yum, and definitely not that world of *experts* from New York." His entire face radiated an inner fire. He needed a cold washcloth for his forehead and maybe some ice on his neck. I hoped he wasn't going to have a stroke. And then he added, "What books do you like? Who is your favorite writer, Crystal?"

"I dunno. Maybe Jack London. I like the stories about dogs."

Shepard's eyebrows shot up in horror. "Jack London!" he shrieked. "No, no, no, no, no!" He twisted his lips and grimaced like he had drunk poison. "Trash! Trash and rubbish! Garbage! The dregs of opposition to the intellectual life of the mind. Oh, Crystal, dear-dear, don't you know that London is a subculture B-grade author of low-minded commercialism? Portentous to the core, a would-be philosopher of Darwin and savagery and Herbert Spencer's so-called psychology, the persistence of force, all of it trapped in London's tales of adventure. Ugh! No refinement, no delicacy, no subtle persuasion. Hits you over the head with a whip of intestine and a dog-bone. You can't really admire him, Crystal. Tell Shepard you don't mean it, my boy."

"I don't know," I said, wishing I hadn't said anything. "Lots of people read his books, I think."

"The most commercially puerile recommendation." Shepard stroked his nose and looked down its length at me. "So, poof poof, huh? Caught me in the coils of a child's saber-thrusting wisdom straight to the means of the matter. The end justification is that London is not past tense yet, he is still being read! God help us! He has been crowned with the incandescence of immortality, while I, on the other hand, have only my genius to comfort me. Is that what you're saying?"

"Gosh no, I—"

"Never mind! I understand everything. Writer versus critic – nasty, ephemeral critic, yum yum *ephemeral*. The pomposity of it becomes you. I, on the other hand, am a genius, after all, a genius abandoned on the frontier of backwoods understanding. Do you understand what I'm saying?"

"Not at all."

"Poof, poof, fortune meant for me to be rich, so I could defray the cost of my mental exertions, but somehow I've managed to baffle fortune and to baffle my destiny – till now! With the Artlife Theater, I will fulfill my early promise. It's not too late, Right, Amoss?"

Amoss nodded his head like he was using it to pound a railroad spike.

"Right Mamie?"

Mamie said, "Yaay!"

"Right, Crystal?"

"Whatever you say, Mr. Shepard."

"Drunk as a bedbug in June," said Amoss wiping his palm round and round his slackened face, eyes and cheeks and even his forehead hanging. So that he looked very old and leathery. Like maybe ninety.

"Barbarian profundity that." Shepard jerked his thumb at Amoss. "In the annals of Oxfordian inclination, I mean the O.E.D., are listed the infamous utterances of Amoss Potter, man of trains forty and four years, whose immortal aphorism shines forth – 'drunk as a bedbug in June.' Amoss, you have a Ganymede's cup of vocabulary and a mind as tenacious as a cobweb."

"Kiss this bumbomb, mushmouth," said Amoss, raising his leg and letting his rear end roar.

"Ugh, disgusting," said Shepard. "However, if that's the challenge, I accept." He raised his own leg and farted so loud I was sure the cushion was torn. I got up and opened a window.

Mamie fell back in laughter and ripped a good one back at Shepard. Amoss tried to match her but couldn't, so he jammed his hand into his armpit and flapped his elbow. Out came squeaky little farts that were, frankly, pitiful. I tried to join in, but had nothing to add to the conversation.

Shepard stroked his nose again, as if soothing it. "Neanderthal. Homo-erectal pithecine, throwback to dark and dreary caves, genetic survivor of the omophagists, those devourers of raw meat, plague of my two-score years, you've proved your head is as full of air as your cacophonous behind and armpit."

"Hee hee hee, what do I care whatcha call me, banananose? You never make no gaddamn sense nohow. You savvy any of his two-bit lingo, Christian?"

"A little bit here and there," I answered. "Not much."

"See, nobody savvies you, Donny. You're speaking educated voodoo."

"Poof, poof."

Amoss burped at him. "That's your language, Donny. Makes as much sense, anyway, don't you think so, Christian?"

"You both have gone beyond me now, " I said. "I haven't even finished high school."

Shepard rubbed his mustache like it itched him. And pointing at Amoss he said, "It just won't take cultivation. It is chromosomally damaged. Don't let it influence you, Crystal. Your broad brow is meant for Johnsonian enlightenment, not for the dribblings that this dear dipsodunce can produce. I, on the other hand—"

"Huh?"

"I mean Amoss, of course."

"Want to see me stand on my head and drink beer?" said Amoss.

"Oh yes!" said Shepard, sounding really interested. "Do it, Amoss. Stand on your head and show them how you're able to create an internal vacuum to defy gravity and suck up beer. You'll be mentally challenged by this, kids."

Amoss shouted happily, "All righty! Hardly a man on this fist of earth can do what I can. Not wartnose here, that's for sure. Stand him on his head it would break his neck. You can't tell it but under those triple chins is a real neck, I swear. His weight would snap it like a toothpick. Hee hee hee. Here I go."

And Amoss drove his head into a couch cushion and turned himself upside down. There he was, his heels booming into the wall, his feet wriggling. Holding himself like that, he sucked beer into his mouth, working his throat muscles and stomach muscles, until somehow he drank whatever was left in the can of beer. He threw the empty can at Shepard, who caught it and held it up like a trophy.

"Isn't he a talent?" said Shepard. "You know of any seventy-year-old men who can do that? I've tried to get him to entertain on street corners downtown, but he's too shy – right, Amoss?"

"Bout as shy as that plum squatting in the middle of your head."

Shepard stroked his nose again, like he was soothing a pet mouse. And he said, "Don't make fun of this noble biscuit. Durante should be so lucky to have a nose like this! It is a badge of great character. Ask any phrenologist."

While he was talking, Mamie went over to the couch and joined Amoss upside down. She smiled hugely at us, her face glowing bright from the blood sinking down to her head. Holding her beer to her lips, she began to suck it upwards like Amos had.

"Just let her try. She can't do it," said Amoss. "It's a gift."

But she did. She siphoned the beer up her throat and into her belly. When the can was empty, she wanted a full one. I opened a beer and gave it to her.

"Show off," said Amoss. "I give her the secret and gaddammit she does it!" He flipped back over onto his feet and threw himself into the chair and pouted as he watched Mamie guzzle the second beer down. Or rather up.

Shepard patted her thigh and squeezed it and said, "Solid muscle. This is a magnificent creature. In her own way almost as magnificent as *moi*. What are you grumbling about, Amoss?"

"I'm hungry. I wanna weeny. Fix me a weeny, Donny."

"You see he has no sense? You don't put hot dogs and beer on top of an ulcer! It's antediluvian! No more sense than God's anointed Noah naked and drinking himself to death." Pointing sternly at Amoss again, he added, "It refuses to listen. It refuses to learn. Do you see why I'm crazy with worry?"

Amoss stuck his tongue out. "It's my ulcer, nosegay, my fuggin ulcer and it wants a weeny!" He stood up and stomped off to the kitchen to make himself a hot dog.

"Well, if you insist, you might as well make us all some," said Shepard.

We shared the hot dogs, putting cheese and mustard on them and rolling them in slices of bread, washing them down with more beer. Afterward I felt sleepy and wished we could go to bed. But sleeping seemed the last thing on anyone else's mind. They blabbed on and on, especially Shepard. He wanted us to know that a genius like him needed to talk in order to make room in his head for all the ideas coming in quick as lightning. He said we must learn about the history of wisdom and integrations of brilliant thought he catastrophically learned by the age of ten. And about certain unsuspected connections between politicians - who spoke the purest cant imaginable and yet were incredulously believed by the stupidest ilk on this earth, your average American, a pointless experiment in greed - and philosophers, whose written tongue twisters were held up by college-cloistered scholars as examples of unparalleled insights into the puzzlements of modern man, yum yum.

As he talked, he drummed his fingers on his great belly, and his mouth seemed to be chewing all the flavor it could get out of his vocabulary. At one point he paused and said, "Of course, this is too far advanced for you to understand. I realize that. But listen anyway, fill your brains with Shepard's celestial phrases. I'm your preacher. I'm your church. Suffer the children to come unto me."

I tried hard, but I couldn't keep up with all he said. I knew he was saying things I should know, but I was too dull to get more than an inkling here and there of what he meant. Still, most of it *sounded* interesting. He was, he said, one of the chosen few. He was meant for a special destiny. But he was two-score years now and still didn't know for absolutely sure what it was he was supposed to do that was so special, but he believed that it was his mission to bring great art to Temple. Which was better than working as a janitor at the college cleaning up behind pseudo intellectuals.

The art movement in Temple might be the bringer of better things, maybe even the start of a larger association that would find disciples all over the world. He would wait and work to see if it happened, and he would be patient, because patience was the most important attribute of geniuses. You've got to let the rest of humanity catch up with you. He would apply his brilliance to the discernment of his destiny, because his destiny was mankind's destiny, and it would come to him one day full-blown, as if from the head of Zeus. Then he would know what the ultimate connection was between him and the spirit of the world.

Up to now he had managed to figure out how to manifest his eccentricities well enough that people who knew him bowed when he walked by. He had dropped out of school when he was twelve because it was a haven of reactionary thought creating mental robots to unfeelingly perpetuate the monstrosity of the capitalist system, with its disgusting pride in natural selection; by dropping out of the army when he was drafted, twisting the intricacies of his thought around the ineptitude of a certain army psychiatrist, who promptly recommended a medical discharge for the mentally unfit unable to slavishly serve their country; by dropping all contact with women who refused to have anything to do with him, who judged him by exteriors rather than interiors, where he shined like the most handsome movie stars, a Gable, a Cooper, a John Wayne; by dropping in on his father, who had disowned him, and convincing the old fellow to leave all his money to the growth of sensibility and culture. The old fellow died and did leave Shepard his money, and it was in use right this moment in the rehabilitation of the theater next door, so aptly named Artlife. What is life without art? Without it the higher purpose is gone and life is nothing but drudgery.

Somehow his own biography upset him and he began leaking tears as he talked, quietly wiping his eyes with a hanky and claiming that he was the only genius he knew who had such depth of soul, such a heart that was too big for his own good. Then he broke down for a while and really sobbed. It was hard to resist him. I had to blow my nose to keep the tears out of my eyes. Amoss was weeping too and declaring himself the only true friend of the truest of friends, that greatest genius of all time, Donald Leonardo Shepard. He threw himself into Shepard's arms and they hugged each other and sobbed over their wonderful friendship. I patted them both on the back to give them comfort. While this was going on Mamie had been rooting over the empty beer cans, raising them to her lips and squeezing into her mouth whatever drops were left.

"More," she said, looking at the three of us.

"All gone," I told her.

"Kritch'n!" she shouted, stamping her foot. "More!"

"Get the splow!" said Amoss. "On top of the fridge."

There were two quart-jars of splow. It looked like anemic tea. I took the jars to the coffee table and opened one and sniffed. The bouquet made my eyes burn. I handed the jar to Mamie. She took a mouthful and swallowed. And coughed. And gave her patented smile - *I'm a wide-mouth frog!*

The splow went round to Shepard, then to Amoss. In a few minutes half of the first jar was empty. Mamie wrestled the jar from Amoss and drank some more and handed it on to Shepard. Suddenly she was on her feet and dancing. Well, sort of. She kicked her feet around like a lumberjack in heavy boots doing a hoedown, while the rest of us clapped and shouted, "Go, Mamie!"

"What a woman!" cried Shepard.

"I'm gonna marry her!" said Amoss.

"More!" demanded Mamie, pointing to the empty jar.

"Get her more!" said Shepard. He chugged towards her, grabbed her around the waist and whirled her. Amoss turned the radio to the polka station. "The Beer-Barrel-Polka filled the room. *"Roll out the bar-rel!"* we all sang. Shepard and Mamie were bouncing around like a pair of mammoth beach balls. The floor rolled and swayed. Amoss joined in and the three of them danced in a circle while holding hands and shouting "Waa-hoo! Yippy! Yowie! Yip, yip yip!" Faster and faster they went and pretty soon they were all dizzy. Shepard fell first, went to his hands and knees then his belly and rolled over gasping. Followed by Amoss who looked suddenly pale. The steam went out of him as he flopped on the floor like a rag doll. Mamie banged into the shelves and knocked some books to the floor and then she joined them, hugging the books, huffing and puffing and giggling.

I watched Amoss trying to get up, his legs and arms jerking as if someone was sticking them with needles. "Ooo, I'm sick," he said. Then he burped hugely, but this one wasn't funny. It was long and wet and thick as taffy. "Tastes ugly," he said, making a bitter face. There was fear in his eyes. "Tastes like salt. Somebody poured salt in my mouth, sticky salt. I know that taste. I know what it is. Here it comes! Look out!"

From deep in his stomach came another ugly burp, and with it flew a clot of blood that hit the floor and splashed over Mamie's feet. Her eyes fixed on the blood as if it was a strange puzzle. What is this thing? Blood flowed from Amoss' mouth, lots more of it. Poured into his lap, foaming with pink bubbles and bits of wiener and other chunks of digestion.

"I'm gaddamn dying," he whispered.

I looked at Shepard for guidance, but he was out cold.

"Hospital," choked Amoss. "Gid me to the hospital."

I glanced at Mamie. She was still fascinated with the blood on the floor. She bent down and ran her finger through a tiny puddle of it, shaping it into a butterfly.

I lost my head. I kicked Shepard and said, "Do something! Amoss is dying!"

Shepard blinked his eyes and looked at me and told me to throw something over the blood. If he saw it he would faint again.

"You faint at the sight of blood?"

"Yes. Cover it."

I ran for towels and covered the blood as best I could. Mamie helped me. Then she picked up Amoss and carried him out of the house, to the car. We followed her. We got into the car. She held Amoss on her lap, while I drove and Shepard sat in back gripping both door handles on each side and moaning, saying, "Beer and hot dogs on an ulcer. He never listens. Turn right at the corner and follow the hospital signs. It's only a mile. Why won't you ever listen to me, Amoss? Now look what you've done."

"My own mind is my own church," said Amoss. "You know who said that? Thomas Paine. A true American hero. I'm sure glad I'm drunk as a headless goose, or I'd be terrified. But I been through this before. They'll open me up and stop the bleeding and I'll be fine. I ain't scared."

"Beer and hot dogs on an ulcer, you harlequin. Serve you right if you died, but you better not or I'll kill you."

"Save me! I don't want to die."

"You'll be fine, dipsodear. Don't worry."

"I ain't scared. Well, maybe a mite."

When we got to the hospital I drove around to the emergency side and parked. Mamie carried Amoss down the sidewalk and through the double doors. A nurse ran up with a gurney and Mamie laid Amoss on that. She stroked his leg and stared at him. His eyes were rolling in his head. Shepard was trembling and blowing his nose and saying he was rich, he would pay, give Amoss the best care possible. But the guy behind the counter kept saying, "What insurance? What is the name of your insurance company?" Amoss made a noise that was a sort of a half-hiccup, "Huck, huck, huck," and more blood boiled out of him. Shepard saw it and his eyes rolled and down he went.

"Get going, nurse!" ordered the man behind the counter.

The nurse and another man in white took off with Amoss down the hall and disappeared with him through some doors. At the same time, a doctor slapped Shepard's cheeks and he woke up. "Save him, save him," he said. "I'll pay the bill, don't worry. Where do I sign?"

Mamie and I went outside and leaned against the car. We waited only fifteen or twenty minutes before Shepard came out, followed by a doctor who said: "He lost too much blood. We couldn't get it into him fast enough. I'm truly sorry. He didn't suffer. He didn't know what was happening to him."

Shepard climbed into the back seat, lay over on his side and sobbed like a heartbroken infant. I had never heard such crying in my life. I had an impulse to slap him and say, "Be a man!" But I didn't do that. It wouldn't have been very sympathetic, seeing how Amoss was dead.

I drove us back to the house and Mamie and I managed to get Shepard inside and into his bed. "You're staying, aren't you?" he said. "You won't leave me alone, will you?"

"We can stay awhile," I told him.

"I can't believe he's dead. It's just horrible. It's awful. Why does this have to happen to me now? Everything was going so well. Beer and hot dogs – you heard me, I tried to tell him. Stubborn old fool. Old nitwit." And then he bawled some more. Then he asked for the jar of splow. I brought it to him, and he told me to leave and close the door.

Mamie and I went out and sat for a while on the porch and stared at the cold stars and the tree shivering the leaves on the branches that were still alive. The dead twigs and branches rattled.

"Kritch'n, Amoss drowd'n man," said Mamie.

"Just like that," I answered, snapping my fingers. The quickness of it was hard to get a hold of. He was alive. Then he was dead. A man having a dance. Then a man heaving blood on the floor and saying, "I ain't scared. Save me!" Where did he go? Where was he now?

After some time we went back inside and I decided to take a shower. Mamie joined me. We soaped each other down like we were trying to soap Amoss' death out of our systems. Our memories. It felt good to have Mamie's hands on me, cleaning me, getting the curse of the night off my skin. And I did the same for her. The slipping of my hands over her skin felt like a renewing ritual. Big life. Broad living. Solid woman that it seemed nothing could kill. That was Mamie. We rinsed off and got out and dried ourselves. By that time I was stiff as a tent peg and couldn't wait any longer to do the no-rain dance.

It was different this time, though. Mamie was soft about it, not dangerous at all. We went into Amoss's room and lay on his bed and caressed each other. We were dressed in moonlight. She was grayish pale white, shiny hair, freckles, sleepy eyes. For some reason the beauty and warmth of her made me choke up and I heard again Amoss' words, "I ain't scared! Save me!" The two things together, Mamie in bed and Amoss dead, got to me and I couldn't stop the tears. It made me mad at myself. We were supposed to be doing the no-rain, and instead I couldn't quit crying.

Mamie pulled my head into her breasts and stroked my back and finally I got control of myself and the sobs subsided. Her breasts smelled so soapy good, I had to kiss them. Then suck them. It was wonderful and sad at the same time. I kissed upward to her lips and clung there a long time to her big, soft mouth. Her legs parted. She pulled me on top of her. Reached down and brought me safely home.

In the calm that came after, I stayed on top of her, loving her so much I had to say it: "I love you more than the whole world, Mamie."

"Yaay, Kritch'n," she whispered.

We had to lie on our sides because it was such a narrow bed. So narrow, in fact, that when Mamie fell asleep and turned over, she pushed me out and I landed on the floor. I knew it was pointless to get back in. I'd have to sleep right on top of her. So I took one of the blankets and went to the living room, where the moon was blushing all over the glass panes and I could see pretty well the way things were, the lay of the land so to speak. I lay on the couch, looking up into the blue air and at Amoss' heel marks on the wall. And that had happened just a few hours ago. And now he was dead. And Mamie and I had come home and did the no-rain dance. Sometimes, when people die, the best thing you can do is the no-rain dance.

Living Hollow

Shepard had Amoss buried in a graveyard at the edge of town. The graveyard overlooked some farmland, gentle hills where silage corn would get harvested in October and cows would be let out to pick at the stubble. There were lots of trees, plenty of shade to keep the grave grass cool in the summer heat. Numerous tombstones in rows stretching from 1860 to 1959. Amoss would have plenty of company. Shepard said he imagined them all in a confab, like in the play called *Our Town*.

There weren't many people at the funeral itself, just Mamie and me and Shepard, Charlie Friendly from the bar nearby, where Amoss used to go, and Mongoose Jim and Kiss of Death Cody, two men of the trains who had got drunk with Amoss plenty of times, they said. Shepard wouldn't allow a preacher to come and give a sermon because it would be an insult to the spirit of his dear dipsodear, who loved God but despised all organized religions. Instead, Shepard talked to Amoss at the graveside and told him how much he missed him after fifteen years of their being together sharing the same roof, the same table, the same ambitious life. He told Amoss not to be shy but to look up Maurice Shepard and introduce himself and tell Maurice that his son, Donald Leonardo, had sent along the best friend he'd ever had to keep his father from being lonely. Time would tell another tale one day, and there would be the three of them, a trendy Trinity, to talk it over before long. Shepard said he was feeling his mortality, a cold shadow resting on his feet and climbing up his ankles, like Socrates drinking the hemlock and feeling the cold poison climbing towards his heart. Shepard hoped when the time came to mingle souls that Amoss would by then have learned a lesson about mule-headedness and that Maurice would have learned to esteem the unique gift of a son's genius.

As soon as Shepard had finished we all took a hand with the ropes and lowered the coffin into the hole. Then we took turns shoveling the dirt on top. And that was that. Amoss was put to rest in a place where no ulcer could ever bother him again.

When we got back to the house, Shepard and Mamie went with the others over to Charlie Friendly's bar. I didn't want to go with them. I knew they would sit around and get drunk and carry on, which I didn't feel up to at the moment. I went into the living room and picked out a book to read to fill my mind with other things than Amoss' death and burial and all the blood and how quick and easy people die, and how quick and easy I might die some day and not have a thing to say about it.

It was that way with me for lots of hollow days after the funeral. I couldn't get my mind off death and Amoss saying, "I ain't scared. Save me!" I kept wondering what my last words would be and whether I'd be scared or not when my turn came to "pass on." Pass on to what? I wondered. I tried to imagine it – me, Christian Peter Foggy, croaked and in a coffin. But I could only get so far – to some brave words I might say on my deathbed, and I would see Mama and Pa crying, and everybody saying how wonderful I was and all that justifying of the dear departed and never saying anything bad about them because it's a curse to speak bad about the dead. I couldn't make myself stay down there, sealed in my casket and being prayed over. It gave me the willies. I told myself it won't happen to me – I will be one of the chosen. The big D won't get me. I'll never really die. Others have gotten out of it, haven't they? I'll go up in a whirlwind like what's his name that Robbie talked about – Elijah.

During that dark time in my life, I came across a book of poems on one of the shelves in the living room. The title was *Intimations of Mortality*, an anthology of poems put together by someone named Professor Steve Kowit. I read a poem by Walt Whitman that said, "The slower fainter ticking of the clock is in me" and I took my pulse and it was definitely slow – 53 beats a minutes. I started wondering if maybe I had heart trouble. Heart disease at my age? Anything was possible. The next line of the poem said, "Exit nightfall and soon the heart-thud stopping." I was getting morbid. My heart fluttered. It made me cough and there was this great thud and a rush of blood into my face and my heart started hurrying. Now it was up to 100 beats a minute! From 53 to 100 almost instantly – that's bad. Was it a chest pain I was feeling, or just gas? I stood up and paced back and forth across the living room floor shouting, "You're acting like a hypochondriac, Christian. Knock it off!" And I did. I knocked it off. Took up the book again and looked for something that would make me laugh, but nothing in there did the trick. Poetry for all its words doesn't do much funny. Lots of it is about death. Lots of it is depressing. Beautiful sometimes, but depressing. "A fly buzzed when I died." "Death will have no dominion." "The little cousin is dead by foul subtraction." "Death thou shalt die." And so on and so forth. It came to me that I wasn't the only one on this planet preoccupied with death. The majority of poets were totally, morbidly, sadly obsessed. What was the point? I don't know. When you're dead, what's it to you? Not even so much as cold comfort. I had to let it go because as another line said, "The pure products of America go crazy." Which was where my head was taking me. But then again what was I expecting from a title that gave me such a warning as *Intimation of Mortality*? Get a grip, kiddo. Hard to get a grip, though. Hard to keep your mind from breathing big D, big D, big D.

Shepard and Mamie spent their days either sleeping, eating or drinking. Mostly drinking. Shepard brought home splow by the case, and he and Mamie drank it like it was holy water renewing their souls. Shepard told her she was a better drinking partner than Amoss, that she didn't talk as much and she listened a million times better, and she never argued. He liked that. Then he would stare at the ceiling and apologize to Amoss if it hurt his feelings. Shepard talked a lot also about how hard it was to be him – a bona fide genius unique in the world. Normal people couldn't understand the misery he went through seeing the world so clearly, having a poet's vision and insight into the mystery of things. Such knowledge tore him to tatters, hurt him to tears. That's why he cried a lot. All his nerves were registering the pain of the world. He talked and talked about his misery until I got sick of it. I mean, it was endless and I was miserable myself. I wanted my home, my mother and father and a simpler, gentler, kinder world, and immortality, but I didn't go on and on about it the way he did talking, talking, talking. Saying ten times a day, "I, on the other hand, am as sensitive as I am large, and therefore I feel things more than others do, even more than that lone, lorn creetur Mrs. Gummidge."

And Mamie never saying much of anything, except to ask for more splow. She sat in the big chair across from him, wearing her stained farmeralls – she had washed them but you could still see the bloodstains, dark shadows on the denim where the bib and lap had held a bleeding Amoss. She held a jar of splow in her hand, out of which she would take a nip now and then and cheerfully smile, while listening to Shepard droning on and on about the hardships of his life. Everything for Mamie was "Yaay" and "Mmmore."

One week passed, then another, and I woke one morning just before dawn thinking I heard Pa calling me to get up and get my lazy ass to the barn and milk the cows. I got dressed and went outside. The tree leaves sounded like rustling water. The wind was carrying the scent of fresh-cut hay from some field far away. I heard the faint throaty roaring of a tractor. A farmer was up and doing already. I envied him.

As I stood there in the freshness of the morning air the sky suddenly filled with butterflies, thousands of them. Millions. Monarchs, black and yellow and red and black and looking like bits of whirling rainbow. They settled on the big elm and pumped their wings, bringing even the dead parts of the tree to life. Watching them breathing in and out like that made me feel peaceful, and I told myself that beauty itself made living worthwhile. Death, as mighty as it is, cannot prevent the rhythmic resurrection of butterflies and leaves on trees and corn in a field and haying seasons. I didn't want to be sad about Amoss or anything else anymore. The butterflies clustered in the tree for thirty minutes or so, and then, like flower petals in an updraft, they rose and flew away. My fear of death seemed to fly away with them.

I took a walk. The streets were quiet, just a car passing by. None of the stores were open, not Charlie Friendly's Bar & Grill or the Piggly Wiggly, or Smithson's Barber Shop, not even the Sunshine Café, though when I looked in the window I could see a waitress making coffee, getting things ready for the breakfast crowd. Walking farther, I came across Cunningham Chevrolet next door to Cunningham Implements. A row of orange Allis Chalmers tractors had their noses toward the street, smiles on their grills saying *come buy me!* There were balers and haybines and hay trailers and disks and harrows, all the implements for farming you might need. I climbed up on one of the tractors, sitting in the seat and holding the steering wheel and wishing I could take it into some field with a baler and bale hay. Far off I could hear that farmer I had heard earlier. I wanted to be him, focused on my work. Even if that work was nasty chores, cleaning cow gutters and such, I wouldn't have minded. Farming, like butterflies coming out of nature, can be good for your soul and snap you out of a funk and maybe keep you from brooding after somebody you care about up and dies. The sun was getting warm. Traffic building up. More noise. A bus hissing as it stopped for a passenger.

A few blocks later, I was going up an alley when I heard a voice calling my name. I thought for a second I was hearing things, maybe Amoss' ghost? But it wasn't Amoss, it was Robbie Peevy. I looked at the building next to me, an ancient red-brick monster three stories high, and there he was, staring at me from behind bars. There was a small vacant lot between us, full of weeds. The morning sun was shining on the building, lighting Robbie's golden hair. I thought of the people in the schoolyard calling him angel, and I could see why they would. More and more he resembled Jesus, I thought. I mean the American version.

"It's me, it's Robbie," he said. "Come here, Christian. Talk to me."

I crossed the lot and went to the window, staring up at him. "I heard you got arrested," I said.

"I've been here two weeks," he said.

"You were in the newspaper: 'Robbie Peevy Returns. Followers Riot,'" that's what the headline said."

"I've seen it," he said. "Did you read the story about how I was a prodigy and how I hypnotized people with my words and how some said I was the Second Coming and others said I was the devil? 'The worst are full of passionate intensity,' the article said. They gave my life history, and they wrote about whether or not some books should be burned. I'm not the only one who thinks there is evil in books, you know."

"Yeah, but who gets to decide what's evil and what isn't?" I asked him.

"Like pornography, I know evil when I see it."

"Yeah? But you were burning everything, Robbie. You even burned Shakespeare."

"Robbie stroked his beard thoughtfully. "To make your point, you sometimes got to exaggerate a little bit."

"Maybe. But that kind of exaggeration got you arrested."

"What, for burning books? You really think it was for burning books? No, no. They arrested me for telling them the truth. That's what they do. They did it to Jesus. And like him I'm being persecuted. They want to put me to death. But I'll be rescued before they get the chance. There are plots against me, Christian. I hear the conspirators whispering in the hall. I see them looking my way. They are making plans to get rid of me permanently. Do you understand?"

"They're going to kill you, Robbie?"

He nodded. "And bury my body where no one will ever know."

"No way."

"Yes."

"No."

"Believe me, if you don't get me out of here, I'm a dead man tomorrow. But I'm not worried because Jesus said you'd come and here you are. The sun in the east and a boy called Christian materializing out of nowhere. What an undeniable omen!"

"Not out of nowhere. I—"

"Do you think it could just happen? Nothing in my life is an accident. I'm fulfilling a special destiny."

"You and Shepard," I said, but Robbie didn't seem to hear me.

"You have been sent to this spot at this moment to help me fulfill it."

"Fulfill what?"

"My special destiny. Aren't you listening?"

"Oh, that. What can I do? I'm just a kid. No one listens to me."

"Christian, you can free me," he whispered. "Jesus will give the power into your hands."

"No, I don't think so, Robbie. I don't want to get in trouble. You got yourself into this, and you got to get yourself out. I'm sorry, but it's what a fellow has to expect if he goes around breaking into libraries and burning all the books. I got to go." I started to leave.

"No!" he cried. "Don't abandon me. Oh, Christian, take this cup away. Listen to me, where's Mamie?"

"She's with Don Shepard. They get drunk every day."

"Mamie's drinking? I don't like the sound of that."

"Me neither, but I don't know what to do about it. They're grieving for a guy we know who died of bleeding ulcers."

"Man is steamed in the decay of the devil's heart. I bleed for man, for he is lost if I do not bleed. Blood washes. Blood cleanses. Jee-sus is the way, oh yes. Get me out of here and I will save ten-thousand souls before I am called to my eternal home in the bosom of my Lord. I'll save Mamie from herself." Robbie had a pleased expression on his face. "Now do you see what kind of prophet I am, Christian? Am I really so bad in your eyes when I can be the instrument that sends countless souls to heaven? Think about it. You know me and you know I'm right."

I stood there thinking it over and decided that the one thing I knew for sure was that I didn't know anything. "I'm not smart enough to figure you out, Robbie," I told him.

Holding his hand out to me through the bars, he said, "Come closer, please. Take my hand. Feel the blessing in my hand."

I took his hand. It was cold and bony. A little damp.

"What we need right now is to save Mamie from the clutches of this alcoholic who is drinking himself and her to perdition. Mamie is in grave danger, deep danger, oh yes, drinking every day and destroying her magnificent soul with the worm of alcohol. Jesus save her! A crooked path is in front of her, I say. A path full of germy dust hiding bad blood and lacerated livers. That way lays death and darkness and the maw of Satan open and hungry for Mamie. He wants her. His teeth are gnashing for our Mamie-girl. Save her, Jesus! Satan wants to suck the marrow of her soul. Don't let him, honey. All she's got is you. It's your duty to rescue her. It's what you were put on earth to do right now. Don't argue. I know these things. Listen to Robbie. Get her away from this Gomorrah. If you don't, it will kill her. Mark my words – the scraph of Camelot speaks to you!"

Leaning his head on the bars, he stared at me for a few seconds without blinking, his wonderful eyes holding me in a kind of spell, his hypnotic voice echoing in my ears. It was hard for me to think straight.

"I can help you," he said softly. "And our Mamie."

"How can you help?" I asked.

"First I got to get out of here, of course. Or my light will shine in darkness no more. Hollow is the future without your tender mercy."

"What can I do? I told you I can't do anything."

His smile looked like a beam of light. He told me to put my hands on the bars. I did, and as soon as I grabbed them I knew how to save him. The bars were loose. They turned in their sockets.

"They're all this way," he said. "Old and loose as a Jew's version of the truth. Jee-sus is the way, amen. The brick and mortar are crumbling from old age. This building is a hundred and fifty years old. Watch this." He shook the bars and bits of grainy brick and red dust rained down.

"A few good wallops with a sledge would break these bricks to smithereens," I said. I was excited now.

"You got it, honey. And especially if Mamie swings the hammer."

He was right, but I still didn't know if we should do it. I told him, "I already have lots of troubles and breaking you out of jail would just get me and Mamie in more trouble."

"Mamie is at stake in this," he said. "You've got to think of that. In saving me, you'll be saving her. I'll take you with me to California. That's where I'm going. No winter in California. Think of that. We'll disappear. I've got friends out there. You'll be welcomed with open arms. So will Mamie."

"California?"

"Golden California."

"Geez, that would solve a lot of problems."

"Bring a sledge and a crowbar. We'll use blankets to muffle the noise. Those guards stay up front and watch TV or sleep. They hardly ever come by to check on me. Pry up a corner, that's all. I'm so skinny now I can squeeze through any place I can get my head through. I'll be out of here like the wind. We won't get caught, I promise you. A sledgehammer, a crowbar, and Mamie. One, two, three and California here we come."

I shook my head and walked away from him. He called out to me, telling me I'd be back, that I wouldn't abandon poor Robbie to his enemies. Jesus would move me and I'd be back.

I went to the graveyard. I sat on Amoss' mound and stared at the trees and the distant cornfield. I told Amoss that I owed Robbie nothing. He had made his own troubles and almost got Mamie and me arrested in the bargain. I shouldn't have anything more to do with him. But maybe they were going to kill him. What did I know? Lots of crazy people doing evil things no matter where you go. And California? Talk about crazy, that's where the kicked-out crazies of the other states went, wasn't it? That's what my pa had said. Land of loonies, he called it. Full of Robbies and probably Mamies and Shepards too. Worse than Wisconsin, which was plenty bad enough. Naw, I told myself, the last thing we needed was to have anything more to do with Robbie Peevy.

Faintly, but clearly it seemed to me I heard Amoss agreeing

with me: "Gaddamn right, kid!" he said.

I stayed gone all day wandering around and when I finally got back to the house, it was nearly dark and I was very hungry. The lamp was on inside. I could see through the window. Mamie and Shepard were sitting on the couch, sharing a jar of splow. They were leaning towards each other, slapping each other on the legs and laughing. Shepard said something that made her howl. Then he was holding the jar to her lips and pouring the splow in like she was a kitchen sink. When he tried to stop, she grabbed his arm and brought it back. He tried to pull away, but she wouldn't let him. Then he was getting mad and pulling really hard. He started yelling at her, calling her a no-good lushy fat twat. When he stood up and slugged her, she let go of the jar.

"Now you see what happens when you mess with Donald Leonardo Shepard?" he said. "You frizzle-headed freaker, you titmouse moron, you fripping jibber-jubber dunciad!" He sucked off the last of the splow and stood swaying in front of wide-eyed Mamie.

Rubbing her jaw, she stood up and stared closely at him. He leaned around her and patted her bottom, then pointed to the kitchen. "Go thou Meemee mine valentine," he said. "Get your master a full jar of God's aqua vitae so I can toast your Olympian legs." He did a little half turn and fell back onto the couch. I heard wood snapping. The couch looked to be broken in the middle.

He was kicking at Mamie's Olympian legs, telling her to get more splow and do it now. She raised her fist slowly and then brought it down, fump! on top of his head. He slumped over like a dead ox. I hurried inside, praying she hadn't killed him. He was lying there with his eyes closed, snoring through his open mouth. Amoss had called Shepard's snore sonic booms, but my impression of the sound was more like hearing the outraged honk of an angry goose. Mamie tottered off to the kitchen.

"That's enough!" I told her.

She glanced at me, curious.

"Splow's no good," I said. "It's ruining you."

"Nup, nup," she said.

"Yup, yup, I say. Listen, Mamie, we got to get out of here before it's too late."

"Nup, nup."

"Mamie and Kritch'n on the go again, wouldn't you like that?"

She thought it over. "Yaay, Kritch'n b-bring it sssplow." She went to the fridge and grabbed another jar off the top. She offered it to me.

"Ugh," is all I said.

Mamie opened the jar and took a big swallow. She set the jar down and put her arms around me. "Kritch'n, mmm-yum, Kritch'n." My feet were off the floor and she was holding me so tightly I couldn't breathe. She gave me a shake that made my legs flip loosely right and left, like I was a Raggedy Andy doll. I whacked her on the sides with my fists but it was like a fly trying to swat an elephant. Holding me against her, she waddled to the bedroom and dropped me on the bed and started kissing me and crooning, "Ko down, ko down, Kritch'n, no-rain me."

I wasn't in the mood, but there wasn't much I could do about it. She took off her clothes and mine, and the whole thing seemed to take forever. I bet it was at least an hour. But it wasn't like when Amoss died, when I was feeling the need to be alive, to feel full of life, and full of love for her too. I didn't feel loving at all. Or maybe it was her being so drunk and sloppy and stinking of splow and pushing me down like I had no choice in the matter. It wasn't the no-rain, it was just sex. And finally she stopped and stood up and went into the bathroom. I lay there thinking that Robbie was right, Mamie was on the road to ruin and I had to do something about it.

Escape

Early the next morning Mamie was sober. She took a long, steamy bath and washed her hair. She was in the bathroom a couple of hours and when she came out the effects of the booze binge didn't show at all. She sparkled. I had washed her clothes in the washer, dried them in the drier, so for the moment she was about as fresh and clean as she could be. I fixed scrambled eggs and toast and coffee for breakfast and while we were eating I told her we were leaving Temple. "It's time to get out of here and find some work," I said. "No point in drinking ourselves to death with Shepard grieving over Amoss. Amoss wouldn't want that either. That would be stupid." Shepard was in his bedroom sleeping. I knew from experience he wouldn't rise until well past noon.

I mentioned to Mamie that I had seen Robbie at the jail. I said we could walk by there and say goodbye to him if she wanted to. Flashing her froggy smile she said, "Yaay, Kritch'n, let's g-go see um." And then she mimicked him singing: "*I got Chris-tian and Mamie go-ing my way; I got tri-umph in Temple today.*" I shook my head in wonder. Always she was full of surprises.

On a side street near the jail a crew was working on a section of sidewalk. They were banging away with a jackhammer and shovels. Standing under the window, I called out to Robbie and he replied, "God be praised! If you hadn't come I wouldn't be alive to greet you tomorrow. They're going to hang me and sink me in the river in the dead of night tonight. I'm talking midnight. I heard them say it. Yes I did."

"How could you?" I asked. "There are doors and walls in the

way of your cell. Maybe you've got super ears?"

"Jesus told me."

"Uh-huh."

"But was I afraid? No! Because Jesus also told me you and Mamie would save me. Look at her, she's glorious. Come close and let me touch you." Mamie grabbed the bars and put her head against them. Robbie ran fingers through her hair. Her curls shot up full of static electricity as his hand passed over them. And he said, "Look at that! She's a lightning rod."

"We come to say goodbye," I told him.

"To say goodbye? What are you talking about, Christian? Where's the sledgehammer? Where's the crowbar?"

"I thought it over, Robbie, and I think your situation has to run its course. They'll just put you back in Camelot for a while, anyway, and you'll get some help and then you'll get well."

"They're going to kill me I tell you!"

"No, they're not. You know they're not."

His eyes were huge. He did look frightened for real. His beard shivering. "I'm telling you—"

"No, Robbie, they aren't going to kill you. Camelot Hospital is just—"

"Camelot is just as bad! Shock treatments, lobotomies, drugs! Don't you understand what goes on in there? Camelot will kill me! Please, Christian, don't forsake me now."

"Listen, Robbie, me and Mame are heading out to find some work. Haying season is here and we need to be moving on out of this place. No more hanging with that Shepard and getting drunk. He's still sleeping it off, and he'll sleep past noon and then start in again with splow and beer. Only Mamie ain't gonna be part of it no more. I'm getting her the hell out of here for good. I've got to be taking care of her and myself. You've got to take care of you and not be depending on me to do something."

"Jee-sus, sear this boy's eyes with the truth! Don't abandon me, honey. Remember how Peter abandoned Christ? Do you want that on your conscience? You'll read in the papers about my death and it will haunt you till the day you die." He took a deep breath and continued stroking Mamie's hair, the curls lifting higher and higher into a sort of poodle puff. "You gonna let them put me away, honey? Stick me in that hollow sock – that Camelot! Where's your heart?"

"Got to think of us, Robbie. You're the one put yourself in there."

"Justice, righteousness, move the boy," he said, lifting his eyes towards the sky. He shook the bars and made them wiggle. I glanced at the workmen. They were watching us. When I looked at Robbie I saw he had tears welling up in his eyes. The tears rolled down his cheeks and I felt real bad for him.

"I'll die in that fairyland, honey," he said. "Give me a chance, won't you?"

I couldn't let go of that tormented look in his eyes. The same sick, hollow feeling came over me as it had the time I did Mamie wrong by showing John Beaver where she was living at the cabin by the Brule. And now this was another one of those moments of truth. Should I act with what my feelings were saying, rather than listening to that rational part of my brain telling me to take Mamie and run? Maybe after all, Robbie didn't deserve what was coming to him – the institution of Camelot with its drugs and shock treatments and lobotomies designed to make inmates into zombies who would behave themselves. A fairyland, as he said, that would kill him, kill his peculiar kind of personality. Maybe, it wouldn't be the right thing to do, even if the law said it was. I mean, what does the law know about the kind of mental fever and fervor that creates a man like Robbie? What the law knows is how to prosecute him, how to lock him up and break him. I had to admit that I liked Robbie as much for his eccentricities as anything. He might be kind of goofy, but so was Mamie, and, if I could see myself as others saw me, maybe I'd look goofy too. The one thing I knew for sure, neither Mamie nor Robbie were faking. Take them or leave them, they were both just simply what they were, bizarre but authentic. Preposterous. But not absurd.

Mulling the whole thing over in my mind, I stared at him and he stared at me, the thoughts seeming almost to come out of his brain into mine like a revelation. God speaking to me. God saying, "Don't forsake your friend. Don't abandon him to the system."

The words were so solid and strong that I felt rooted to them and there was no way to run away then. It was borrowing more trouble, but I knew I'd never live with myself if I turned my back on Robbie and let Camelot have him. I glanced again at the workmen and thought about asking to borrow their jackhammer. Then I thought maybe I should go over to Cunningham Implements and ask to test-drive a tractor, and get a chain, and pull the bars off. Free Robbie that way and then steal a getaway car. While I was planning things out, Robbie let go of Mamie and shook the bars in frustration and said, "Let me out of here!"

Mamie grabbed the bars and shook them too. She kept shaking them and chips of cement and bits of brick rained down.

Robbie caught her wrists and said, "O Jee-sus, Mamie, I wish you could just pull them off the wall. Shake them until they fall. Free your Robbie from this horrible temple of hell."

"Not even Mamie can do that," I said.

"Yaay, Kritch'n, I c-can," she told me.

"No way." I knew that no one in the world could pull those bars out by hand. I knew it in that part of my brain laughing at the idea. But then again, people have picked up cars that had rolled over and trapped a loved one. They've broken down doors and carried two-hundred-pound victims out of burning buildings. There was a guy who had picked up one end of a bubble-glass helicopter that had crashed into a drainage ditch and he saved the pilot inside, who was trapped under the water and drowning. There had been pictures of it on TV. People could do unbelievable feats of strength if their bodies and minds were totally into it. Maybe Mamie could rip those bars off, I told myself. She was gripping them, her hands and arms so tight that the muscles in her shoulders and back were swollen and curved, like a bull pawing the earth and getting ready to charge. Everyone was watching her, Robbie, myself and the workmen. All of us wanted to see what she would do.

"Rip 'em out," I whispered in her ear.

Rattling the bars again, she caused more brick dust to fall, more pieces of it crumbling. She climbed up the bars and took a hold of the upper right-hand corner. She placed her feet against the wall, so that she was squatting in a crablike triangle. Taking a deep breath and blowing it out, she pulled on the corner, but nothing moved and it seemed certain that Mamie had met her match. One of the workmen laughed. Another one said she looked like a monkey. The one with the jackhammer said. "I wish she could do it. Do it, baby. Come on."

Mamie kept increasing the pressure, pulling so hard her face turned as scarlet as a pomegranate. Her arms bulged against the sleeves of her shirt. Her thighs stretched the seams of her pants. You could see the white seam thread at the point of parting. She grunted and growled like a frustrated bear. And nothing was happening. I got scared for her. I was sure that if she kept it up something would break inside her. She would break her back or bust her heart.

"She'll kill herself, Robbie," I said.

"No she won't. She can do it. I can feel the wall surrendering. Listen, do you hear that? The wall is shaking."

"I think I hear something cracking."

"Jee-sus, give her strength. Burn the power of your heart into her flesh. Give her the spirit of Samson, the power he used to pull the pillars down."

Yes, I could hear a deep cracking coming from the upper right part of the wall, where Mamie was concentrating all her pulling. Fine lines appeared in the ancient brick, fissuring outward like spider legs.

"Holy Murphy, she's doing it!" said one of the workmen.

All three of them started cheering her, "Go, baby, go!"

Some people passing by stopped to watch, and they got so excited that they started yelling too. I heard car doors slamming and more people joining the chorus of shouts and cheering and whistles. The thin cracks got longer, running in all directions from the corner. The yelling was awful loud and I got worried someone from the front office would come back to the cell to find out what the noise was all about. I looked at the man holding the jackhammer and cupped my ears toward the front of the jail. He understood me and started hammering away, trying to drown out the shouting people, a half dozen of them by now and more coming, watching Mamie stuck on the side of the building like she had conquered the law of gravity.

She kept the pressure on and the cracks got wider. The sight of her was breathtaking – light blazing in her hair and making her whole head look like a little sun producing its own nuclear fire. Dusty cement and brick rained down along with chunks as big as gravel rocks. The corner was bulging, giving way, and then it abruptly fractured and the bar erupted through and was bending toward her chest. Her legs were straining to straighten, the crossbar popping from its anchor, then a second bar bursting through and more brick disintegrating. The corner was a good six inches from the wall and wide enough for Robbie to squeeze his head through. Then the thin rest of him. He slid beneath Mamie's right leg as she pulled and held her position, until he had fallen into my arms. Then she let go and the bars boomeranged back a little, leaving a smaller gap than before.

"I'm a free man!" Robbie cried out. "If I ever get the chance I'll repay both of you. You can count on it."

"You don't owe me nothing," I said. "Mamie, on the other hand—"

The crowd behind us was cheering so loud that they overwhelmed the noise of the jackhammer. The eyes looking at us shined like they had seen a miracle, an honest to God one. People clapping and whistling. Some hugging each other. Some standing rigid and disbelieving, their faces shocked. No one protested, even though what Mamie had done was wrong, according to the law. No, it felt too tremendous to be wrong. A great wonder in its own way.

Mamie had jumped down and I was hugging her and calling her Queen Kong. She was shuddering in my arms like a volcano ready to burst. Her marvelous muscles unable to relax yet. The crowd came towards us. The jackhammer man slapped Mamie on the shoulder and said, "If I live a hundred years I'll never forget what you just did. No one will believe me when I tell them. Wish I had a camera." Other people reached out, wanting to touch her. Maybe some of them weren't certain she was real. Or maybe they were hoping some of her magic would rub off on them. Whatever it was, more and more people were reaching for her. She was happy about it. Smiling and reaching out to touch them back. It was like a bunch of kids had cornered Santa Claus.

A girl pulled at my arm and asked, "Who is she?"

"I don't know who she is," I answered.

"Feel her," said someone. "Ain't she feel wonderful?"

"I can feel her energy."

"I can feel her muscles bulging like volley balls."

"Trembling. Feel that trembling?"

"She sure give 'em hell."

"Who? Who is she?"

"Did you see? Did you see what I saw?"

"She feels like electricity."

"Touching her makes me feel stronger somehow. She's holy. She's from God."

"What the hell are you people doing out there?" said a voice from inside the cell. "What have you done? Look at this!" A policeman had a hold of the uprooted bars and was shaking them. "You're them goddamn book-burners! Don't nobody move!"

That's all it took to break up the love-fest. People ran away in all directions.

"You're under arrest!" the cop yelled.

Mamie, Robbie, and I tore across the street and down an alley. Behind us we could hear more cops yelling, saying, "Halt! Halt, or I'll shoot!" Shots were fired. A long-legged man sprinted by us. "Holy shit, they're crazy!" he cried.

We went between some houses and crossed several streets. We didn't stop until we got to Shepard's house, where I figured we could hide until dark and then get out of town. But when we tried to go in, the door was locked.

"Where the hell is he?" I wondered. "He's supposed to be sleeping." I pounded on the door. I looked in the windows. No Shepard. Or maybe he was dead.

"Teef! Teef!" I heard someone yelling from across the street. "Teef! I see you, teef!"

It was a tiny woman, maybe fifty years old, standing on her porch across from Shepard's and shaking a broom at us and calling us thieves. I remembered seeing her before. She had a little dog that barked a lot and a husband in a wheelchair.

"We live here, ma'am," I said. "We got locked out accidentally."

"She looked fiercely at me, like I was a liar. "I not see you ewer before dis time," she said. "You look a teef to me, I tink."

"Honest, we live here. We've been here a couple of weeks. I've seen you before. Don't you remember?"

Her face was softening. I thought things were going to be all right, but then I heard sirens heading in our direction. "Ya, my hoosban call dem," said the woman.

"That's it," said Robbie. "Can't stay here!"

He took off in the direction of the rail line and we went with him. Past the train station, we plunged into the woods. Mamie was in the lead now and she led us on a winding path, over a creek and deeper into the trees to a place thick with undergrowth and live oaks. We paused to catch our breath. I listened for sirens, but couldn't hear anything other than our panting breaths and the wind rustling the tops of the trees and the gurgle of water behind us.

And I said, "We're safe, I think."

"We outfoxed 'em," said Robbie. And then he said, "God will bless you for what you've done. I'll carry you first in my heart for it. I'll take care of you in California. I'm taking you to that golden land. All we gotta do is get out of these woods and head west. It's easy."

I shook my head and told him we weren't going. "California is no place for me and Mamie," I said. "We don't have nothing to do there. What we know are cows and farming. What we know is Wisconsin. We've got to stick to what we know."

He thought it over for a little while, stroking his beard and looking at the sky. "And that's true too," he said. "It might be the worse thing to haul you and her off to a foreign land like that. But I'd sure like you to go. I'd like it, but I can see in your face that you won't. Well, that's okay. Maybe this is a mission I'm supposed to go on alone. Maybe Jesus has another mission for you."

"Maybe so, but I would as soon have things calm down now. There's been enough excitement this past month to hold me for the rest of my life."

Robbie took one of my hands and took one of Mamie's hands. He leaned toward us, his face shiny, eyes fixed on a point above our heads. "We'll be missing each other," he said, "But we'll still be connected. Jesus says, 'Listen to the wind because I am the wind. Listen to the song because I am the song. Feel the rain and you are feeling me. Take a breath and you are inhaling the inspiration, the breath of God. I am in all things. Reach out and feel me anytime you want. Caress a leaf and you caress God. Drink living waters and you drink the living God. When you eat food to sustain you, you eat the sustaining God. You will see me when the clouds drop their tears on the earth and wash your sins away, and in the smile of a baby you will see the innocent love of Christ. When you fall in love for real it's because Christ is a living presence in your soul. My great commandment above all others is - love ye one another. If you will do that, the world will heal and you will see with new eyes the connective brotherhood of all humankind.' And you will see your Robbie too, because I am a piece of Christ and so are you. Yes, Jee-sus is in you, and invisible threads of love bind us together no matter where we are. Praise God!"

He paused a second, looking higher above us, like he was listening to the rest of his sermon, or reading it on the sky. "And what you did, Christian, was done for truth. And truth is what Robbie done was done for truth too. Truth is that there are books that should be burned for their evil teachings. Evil, like good, is taught through the word – and evil words must be burned before they infect more innocent minds and stretch the reign of Satan. Remember, a book can make you yearn for loving kindness and can teach you what is wise, but it can also teach the opposite. It can make you respond with the evil of original sin hidden in your heart. It can make you stupid and mean as a cannibal. If a book can inspire and improve a boy, it can also depress and corrupt him. Burn the corruption. Vomit the evil word and burn it. Truth is, we only need one book for our true pleasures, those pleasures that will bring us closer to God. Jee-sus is the way."

He put his hands on top of our heads and blessed us. His sermon continued. "And even if you never see me again, honeys, it don't matter. We've done what we were supposed to do for each other, and now we've got to part. But I'm sure gonna be with you, because I'm part of Jesus and Jesus is part of you. Everywhere are pieces of Jesus. Mamie is a bigger piece than normal. She's a special piece of Jesus, and her special mystery will unfold before you. You'll be amazed when it happens. She's not an accident. There are no accidents. And look here, I'm gonna be everywhere with Jesus guarding you and Mamie. Yes, Lord, wherever you go and feel that movement in your soul, you're feeling me and Jesus. And if you hear people talking filth and corruption, you tell them in the name of Christ don't do it because they are pieces of Jesus. And if you come on men fighting and you say to them that they are punching the face of Jesus, they will stop and listen to you. I guarantee it. And if you know a man who ain't crazy but is getting sent to Camelot and you set that man free, it's because he's a piece of Jesus. When you help the sick and give shelter to the homeless and stand up for the coward and carry the weak and love the unlovable and forgive the unforgivable – it's because they are all pieces of Jesus. And you are a piece of Jesus, which makes them all a piece of you. Praise God!

"And don't go falling for the lie of the American Dream either, honeys, the dream of give me this and give me that and I'll be happy. That dream ain't got nothing to do with happiness or Jesus. That dream was placed here by the devil. It leads you straight to hell and fire and brimstone. Don't get caught up in that false dream. Say no to it. Say, 'Get behind me, Satan,' and get on with being a piece of Jesus. It's simple. Just act like Jesus would, because that's all he wants of you. If you find evil, burn that evil. Jesus would."

He lifted his hands from our heads and turned away. He walked west, tall and skinny and fair-haired as any ghost might be - that was Robbie Peevy, mad about Jesus Christ. But maybe not mad.

We watched him disappear into the trees, and then it was time for us to go too. We turned southeast on a route I figure would bring us back to the railroad tracks, eventually. From there to the farm roads, the back roads, where the hay was waiting and the milk cows and the endless chores and some overworked farmer (a piece of Jesus) needing me and Mamie to help him carry his load.

Teddy Snowdy & His Mommy

Mostly it was just a lot of walking along dusty roads, heading east and heading south, taking us farther away from trouble. We had to spend the first night outdoors, and except for the dew settling over us, making us wet, I enjoyed sleeping with Mamie once more beneath a tree, with piled pine boughs for a bed. When we got up in the morning, the sun was already putting out enough heat to make our clothes steam as we walked through the countryside. Hay and cornfields were everywhere, big barns and silos and big white houses rising in the distance. Farmers making second crop. The clatter-siss-click of the haybines, the serious roar of the tractors, the hiss of the hydraulic pistons as the knives were raised and lowered at each turn – it was all music to me, though I had never thought of it as music when living at home. Smelling the fresh alfalfa mixing with the odor of engine exhaust and hot oil and the methane traces of cows at pasture clipping the grass low, I breathed deeply and said, "Ah, Mamie, don't it smell good?" And she bobbed her head in agreement as she sniffed the air and smiled benevolently on the fields stretching in front of us.

The farms where nature didn't always get to have its way were full of clean lines, windbreaking shade trees around the houses and along the driveways and the woods at the edges of the fields, and all the restful hues of resurrected green. It made me want to go tell every farmer that he had done himself proud. Oh, I was missing home, missing the land, the cows, the whole family around the dinner table passing plates and fussing about something. Even the morning and evening chores I truly missed.

We stopped at the houses, asking farmers if they could use a hand, but none of them needed us. The sun was between 11:00 and 11:30 before we got a lead from a farmer we stopped in a field, where he was raking hay, and he said that we should go east on County Road 6 and there would be a sign on a barn saying SNOWDY DAIRY FARM. Mr. Snowdy was looking for hay buckers and someone to help with the dairy. I thanked that fellow and we took off east as fast as we could walk. We were both awfully hungry and thirsty by then.

It took about thirty minutes to get to the Snowdy farm. From where we stood on the road, I could see the farm was a bit different from most of those we had passed, the land more hilly, and the house small, a one-story shingled house painted dark gray, which I understood would help hold the heat in winter, but would also hold it in the summer when you didn't want it. Attached to the house was a cinderblock addition, long and low, only two feet high, the rest of it underground creating a basement. The house stood on the highest point around, so you looked up at it from the road or from the fields. A trio of great cottonwoods dotted the yard, their branches spreading out and helping to shade things, though not much at the moment with the sun's rays coming straight down and baking the asphalt roof.

Fifty yards west were a barn and a silo. The silo was one of those shiny tile types, cinnamon colored, with an open top. The barn was painted white, and it was set on the side of a mild slope, where it had good drainage. There was a shabby machine shed a few yards up from the barn and a wire corncrib and a chicken coop. Next to the coop was a garage that leaned to the east and needed painting badly. It looked like a heavy snow might bring it down. The field west of the barn was all alfalfa. It was knee-high and overripe, purple flowers blooming and some of them going to seed already. I knew those leaves would not be as tender as the cows liked them to be. The leaves would also be giving up protein with every passing day, and they would probably shatter once the hay was dried. A good farmer would have had that field down at least ten days ago.

"Want to cut some hay, Mamie?" I asked her.

"Yaay, Kritch'n," she declared.

We walked up the driveway and looked inside the machine shed. A Massey-Ferguson 65 Diesel stood at the door, its nose out, looking ready to go. A 4-bottom plow stood behind it and a 13-tine Tiller and a New Holland baler, a disk and a harrow and a seeder. Mamie climbed into the seat of the tractor. She turned the key in the ignition and the engine came to life instantly. Working the throttle up and down, Mamie played with the RPMs and ran them up until the engine hummed like it was ready to take care of business. I jumped up behind her and told her to turn the motor off. Snowdy hadn't hired either of us yet. As the noise died away, I heard a door slamming behind me.

And a squeaky voice said, "If you're gonna steal it, I'll give you a running start. Go head, go head." I turned and saw a short man with a heavy mustache. He was smiling hugely, showing the top and bottom rows of all his teeth. Which totally dominated his face, making his upturned nose and beaded eyes and bullet-shaped head look small as a child's. In his hands was a rifle. He was making motions with it and saying over and over, "Go head, go head."

"We're not stealing anything," I said. "We heard you was looking for hands to make hay and help with the dairy."

His eyes squinted distrustfully. He looked us up and down.

"We've got lots of experience," I said.

With one hand the man brushed the corners of his mustache, while the other tucked the rifle under his arm. The barrel pointed to the ground. "You're too skinny to be much use," he said to me.

"I was raised on a farm. Everything you see is muscle," I told him.

He clicked his teeth and laughed loudly and said, "Who's the mule?"

"We're partners. We travel together," I said. "We work the harvests and such."

He nodded and then said Mamie could stay, but I had to go.

"We're a team," I said. "If I go, she goes."

"A team?" The man laughed again, his teeth clicking and bulging like they might jump out of his mouth and bite me. His eyes behind wire-rimmed glasses were pinpoints, two tiny beads of

170

pewter.

A gray-haired woman appeared on the porch. "Teddy," she called. "Who is that?"

"They're a team, Mommy," he said. "They want to help with the hay and the cows."

"Oh good!" she said. "Now maybe we can get something done. Are you two hungry? What's your names? Come on in and eat."

"You're not hungry, are you?" Teddy asked.

"We kind of are. We didn't get any breakfast."

"Yeah, they're hungry, Mommy." He stared at Mamie and said, "I bet she eats like a damn Holstein hay-burner."

"Well, come on in and eat," said the woman. "I got fried rabbit, squirrel and chicken in the fridge. There's plenty of bread and potatoes. We'll fill you up."

We followed Teddy toward the house. While we were crossing the yard, a pair of crows flew overhead, clucking noisily. Quick as a gunslinger, Teddy raised his rifle and fired twice from the hip. Both birds plummeted like black sandbags falling out of the sky.

"What a shot!" cried Teddy. "Am I good or what?"

"You're good," I said.

"Better believe it, buddy." Patting the butt of his rifle, he called it his big boy.

Out of the corner of my eye I caught the movement of two orange tabby cats. They pounced on the dead crows and dashed with them under the machine shed. Teddy hadn't noticed them until it was too late.

"Okay," he said, glaring. "I saw that." He looked at me as if it was my fault and he said, "I'm going to make hats of those cats."

We went inside and Mrs. Snowdy fed us cold rabbit and cold boiled potatoes with butter and bread. There was plenty of milk. Mamie and I stuffed ourselves shamelessly. The table we sat at was made of blond oak. In one corner there was a carving that said: BEN SNOWDY 1940.

"That's my husband," Mrs. Snowdy told us. "He made all the furniture in this house. He's an artist and too sensitive to live around Teddy."

"He's a jerk-off," Teddy whispered in my ear.

Mrs. Snowdy heard him. "He can make artistic furniture, Teddy. Can you?"

"I can do other things, Mommy. Hey, who runs the farm since Daddy is gone? *I* keep it going. He sits in his stupid cabin in the woods and makes stupid furniture for stupid people who never pay him." Teddy's lower lip had curled into a toddler's pout. "You can't trust a guy like that. You never know what a guy like that is going to do."

"The deal was," Mrs. Snowdy explained, "that Teddy could stay and run the farm and fill the house with his little animals, so long as he was nice to his mommy and didn't tell nasty stories about his sensitive daddy. So Teddy, what are you doing again?"

"I'm not telling nasty stories about him. I'm just telling the truth, Mommy." Teddy was whining like a little boy, his voice shrill and painful to hear. He was somewhere around forty years old, maybe forty-five, with gray hairs sprinkled through his crew cut and mustache. There were dry wrinkles around his eyes. The skin sagged beneath his chin. Two large tendons tightened on his neck when he talked, looking like a pair of banjo strings.

Mrs. Snowdy had a smaller version of her son's grin. She threw her head back and laughed as he whined. And she said, "You can be such a baby, Teddy."

He perked up at the tone in her voice. "But who's your favorite Teddy, Mommy?"

"Oh, go on," she said. "What a child." She sat in a rocking chair next to a table and lamp and started rocking back and forth, filling the house with the creak of aging wood. Teddy was at the table with us. His rifle was across his lap. He eyed us narrowly as we ate. Mrs. Snowdy asked us our names, and when I told her she said, "Mamie, that's a sweet name. My name's Lily." She paused a moment. Then said, "Mamie – Teddy. It rhymes. Mamie – Teddy. Can you cook, Mamie?"

Mamie thought about the question. She looked at the ceiling as if the answer might be there. Her tongue was working around inside her cheek. The quiet lasted a few seconds, until Mrs. Snowdy said, "That's nice. I'm glad."

So I said, "Nobody can cook fresh trout with the trimmings as good as Mamie. She's a wonder in the wild, getting herbs and greens and knowing what to do with them. You bet she can cook."

"Oh, that's even better," said Mrs. Snowdy.

Teddy tapped my hand and said, "I've shot fifty-four deer in my life. How many you shot?"

"None," I answered.

"None! That's pitiful. That's anti-American, man! Mommy did you hear him? By the time I was his age I'd killed a dozen. None. Poo!"

"Teddy has always been a go-getter," Mrs. Snowdy told us. Then she looked at Mamie again, and she said, "Can you keep a clean house, Mamie?"

Mamie rolled her eyes and thought about the question.

"I'm a big game, slash, little game hunter," said Teddy. "I don't play favorites. I've shot thirty coyotes, four honest to goodness wolves. And ten bald eagles. Got to shoot them or they'll snatch your chickens right out of the coop. Worse than foxes them bald eagles are. I've shot eleven foxes over the years. Got all eleven on the run. And lets see—" He closed one eye in a heavy think. Stroked his chin and added, "A blue heron, fifty goldfinches, seventy-two ducks, sixty-five geese, forty red-tail hawks, two hundred and twenty crows. How many you shot, Christian?"

"I've trapped a few mink and rabbits and gophers," I said.

"That's shameful."

Mamie started to say something, but Mrs. Snowdy spoke first. "That's nice," she said, and went on to ask Mamie was she good at scrubbing floors, doing dishes, dusting furniture, changing bed linen once a month, making jam and cheese, washing clothes, baking bread, sewing, and could she do all that and milk cows too? Mamie thought hard, working her mouth up to answer. She looked at me. I didn't know what to say. It didn't matter. Teddy interrupted the conversation with another list of animals he had killed. When he finished, he stared at me in anticipation.

"You're quite a killer," I told him.

Standing up, he took my hand and told me there was something I had to see. He led me toward the hall. Mamie followed.

"Did I ask you if you sewed?" said Mrs. Snowdy. We came to a door at the end of the hall. Teddy opened it and motioned for me to go first. He turned on a light, and I saw steps leading to the basement. I walked down into a showroom full of animals frozen in a last second of flight or leap or crawl or bite or claw. All had their mouths open on the edge of making some kind of noise. From the ceiling hung hawks and eagles and crows, a blue heron, even a seagull, and four goldfinches set in formation – two in front, two behind – flying nowhere forever. Sparrows and swallows, woodpeckers, hummingbirds, robins, and blue jays dipped and darted from corner to corner. A king snake lashed out at a titmouse, a hawk closed in on the king snake. Rabbits ran from eagles. Badgers chased woodchucks. Cats pounced on sparrows. Gophers fought each other. And along every wall from floor to ceiling were shelves covered with the heads of deer, wolf, coyote, fox, badger, mink, skunk, muskrat, raccoon, dog, and cat. Teddy pointed his rifle at each animal, named it, and told us what kind of shot had brought it down. An hour passed before he finished the list.

Then he took us into a workroom, where there was a long, high bench full of tools and wire models with skins draped over them. Papier-mâché heads of all sizes with wire ears and necks were everywhere. There was a gun rack on the wall above the bench. A dozen rifles hung there, a couple of pistols and a Bowie knife. Teddy named each weapon for us. All of them were his "big boys."

When we went back to the showroom, Teddy declared that he was going to be generous and let me sleep there. He would give me a mattress and some blankets, and I could lie in the corner and watch the animals chasing each other. "I've done it lots of times," he said. "It's a pretty powerful thing to see. It gives you a real feeling for nature, what it's all about. It's an education is what I'm saying."

"Where would Mamie sleep?" I asked.

"With Mommy. She's got a queen-size bed. It's a luxury."

When we got back to the dining room, Teddy told his Mommy about the sleeping arrangements and she patted Mamie's backside and said, "Of course you can sleep with me. I got plenty of room and I don't snore. Do you? It don't matter, I'm a sound sleeper. I sleep like the dead." She paused, chuckling. Her mouth opened again to speak. But then she looked puzzled, as if she had forgotten what she had wanted to say.

That afternoon, Mamie and I and Teddy worked in the hay field. Mamie drove tractor, pulling the haybine cutting alfalfa. Teddy followed behind her, holding one of his big boys at the ready and shooting the birds and mice that got spooked as the tractor passed by. I came behind Teddy with a gunnysack. It was my job to bag all he shot. Before the afternoon was over and it was time for chores, the sack was better than half full.

After milking cows and eating supper, I was pooped and wanted to go right to bed. I told Mrs. Snowdy that if it was all the same to her, I would just as soon sleep out in the loft. But she and Teddy wouldn't hear of it. They said it was cool sleeping in the basement. The mattress was already on the floor and covered with a quilt. No ifs, ands, or buts, I was sleeping in the showroom. I wouldn't be lonely. I'd have lots of company.

Too tired to argue, I took a shower and went to bed. My head was buzzing with fatigue and the aftereffects of Teddy's rifle going off constantly all afternoon. I was almost asleep when I heard Mrs. Snowdy yelling, "No, no, Mamie! You can't sleep there! It isn't Christian!" The light came on and I heard Mamie's steps pounding down the stairs. Mrs. Snowdy was after her, saying no no.

"You sleep with me," she said.

"Nup, nup," said Mamie. She threw herself beside me. Her hair was still damp from her shower. Her face glistened in the light. "I sssleep Kritch'n," she said firmly.

"She's used to us sleeping together," I explained.

"Well, I never," declared Mrs. Snowdy.

Mamie rolled me up in her arms. "Kritch'n, Kritch'n," she murmured.

"Teddy!" cried Mrs. Snowdy. "Teddy, come down here this instant!"

When Teddy came downstairs, his mother pointed at Mamie and me cuddled up on the mattress. "This won't do," said Mrs. Snowdy.

"Well," he said, "they're a team, Mommy."

"But this is immoral, Teddy. It's unchristian."

"She'd sure make some fine big babies," he said, stroking his chin thoughtfully.

Mrs. Snowdy's eyes looked at him. "Then you like her, Teddy?"

Teddy bent down and looked Mamie over. He rubbed the tips of his fingers with his thumbs, as if he had pieces of Mamie there and he was testing her texture. It was hard to tell what he was thinking. Behind his glasses, his pupils were no bigger than lead buckshot. "She'd look like an inspiration if I could stuff her. Put her standing in the corner on a bit of pasture, next to a stuffed cow. I'd call it 'Super Milkmaid with Holstein Cow.' Oh, think of that! Imagine it! Talk about art! If I was able to do it, I would be in the *Taxidermist Quarterly* as taxidermist of the month. Maybe the year. I'd win Best in Show."

"That's *not* what I had in mind when I asked you if you liked her, Teddy. Quit fooling around." She shook her head and said, "He's such a teaser."

"But, Mommy, think of it. Picture it!"

"Stop that right now, young man. I don't think you're funny."

Teddy hung his head a little, but continued to stare at Mamie hungrily. His mother sniffed and snorted and finally grabbed him by the hand and hauled him back up the stairs, and the light went out.

I whispered to Mamie, "'Super Milkmaid with Holstein Cow.' She wants to marry you to her son, and he wants to stuff you. Oh wow!"

We laughed crazily for a while. After we calmed down, I laid my head on Mamie's arm and looked at the animals shining in shadowy grayness, mouths open in silent laughter. After some minutes passed, the joke faded and I realized I wasn't looking at animals laughing at all. What I saw were dozens of silent screams captured in an instant of dying.

Immaculate Reception

We stayed on with the Snowdys for the rest of the summer and fall. We filled the barn with hay and the silo with silage and disked the corn stalks under to get the land ready for harrowing and planting next spring. We took over all the chores in the barn – milked the cows twice a day, cleaned and sterilized the milkers, shoveled the manure gutters, took care of the calves, whitewashed the walls, kept the machinery repaired and running.

Once Teddy saw we didn't need him to boss us, he stayed out of the way and spent his days either hunting the woods or stuffing what he had killed. He would bring his latest creation to his mother and she would always praise it. She would tell him that some squirrel or crow or beaver or toad looked so lively, she wouldn't be surprised to see it run away. She told Teddy he was an artist, just like his father, except that his father was an artist in wood instead of animals. But they were alike as two peas in a pod, so it was no wonder they couldn't get along.

Ben Snowdy came by once or twice a week and visited his wife. Sometimes he would stay to dinner, if Teddy was off tramping the woods, and now and then he would stay all night and sneak away early in the morning, doing his best not to let his son see him. Whenever Teddy was around and Ben was there, Teddy would stay as close to Mrs. Snowdy as a Siamese twin. It looked strange to see her trying to talk to her husband around Teddy's shoulder, her face popping out one side of him or the other. On those occasions, Ben didn't stay very long. His cabin and workshop were just a mile down the road, and sometimes he would bring a piece of furniture he had just made, a small table or chair, one time a hall tree, to show his wife. She would always praise him as much as she did Teddy, making a fuss over what a wonderful pair of artists she had in her lucky life.

I liked it when Ben was there. He always asked about the cows and made compliments to me and Mamie about how much better they looked and milked since we had taken over. He was short, like Teddy, but not as thick in the chest and arms. There was a quiet light of kindness in his eyes that made him seem to walk within a cocoon of calm air. He didn't have those big, hungry teeth, and he wasn't forever smiling at nothing; nor did he have Teddy's high-pitched voice, which could set your teeth on edge and make you want to throttle him. Ben's voice was deep and gentle; it fit the rest of him. In all, he seemed a self-contained, straightforward, no-nonsense fellow, who, for whatever reason, had stepped aside and let his son run the farm his own way. I felt that Mrs. Snowdy, who doted on Teddy like he was a treasure, had arranged all three of their lives so she could have the best of her men and they could still have a share of her.

In mid-October I got sick. It wasn't much, a little fever and sore throat. Mrs. Snowdy mothered me, while Mamie did all the work. When Teddy saw I was sick, he made faces and said he couldn't stand sick people. He claimed he had never been sick a day in his life, and he couldn't understand why anyone would let it happen. It was a weakness for which I, and all others like me, should be shot. He said only the fittest should survive in this dog eat dog world. After he made sure I knew his opinion and had been seared by the unforgiving gaze of his contempt, he took up his rifle and said he would be gone a couple of days, and I had better be well when he got back – or else.

I had been a lot sicker a couple of times in my life. Once I had pneumonia and another time a bad case of German measles. So a fever and sore throat didn't worry me much and, in fact, I enjoyed the opportunity to stay in the sack all day and get babied by Mrs. Snowdy. She made hot soup for me and put cold cloths on my forehead and read me homespun stories out of the *Saturday Evening Post*.

178

One day Ben came over to visit. He and Mrs. Snowdy sat beside me and talked. She asked him if I reminded him of anyone. He thought a second and said, "Oh, you mean Teddy, when he was little. Yes, he was a sickly boy. Many was the time I stayed up nights with him, putting cold cloths on his head and listening to him whine."

"So many times I've lost count," she said.

"He told me he was never sick a day in his life," I said.

Ben shook his head. "You know, Teddy wants to believe he's a special person, an artist in his own way making his mark."

"He is," said Mrs. Snowdy.

Ben held up his hand. "Let me finish, Lily. You see, Christian, according to Teddy, if you're sick, then you can't possibly be special. Illness proves that nature or God has lumped you with all the rest of us mediocres. A long time ago I made the mistake of telling him about a philosopher named Nietzsche who came up with an idea that every once in a while a superman was born. He called him an *Ubermensch* and said he was beyond morality, or made up his own morality, something like that. But anyway this superior man was born to rule over the rest of us and his goal is to weed out the weak, so that only the strong continue to breed. Well, that notion took Teddy over. He insists on being an *Ubermensch*, one of the chosen, a man larger than life and immune to anything that afflicts lesser mortals. But to tell you the truth, he was periodically one of the sickest kids you can imagine. Every childhood disease seemed to own him. It's a wonder he didn't die. He conveniently forgets things like that." Ben paused and looked around the showroom at all the animals frozen in time. "But, you know, I have to give him credit," he continued. "I mean Teddy's sheer force of will made his body into a paragon of health - out tramping in those woods and sleeping outdoors when it's cold, honing his senses so he can track and shoot his prey. He's a mighty hunter now. He's a god of the forest. The Old Testament type full of fire and anger."

"He told me that only the fittest should survive," I said. "Sickly animals should be shot. Even human beings."

Ben chuckled softly and slowly blinked his eyes. And said,

"There's that damned old *Ubermensch* influence, you see? Maybe I should have read him the Beatitudes instead, ey? But you have to admit that Teddy turned himself into a superior specimen of sorts. He started working on it when he was around eleven or twelve and started exercising fanatically, taking long walks and doing pushups, pull-ups, sit-ups, doing squat thrusts and standing on his hands. All those things. I watched him day after day working on being healthy. He never let up and it paid off. He hasn't been sick a day since somewhere in his early twenties. Let me tell you something else. When he was just a shaver he told me he saw a little bear in the woods and was going to shoot him. I told him to leave that bear alone. Its mother was probably around somewhere and would eat him. But he snuck off with one of my rifles and he shot that little bear. First thing he ever killed, and it was a bear, half-growed like him. He gutted it and lugged it home and wanted me to tell him how to stuff it. But I had no idea how to stuff an animal. It made him mad as a hornet. He's been mad ever since. Remember that, Lily?"

"He has a terrible temper all right. Can be a little monster."

"To say the least."

"But he has a good heart too. Teddy loves us, I'm sure. He loves you, Ben, and in time he'll grow to know it. Just give him time."

"He's forty-three, Lily."

"Give him time."

Ben winked at me. "But you know, I would have thought by the time a fellow was his age he would come to realize his father wasn't the real enemy. Usually sons get over that notion by the time they hit thirty. I know I did. Once I hit thirty and had absorbed the ways of this world, my father and I became pretty good friends. We stayed that way until the day he died."

"He doesn't hate you," Mrs. Snowdy insisted. Her tone was impatient.

Looking again at the animals crowding us, Ben said, "Since he started stuffing everything in sight, I've never quit wondering why. I mean, what possesses the fellow? What do you think, Christian? I mean, look at all this." His hand swept the air.

I told Ben it was hard to know the why of it. "I know plenty of hunters who think nothing of killing. Killing is natural, a man thing same as a lion or tiger thing, and I've trapped for years and killed animals without it giving me a bad conscience. But something about Teddy's way doesn't set well with me. It reminds me of loggers going into a forest and clear-cutting everything, leaving nature ruined in the process. Also it reminds me of the cold viciousness of a guy I know named John Beaver who I saw skin a mink alive. He has the kind of meanness I've heard that some men have in war. Killing and taking pleasure in it. I've seen Teddy not finish an animal off because he didn't want to mess up its pelt, though a tap on the head wouldn't have harmed the fur. He never seems to mind waiting for something to die. That's a trait I don't admire."

"Me neither," said Ben.

"A man who skins a mink alive is a maniac!" said Mrs. Snowdy. "He's worse than a viper, and not to be compared with Teddy, do you hear? The very idea that he enjoys watching some poor thing suffer! He's not like a normal person, I know that. He's an artist, like Ben. He has to think about his art and make sacrifices. Would a beast dedicate himself to the creations you see in this showroom? Certainly not. Teddy is a creator like God – a creator, do you hear me? Look how lively these animals seem. They're absolutely beautiful, don't you think? They're as much a work of art as . . . as . . . name an artist, Ben."

"Rembrandt."

"As Rembrandt."

Ben said, "It's true, Lily. They do have a terrible beauty in them."

She gave Ben a tender look. "Do you remember when our little Teddy used to climb in bed with us on those cold winter mornings?"

"Yes, and we would cuddle him and warm him up. Those are nice memories."

"And treat him like the only boy on earth. And he was that to us. And could that darling be compared to some viper who would skin a mink alive?" She shook her finger at me. "And shame on you. You're just a regular boy, an ordinary boy making judgments about something far above your head. You're no Rembrandt, and you might do harm to a person's reputation talking like that. What do you know about art or artists and the artistic temperament? Not a thing. I've lived with him for over forty years. I know him inside and out. Don't tell me!"

Mrs. Snowdy harrumphed. Then she softened a bit and I saw her looking at a lynx licking its paw. "See, I remember that one. It was sitting in the front yard under the elms, cleaning its paw like that. Tell me it isn't lovely. Teddy shot it as it sat there and look what he's done. He's made it immortal."

"Don't pay me no mind, Mrs. Snowdy. I've got a fever," I said. Adding, "What do I know? Yeah, shoot, I know nothing."

Later that evening I finally wrote my parents and told them where I was and what had happened to Mamie and me. In my letter I asked for their advice and asked what the situation was with John Beaver and the law. I apologized for all the worry I'd caused and tried to explain the difference, as I saw it, between right and truth, and how what I had done seemed like a moment of truth thing at the time, though according to the law it wasn't right. I told them that so much had happened since then that it seemed I had already lived a lifetime. Yet there was tomorrow, and I didn't know what to do about it, or any of the tomorrows coming up. Would I always be a wanderer now? An outcast? At least they hadn't named me Cain. Or Ishmael.

A day after my letter went off, Shepard came to get Mamie. I heard him groaning and wheezing and his heavy steps making the stairs creak and crack. His breathtaking nose led him into the room where I was still in bed, but my fever had broken and I was feeling better.

First thing he said was, "No wonder you're sick, Crystal. Look at this place. Ugh and yuk! Neanderthal lives! What a disgusting means of inducing catharsis. Is the mad hunter gone, I hope? Is he off creating havoc on poor beasties like these?"

"As far as I know," I said. "So how come you're here, Mr. Shepard? How did you find us?"

"Ben Snowdy was in town. I ran into him at Charlie Friendly's. He told me all about you and Mamie, how you're running things. But the autumn ebb tide is over and winter is nearly upon us and the Snowdys won't need the two of you. One of you is an extra mouth to feed and I'm here to take her off your hands."

"Mamie?"

"Of course."

He kept staring at the animals as he talked. And then he said, "These poor creatures are indications of mental aberrations of vast and potentially lethal proportions that may overflow one day into homicidal proceedings. The indications are all there and there and there." He jabbed his massive finger at the displays. "Hmm, I have always heard that Teddy has arranged a Great White Hunter's delight in his basement, but this is quite beyond even my exceptionally superior imagination. There is a continual flagellation going on in here. This is a microcosm of how he sees the world. Cat chasing rat, snake fanging mouse, hawk seizing snake, lynx pouncing on calf – kill kill kill - everything in the cosmos living by killing. Even the lynx licking his paw there looks like he's just finished a bloody meal. Look at the wicked eyes of the birds, look at their beaks bent like fishhooks. Can the deadly creator be more blunt. Is he behind all this and holding his thunderbolts, timing them for us? Hmm? So where's my Mamie, Crystal?"

"She's in the barn," I told him. "She might not want to go with you, though. She likes the cows here plenty."

Sticking his fists into his eyes he groaned and said, "Ohhh, I knew it, I knew it. Child of nature, of course she's going to thrive in this environment."

"She's wonderful with those cows. They milk heavy for her."

"The dirty pied perpetrator working his charms on her, his bovine charmers helping him, of course. It's true, isn't it? Teddy wants Mamie for himself."

"I don't think so," I answered. "Teddy just wants his Mommy."

Shepard sat in the protesting chair next to me and leaned over, saying quietly, "You are aware, Crystal, aren't you, that Ben and Lily are in the middle of . . . are the progenitors of . . . a salient Oedipal complex the size of a whale's member? Yum yum. Little Teddy agitated them asunder. He has gonadal heat for his mommy. Classic Freudian case. I should write a book about this ménage and get famous, hmm?"

"Mrs. Snowdy thinks Teddy is a god. So does Teddy. Ben wonders where he went wrong. He thinks it's because of a guy named Nietzsche."

"The *Ubermensch*."

"That's it."

"It's not that so much as it's the follies of parental permissiveness. Poof poof, Teddy is a perverted Hippolytus chasing Phaedra. Ben is a poor, blind Theseus. But none of them is noble enough for *tragedy*. I won't have it! Perverts are never noble, Crystal. Nothing to be done about it, as Gogo, or is it Didi, says?"

"Who?"

"General reference to Beckett's losers waiting for God."

"I don't know them."

"Someone has neglected your education, son."

"Is there really nothing to be done about these Snowdys? I suppose not. But I feel really sorry for Ben. I see it in his eyes sometimes, like he knows it's hopeless. He stares at me like I'm sort of the son he wanted, instead of the one he got."

"Punitive genetic excess," said Shepard. "Followed by inappropriate nurturing."

"We're going hunting in November. Teddy knows a place he guarantees will be full of deer."

Leaning back, Shepard gazed down his nose at me. He needed to clip the hairs inside his nostrils. Needed to wash his hair too. It was tangled all over his head and standing out in tufts in some places as if he had just come through a windstorm. He rubbed his belly and said that hunting was fine for me, but what about the future for Mamie? He said the Artlife would be ready to open by the first of the year. The projector had been purchased and he had a brilliant idea that he would train Mamie to run it. Give her a trade that would be useful. Mamie Beaver – projectionist. She was a tad slow, so it might take some weeks for her to learn, so it would be best if she went back with him now and got started.

Didn't I want her to have a chance to be something other than another dung-flavored farmer?

"You got it all wrong," I told him. "It's up to Mamie, not me. You got to ask her about it. She knows her own mind better than you think. But listen, tell me what you know about Robbie Peevy. You know we broke him out of jail, right? Did he ever get caught?"

"Little Anna across the street told me she saw you trying to break into the house that infamous day. She described Peevy and Mamie - so as usual I know everything. Yes, they chased him with dogs and state police and tracked him for a week through those woods. They had him surrounded, but they never found him. The dogs were chasing their tails – all baffled. In the repositories of those impoverished minds belonging to his followers Robbie climbed Jacob's ladder." Shepard made a sour face. "Those true believers have dubbed it his Immaculate Reception, yum yum. One of that ilk told me that Saint Robbie metamorphosed into pure spirit and flew to Abraham's bosom. Good grief! There's a movement afoot to have that dissembler canonized and a church named after him. The Church of Robbie Peevy of the Immaculate Reception. Suffering succotash, what will they think of next?"

I was happy to hear he'd gotten away. "Good for Robbie," I said.

"Bad for the rest of us," said Shepard. "It's ignorance and fear and the abysmal standards of puritanical terrorism clogging the free flow of ideas and destroying my right to think and your right too, and giving power to the pusillanimous ilk that would make automatons of us all if we don't watch out. Those are Peevy's followers. They say that the fact of one girl pulling the bars off the jail is proof without peer that Robbie stands at the right hand of Jesus. Oh, poof! They don't know the Mamie you and I know."

"Then the followers know her?"

"None in a million. They think she was an angel sent from the Lord. Such asininity depresses me beyond measure, Crystal." He stroked his nose for comfort.

At the top of the stairs, the door opened and Mamie came down into the basement. Shepard stood up and held out his arms. "Look who has come for you!" he cried.

But she went right past him and knelt down to put her cheek on my forehead. "F-fever g-gone," she said.

"I'm fine," I told her. "Just being lazy. Here's Shepard. You remember him?"

"Mmm-milk fever," she said. "D-d-down cow."

"A down cow?"

"Yaay." She put her finger on my neck on the jugular vein.

Shepard sounded close to tears. "Doesn't she remember me? Her old boozing buddy? The one who adores her so?"

"There's a cow in the barn with milk fever," I explained. "We've got to get calcium into her jugular or she'll have a heart attack and die."

"I can't see how she could forget me like that," he continued. "Maybe she's just too dumb. Maybe she has the two-week memory span of a dog."

Mamie caught him by the shoulders and said, "Shep, shut up now." She turned him around and pushed him toward the stairs.

"Did you hear that?" he cried out. "She told me to shut up! She remembers me!" He was grinning over his shoulder at me, showing his wet gap, his walrus teeth as she bulled him up the stairway.

Down Cow

Jewel was down and hurting. On the walkway behind her was a fresh calf wobbling about, not at all sure what it was doing there. It was a heifer, mostly opal white like her mama. Her eyes were big with amazement as she stared around the milking parlor. I took her to the front of the stanchion to see if Jewel would try to get up and lick her baby. And Jewel did try, but one of her hindlegs wouldn't work. It was curled near her stomach and was obviously useless.

"This isn't milk fever," I said. "That leg is paralyzed."

"The poor bovinity," said Shepard. He kept patting her hip. "Will she die, Crystal? Don't let her die in front of me. Another witness of death would kill me. O fate, why did I have to come to this Snowdy farm today of all days?"

I opened the stanchion so Jewel could get her head out. Then the three of us pushed and pulled and jerked her out into the aisle, where she had more room to rock herself and maybe get up. With us to help, she tried it, but all she could do was thrash around and flop back onto her side helplessly. After a while she got too depressed to try anymore. She tucked her head over her shoulder and closed her eyes. It was her way of saying, "Go away, I die now." In fact, the way she had positioned herself was exactly like cows do when they've got milk fever, which made me think it was that *and* a paralyzed leg. I took her temperature and found it low.

"By golly, you're right, Mamie, she's got milk fever."

Mamie went to the medicine cupboard and got a bottle of calcium and the tube and needle. I put a nose clip on Jewel and tied it to one of her back legs, so that her neck bulged out and I could see the artery. It took only a couple of tries till I hit the jugular inside just right and the blood came spurting out. It looked like a tiny red fountain arcing over my hands.

"Aghh," groaned Shepard. "Blood, ohhh." He stumbled backwards into the wall and slid down it with his eyes closed and then eased over onto his side. I told Mamie it was a good place for him to be; we could wake him later. She turned the calcium bottle upside down and let the air out of the tube. I fitted the tube to the needle in Jewel's neck. We let the calcium go in slowly so she wouldn't go into shock or have a heart attack. Twenty minutes later the bottle was empty. Jewel was shivering, but life was coming back into her eyes. I untied her nose and she lifted her head high. She was very alert, eyes searching for her baby. Amazing stuff – liquid calcium. We tried again to get her up, and she was willing, trying her hardest; but the leg stayed dead and she stayed down.

"Sciatic nerve damage," I said. "I've seen it before. It's bad, Mamie."

While we were standing there wondering what to do, Shepard woke up and said, "Is there going to be any more blood? Please warn me. My sensitive constitution can't help how it reacts."

Mamie and I pulled Shepard to his feet. He stood leaning against the wall and shaking. "Poor beastie," he kept saying.

The door banged and Teddy came in, rifle in one hand and a dead woodchuck in the other. He threw the woodchuck down and said, "*That* for three days of freezing my ass off! It's like a ghostland out there – there's nothing! Where the hell have all the specimens gone?"

"Maybe you've shot them all," I said.

"Shut up," he said. Walking over to Jewel, he poked her with his rifle. "So what's her problem?" he asked.

I explained about the milk fever and the bum leg.

"She looks all right to me," he said. "She looks fine. She's just being lazy. You two are just too namby-pamby with these cows. Get up there, you!" He goosed her with the rifle. She rocked and thrashed but it did no good.

"So that's the way you want to be!" Teddy bellowed. "Huh?

Okay then, okay for you. I got a trick to put some mustard in a lazy cow."

"She's not being lazy," I said. "Her sciatic nerve is crushed. I've seen it before. There's nothing you can do but wait it out and see if it repairs itself."

"Oh bullshit, buddy! She's being ornery and lazy! I've had cows pull this shit on me and I always got them on their feet once they figured out that I meant business."

"No, Teddy."

"Step back! Who's the boss around here?"

Teddy got an extension cord and shoved a piece of bare copper wire into the female end of it. Then he plugged the other end into the socket and zapped the wire on Jewel's spine. A tiny blue light crackled in the white hair and the cow threw herself forward frantically, legs flashing like mower blades all over the cement floor. Zap! He hit her again, zap zap zap! The blue light arced and sizzled and Jewel tried to get up each time but was unable. It wore her out, until she couldn't respond anymore to the continuous shockings. All she could do was moo long and hard. More a moan than a moo actually. Zap! Zap! The blue arc kept flashing and a wisp of smoke rose from a bare spot on Jewel's back. At last she couldn't even moan. She stuck her tongue way out and twisted her head the way cows do when they're terrified and in great pain.

We were all stunned. I had never seen anything like it before and it froze me in disbelief. I looked at Mamie. She shook her head and said, "Nup, nup." Reaching down she unplugged the extension cord.

"What the hell do you think you're doing!" Teddy shrieked. "This is my fucking farm and my fucking cow, and I'm the one in charge here, not you, fat girl! You plug that in or you're fired! Get out of here!" His mean teeth bit the air as he yelled. He charged at Mamie, teeth snapping as if going for her throat. She stared down at him. Just before he reached her, he stopped in his tracks, his mouth frothing at the corners. Mamie wrapped the male end of the cord around her hands and ripped it off.

"How dare you do that!" He turned in circles stomping his

feet.

She dropped the plug in the gutter.

"Where's my rifle?" he said, staring around her to where he had propped the rifle against the wall.

Jewel's eyes were bloodshot and bulging with terror. Shepard was sobbing and begging in a whisper for Teddy to stop hurting the beastie. I was still frozen in place, but I managed to tell Teddy not to mess with her. I meant Mamie, but he thought I meant the cow. He turned and kicked Jewel in the rump and told me not to tell him what to do with his property.

Next he turned on Shepard and said, "What you crying for, you big baby? What you doing here, anyway. God what a blubberpuss. Guys like you make me sick.

Shepard took out a hanky and blew his nose, wiped his eyes, and told Teddy, "I've come, ub, ub, come for Mamie, *you bucolic cretin!*"

"Come for Mamie? You can have her, Baby Huey. She don't work here no more, she's fired. Don't take that crap from nobody, nosir, no way, not this old boy. My farm, goddammit! Kill that goddamn cow and stuff her if I want to. Nobody tells me!" He glared fiercely through his glasses, eyes magnified at Shepard. "Look at your face, fat boy. Snotty nose, boo hoo hoo, crying over a dumb cow. Don't you know that millions just like her go to Packerland everyday? Get their throats cut, get made into hamburger and roasts and steaks and you eat 'em. Don't you know that? Meat! That's meat on the hoof, you dumb, fat shit! You cry every time you eat a steak? Haw haw! If you don't look silly, a big bozo like you bawling like that. You belong in some cartoon, Baby Huey." Teddy chucked his elbow at me. "Ain't he silly, Slim, crying over a cow? Big sissy. He ought to see them smelling blood in the slaughterhouse and moaning and coughing like they do, their big eyes rolling as they go to meet the man waiting to shoot them between the eyes."

"He's just got a soft heart," I said.

"Well, what's he doing round here then? Soft hearts don't belong on no farm!" His voice was so shrill he was making the wax bubble in my ears.

"I had no intention of witnessing your despicable infamy," said Shepard. He was staring contemptuously down his nose at Teddy. "I'm in this barn by accident."

"What you want with Mamie, anyhow? She's got less brains than this brainless bovine she's working on."

"She has more brains in her earlobes than you have inside that entire cranial corruption you call a head," Shepard answered. "You despicable excuse for a man! You have the intelligence of an inebriated bully afflicted with the conscience of a Nazi. This display of your harassing cowardice fills me with infinite loathing. In my estimation, you are the first man I've ever met whom I would christen imminently clubbable!"

Teddy stuck his tongue out and said, "Who cares what you think?" He went to the wall and picked up his rifle and pointed it at Mamie. "You like staring at me, fat girl?" he asked. "You think you can stare me down? You think your size scares me? Think again, fatty-fatty two by four! Stop staring at me or I'll blow your fucking head off! Then I'll stuff you and this worthless cow! I swear to God I will."

"The fellow's mad as tyranny," said Shepard.

"I'd have my Milkmaid with Holstein then. That's an image hard to resist. I'm gonna have to have it." The rifle shook in his hands.

Mamie wouldn't quit staring at him and he kept raving about what a temptation she was providing him, and how he was going to stuff her for sure, no doubt about it, and add her to the displays in the showroom downstairs and sell tickets to see her. People would come from far and wide to see something like that. As Teddy described all he would do, Shepard moaned and wiped his eyes and cursed "the frothing dog's excess loquacity" and warned him of "protracted and painful consequences" if he didn't lower the gun. But Teddy ignored Shepard, until Shepard lost heart and tottered over to Mamie and pleaded with her to quit staring at Teddy.

"Just come away with me," he said, "from all this sordid, smelly, primitive ick, where cows are beaten by the likes of this devil's minion. Come away from all this saponaceous shit and Teutonic terror with blood in his beady eyes. Come come, Mamie from this inspissated gloom. Won't you come? He tugged at her, but she stayed solid as a fireplug, her eyes boring into Teddy.

And suddenly he screamed at her to get out. "You and Baby Huey, out, out! Tempting me ain't cute no more, fat girl. You're fired and I'm ordering you to get out of my barn and off my farm!"

"Who's fired, Teddy?" I looked behind me and saw Ben and Mrs. Snowdy. "Who's fired?" she said again.

As soon as he saw his parents, Teddy puffed up his lower lip and pointed with his rifle at the broken extension cord. "Look, Mommy, look what Mamie done," he said.

"Your son was electrocuting this helpless cow," said Shepard, his voice full of outrage.

"I wasn't either electrocuting it. I was trying to make it get up. Lazy bitch."

Mrs. Snowdy clicked her tongue at Teddy. "Why, Teddy," she said, "wherever did you learn such a cruel thing?"

"What's cruel about it, Mommy? If I don't get that cow up, it's gonna die. That's what's cruel."

"You've got a point."

"That's right. You know, sometimes a farmer's got to be harsh for the cow's own good."

Ben pulled the piece of copper from the cord and held it up. "This isn't anything I ever taught you, Teddy. This isn't just a kick in the ass or a jab with a pitchfork. This is a hundred and twenty volts of fire. You've stuck your finger in a light socket. You know what it feels like."

"All I know is it works good. When I tell a cow to get up, by god she gets up. I'm the farmer running things here. I'm the boss. Am I the boss or not?"

Mrs. Snowdy nodded. "You're the boss, honey. No one disputes that."

"Yeah, and I've kept things going without them, Mommy." He pointed the rifle at us and his father. "I'm a better farmer than Daddy could ever be."

"Too bad it isn't true," said Ben. "This plan of Mommy's letting you run things has only made you worse, far as I can tell."

192

"Worse than what? You're the one causing all the trouble. You never liked me. You always wanted her for yourself, and you hated her paying any attention to me." He pointed his rifle at Ben. "You never know what a guy like that might do! Watch out!"

Jewel started trying to get up again. We gave her room as she rocked and threw her head forward and kicked her one good leg out behind her. Her efforts got her nowhere.

"That's sciatic nerve damage," said Ben.

"That's what our Crystal Christian told us," said Shepard.

"Yeah, he's right. That nerve runs right down over her hip to her lower leg. It gets pinched from calving. Most cows don't get over it."

"So there," said Teddy. "Daddy says so hisself. Best to save the critter from pain is what I say." He turned the rifle onto Jewel, putting the barrel between her eyes.

"Hold on!" yelled Ben.

All of us yelled except for Mamie. She reached over and caught his wrist with one hand and snatched the rifle away with the other.

"Oww, you goddamn buffalo," he hollered. "Lemmee go!"

Mamie let him go. Rubbing his wrist, he showed it to his mommy and said "I'm paralyzed."

Mrs. Snowdy wasn't very sympathetic about it. She gave his ear a twist and said, "You scared hell out of me doing that, Teddy!"

Teddy made a squealing sound and petted his mommy's arm. He grabbed her hand and kissed it.

Ben said there was no reason to shoot Jewel just yet. "Some cows do come out of it, I've heard. Just none of mine ever did."

Teddy turned from his mommy and sneered at us. "Go ahead, you can all be against me," he said. "I don't give a damn. I'm still gonna be stuffing this cow, you'll see. You'll let her die slow and suffering and all, and in the end you'll be meaner than I ever been. I know animals from nostril to asshole, and I know when they're gonna die, and this one is gonna die, I tell you."

"Maybe Teddy's right," said Mrs. Snowdy. "He does know animals after all."

"I am right. And I'm sorry I had to hurt her, but I had to see if there was a chance she could get up." He smiled at his mommy and she smiled at him. It was like two forests of teeth in love.

"Can I have my rifle back?" he asked meekly.

"Of course you can," said Mrs. Snowdy. Taking the rifle from Mamie, she handed it to Teddy. He picked up his woodchuck and followed her as she left the barn. I could hear him complaining to her, saying she should watch out for that Mamie. "You never know what a girl like her might do."

"That fellow is a menace to sanity," said Shepard. "I suppose we should pity him, but primarily, I think, someone should take a stick to his behind and let the pity come later, if ever."

Ben asked if we were leaving. "That was just a little Teddy-fit," he said. "Don't let it bother you. No harm done, ey?"

Shepard disagreed. "No harm, my foot. It's dangerous here. That man is a threat, a walking time bomb, stupid and depraved and evil. You can stay here, Ben. But both of you must come with me. Of all the anfractuosities of the human mind, none is so blunt as its love of killing, none so primitive and sure, driven into our antediluvian blood, yum yum, by the needs of hunger, basic as instinct, basic as lion tooth and tiger claw. Doom is lurking in those pea-sized eyes of his. I beg you to listen to me, sapient sage that I am, Teddy Snowdy is a fractious monster. Run for your lives!"

"Oh now, listen," said Ben. "Teddy's got his problems, but he's no Lizzy Borden, Donny."

Shepard's eyes pinned Ben with a glare of contempt. "Even with my uncanny gift of lexicography, yum yum, I cannot *exaggerate* the perversions I've seen here today, Benjamin Snowdy. I'm sorry that you've forced me to say this to your face."

"Whyn't you just go, Donny. I'm not in the mood for anymore, okay?"

"Well, so truth's a dog, must to kennel. I'll leave, if that's what you want. Yes, my Tiresian insight goes unappreciated here, I can see that. Mamie plays with a cow's leg. You tell me I exaggerate. Christian bites his lower lip and defends me nothing, even though he knows I'm right. One word more. You have a butcher in your midst. Beware. His mind is a carving block and remember this -

that worms eat men, but not for love."

Shepard tossed his bushy hair, petted his nose, and, with great dignity, waddled past us and out the door.

I knew in my bones that he was right. And had it been just me, I would have gone with him. But I couldn't leave Mamie and she wasn't leaving Jewel. Not only Teddy, but few farmers would give a down cow like Jewel a chance to recover. It was the nature of the business to be cold when you had to – to kill a cow when she couldn't earn her keep. Soft-hearted farmers had it the toughest. They would hang on and nurse a cow to the end, and if it died, the soft-hearted farmer looked like a fool wasting time and money, when everything in farming is marginal at best. But more often than not, a down cow will live, if given a little time to recover. I had seen it happen plenty of times, cows coming back from death's door. My pa was a soft-hearted farmer. He hated to give up on a sick cow. He always felt he owed it to her to try all that he knew to make her well. He said she was the supporter of a farmer's dreams and gave more than she got and there was a union in nature between man and beast, a union that too many farmers forgot in the heat of running a *business*. Pa insisted farming wasn't a business, it was a way of life. It was practically a religion.

I pinched a cowlift over Jewel's hipbones. Then we took a chainfall and hooked it to an overhead beam and then to the cowlift. Mamie cranked the chainfall and got Jewel's hindend off the floor, but Jewel must have thought we were going to torture her more, because she hung loose, her head down, her butt in the air, and she wouldn't make an effort to stand at all. We petted her and loved her up, talking soft and trying to convince her we meant well. But she was having none of it. She hung like a rumply old rug waiting to be beaten.

Ben said the thing to do was get her front-end even with her backside and see if she would let her legs down then. He went out back to the old scrap pile and got a four-by-six long enough to go under the cow. Ben and I got on one side of the board and Mamie on the other. We heaved together and got Jewel's forelegs up all right, but she stayed limp, her front legs drawn up. She looked very depressed about the whole thing. So we let her front-end down again.

While we stood there trying to figure it out, Mamie got the baby heifer and showed her the teats, squirting some milk on her face to get her interested and giving her tail a little tickle. It was just the coaxing Jewel needed. She looked at her calf and came alive, rising up on her front legs and mooing softly, telling the baby to suck. The calf reached in and caught hold of a teat and gave a tug. Jewel was up, leaning a bit to the left, where her leg dangled, but the rest of her worked well enough. We left Jewel and her baby alone. We talked it over and figured we would have to keep lifting her up and down several times a day for a while, and we'd have to massage the bad leg to see if the nerve would come alive again. Ben said if Jewel wasn't standing on her own in ten days, then it was permanent damage and he would have to let Teddy shoot her.

Mamie's Obsession

Time went fast. And Jewel was not getting well, no matter that Mamie took over completely and stayed with the cow around the clock, raising her five times a day and massaging the bad leg and the hip, kneading them, trying to find that magic spot, that chemic heart that would bring the nerve alive and put Jewel on all fours. Each time Mamie massaged up and down the muscles, she would grab the leg and force the tendon to stretch out, pulling it back as far as it would go, before letting it spring forward again. She did this many, many times a day. Then she went back to digging her fingers into the muscle and working at it like it was a mound of bread dough. I tried it myself, kneading the muscle, but my hands started cramping after five minutes. So I stayed out of the way, doing most of the chores and milking and letting Mamie give all her time to the down cow.

Ten days went by and it looked to me like we would have to do what Ben had said and let Teddy put Jewel down. Not only was the tendon still drawn up and shriveled but the cow's hips were being chewed to pieces by the cowlift and had become raw and bloody. To help this problem, Mamie wrapped the hipbones with rags smeared with Bag Balm, but it didn't do much good. Still, Jewel milked all right, and she ate and drank good, so it didn't make sense right then to go ahead and shoot her, tenth day or not. Bleeding hips and all, she had a lot of life in her yet. Teddy was insisting that ten days was enough. Ben said he was afraid Teddy was right. I argued for giving the cow more time. She was milking well and earning her keep, so why not?

"But look," said Ben. "Her hips are turning into hamburger. She's in pain, Christian, and it's just going to go on till she has to

197

be shot anyway. So what's the point? We're not much if we let our animals suffer that way. I'm afraid I have to insist now."

Teddy already had his rifle, so we marched down to the barn with him. On the way, he pointed out to us how stupid we were for not listening to him in the first place. The cow would be dead now and not have had ten days of Mamie pestering her.

"I suppose so," I said, hating to agree with him.

He clicked his teeth at me. "You're all right, Slim," he said. "Most people don't want to admit when they been wrong."

When we got into the barn, Mamie was standing in front of the cow, giving us a look of warning.

"Now, Mamie," said Teddy. "I'm gonna shoot that cow. So you step out the way."

"Booshit," she answered.

"See there, Daddy? See why I fired her? She won't take orders. That's my cow and I'm gonna shoot it, by God."

"Booshit," said Mamie again. She took a step towards Teddy, and he backed off.

Ben said, "Talk to her, Christian. Make her understand."

So I did. I went through the whole thing about it being ten days and about Jewel being in pain and going to die anyway, so it was cruel to keep her going. If Teddy shot her, she would never know what happened. It would be over in an instant. It was the right thing to do. After I finished my speech, Mamie cocked her head to one side and looked me over. She was sizing me up and I felt that she found me wanting.

And to me she said, "Booshit, Kritch'n."

"Well, Mamie, dammit, she's not your cow."

She didn't reply. She set her feet and crouched like a wrestler ready to do battle with all of us if she had to.

"Let's not fight over this," said Ben. "Give her more time. I'm sure Mamie doesn't want to prolong Jewel's suffering. She wants to do the right thing."

"I could wing a shot in there before she knows what's happening," said Teddy in a whisper.

Ben shook his head no. "That's too dangerous," he said. "And from the look of things, you'd probably be forced to shoot Mamie too."

"Then I'll take care of business when fat girl's asleep." Teddy pivoted on his heel and left the barn.

Ben and I followed. I was feeling rotten for taking the side against Mamie, and I wanted to make it up to her. Not that I thought she was right. Ben and Teddy had right on their side. But she wasn't wrong either. It was the thing about truth again. They had right. She had that moment of truth thing.

When I got to the house, I asked Mrs. Snowdy if she would make some lunch for Mamie for me to take to her. Mrs. Snowdy fixed me a basket of cold chicken and buttered bread, which I brought to Mamie as a peace offering. She sat and ate with me and acted like nothing had happened. But when we finished and I started to leave, she caught my hand and said, "Kirtch'n, y-you know w-what I d-do?

Did I know what she was doing? I thought I did. "Yaay, Mamie, I know," I told her. "But the cow, she's suffering, and it's bad if you let an animal suffer, you see?"

Jewel was resting on her side, her head in the stanchion, chewing her cud, pretty much the picture of the contented cow, except for the gashes around her bloody hipbones. Mamie nodded towards Jewel.

"S-suffer?" she said. ""Nup, Kritch'n. W-why you s-say that?"

"Never mind, Mamie. I'm for whatever you want."

The days went by, one after the other, and nothing changed with Jewel. Mamie stayed always in the barn, and some nights I stayed with her. I would sleep and wake and offer to stand watch while she slept, but she always turned me down. She didn't want Teddy to catch her off-guard. When she slept was a mystery to me.

Most nights I would leave her around ten o'clock and go back to the house. Teddy would be there, sitting at the table, having his cereal before bedtime. He would growl at me about how the stupidest farmers he ever met were those who made pets of their cows and then couldn't shoot them when it was necessary. I'd tell him that according to my pa, catering to a cow when it was sick wasn't stupid; it was the least you could do considering what the cow had done for you, giving you a milk check every month. Teddy would holler at me that what I was talking about wasn't the same thing as what was going on with Jewel. But it was. He just didn't see it. He would say also that we should let Mamie starve, not feed her down there, and she would eventually get hungry and come to the house. And then he could sneak down to the barn and quick as a bullet get the job over with. Mrs. Snowdy always told him to get those thoughts out of his head. She wasn't about to let that brave girl starve.

Mamie went on and on with Jewel, lifting her, feeding her, milking her, putting her back down and rubbing the sores on her hips with Bag Balm. And of course, she exercised Jewel's leg tirelessly.

An entire month went by. We had a nice spell of Indian summer just before the rains came and knocked the leftover leaves to the ground. And then came a light dusting of snow. The trees became a ghostly gray, and the hay stubble went from gold to brown to black. And even after the snow stopped, the clouds stayed on and let loose a shroud of mist that hung in the air and made it gloomy.

And what was worse than the weather was the decline of Jewel. She was losing weight and her milk was down to less than a gallon a day. Her hips looked like a dog had been chewing on them and she had developed a deep cough. I was all on Teddy's side for shooting her now. I even thought about doing it myself, and I told Mamie she was as mean and cruel as John Beaver himself not letting the suffering cow die. What I said made no difference to her, and I couldn't get up the gumption to transfer my opinion into action.

By then it wasn't five times or a dozen times a day that Mamie massaged Jewel's leg – it was almost constantly. Whether the cow was up on the chainfall or down, Mamie pushed and pulled and kneaded and stretched. I had never seen anything make her tired before, but I saw her tired now, and getting more and more tired each day. Her complexion turned from rosy to ashen and there were deep circles under her eyes. Her clothes got baggy from her losing so much weight. The cow was dying, and I began to fear that Mamie was dying too. I tried to help, but just a few minutes of doing what she was doing wore me out completely. I didn't see how she could go on. Every body has its limits. I yelled at her that she was going to kill herself over a stupid cow, and wouldn't that be the dumbest thing ever? I said she wasn't brave and kind, just stubborn and stupid. I got mad at Jewel for not getting well. "Stand up or die!" I screamed at her. And I said, "There's nothing stupider than a stupid cow, unless it's a stupid Mamie Beaver!" I said a lot of things like that. I wasn't being the friend Mamie needed.

But she didn't seem to mind. All her single-mindedness was focused on the cow, and nothing else got to her. It got so bad, I just couldn't stand to stick around and watch her, so I started staying away from the barn. I still brought food to Mamie, but I didn't stay to eat with her. I milked and did chores, and then I got out and tried my best to not think about her down there, digging her hands into that shriveled leg, feeling for the nerve that had withered. But trying not to think about her made me think about her more than ever. I spent a lot of hours wondering if she had gone fully crazy at last. I thought of all the forms of craziness I had seen since running off with her, from John Beaver to Mike Quart to Robbie Peevy to Shepard and Amoss and Teddy – not one really normal mind in the bunch, as far as I could tell. But then I tried to think of what was normal, and decided that I was the only one. No one else, just Christian Peter Foggy. And that kind of thinking made me laugh and tell myself that *I* was crazy. So I said crazy is normal and everybody belongs in Camelot where things are simply normal, just like in Madison and Minneapolis and Cloverland and . . . everywhere. The thoughts piled in till I couldn't sort them and could only see in my mind the way Mamie was fading away, getting thinner, her eyes turning into two gray lumps of clay, her hair looking like wilted maple leaves. An acid smell rose from her skin, a mixture of manure and damp cow and spoiled milk. Only her hands stayed the same, long-boned and muscular, with freckled backs and tiny golden hairs standing up as if full of electricity.

Every night in bed I made the sign of the cross to get God's attention, and I prayed for Mamie, prayed that God would snap her out of it. I also prayed to Robbie, just in case he really had had an Immaculate Reception and what he said was true about all of us being a piece of Jesus. Many nights I prayed myself to sleep, and in my sleep I had nightmares of cops chasing me and Mamie, and I was always riding her bloody hips and clinging to her hair, screaming at her to run faster and faster. She would leap over boulders and logs and ponds and go higher and higher with each leap, until we were going over whole barns and trees. I would feel the sickening sensation of being so high and knowing we were bound to come down in a crash – but we never did. We'd hit the ground, and the ground was like rubber that would bounce us higher than ever, boing . . . boing . . . boing, like on a pogo stick up and down, up and down, until somewhere in the dream we would come to the Snowdy farm. Teddy would be there with his rifle. His teeth would come at us, clicking as they came, and they would catch my foot. My foot would disappear, and then my ankle and then my knee, and down we'd go, both of us, swallowed by Teddy's teeth. He would take us to the basement - make us into papier-mâché figures.

Night after night I had the same dream, until I didn't think I could stand to sleep anymore, it was too terrifying. But then again, I couldn't stand not sleeping either. I wanted Mamie to come and lie down beside me. I wanted Jewel to die. I wanted to go to California. I wanted to believe it was true that I was a piece of Jesus.

One day a letter came from home. Mrs. Snowdy brought it to me. "You got kin in Cloverland?" she asked, turning the envelope in her hands.

I took it and went downstairs to read in private. But then I saw Teddy was working at his bench, rubbing the inside of some skin with borax. He had been working hard for days, preparing balsawood and papier-mâché bodies for some animals he was ready to stuff. I had to admit that Teddy was talented when it came to carving balsa. To me the figure he made looked like a piece of woodcarving art he could have sold in some gallery. Sewing the skins and fur over the figure only made them ugly, in my opinion. He thought I was nuts, of course. He said he turned straw into gold, and only an idiot would want to leave it straw. It was an eye-of-the-beholder kind of thing, only I was dead sure I had a better eye than he did.

When I came into the workroom, he said, "Hey, that goddamn cow dead yet? No? Well, it's gotta be soon now. She's coughing and has a fever. Next thing she'll have pneumonia and then forget it, she's a goner. I see her standing over there in that corner with her head down and those two wolves chomping at her hindquarters, trying to hamstring her. Or maybe put them in front, going for her throat. There's a picture for you! Don't you think I've got magic in my fingers, Slim?"

"Yeah, magic," I said. I hurried back upstairs and out to the peaceful loft in the barn. I settled myself into the hay and opened my letter.

Dear Christian Peter,
This here is your sister Mary Magdalen writing for me and Mama. We get to go first, Papa says. First I got to say something myself that I wish I could say it to your face. Christian, brother mine, I am so proud of you I could just cry and cry. God will bless you, I know he will, and keep you safe from harm. Your letter explained so many things that John Beaver left out. Like he didn't mention a word about you hitting him because he was scalping Mamie. Not a word, the skunk. He said you hit him because there was a plan for the two of you to rob him and steal the truck and run off. Don't think for a second we believed him. We know you better than that. We have faith in you that you did what you had to do, and your letter confirmed what we had guessed but didn't know the details. You saved Mamie. Pa calls you our righteous Samaritan. What a brave thing for little skinny you to do. Our little Christian just like a knight in shiny armor. I pray Rosary for you every night before bed.

And now Mama wants me to write this. That when you left she just cried and cried. She misses you, her baby boy. When your letter came she just sat down and cried and cried. She prays to Saint Jude every night for you. She says Rosary for you every night. She thinks this is a good time for you to think of becoming a Catholic instead of following in Pa's footsteps. Because nobody should make up his own religion based on Shakespeare and Emerson and Deism. Except Pa. (He said to say that.) He is giving Mama a lecture now, so I want to say that your letter sounded like you might be depressed. We know things have been hard for you. We wish there was some way of making it better. Please have faith in God and remember that the Lord loves you like we do. Be thankful for what you have right this minute. At least you are safe and have a roof over your head and food in your belly. You can see. You can hear. You can feel. You can smell. You can write us letters, which you better do a lot more.

Mama wants to say that it is all right if you want to have a religion like Pa. Just so you believe in God is the important thing. They both agree on that. Mama says she has been so tired lately but cannot sleep for worry of you and she cries and cries. Her bladder has hurt a lot too. And her arthritis and that sciatic nerve thing are killing her. She thinks the extra pain is from worrying about you. And from her heart aching because she misses you so. She says to be good and work hard for those good people who gave you and Mamie a job. She is glad they are such nice farming folks. She is thankful to God that you and Mamie are healthy. She wishes you would write more often because she worries and cries about you and can't keep from crying all the time. (Not all the time.) She wants to know if Mrs. Snowdy is a good cook and does she sew your clothes when you tear them? Calvin is standing here waiting to write for the boys. So get ready for two cents worth of nothing. Bye, brother Christian. Write soon! XOXOXO

Mary Magdalen and Mama

Christian, this is your big brother Calvin. Don't lisen to Mary Magdalen, she is much a brat as ever. So Christian, you hit Beaver on the head with a club he told us. Good for you. All us brothers say good for you, we aint gong to pick on you no more when you come home. So Christian, you stoled his truck and recked it. Was he mad! He come here and yelled about how bad you was but pa stuck up for you. And he come at pa to hit him and pa picked up a rock and said he would send him to hell in a hurry. Cush and Cutham and me come running to beat up Beaver but pa said we should not unless Beaver didn't get off our land. Beaver swared at us like a devil. We itch to poke him bad. Cash and Calah come in from the field on the 350 in 4 geer storming along, the loder bouncing in front. You know Calah can be meen. He saw Beaver and us with our fists up and he put the 350 bucket down and lit out after Beaver. He chased him all over the yard. Beaver run in circles. His face got red as fire. We laughed so hard we fell down. Even Pa could not help hisself laughing. Beaver jump in his truck that you recked but it runs still tho it sounds clunky junky and Calah put the bucket on his bumper and pushed him down the driveway. We seen no more of him for now. So Christian we stuck up for you. Teached that mongrul not to mess with Foggys. You should be proud of us. All the brothers says hi. Sugar had a heifer last week, she is milking heavy.

Your bros Calvin Cutham
Cush Calah Cash

Christian, my son,

Well, son, I have mixed feelings about it all. We cannot live in this great country of ours without being lawful. But when the law is on John Beaver's side there is something rotten in Denmark and no two ways about it. He told us his side and now we got your side. We always knew that your side would be the truthful one. Beaver says he has the law and will put you in jail and throw away the key. So you better lay low for now, son. The Deity's anger will come on John Beaver one day, I predict. He is a evil man and I admit I was wrong to tell you to give up Mamie to him. Now I tell you to NOT give up Mamie to that low living son of a cloven hoof. Your conscious can be clear, my son. Remember what

Hamlet said, Let the doors be shut on him, that he may play the fool nowhere but in his own house. Not that I believe he is a fool, he is crafty as a weasel. But he won't learn anything from us and neither will anybody else. The doors are closed to him. I know in my heart that the Deity is on your side. And John Beaver has not dreamed what Horatio knows. I seen him drive up and down in his truck that you smashed the side in. I know he wants to stop and see if we heard from you. He don't stop though, not yet anyway. You know Calah. He sees John Beaver go by and he runs to the tractor to get it ready to run him down. All the boys want to beat him up. I have to get on them not to chase his truck. You know how they are. They like to punch each other round and roll in the mud. We have had lots of mud this fall and now some snow. I bet you have too. But it is one thing to play grab ass with each other and quite another thing to take on a man the size and meanness of John Beaver who would cut your gizzard from ear to ear like he would pluck a chicken. Then I would have to shoot him to save the boys and I would go to jail and rot. I can not say what will come of it. All I can says is stay put and lets see if this don't blow over and John Beaver gets tired of acting like the second coming of Job. No one believes him anways. I talked to my old friend Ken Maydwell the other day. He says no one believe Beaver but that don't matter, since you hit him and steal his truck the law would have to pinch you for it. So he agrees that you should just stay low and lets see how things turn out. He said you sure outsmarted him the day he met you and you had just laid Beaver out like a dead dog. I told him you were the smartest of all my boys. You didn't get your mother's side in you from all her weird brothers and her pa, so it didn't surpise me that you outsmarted him. He didn't get mad about it. Ken is a good guy. He says he hopes you can keep outsmarting John Beaver. He thinks Beaver has a lot of killer in him. I am not worried about it. Any son of mine who could not outsmart that bastard I would have to send back to his maker for a new transmission. Calvin told you about your cow Sugar. She is fine. Trigger had a heifer too and she is already milking 60 pounds. She might look like a horse but she milks like the queen of cows. We put up 10,000 bales this year. The Massy Harris 44 snapped an axle when Cush popped the clutch too hard. Cutham saw him do it but Cush tried to say he didn't do it. They had to wrestle for an hour before Cutham won and made Cush confess. Anyway we had to pull the whole differential off to fix it. I guess you know Cush had to give his soul to God because I had his ass for a week and might keep it a month. Be careful out there and write us some more. We let you know what Beaver is doing.

Jacob Foggy Your Loving Papa

It was a big comfort to me to know that my family so totally believed my version of things. I was sorry about Mama's aches and pains and worrying and crying so much, but what could I do about it? I prayed to Saint Jude to help her.

I walked around outside and then went into the barn and watched Mamie working Jewel's leg. All of a sudden I hated Mamie. She was the cause of my family's trouble with John Beaver. If it

205

weren't for her I would have been home where I belonged, instead of running around the country with John Beaver and the law after me. And her obsessed with a dumb cow! Not eating or sleeping or caring about me and letting herself go to the dogs. She stank worse than a civet cat and she looked like an exhausted ghost. And I didn't exist for her either. I had given up everything for her, my whole life gone to save her. Some kind of thanks I was getting. I told myself that for two cents I would leave her and go back to my family and take my chances.

That night in bed I started having the same nightmare about Teddy eating us and making us into papier-mâché figures. But the dream was interrupted by someone shaking my shoulders. The first thing that came to me was the smell of putrid cow needing to get hosed off. I opened my eyes and saw who was shaking me. It was a dark silhouette with an imploding pumpkin head. It was Mamie. She threw the covers off and pulled me into her arms.

"Kritch'n, come," she said.

I followed her up the stairs and out the back door. The shock of the winter forecasting November air made me gasp. Grabbing my hand she pulled me running to the barn. When we got inside, she pointed to Jewel. And there she was, that big white cow staring me face to face, standing in the aisle – standing on her own! She raised her head and greeted me with a moooo. I could smell the cud on her breath. I grabbed her neck and hugged her hard, "You old bossy," I said. "You're standing on you own." Jewel raised her neck for me to give it a scratch. We fussed over her like a pair of mother cats, brushing her down with the curry comb and washing her with wet rags soaked in a bucket of water, drying her with straw, making her shine like a polished opal. Except for the sores on her hips, she looked grand.

"What you've done here," I told Mamie, "is made yourself a miracle. This cow should be meat on hooks by now, her hide inside Teddy's dampbox. But she isn't because you wouldn't give up on her. You knew what you were doing, even though all of us thought you were wrong. It's a miracle, I'm saying, and I'll never doubt you again, Mamie. You are magic. Mamie is magic."

I kissed her smelly face and kept calling her magic. She smiled and nodded her head like she believed it. My fair opinion was that nobody in the world was ever quite as special as Mamie Beaver that wonderful night. Not even Dr. Einstein.

We put Jewel back in the stanchion and gave her and the other cows fresh hay. Then we went back to the house and down to the basement. I jumped under the covers and held them for Mamie, but she took her clothes off and started to leave.

"Where you going?" I said. "I want you here with me."

Turning around she smiled and sniffed at her armpits and pinched her nose and said, "Woo woo."

"Who cares?" I told her. "You just smell like a farm. I'm used to it. Get in this bed with me. Shower tomorrow. I've been missing you, Mamie."

Looking down at me, her eyes were thoughtful. Her face might have been a hundred years old it was so full of shadows and fatigue. Finally, she came under the quilts with me and wrapped me up. I hugged her like I was hugging life itself. She exhaled cow and hay and manure and her Mamie self. Which was the smell of earth and green fields and the morning air straight from the breath of God. I was ashamed of doubting her and hating her for a while. But of course, I never really meant it. In my heart of hearts I had always had faith in her. I had always mostly believed.

Ambush

The first big storm ambushed us on the 23^{d} of November. High winds knocked over trees already loose from having so much rain that autumn. The power was out for ten hours, and we had to do the morning milking by hand. Snow blew across the land, covering it so well that stubbles of hay and undisked corn stalks could no longer be seen. The drifts piled as high as four feet on the north and west sides of buildings. The temperature dropped nearly to zero and stayed there for three days straight. Then warmed to twenty above.

There wasn't a jacket on the place Mamie could wear, nor a hat. So Mrs. Snowdy took some of her unfinished quilts and made Mamie a motley-colored quilt coat with a coyote collar. Teddy gave me one of his old chore jackets made of corduroy and denim with an inner lining made of felt, and he gave Mamie and me each a fur cap that pulled down over our ears. He called them tabby caps. They were blond and orange striped with tails hanging in the back. I recognized them as the two cats that had stolen Teddy's crows the day Mamie and I had arrived. They were warm enough, which is what we needed, a little bit of warmth against the aching cold of Wisconsin.

One morning Teddy woke us two hours early to do chores. He said we were going deer hunting. It was the last week of the season. Ben Snowdy arrived to help out. He was going with us. He and Teddy were getting along pretty well, chattering like a couple of old beer-drinking buddies about the great hunting weather and how the snow would enable them to track whatever deer were out there on the South Range. They talked about their old hunting trips, the six-pointer Teddy had shot some years ago, the clean shot from Ben that had brought down a four-pointer, and so on and so forth. They complimented each other and patted each other on the back. It was quirky to hear them being so kind to each other. Such a change was weird to witness, especially from Teddy, who had been almost soft to Mamie since she had brought Jewel back from the door of death. It made me think that Teddy could be likable, if he wanted to be, if he would simply put his mind to it.

After milking, we went to the house for breakfast. Mrs. Snowdy gave us fried eggs and bacon and potatoes and bread and coffee. While we ate, she bustled about offering us more of everything. We weren't to leave the table unless we were ready to bust. As she went back and forth with her coffee pot in hand, she would touch Ben on the shoulder and then touch Teddy. She would play with Ben's hair a little. Then play with Teddy's. She would whisper something to one, then whisper something to the other. I heard her say wistfully, "This is how it should be with my two men." Her face was pink with excitement, her men going out on the hunt, bringing home meat for the table. Like men should. The way nature meant them to be all along. I had never seen her so full of energy and good humor. She laughed at everything, her own thoughts at times it seemed, floating out of her mouth, chuckling over the novelty of her son and husband being nice to each other. She laughed hardest whenever one or the other made a little joke. "Look at Mommy moving like she's got the skitters." "Lily, you are in overdrive gear chasing light speed today." You'd think she'd never heard anything so funny. Yes, it was certainly an unusual sight – the three of them sort of thick as thieves as the saying goes – and I thought what an amazing family they were. It even made me think that deep down Teddy really loved his daddy. I was happy to watch them being close. I took it as a good omen for what lay ahead.

It was not quite day when we left the farm, a lip of light graying the southeast rim of the world. Clouds blanketed all the horizons and let loose scattered flakes of snow. Mamie and I huddled in the back of the pickup, while Ben drove and Teddy kept his carbine semi-automatic ready to fire in case he saw something that needed shooting. Now and then he would roll down his window and blast a stop sign or some farmer's no-hunting sign. Then he would roll the window up and reload. A lot of metal was turned into scrap by his enthusiasm before we got to where we were going.

It was an area of forests and back roads and clearings, only forty to fifty minutes from the Snowdy farm. We turned off the main road and followed a snow-covered trail for a mile or so, until we couldn't go any farther without getting stuck. On our left was an eighty-acre meadow surrounded on three sides by trees. Straight ahead and to our right were snowy forest, barren trees and spots of wind whirling the snow, making it look like the dancing ghosts of bees. The wind pelted our bodies, nipped our faces. Even bundled in my chore jacket and tabby cap, I was freezing. Especially my feet. I kept kicking one of the tires to warm my toes. Mamie stood still and looked longingly towards the woods horseshoeing around us. Ben, like me, was kicking the tires to warm his toes. Teddy seemed to think we were weaklings. He didn't even wear his hat or gloves. He was kidding us, calling us pussies, saying how when you lived in the great outdoors the way he did, you could go bare-chested at twenty below. Then he told us his plan for flushing out the enemy.

Ben and Mamie and I were to go in on foot a hundred yards west and circle back, until we were coming east toward the meadow. Where he would be waiting in ambush for whatever came out of the trees. Ben complained that if anyone should wait in ambush it should be him because Teddy was younger and stronger, so he should go in and circle back. Teddy lost all of his recent good humor. He glared at Ben and said he was damned if he would. It was his plan to come to this spot and have us drive the deer to him. He made the plan. He told the plan. He had had the plan in mind for weeks, and why was Ben always trying to be the boss and make people think that Teddy didn't know eggs from buttercups? Teddy was shaking his finger, almost tapping Ben's nose with it, and suddenly Ben grabbed the finger and held it, shocking Teddy into silence. The two men stared at each other, Ben still squeezing

Teddy's finger tightly. Finally, Teddy blinked and said, "Daddy, ouch." Ben let go. He turned and waved us forward.

"Let's go get Teddy a deer," he said.

"I'll set up a flanking fire. I won't miss, I promise," said Teddy as we walked away.

It was hard going, with better than a foot of snow to tromp through until we got out of the meadow and into the trees, where the snow wasn't too bad. Still, I was breathing hard and so was Ben. None of it bothered Mamie. She ran ahead of us like a bloodhound tracking left and right, leaping over little drifts and shrubs, then circling back behind us and running on ahead again.

"She's such a happy one mostly," said Ben. "Wish I had that kind of energy. It exhausts me just to watch her."

"She's got more energy than all three of us put together," I told him.

"She's like nobody I ever knew or heard of in my life. I can't make up my mind about her. Is she touched or no?"

I shrugged. "I don't know, Ben. I thought I knew the answer once upon a time, but I don't know anymore. All my life I'd heard she had molasses for brains, that she was retarded and hopeless. She couldn't learn anything, couldn't read, couldn't talk without it taking an hour to bring out a sentence. But I'll tell you she's not that simple. She's a mystery, I mean. You know, when she really wants to, she can talk perfectly. It depends on what she's heard a moment before." I told Ben about the lines from *Blithe Spirit* that Mamie had memorized instantly. "Ghostly spectre – ghoul or fiend/ Never more be thou convened/ Shepherd's Wort and Holy Rite/ Banish thee into the night."

"She said all that?"

"Every word perfect. See what I mean?"

"That thing with the cow, with Jewel," said Ben. "How would a retarded girl know to do what she did? Not likely, I think. I can't make up my mind if she knew more than the rest of us or was she just too stupid to quit? It seems she understands cows like she's been one herself in another life. They've never been healthier or milked better, not even when I had them. And I'm good with cows. I know how to take care of them. But Mamie's got a special touch, no denying it. She's like a genius with them. Is there such a thing as a retarded genius?"

"I've never heard of it, but there's a lot I've never heard of," I answered.

"Actually, I suppose I could be talking about Teddy in some ways," he went on. His breath was steaming in the air and so was mine. We slowed down. Like a child playing peek-a-boo, Mamie kept coming in and out of sight through the trees. "There is retarded, and then there is retarded. Teddy is good at only one thing – his taxidermy. In every other way I can think of, he acts a wee bit mentally impaired. Always has. Take the cows now. He was raised with them. He should know better how to handle them. But he won't learn. Since I left him to run the farm, he's hired God knows how many hands to help him. But none of them last very long. They just can't stand Teddy. Only you and Mamie have ever stayed this long.

I wanted to ask him why he didn't just stay home and kick Teddy's ass once in a while, take over like my pa would, but I didn't want to spoil what a good talk we were having.

"Yeah," he continued. "I'd take your Mamie, retarded or not, whatever faults she's got. Any farmer would. She's fascinating. She gives me a feeling like I used to get when we had Morgans to pull the plow – sweet, gentle, real power. I'd like to bring those days back again. Things were tough, but it all seemed worthwhile. If I'd had a gal like her instead of Teddy, well, who knows where we'd be now? But better off, I betcha." Mamie streaked across our line of sight and vanished once more.

"If there's any deer in here, she'll find them," Ben said. He looked at me and said, "So what do you think about this Freudian notion that it's the parents' fault if their kid turns out to be a monster? If that's true then it's a good thing Mamie wasn't our daughter, huh? We probably would have ruined her for sure, made a female Teddy out of her."

I was on the verge of telling him about John Beaver and that if such a father as he couldn't ruin Mamie, no one could. God only knew what she might have been with Ben Snowdy as her pa and Lily Snowdy as her mother – parents to really nurture her gifts and help her realize them fully. Whatever those gifts were. I still wasn't sure.

Mamie came back into view and stopped. She got down on all fours, face close to the ground as if she were looking for something in the snow. When we caught up with her, she was kneeling on a frozen creek. She held what looked like a yellow flake of ice in her hand.

"That's a tooth," said Ben. "Look at it. How do you like that? Broke right off. Must've wanted a drink pretty bad, poor fella."

"A wolf do you think?" I asked.

"Maybe, I don't know. Not many wolves left in this part of the world anymore. All of 'em gone to Canada. Look at the bite marks he left. Frustrated and tired of eating snow, so he knocks out a tooth on the ice trying to get at the water below. It looks old. Maybe he's on his last legs." Ben tapped his own teeth. "Nature takes the bite out of all of us eventually. Mine get anymore tender I'm gonna have to start eating pabulum." In the gray light, Ben looked every minute of his age and older. Long creases made his forehead like a washboard. A nest of wrinkles webbed his cheeks and lips. Silver hairs bristled on his jaws and chin. Mamie gave the tooth to him. He dropped it in his pocket and said he would polish it up and put it on a chain for Lily to wear.

After another twenty yards or so we turned left and walked in a wide circle and started back. We spread out and walked towards the meadow. I didn't hear any deer as we made our way, but as we got near the clearing not far ahead of us I saw a small doe, which was no good since we were allowed to shoot only bucks. We kept moving toward her. Mamie was a few feet to my right and Ben a few feet to the right of her. He hollered for Teddy not to shoot – a doe was coming out. As soon as the doe hit the edge of the trees, she broke into a frantic run. Teddy bounced up from behind a drift and started firing.

"Doe! Doe!" shouted Ben.

But the spray of the carbine was too loud for Teddy to hear. As the first bullets whizzed by, the doe spun round and headed back for the trees. Teddy spun with her, raining a storm of bullets as he turned. I could hear lead slapping the trees and I could see twigs shattering and falling like a plague of centipedes. Everything happened so fast I never even thought of taking cover. Teddy held the carbine at his hip and kept his trigger finger in motion, firing in the same zig-zag pattern the deer was making as it ran towards us. Out of the corner of my eye, I saw Ben go down. He was clutching his chest. The doe was hit too. She staggered in the snow but didn't fall. Teddy ran out of bullets and changed clips and ran after the doe, giving her another burst. Her hindend exploded. She kept trying to crawl away, using her front legs to inch her body along. She went down and got back up, her front hooves flailing at the snow, trying to dig her way to safety inside the trees.

The firing stopped. Teddy was cussing and banging his fist on the side of his rifle. "Jammed!" he shrieked. "Jammed, the goddamned thing!"

The doe quit struggling and stood there in front of us, her spindly front legs stiff at the knees and quivering, her head up, her tongue out, her eyes huge. Her bloody bottom steaming in the snow. Mamie went to the doe and caught her by the head and stroked her gently. Then took her head to one side and gave it a quick twist. Something popped and the doe went limp. Mamie left the doe and walked over to Teddy and snatched the rifle from him.

"What?" he cried. "Again? Again you take my gun? You two-ton turd, gimme that right now!" He kicked her in the shins and punched her face, but it was like he was hitting her with clubs made of foam rubber. She tossed the rifle behind her so that it spun through the sky up, up, and up, like a dark spear doing cartwheels. Teddy was screaming in her face, his huge teeth snapping. She took hold of him by the crotch and neck, turned him upside down, and rammed him in the snowdrift so hard he went out of sight, except for his boots and red socks flailing, having a tantrum.

Mamie hurried over to Ben lying bloodied and looking dead. She picked him up and hustled with him to the pickup truck. Somehow I got my numb brain to order my numb feet to move and run after them. As I climbed in behind the wheel, I looked back across the meadow, and I saw the body of the doe between a pair of maples, its bare branches reaching towards the sky as if protesting or pleading. Behind the deer was a pool of blood soaking up the snow. A few yards into the open was the drift and Teddy's boots sticking out of it still pounding the sky. I wondered if he would suffocate. Mamie nudged me and jerked her thumb toward the main road. To hell with Teddy, we had to go. I looked at Ben draped across her lap, washed in his own blood just the way Amoss had been.

"Shades of Amoss," I said. "Why is this happening?"

"Kritch'n, go!" she ordered.

It took us thirty minutes to get Ben to the hospital in Park Falls. At the emergency room it was a replay of what had happened with Amoss. Ben was put on a stretcher and wheeled away down a hall and through some double doors. A man in a white coat shoved a paper on a clipboard at us and asked about insurance. I backed away and said, "I don't know nothing. We found him like that."

"Well, who is he?" said the man.

I told him to get a hold of Lily Snowdy. Mamie and I left the man looking puzzled and suspicious and saying we had to stay because there had to be an investigation. He followed us out to the parking lot.

"I've got your license number," he said as we pulled away.

We drove back to the Snowdy farm. It took us about an hour to get there, and as we pulled up Teddy himself came out the back door, carbine in hand. Mrs. Snowdy came with him.

"Get off! Get off my land!" Teddy bellowed.

"How could you do that to my boy!" cried Mrs. Snowdy. "Shame on you!"

"Hold on!" I told her. "How the hell did he get here so fast?"

"No thanks to you, some hunter rescued him. He almost asphyxiated!"

"Get off!" screeched Teddy.

"He shot Ben! Shot him in the chest!"

"What? What did you say?"

"I never did!" said Teddy.

"Shot him bad. We took him to Park Falls. They need you to sign papers."

"Ben! Shot?"

"Shot him in the chest."

"He's alive?"

"He was when we left. But he's lost a lot of blood."

She looked at her son. "You shot your father! You shot my husband!"

"On accident, Mommy!"

"He shot your Ben, Mrs. Snowdy," I said.

"On accident! I was shooting at a deer. I was gonna tell you about it. This deer—"

"Shut up you! How bad is he, Christian?"

"Not good, Mrs. Snowdy. Not good. Look at Mamie's coat. That's his blood."

When she saw the blood she went nuts. She turned on Teddy and started pounding him with her fists, punching him so hard his glasses flew off and blood spurted from his nose. "You you you!" she screamed, smacking him with all she had, driving him back to the pickup, where he turned and leaned across the fender, letting her pound on his back until she was exhausted.

When she finally stepped back, he peeked under his arm and said, "It was on accident. I was gonna tell you, Mommy. It was on accident."

"Shut up," she ordered. "Just shut your stupid face! Get in that goddamn pickup and get me to that hospital!" She kicked his rump. "Move!" she told him.

Teddy scrambled in the snow and found his glasses and jumped into the pickup. Hit the starter. Mrs. Snowdy got in, took another whack at him, and pointed towards the road. They shot down the driveway, the back end of the pickup fishtailing, the engine roaring. I could see Mrs. Snowdy continually smacking Teddy and yelling something in his ear.

In front of us was a road with several inches of hard-packed snow making walking treacherous. On both sides were ditches banked with more snow. Long, slow-rolling fields met lines of trees farther out. Here and there barbed-wire fencing enclosed plots of

216

pasture. I knew that inside the barns we passed were tons of hay. The silos were packed with silage, and the machinery was greased and put away for spring. Chickens huddled in straw nests inside their coops. Outside Dutch doors cows stood in line, wanting to get back in the barn where they could eat and be warm. And I knew that it all seemed quiet and calm – everyone and everything settled in for a long winter's nap. Time to rest. And I knew also that what I looked at was a lie. The cold would cause pipes to freeze and break, milkhouse drains to plug, water cups to ice up, frozen manure to break the links in barn cleaner chains. The cold would make batteries die and tractors not start and hydraulic lines get so sluggish the frontend loader buckets wouldn't raise or lower. The cold would give the outside heifers frostbite and even kill some of them from dehydration because they wouldn't get enough water. And the fires would roar up chimneys and cause fires, and some farmers would watch helplessly as their houses burned and curse themselves for using green wood. Some fan or exhaust motor or overloaded fuse in a barn wouldn't be able to take the load of twenty-four-hours-a-day running the exhaust fans, and there would be a spark, a cobweb would flare up and catch a bit of hay, and in an hour the barn would be black boards and ashes, and the cows and calves would be dead. Winter was always a fooler. It never was or will be a farmer's favorite time of year.

My thoughts went back to Ben and how it must have hurt to get smacked by a bullet in the chest like that. In my mind I saw him falling and saw the deer's rump explode, saw the twigs and bark showering down. Could have been me all bloody and dying like that. Could have been Mamie. Snow like a raspberry cone underneath her. And did Teddy mean for it to happen? I wondered. Teddy had said he would wait in ambush, set up flanking fire, but had he meant ambush for the deer or for Ben? Could any son, even a Teddy, shoot his father?

And I asked myself where are we going? The road stretching out like a white ribbon in front of us going west or east forever, it seemed, leading us somewhere new again, maybe even crazier than where we had just been. I didn't know. I only knew we had to get there. Find shelter. Food. And keep our exiled selves from freezing.

Good Country People

Mamie and I made about ten miles before it started getting dark. The clouds had cleared away, the sun glittering white gold like a jewel in a blue icebox. A narrow road ran off to our right. Barren trees lined the north side of the road – tall, thin poplars in tangled columns all the way back to a long, white building that looked like a warehouse. We headed for it to get out of the freezing air. A half-mile or so east we could see a farmhouse with a barn nearby. In every other direction there was nothing but snowy fields or naked trees.

The warehouse had some steps in front leading to a loading platform and a sliding door that wasn't locked. We jerked the door back just far enough to squeeze inside. In one corner beneath a window were a desk and a chair coated with dust. A Sears-Roebuck catalogue and some farm implement magazines were strewn over the desk. I picked up the catalogue and shook the dust off of it. The year on the cover said 1941. Everywhere else there were gunnysacks wall-to-wall, stacked six or seven feet high, with narrow walkways crisscrossing and winding in and out like a maze. We made our way from the front to the back of the stacks and found a small window and a door opening onto a yard, where an ancient iron-cleat tractor sat rusting away near a heap of equally rusty harrows and a stock tank and lots of rolled barbed wire and pieces of tin sheeting. A pile of old gears sat next to a stack of rotting two by twelve planks. The yard was a junk pile of someone's leftover dreams.

Mamie and I made a gunnysack bed next to the window. We covered ourselves with gunnysack blankets, and laid our heads on gunnysack pillows. Snuggled together, trying to ignore the rumblings in our stomachs and the memories of the hunt, we looked at the pictures in the Sears-Roebuck catalogue, old pictures of fashions gone by. We turned the pages and pointed at the things we wanted. I was surprised to see that Mamie wanted all the dresses. "That one, that one, that one." I had never thought of her in a dress. But I promised I would buy her one someday, and some high-heel shoes, and a hat with a feather, and a pair of gloves that went up to the elbows. She tore out all the pages of things she coveted and stared at them as if she could will them to appear in the room. I went on looking for my own kinds of wishes, boots, blue jeans, cowboy shirts, until it got too dark to see.

In the middle of the night, I woke up so hungry I was ready to eat my own arm. I went outside and ate some snow. Which didn't help at all. The air was bitter cold, the sky ladled with the Milky Way. A full moon gave a bluish blush to the snow. Distant trees pointed black fingers at each other. Two hundred acres away I could see a yard light, a tiny, winking point, like a hovering star. I wondered if the farm underneath that light had a milkhouse and a bulktank full of milk. It seemed like it would be an easy thing to sneak over there and fill my belly, and maybe steal a pail of milk to bring back to Mamie. I decided it was worth the chance and I started down the road, the light providing a beacon leading to what might be the Promised Land. I didn't get very far before Mamie showed up. She had a gunnysack in one hand.

As we got close to the farm, we could see that the barn was old and small and had no signs of life – no trampled snow, no manure pile in back, and no fenced-off yard for cows. It was not a dairy. I told Mamie that we might as well go back to the warehouse and wait for morning and move on. There wasn't even a chicken coop for eggs. I turned around, but Mamie went toward the house.

Catching up with her I whispered in her ear that we might get shot trying to go inside the house to steal food. She wouldn't listen. I tagged along behind her, unable to think of anything else I could do. We scouted along the outside of the house, until we came to a pair of cellar doors. They weren't locked. We opened one door and climbed down some cement stairs that led into pitch darkness. I stopped at the bottom and heard Mamie moving around. The air was cool but definitely warmer than it was outside. Beside me I felt a damp cement wall and some shelves stacked with glass jars. A light came on and I saw Mamie standing beneath a bare bulb, her hand letting go of the chain switch. We looked the place over. There were hundreds of potatoes in open bins. Onions brimmed from burlap bags. Meats, mostly hams and bacon slabs, hung from the ceiling. The shelves were full of canned tomatoes, corn, green beans, peas, beets, carrots, pickles, and watermelon rinds. Gallon jugs of apple cider made a column across the floor beneath the shelves. I felt like I had morphed into Ali Baba.

"Shazam," I whispered.

Mamie plucked a smoked ham and a slab of bacon from the ceiling. I grabbed a jar of watermelon rinds, some potatoes and onions – stuffing all of it into Mamie's gunnysack. I took a jug of apple cider too. I told her we had enough and probably what we took wouldn't even be missed there was so much food. She turned out the light and we went back up the stairs, closing the door behind us softly, hardly making a sound. Home free so easy, I thought. Sliding along the house towards the driveway, I was about to leave when I felt a rap on the top of my head. Mamie grabbed me by the armpits and picked me up, held me to a window. Inside I saw a big table. On it I saw the outline of a cake, a double-layered one. Mamie smacked her lips and said, "Yum yum, Kritch'n."

"Not worth the risk," I told her.

"P-poof, poof," she replied.

Putting me down, she snuck around to the back door and slipped inside. I picked up the gunnysack and followed. The kitchen was warm and smelled of good things, like coffee and baked bread and fried ham and chocolate frosting. There was a cloakroom to the right of us and a refrigerator and stove straight ahead. Next to the stove was the entrance to the dining room. In the silence I could hear a clock ticking somewhere. I opened the refrigerator and found a bottle of milk and took it to the table, where Mamie was already devouring the cake. She smiled at me hugely, displaying a mouthful of chocolate teeth. The sight made me giggle. I stuffed the tabby-cap into my mouth to stifle the noise.

Before I could get a bite of the cake myself, car lights slashed across the window. A second or so later a bedroom door opened behind us, and a woman entered the room. She flicked the light switch on and the room lit up. She was in mid-yawn and her mouth froze open as she caught sight of us. She was wearing a blue terrycloth robe and fuzzy slippers. Her ankles were bony. Paper curlers in her hair made it look as if she had horn nubs coming out of her head. Her hands had gone to her cheeks, framing a face out of which two enormous eyes bulged in disbelief.

Out of the bedroom came a golden Labrador yawning and wagging its tail. It had sleepy eyes and a pet-me disposition. It sniffed my knee and I reached down and stroked its back. It stretched and yawned loudly. The woman still hadn't managed to scream or do anything. Behind her a grandfather clock tick-tocked slowly. And then there were heavy footsteps and a man walked in through the back door. He turned on the kitchen light and said, "What a night, Marge. I'm pooped." We could hear him taking his coat off and hanging it in the cloakroom. Then he was standing in the doorway of the dining room, looking at us. "Who are you?" he said. "Who are they, Marge?"

"I don't know, honey," she said. Then she blinked and seemed to wake up. She started shouting, "They're robbers! They're robbers!"

"Robbers?" said the man. He jumped back into the kitchen and we could hear him rummaging in one of the cupboards. I figured he was grabbing a cleaver to chop our heads off.

"Run for your life!" I yelled.

We bolted from the dining room and ran through the kitchen, where the man was standing with a pot in his hand. He walloped Mamie on the shoulder as she went by, and then walloped me on the elbow and made my crazy bone go wild. When we got outside we headed for the open field in the direction of the warehouse. Behind us I could hear the man yelling, "Sic em, Emma! Sic em, girl!"

And Emma did sic us. Sort of. In any case she came barking

after us. When she caught up with us she zoomed by, yip-yapping at God knows what, the moon maybe. She started zigzagging and leaping like she was on an airport runway getting ready to take off and fly. She ran so far in front of us that she became hardly more than an inkblot bouncing across the snow. We lost sight of her, but we could still hear her barking. The barking got quieter and quieter. Then louder and louder. As she came back into sight, I saw her stop and turn in a circle chasing her tail and growling. Then suddenly she was barking loudly again and jumping upwards like she was on a pogo stick. It looked like she was trying to bite the huge, hanging moon in the sky. I walked up to her and said, "Emma, what are you doing?" When she heard me she sobered up. Shaking her head, she barked seriously and circled around me.

Suddenly she dove in and grabbed one of my pant legs, shaking it like a rag and causing me to lose my balance. We tumbled into the snow together, Emma yelping as if I had shot her. I could hear the man yelling, "Emma! What's wrong? Where are you, Emma? Don't you hurt my dog whoever you are!" Fifty yards away I could see that the man hadn't left his porch. The cooking pot was hanging in his hand.

I lay there a few seconds while everything got quiet. Emma was looking at me sheepishly. Then her eyes fastened on my tabby cap a few feet away. She leapt up barking and she pounced on the cap like a pissed off lion. Sinking her teeth in she fought that tabby cap as if her life was at stake – shaking it wonderfully, rolling over on her back as it got the upper hand for the moment, then on her feet again more furious than ever, stomping the tabby cap, tossing it in the air, leaping after it as it tried to get away, snatching it not a moment too late and pulverizing it with a tremendous tearing of her teeth. When she finally finished, little remained of the cap but some patches of hide and fur. Satisfied that it was dead, Emma backed off and barked a few times in triumph. Jumping in she gave the pieces a few more bites and flipped them contemptuously over her shoulder.

"Good girl, Emma," I told her.

She came to me wagging her tail and panting. I kept calling

her a good girl, the fiercest fighter dog in the world. She whined and put her head under my arm. I gave her a hug and scratched her chest. Mamie picked up the remains of my cap, a scrap that looked like a beanie. She put it on my head. It felt wet and sort of slimy and I said to Mamie, "Feels like I'm wearing a dead man's scalp."

She snorted laughter and pointed at me and said I looked funny.

"Oh yeah," I said. "Real funny, Mamie. My cap is ruined, so now my head and ears are gonna freeze. I got a bump on my elbow where that damn pot hit me. It still hurts like crazy. And so does my knee from falling over this dumb dog here. And you know what, I'm still hungry. And dammit, you ate that chocolate cake and I got not even one measly bite. We could have been back in the warehouse by now and eating ham and drinking apple cider, instead of being chased by this brainless Labrador. And all because of you and that bloody cake!

Mamie pulled me into her arms and squashed me.

"Lemme go!" I told her. I shook myself loose and started limping toward the warehouse. Mamie and Emma followed. I turned on the dog and told her to go home. I tried to kick at her, but it made my knee hurt more, so I made a snowball and threw it at her. She liked it. She tried to catch it in her mouth. "Stupid dog," I said and trudged away.

It was a relief to get into bed and pull the gunnysacks over me. Mamie got in too, and Emma went round and round between us until she had the place to her liking. She settled down with her chin resting on my stomach. She whined softly and wouldn't quit until I petted her head and told her she was a good girl. I told Mamie that we didn't dare sleep too long, in case the man came looking for his dog in the morning. She reached over and patted the gunnysacks close to my sides, tucking me in. She pressed her head against my shoulder and soon fell asleep, her breath still smelling of chocolate.

It was Emma's leaving the bed that woke me in the morning. I cracked my eyes open a sliver and saw the man from the house standing over us. Emma yawned and stretched. She reached her head up to him for a pat. He scratched her nose, all the while looking from me to Mamie and Mamie to me. His brow was furrowed, his eyes sad. He was a worn-out looking fellow, with a face full of deep lines beneath a stocking cap that covered his ears. He was thin and not very tall. His hands had the look of burnt cowhide, cracked and dark. He must have stood there for a full minute before he took Emma and went away. A few seconds later I heard a car door slam. Then I heard footsteps again. The man had brought his wife to see us. In her hand was a jug of cider. In his hand was a bulging gunnysack.

"See?" he whispered to his wife.

"Poor things," she said, setting the jug down.

He dropped the gunnysack on the bed between Mamie and me. Neither of them said another word. They left and soon I heard the car pulling away. I looked over at Mamie and nudged her. She opened her eyes.

"We got the food," I said. "They give it to us. Those people we stole it from."

She rubbed her eyes and yawned.

"Aren't some folks great?" I said.

We dug into the gunnysack and made ourselves a breakfast of cold ham and watermelon rinds and apple cider.

And then it was time to get going.

Outside, the sun was a foot or two above the horizon. It was so cold I wouldn't have been surprised to see our breath freeze and fall on the loading platform. In our sack there was still a lot of food, but when it was finally gone we would be right back where we had started. Nothing to eat, no place to go. I told Mamie there was nothing to do but make our way back to Temple and stay with Shepard.

We followed the road for about a quarter mile, then came to a crossroads and turned west. Looking back, I could see where the house sat, all but invisible at the top of the hill, far away, surrounded by glittering snow. And I had a notion that maybe my mother's and sister's prayers had led us to such good-hearted humans. Or maybe it was the piece of Robbie that he said was attached to us and everyone else in the world. Maybe his spirit had guided us there, who knows? All these tiny miracles coming our way, making Teddy's bullets pass us by, finding us shelter and prompting two strangers to feed us when we were on the verge of starving. The road stretched before us thin and white and feeling endless. It was a fair walk to Temple yet. But our bellies were warm, and our memories of the man and woman and their dog Emma, living in the white house on the white hill, were as warm, I'm convinced, as memories (or blessings) will ever get in this go-round life.

Anna Gulbrenson

We walked all day, not daring to stop, it being so cold that anything not moving was bound to freeze, and we finally made Temple about an hour after dark. We got to Shepard's soon after, but he wasn't home. His bedroom window wasn't locked, so I opened it and we crawled inside. It was fine to feel the warmth of the place and to see the familiar mess of books in his room. But when we went into the living room and turned on the light, something was missing. There weren't any books. No crates of books stacked up, no books on the shelves – no shelves even – no books on the coffee table, and none on the couch or chair or floor. In the kitchen on the table, was the dictionary and sheets of paper covered with words and definitions and "yum yum" written beside them, but everywhere else I looked – no books. I was puzzled. "Maybe those book-burning Christers raided his house," I told Mamie.

We would have to wait for an answer, so in the meantime we emptied the gunnysack and fixed ourselves some fried ham and bacon and potatoes and more watermelon rinds and cider. Then we took a hot shower together, scrubbed each other and came out pink and squeaky-clean. I grabbed a pair of Amoss's overalls and a blue work shirt and put them on. And a pair of his woolly socks. Mamie dressed in Shepard's overalls and checkered shirt. The overalls were baggy in the belly but fit her well enough. At least they were clean. We threw our dirty clothes in the laundry for washing later.

Not long after we heard a pounding on the porch – *boom boom boom*! – and Shepard's voice calling. "What incubus within wastes Edison's glory? Speak out, housebreaker, lest my wrath I unleash!"

226

When I opened the door, Shepard took two steps back and turned as if he were going to run. Stopping in mid-stride he cried out, "Crystal?" His head whipped back around, his surprised eyes fastening onto me. "Is that you? Yes, it is. It's Crystal! Where's Mamie? Tell me she's in there!"

"Sure she is," I said.

Mamie peered over my shoulder. "Yaay, Ssshep," she greeted him.

"We've come to wear out our welcome," I told him.

"You've come back to me, my precious pride, my metronome of love, oh yum yum!" He tore open the screen door and pushed me aside. Clutching Mame, he kissed her on both cheeks and cooed, "Soo happy, happy, happy you're here." Then he broke down in tears and shoulder-heaving sobs that went on for at least half of a minute before he whipped his hanky out and wiped his face and blew his nose and said, "I thought I had lost you for forever to that vicious imp of an ilk. I'm so glad you came to your senses and left him. We've got to celebrate!"

He motored to the kitchen and came back with a jar of splow. We each took sips of the vile stuff as we sat around the coffee table and I told Shepard about what Teddy had done to his father.

Shepard kept nodding his head wisely. "It seems inevitable now," he said. "You know, looking back at the events of their lives, a man of my extraordinary gifts should have predicted such an acidic super sulfate savage show, and if you'll recall I did say something to the effect that Teddy's mind was a carving block of perverted Oedipudal cravings." Shepard's finger shot up and he shouted, "Beware of mad little bastards who want to sleep with their mommy! And yet it was – ahem, I say – perhaps it was a lavation for them both, a washing, a cleansing – to make clean. I mean if Ben lives through it, he will be purified, you see. No more meretricious show for the sake of his shrinking Lily. She who has had the man long-chained to her pubic hairs from the beginning, even before Eden was breached by the birth of Theodore, her monstrous teddy of a baby. Who still is and ever will be. Take note, Crystal, of everything I say. Such profundities come never when you're not around me."

"Yeah, but you should have seen how Mrs. Snowdy smacked Teddy when I told her what he had done. She hit him so hard his nose bled. I'm telling you she went nuts. I bet she'd never hit him in her life. He was really stunned, you could tell. He looked like he thought he was dreaming, having a nightmare."

"Good for her," Shepard said. "I'd have physically sanitized that flim-flam clot of garget long ago. In fact, I would have divined what was coming and pinched his head off when he was birthed. Such clairvoyance would have saved a world of woe and made a morsel of his potent curse. The thing is, Crystal, when my blood is up I am magnificently awesome."

"If you say so."

"I do say so. There is no denying the fact that I am capable of terrifying acts of corporeal desecration. You have never seen me with my blood up. He's lucky it was Lily punching him and not yours truly." Shepard's eyes narrowed with the toughness of his talk. His walrus teeth probed viciously from under his mustache.

"Well," said I, "lucky for him you weren't there."

"That goes without saying. Indeed, Teddy has the luck of the devil. Can you imagine how I would have crushed him?" Shepard grabbed himself in a bear hug and growled.

"He's no damn good," I said. "Someone should have crushed him long ago."

"Son of a cloven hoof. Lower than snakeshit in a ditch. Less than the most contemptuous hoi polloi. Hoi polloi – the masses, the common humph."

We spent some minutes dragging Teddy Snowdy through the gutter. And then Shepard switched the subject to the Artlife and what he was doing there. On schedule, he said, and ready to open in January. Or February at the latest. He had bought paintings by Wisconsin underwood artists, which he was hanging on the walls for customers to buy. A few telling totems had arrived from British Columbia, Wolf Clan, Crow Clan mixtures full of beaver, salmon, hawk and frowning gargoyle incredibles to scare ghosts away. First-rate underwood art every one of them from three to five feet high. He would put totems on the map for the lower forty-eight, and people from Maine to southern California would plant them on their lawns as spiritual guardians of the house. Just like the Greeks did with Hermes, those phallic symbols offering sexual potency. And he had all of his books lined up on shelves over there in the lobby as well. We had come at a perfect time to help. We would work together and together watch the dream unfold. We would sell books and paintings and sculptures and tickets. Tickets to see the best movies ever made – true art, nothing less. Movies that the ordinary ilk could imitate with no shame. No *Billy Buck Does Dodge City* or crap like that.

"Laurence Olivier! Ralph Richardson! John Barrymore! Garbo! Bogart! Gable! Cooper! Vivian Leigh, yum yum, and more ad infinitum! Pure strokes of genius all. Not only fortune, but fame would descend upon Donald Leonardo Shepard, the Great Creator, the Shakespeare and Milton of his time. No brag, just fact. Tee hee."

While Shepard was talking, Mamie killed the jar of splow. She licked the rim and handed the jar to him and said, "More." And I was thinking, oh no, here we go again.

Shepard got up and got another jar and passed it around. Just smelling splow was enough to make my head spin. "What is this stuff anyway?" I asked.

"Splow? It's God's elixir. It's wood-brewed by leprechauns living deep in the forest lighting fires underneath copper kettles filled with sweet corn and winter wheat and steel-cut oats. When the process is ripe God's elixir egresses the tube one drop at a time into a jug very slow plip, plip. Add the *p* to *slow* and you've got *splow*. Savvy?"

I nodded my head.

"But listen," said Shepard. "I've gotten to be good friends with Anna Gulbrenson across the street, that vigilant pixie who called you thieves that day you were unable to get into the house. She's the astronomer of our little enclave here. Nothing escapes the keen probing of her eagle eye. You've got to meet her. It's destiny, I'm telling you."

And he went on to tell us that Anna had been helping him renovate the Artlife. She also gave him daily reports about whatever transgressing perpetrator might be slinking by, all of them wanting to look up her dress, of course, all of them thieves and murderers looking for nefarious opportunities.

"She is a Sargasso Sea of unfathomed motives," he said. "Unfathomed motives, I say – unfathomed motives lying deeply within the depths of that suspicious bosom of hers. Neurotic to say the least, but also a dear little thing full of energy and a willingness to work that defines the very word itself." He glanced at me, blinking his eyes and rubbing his nose with pleasure and giving me a gummy, gap-toothed grin. "It's time you two met the nemesistic Anna Gulbrenson. A tart, she is, and a hag - part pixie-harridan, and three-fourths valentine with a heart as big as the word gloriolisciosus. You'll love her! I'll be right back!"

He rose puffing and snorting and left the house. I watched him chugging across the street to Anna's house. A few minutes later the two of them came arm in arm, him leading her sideways into the living room. It would have taken three of her to make one of him. Tiny she was, but not quite a midget, missing maybe an inch or two to fit that category. She came in rubbing her hands and saying, "My oh my, fweezing off my toot-toot. Vut a cold vinter."

When he introduced her, she shook her finger, saying she remembered how we scared her half to death that day she yelled at us. "I tot you ver teeves!" She threw her head back and laughed loudly, her eyes closing, her salt and pepper hair shaking all over her shoulders. "Teeves!" she repeated. "Ha! Ha!"

We all laughed with her. To me she looked to be about forty-five or maybe fifty, somewhere in that range. She had crescent eyes, high cheekbones and thick eyebrows. Her skin was very pale and contrasted wildly with the bright red lipstick gashed across her mouth. Her teeth were too perfect to be her own. She had what I would call a choir soprano voice.

Coming close she chucked my chin and said, "Vut a mama's boy you are. So pwetty I take you home vit me."

"You see why I named him Crystal?" said Shepard. "Tee hee hee! Anna understands. Anna knows. Don't you, Anna? Sit your little toot-toot down. Let me get you a glass of splow."

She stared at Shepard suspiciously as he poured her a glass. "A dwop of dat voud kill me, mister," she said. "Vut you got dat for doink?"

"Nectar of the gods, Anna. One-hundred-fifty-proof. Smooth as Halley's Comet streaking through the vacuum of eternity. Just a tad, my dear. Go ahead. Wet your tantalizing tongue."

"You vant to get Anna dwunk. I know you. Vant to see vut Anna's got up dis dwess. Gimme dat. I dwink it. Oh, vut a bad boy." She took the splow, sipped it, made a face. "Oh ho ho, dat's not so goot as aquavit, but I like it! Oh ho ho. Sit down, let's dwink some mo."

Happily Shepard eased his bulk beside her and took a long drink out of the jar. Anna turned her attention to Mamie and me. She wanted to know if we were brother and sister. I told her we were cousins. She said I looked like an unfed version of Mamie, which was news to me, as I never thought Mamie looked even a little bit like me.

"Occasionally in the course of time some people grow to look like each other," said Shepard. He agreed I had some of Mamie in me, especially the open sheen of my blue eyes, the wide shine of my forehead. Put some freckles there and it would be exactly like hers, he claimed.

Mamie was smiling broadly at Anna and Anna said, "Hey, pwetty one, you got a gap in you teef. Vunce I had a gap like dat. Da men, it dwives dem cwazy. Sexy vooman vit a gap like dat. Dem damn dentist pull my teef out all gone because I got a gum infestation. You vant to see?" She took her thumb and forefinger and popped her teeth out. "Thexy, huh?" she said, batting her eyelids at us and laughing. The teeth went back in. She took another sip of splow and made a face like she was dying.

Then she said, "So! Tell to Anna, tell me vut you be. Novegian, I tink. And some Iwish?"

I shrugged. "Heinz fifty-seven, I guess."

"Nope. Novegian. Iwish. Dats vut you be. Anna knows dees tinks."

Shepard got some glasses and poured us all a shot or two, saying it was time we drank like civilized human beings instead of swilling out of the same jar. Every time Anna would take a drink, he would tip more splow into her glass. She accused him of wanting to get her drunk so she would pass out on the couch and he could look up her dress. Take advantage of her.

"*Oh Anna, oh Anna, oh Anna oh!*" he sang.

She giggled and called him "dewil" and slapped his knee over and over. They roared laughter into each other's faces. The sound made me think of two braying donkeys. She turned away, wiping her eyes with the heels of her hands and saying, "Oh, my oh my, sooch a time we hawink."

There was a scratching at the door and Anna jumped up to open it. "Vut you doink, Chee Chee?" she said. "Twyink to fweeze you little toot-toot? Get in heah." She was shaking her finger at a pug nose dog with big black eyes, eyes that looked dipped in maple syrup." Picking the dog up, she pretended to spank it, while it squirmed happily in her arms, its pink tongue trying to lick Anna's face off.

"Dis my Chee Chee," she told us, holding the dog out for us to see. "Is she pwetty?" Chee Chee looked back and forth from me to Mamie to Shepard, her little head and ears quivering with excitement. Anna sat down with the dog in her lap. She gave it a lecture. "So you make it too much noise fo Sowen daddy, ya? And he can't vatch dat telewision, ya? And he kick you out, got-dammit him, in the snow. Po baby-vun, you come to Mommy. Naughty, naughty, but Mommy lowes you anyvay. But don't you cwoss dat stweet alone. Comes a auto smash you like Chee Chee pancake, ya. And den all gone Chee Chee, poof like dat, no mo. Vut a bad papa you got. Some day I bweak dat telewision vit a baseball bat."

Shepard was smoothing his mustache and putting on his wise man face, his nose hoisted like a monument. His eyes with a look of superior superiority. "Television, humph. Television is an instrument providing painless lobotomies to the masses. Television turns their minds into the semblance of shredded cabbage. No longer is religion the opiate of the people. Now the opiate is television. The long slide to arrogant ignorance is well underway because of that loquacious instrument. The death of the novel, the death of critical thinking, the death of writing anything worth reading, the death of perspicacity and discernment and acute wisdom will be the by-products of television. Curse of earth. Shrinking the brain cells of whomever it touches. Driving the pure products of America crazy – i.e., TV. Television." Proud of his speech, Shepard's eyes swept over us like a pair of giddy pilot lights.

"Pure products of America go crazy! I know that from somewhere. I read it in one of your books."

"William Carlos Williams, dear boy."

"Opiate! Ya!" said Anna. "I tell dat to Sowen. Dat tink make him a wegtable! Shwedded cabbage." She drained her glass again and said she had changed her mind about splow. It was better than aquavit. Splow should be the opium of the people! Everyone would be friends then.

Shepard poured her glass full. "The genius who makes this libation," he said, "is a local backwoods boy named Bob Thorn. Let's drink to him."

So it wasn't leprechauns? We toasted Bob Thorn.

Shepard shifted his attention to Mamie. "By the way, my mastodon beauty, goddess of my stupendous soul, my Valkyrian heartthrob, Bob Thorn knows you. He says you are on his shit list for good. Apparently you wounded his pugilistic pride. He said you outwrestled him. Tee hee!"

"Yeah, that's true," I said. And I told him what happened the day of the book-burning, when Bob Thorn tried to tackle Mamie and she tossed him into the bushes.

Anna pinched Mamie's leg and told her she didn't sound like much of a gentile lady.

"Genteel," corrected Shepard.

Mamie pinched Anna back. "Ooch, oh my-my, Bwunhilde, dat make a bwuse on po Anna. Don't be a naughty vun. Let's be fwiends." She patted Mamie's hand carefully. "My my, oh my, is it varm in dis woom, or is it yoost me?" And down went the splow in noisy gulps.

"More, my dear?" said Shepard, holding the jar out.

"Oh my, oh my. Vell, vhy not?" He filled her glass again. Some of it went over the edge onto her lap. Chee Chee licked at it. "Dats not fo you, Chee Chee. Bad dog. Oops, look out, my teef."

She jammed her thumb against her teeth. "Sometimes dey fall out. Den I talk funny some. Oh my."

"Den I talk funny some. Oh my," said Mamie.

Anna's brows shot up. "Hey, dat's pwetty goot. Can you do udders? Is she a comic?"

"Mamie can do just about anybody," I said. "She's a mimic."

Anna thought about it a second. "Ya, so vut dat do fo you? Makes you money?"

"Well, it's just a neat trick is all. Because I mean otherwise she doesn't talk so good. Just when she's mimicking."

"You know vut I say? Vagner vud put dis vun in a opwa. Bwunhilde."

"Brunhilde, indeed. A treasure, a magnificent example of a creature created perfect." Shepard's mustache shivered as he stroked Mamie's leg. "I'm going to teach her to run the projector. I'm going to give this precious one a profession, a future. I'm going to teach her to read and write. I'm going to rescue her from her abyss of ignorance. I'm going to give her knowledge that is inextinguishable. I'm going to release her from those dark caverns of unenlightenment where Plato's cave dwellers mark the passing of shadows on the wall. On the other hand, I'm going to unchain her mind and take her up the path into the sun of illuminated knowledge, wisdom, foresight, common sense, the inspiring breath of imagination. On the other hand, I'm going to give her words – words! – to fill the hollows of her mind, transforming her, metamorphing her into an irresistibly sapient example of pulchritude and pride. This daughter of the earth, the contours of cosmic soul beaming through her smile, the power of a goddess dripping from her fingers, she the manipulator of tomorrow holding the whole world in the palm of her hand. On the other hand, I'm going to—"

"Ya, ya, okey-dokey, vee get it," said Anna. She jerked her thumb at him and said to me, "You unnerstand dis man?"

"Sometimes."

"Den I put you in dis pocket." She held out her arms. "Gimme hug. I giwe you sooch a sqveez, you pwetty boy, so polite." She caught me suddenly and kissed my cheek. The movement threw

Chee Chee on the floor. She scrambled up on her short legs and gave my ankle a nip. I kicked her under the chin, which made her yelp and back off.

"Don't be a naughty vun," said Anna, picking up Chee Chee. "Mommy can kiss dis pwetty boy if she vant to. I spankee you, you don't be nice to him." She squeezed the dog till its tongue stuck out as far as it could go. "Oh my," said Anna, "vut a time vee hawink. Sowen should come. I tell to him, 'Sowen, life too tough, ya? But nuttink happen so bad dat vee can't vait for sometink betta to come along. Dat vheel come up to fowtune again fo us, and den vee be happy.' Dat's vut I say to him, but he don't lissen. He cwies he is a wictim. See now, vut a time vee hawink? Instead of vatchink telewision!"

"Have one more," said Shepard.

"Okey-dokey." Anna tilted her glass and let the last few drops fall on Chee Chee's tongue.

I recalled seeing Soren in his wheelchair, and I asked Anna what had happened to him and learned that he had broken his back in a shipyard accident. It had partially paralyzed his legs. He could stand up and shuffle along with canes, but he hardly ever used them, preferring to stay in his chair. Anna was ashamed of him.

The dog kept bugging her for more splow and Anna let her lick from the glass. "Oh my my, vut a time vee hawink." Anna fanned her face with her hand. Then she said we should sing God bless America. She wanted Mamie to sing it. But Mamie refused. Anna claimed that she was once a singer and dancer, a hoofer on the stage. And she was once a stunning beauty, she said. Men always wanting to look up her dress. Lots of times she let them. Why not? But now she could go naked in the street and no man gave a damn. It breaks your heart when men stop turning their heads to look. She asked me if I believed she was a beauty once.

"You're still pretty pretty," I said.

"Gimmee kiss!" She grabbed my head and planted a sloppy kiss on my mouth and laughed about it. She said I knew how to flatter a girl and she could tell that with my looks and manners I was going to get a lot of nooky when I grew up. "But look at dees legs!" she said. She pulled her skirt up over Chee Chee's wobbling head and stuck her legs out, rolling her tiny feet to show us what she had. "Not bad fo an ol lady, ya?" They were chubby and very white and blue veins showed through like lines on a map.

"Hmm, prime," said Shepard.

"Real nice," I said.

"Vut a polite boy. I put you in dis pocket." She kept saying how the boys used to chase her and how she used to be a sexy broad, a dream girl that men drooled over. But now no one looks at her that way because her breasts were falling to her belly button and her skin needs tons of moisturizers, and the wrinkles on her face are getting as deep as canyons. But what can you do? Nothing. Old age is the same dirty trick played on all of us. She stood up and tucked Chee Chee under her arm. Chee Chee's eyes rolled and she grinned, her tongue lolling out the side of her mouth.

"That dog's drunk," I said.

Anna stumbled to the door, hiccupping and saying, "Oh my!"

Shepard followed her. Bowing her through the door like Sir Walter Raleigh and saying, "O vision of pulchritude, yum yum. Pulchritude – from the Latin *pulcher*, beautiful, yum yum, dear female dipsodear making drunk my smitten heart."

"I twade Sowen fo you. Coochy, coochy!"

Shepard pounded his chest and gave a Tarzan yodel. They walked across the street together. Both of them unable to get words in edgewise through whatever the other was saying.

Words - lots and lots of them, and laughter fanning the freezing air, escorting the unlikely pair of dipsodears up the walkway. To the front door. Under the porch light he kissed her.

Secrets

Throughout November and December we stayed busy getting the Artlife ready for the grand opening. Painting the walls inside took the longest time, up and down ladders day after day with paint bucket and brush rollers. It was really boring hard work. Shepard had sent the seats out to be upholstered, and as they came back, we bolted them down auditorium style, about a hundred of them. We varnished the stairs that led to the projection booth. We cleaned all the carpets. We put in a popcorn machine and a candy counter and a refrigerator for apple juice and orange juice and cranberry juice. In all, we transformed the place, made it from a dingy, water-spotted, paint-peeling dilapidation into a pretty respectable house of art – what Shepard referred to as his "hall of inspiration."

While we were working to get the theater ready, Anna kept coming over to lend a hand. She had no problem with grabbing a paintbrush or a hammer or a saw and going to work on whatever needed doing. She could stay with it all day and keep up a constant rain of chatter too. Chee Chee was usually there ready to nip our ankles if they caused her any insult. Even Soren came over in his wheelchair sometimes to help out. He wasn't the talker Anna was. Nor did he have an accent like hers. When he spoke, he spoke slowly and to the point, like he only wanted to say it once and not waste words while he was at it. He had an old man's voice, full of gravel and always a bit of grump in it. His shoulders were broad and straight and thin as I-beams and his hands were large, the fingers thick and strong-looking, out of proportion to the shrunken rest of him - his skinny legs, his concave-nothing belly. His face was pasty pale from lack of sun. His eyes were deeply shadowed, like black holes out of which no light escaped.

It seemed every time he would come over, Anna would try to pick a fight with him, and she wouldn't let up until he exploded and responded one way or another. Sometimes even then she wouldn't quit. She'd always turn away and smile impishly when he yelled at her. There wasn't much for her to pick on, but she made the best of it, saying to him what a slob he was because he dripped paint on his pants, and how he could never learn to hold the brush so the paint wouldn't run up the handle, and how he cleared his throat so noisily it made her sick, picked his nose so much it made her sick, when he coughed the bubbling mucus in his lungs it made her sick, broke wind so often it made her sick, the smell of his feet made her sick, the dandruff in his hair made her sick and so on and so forth. Stuff like that, almost always the same complaints every day, like she needed to rile him, make him mad to see if he still had any fight left in him - if he was still *alive*.

One day I asked him how he broke his back. He tried to tell me, but Anna kept interrupting, wanting to tell the story herself. He let her talk for a while. Then he grumbled at her, telling her she had diarrhea of the mouth. She fired back that he sounded like a senile old goat.

"You stupid bitch," he said, his voice slow and reedy with anger. "Shut up and let me talk. It's my goddamn story, not yours."

"You don't know fo shit!" she said.

"I don't know for shit? Was I there? Or did it happen to someone else? Did it happen to you?"

She kicked his wheelchair. "I know the twuth."

"So do I. You think because you *heard* the story that you remember it precisely. You need to shut up, Anna, and listen better."

"You shut up, you old goat."

"I'm gonna punch you."

"Twy it! I'll punch you back. Phooey on you. Go 'head tell you stowy. Old goat." Anna had a brush full of varnish in her hand. She flipped the bristles and spattered Soren's face.

"You want to blind me?" he said.

238

"Now you got fweckles like Mamie," she said. Her laugh echoed off the high ceiling.

"You think it's funny to pick on a crippled man!"

"Ah phooey, you big baby. Tell you stowy."

Soren looked at me, his dark eyes seeming to sink to the center of his skull. His face was covered with shiny dots of varnish. "What do you think of a woman who gets her kicks out of picking on a man in a wheelchair?"

I didn't want to get in the middle of it. I looked at Shepard, hoping he would help me out. Switch the subject or something.

"These epithalamiums must cease and desist," he said. "These nuptial songs must end, must give pause for more serious literary endeavors, like painting the shelves or varnishing the rails or—"

"Sooch a big baby!" said Anna.

And Soren said, "Nit wit! Shut the fuck up!" He wheeled his chair around so his back was to Anna. She rolled her eyes and grinned like a mischievous child. She had riled him good, forced him to show her that there was giddy-up in his old carcass yet.

"I'll tell you how my back was broken," he said. "If that dumb broad will keep her mouth shut for a second." He glanced over his shoulder at her, eyes searing her. "I worked twenty-nine years as a crane rigger, Christian. You see these hands? These hands used to know how to work. I didn't miss a day of work for over twenty years."

Checking his hands I noted again how muscular they still were. They still looked powerful, unlike the rest of him.

"One day I was with a rigger named Neil Connolly hooking up forty feet of scaffold to take away from the side of a ship. We didn't know that the pipes holding the scaffold welded to the ship's side had been cut away already. You're not supposed to burn the welds until the crane has hooked up and can hold the scaffolding in place. That particular section weighed a couple of tons, and it was just standing there by itself, forty feet high and narrow, ready with the slightest nudge to fall over and crush us. The gantry was coming down the rail tracks behind us making the quay sway. Sort of rippling from all the weight, you could feel it through the bottom of your boots. Those gantries are monsters a hundred and ten feet tall with a hundred and sixty feet of boom jutting out. They create little earthquakes wherever they go. Neil was climbing the scaffold to hook up the chokers. I was climbing up behind him. We didn't get there. Halfway up I could feel the vibration of the gantry as it got closer and closer. And then I felt the scaffold twisting and saw that some stupid burner had cut the welds. I yelled jump! just as it started over. Taking Neil and I with it. I was slammed onto the craneway right next to a bunch of barrels that blocked the piping from falling on me and smashing me to death. But Neil wasn't so lucky. He was buried under a pile of two by twelve planks that had been stacked at the top of the scaffold making it top-heavy as hell, of course. Neil's liver was ruptured and a bunch of other stuff. He lived about thirty minutes. When the other workers uncovered him, I looked over at his bloody body and yelled, 'Neil! Neil! I can't feel my legs!' He opened his eyes and looked at me for the last time. 'Oh, shit, Soren,' he said. 'Oh, shit.' Those were his last words. Neil was a victim of hurry-up money. Can't take two minutes for a crane to hook up and make things safe before you burn the welds and free the structure. Hurry, hurry, that's what bosses want. Saving five minutes is more important to them than you are. Grind up Neil. Grind up Soren. Grind up you too, and throw you away if you let them. You understand what I'm saying?" He shook his head at the bitter memory and wheeled away from us, across the entrance and out the door, his workman's hands pumping the wheels with murderous energy.

"Immutable web of history recycling the same stories down through the ages," said Shepard, his voice choking. "A never-ending story of the pecking order and men like Soren who pay the price of hurry-up money."

"I could hawe told it jus as goot," said Anna.

I had written my folks again just before Christmas and told them about our bad luck with Teddy Snowdy, and our good luck with the country people who fed us, and our who-knows-what-luck living with Shepard and working for him. I said how we were doing renovations to get the theater ready and Mamie was learning to run the projector and would have a skill to offer the workaday world. I told about Anna and Soren and Chee Chee too. In January I got a reply.

Dear Christian,

This is your Mama. Thank you for writing for Christmas. It wasn't the same without you. I sat and cried of a broken heart because I miss my little boy. The Lord above has a reason for all this I am sure but it breaks my heart. I wish you could come home now but Papa says you better not. As John Beaver is crazy and scaring us half to death. The boys take turns watching for him with the gun in their hands. He comes two or three times a week and stands in the snow at the bottom of the hill and cries out for his Mamie. Papa says things will get better with time. I pray he is right. I pray on my knees on the hard floor praying that John Beaver wont kill us and that you are safe wherever you are. I say Rosary every night on my knees on the hard floor. It hurts like the dickens. Which is good because God and the Saints listen better if they know you are willing to pray to them in pain. This is common knowledge for Catholics. All suffering of any kind is ultimately good for you. My arthritis and bad sciatic nerve is earning me less time in Purgatory after I die. You should pray too Christian. Pray to Saint Jude. He is the one for you. Ask him for the faith to make you a Catholic. I always thought you might be the one boy who would come to the True Faith like Mary Magdalen did. I pray all the time that Papa will convert but after all these years it would be a miracle. Which the Holy Mother would have to make happen. But you are perfect for it Christian. You are the smart one. I am always proud of you in school. I always hoped you would become a priest. This would win me a place in Heaven guaranteed. Mothers of priests automatically go to Heaven. That is the deal. They are special above other mothers in Gods eyes. Mary the Mother of God would welcome me at the gates. Wouldn't that be something! It is a dream I have. It makes me feel my sufferings are all worth it. It keeps me from crying so much except when I think of you out there in the cold cruel world without your mother and father to protect you. Pray on your bare knees on a hard wooden floor for guidance from Jude, Saint of lost causes. Pray till you are in pain. He will listen then.

Love, Mama

Hey Christian,

So what do you think? John Beaver cant get up our driveway hill to get nobody. We watch him and shoot over his head if he tried to get up the hill. Cutham shot close enuff to kick snow in Beavers fool face one day but Pa says not to do it no more we might kill the booger and go to jail. If Beaver comes with a gun then we get to shoot his legs otherwise we dunt get to shoot him darn it. We hope he comes with a gun. He yells Mamie Mamie like a crazy echo chamber down there at the bottom of the hill. You should see him with his arms out like a big calvry cross yelling for her. Where is my Mamie? What did you do with my Mamie? Give me back my Mamie. And we tell him she is not here so he rolls in the snow and cusses and looks like Frosty the Snowman. We throw snowballs at him but he dunt care. He throws snowballs back at us and says words not fet for cows. They should take him to camlot and wash his mouth out with soap. He is a crazy purson. What a goon. But dunt be scard you are the little brother and your big brothers are looking out for you. We have a sprize for Beaver. We cant tell you what it is yet but boy will he be sprized.

Calvin Cutham Cush Calah Cash

Brother Christian,

We sure miss you bad. As I told you before you are our hero. At Christmas we sang the Battle Hymn of the Republic just for you. And we read the part in your letter about the man and his Dog Emma who chased you and tore up your hat that you said Teddy made out of a cat who stoled the crow that he shot. What a nice man that fellow was to see you weren't a crook really and give you and Mamie food so you won't starve. Mama and I said three Hail Marys in his honor that God may bless him and his wife Marge and Emma the Golden Labrador who was sure a sweet thing for a dog. I want a dog but Pa says the cats in the barn are enough. We can keep them because they eat the rats and mice. A dog would do that too wouldn't it? Anyway there are some good people in this world aren't there Christian? You've had some bad luck in meeting some of the worst but you've met some of the best too, thank God, and that I am sure has kept you from becoming one of the tough guys who hates everything and wants to carry a knife or a gun. Isn't that right? This great adventure of yours has a purpose beyond what any of us can see right now. Of this, there is no doubt in my aching heart. Take care of Mamie. Aren't you sick of all the snow? I sure am. Happy Birthday, sweet sixteen. Sorry to tell you that so late. Have you been kissed yet?

Love, Mary Magdalen xoxoxo

Dear Son,

Well Christian its tough times all around. I know what Beaver wants to do. He wants to plague us into making you give back Mamie. But this we will never do. The Deity is on our side. He has told me in a dream that he has his eye on us. So I don't want you to worry. You have made us special and we will be worthy of it. We will keep that bastard at bay until he gets tired of his silly game or freezes to death out there at the bottom of the hill. The boys sure want to beat him up bad but I don't think so. He would cut some one. He is crazy but not so crazy to bring a gun. Then we could be in the right to shoot him in self defense. I think he is playing for our hearts when he cries out for Mamie so sad and rolls in the snow so we will feel sorry for him grieving the loss of his daughter. It sure don't work on me and the boys. All we want to do is boot his ass to kingdom come. He gets to Mama Ruth though. And a bit to Mary Magdalen. They feel sorry for him some days he cries so pitiful. But they would never tell him even the time of day, so don't worry. A female might have a soft heart for a man's troubles, but if they are protecting some one they love then their souls are hard as cast iron pots. That is woman for ye.

Beaver lets the boys hit him with snowballs sometimes. He stands there with his head down like a martyr. But you know the boys. When Beaver stands there they get bored and start throwing at each other. Beaver hears them squeeling and having a good time and he can't help but quit the martyr stuff. He

242

gets excited watching them and starts yelling for Calvin to watch out for Cush sneaking up behind, or telling Cutham to rub Cashs face in the snow, or telling Calah he don't throw no harder than a girl. As the war goes on they forget who they are and who John Beaver is. And he forgets too and starts throwing snowballs at them. Back and forth the snowballs go. Just a bunch of kids having fun. It has happened two or three times now and it is something to see. I just shake my head because what can you do with something like that? But you can see why I don't believe him when he wails for Mamie. It's hard to take some one like that serius. When they get all tuckered out from the snow wars, the boys get nasty and ask Beaver what does he think he is doing on their hill? He comes to his senses and cusses them good and goes down the hill to stand in the road and yelp like a dog.

What a clown. But I am not fooled. I know he is still a dangerus fellow and not to be taken with a grain of salt. I wish I could tell you when it will be over but only the Deity knows. I do know that it will be over some day. Everything ends some day. In the meantime you are safe and making a living with Mr. Shepard there, who seems to be a funny kind of fellow but also a good one. I would like to sit and talk to someone who knows so many words as you say he knows. Did he really read the dictionary cover to cover? You said he likes to say yum yum when he uses big words. I would like to hear that. It is a feeling I have had myself a time or two when I read Willie S. about Horatio and Hamlet or Emerson using such wonderful words as they do. The words seem to have a taste that makes my mouth glad to say them. "Oh, that this too solid flesh would melt into a dew!" yum yum. Yes. Try it in your mouth and I think you will understand Mr. Shepard better. Does he know quotes like that? Does he know any from Emerson? "Belief accepts the affirmations of the soul, unbelief denies them." I think that is how it goes. Can he whip the Bible on you? "All the horns of the wicked he will cut off, but the horns of the righteous shall be exalted." I walk around the farm with pieces of paper in my pockets and I memorize this and that. Keeps the cobs off my mind now that you are gone and we don't discuss these things anymore. Miss you sorely. Until we meet again, my son, lay low.

Your Papa who loves you

It made me feel real bad to know that John Beaver was plaguing my family like that. But I had no idea what to do about it. What Pa advised seemed to be right – lay low and see if time would settle Beaver down. I had my doubts that it would though. He wasn't a normal human being, who would get tired of the game eventually. I knew one thing in my heart for sure – he would never get Mamie back, not because of anything I could do about it, but because of what she could do. Mamie's mind had no connection with John Beaver's. She had cut herself off from him for good. She was a million light years above him, beyond him, like they were separate planets. If he only knew how wide the gap was between them, maybe he would give up trying to get her back.

But I also knew that there was no way to make him understand it. Even I, who knew her better than anyone, could not understand her, not what she was really. Or how she could do what she could do, which was anything she put her mind to. Retarded girls weren't like that. Retarded girls were – well, *retarded*. But where Mamie fit in the scheme of things, what category or label she had was impossible to tell. In the up and down scale of human beings she was a mystery. And probably always would be.

So Shepard had taught Mamie to run the projector. It was an old machine, but it looked pretty good because he had sent it to Chicago to have it overhauled. He called it Powers after the nameplate on its side: Powers Electrical Chicago. It stood on a base that had four little wheels that could be locked in place. A solid column stood on the base, like an elephant leg on a swollen elephant foot. The body of the projector was as large as a fifty-pound bale of hay. Jam a short pipe into one end of the bale and it might resemble the lens. Add a pair of twelve-inch pipes shooting up diagonally at each end of the bale so that they stick out a foot or so. Bolt a pair of twenty-inch clutch disks to the pipes and you would have a fair resemblance of Powers – bale of hay for the body, pipe for an eye, clutch disks for ears. And inside Powers, under a metal cover, there were numerous tiny wheels and gears that the film wound around, like a thin, gray tapeworm. To me it was quite an impressive machine. But for Mamie it turned out that Powers was much, much more than that.

She learned the mechanics of Powers the first time Shepard showed them to her. He ran the film through and wrapped it round the back reel. He released the lock on the wheels, slid the projector forward to a little window, turned it on, and adjusted the focus. The name *HAMLET* hit the screen. He adjusted the sound so the music wasn't so full of static. Then he turned it off and ran the film backward until it flapped loose around the front reel. Mamie didn't have to ask how to thread it through again. She grabbed Powers, unlocked his feet, rolled him back. Then wound the film like she had been doing it all her life. Rolling Powers forward into position, she fine-tuned the focus and the sound and the movie was ready to be shown.

"My God, she's inconceivably incredible," Shepard said to me. "What unqualified potency of mind. What effulgence, ahem, effulgence – to shine with brilliance. And in my own brilliance I recognize and predict she is the *sine qua non* of any further intellectual evolution, yum yum. Who says retarded? Who says slow? Who says on the cusp of cretin? None are applicable to *my* Mamie. He pinched her cheek. She petted his nose. I went back downstairs and left them to their mutual admiration association.

A couple of hours passed by, and I was alphabetizing the authors of the books on the shelves and half-listening to the movie playing, Laurence Olivier giving his speeches, some of which I recognized because my pa had memorized and often quoted them. When the movie was over, Shepard came down from the booth. He was very pale and his hands and fat cheeks and jowls were trembling. I asked him if he was sick.

"Mamie," he answered, his voice hardly more than a whisper. "You won't credit what I saw her do, what I heard her say. No I must not tell you yet. I must think about this first for a while. It is a new form, a new art, a new species, a wonder worth, perhaps, millions of – dare I say it? - dollars. Mamie is a mock moon, Crystal. A heavenly body has fallen out of the sky and come to Earth to live among us. A phenomenon extraordinary with portentous implications. The possibilities are overloading my brain cells. I must go away and ponder my navel. I must open myself to the answer of how, what, why, where in the world?"

"Huh?" I said.

He waved me off and went out the door. I saw him heading for the house, his fingers playing a little tune in the air, his mouth steaming with frosty words. And so I ran upstairs to see what Mamie was doing. Nothing much at all. She had an oil rag in hand and she was cleaning Power's little wheels and gears. I asked her what she had done to shake up Shepard.

"Nnnutt'n," she said.

"You must have done something," I said. "Did you do the no-rain with him?"

"Nnnutt'n," she said.

"You know, Mamie, if a guy was sober, you could scare him to death with the no-rain. You got to be careful. Most won't understand it like me. Like I did that first time with the knife in your hand?" She looked at me with puzzled eyes. Then went back to rubbing Powers all over. I watched her work on the machine, and I knew the no-rain idea was way off.

"You like Powers?" I asked.

"Yaay, Kritch'n!" Grasping the projector in her arms she picked it up. She hugged it, kissed it, and grinned at me from between its reels. When she put the projector down, she came to me, grabbing me by the shoulders and staring into my eyes. "P-Powers t-teached m-me," she said. "I luf him now."

"You love him?"

"I luf him now."

She let me go and went back to Powers, oily rag in hand. She hummed a made-up tune that made me think of bright mornings at home, listening to Mama and Mary Magdalen singing as they cleaned the house. Next thing I heard was Mamie singing like Ophelia in the movie – *Hey non nonny, nonny, hey nonny*, the words coming from her mouth as crisp as winter. She glanced at me and in her eyes I saw *secrets*.

"What's going on?" I said.

She put on her frog smile. If she wanted to, she could lick her earlobes.

"What are you up to?" I asked.

"*Hey non nonny, nonny, hey nonny–*"

"Are you being Ophelia?"

She kept singing. And try as I might, I couldn't get anything more out of her.

We finally had our grand opening on Valentine's Day in February. It wasn't much of a success. I sold only eleven tickets in all for both the showings of *Hamlet*. Anna came over to help at the counter and with selling popcorn and drinks. A sign on the wall in back of her said SHEPARD'S ARTLIFE SELLING YOU HEALTH BOTH INTELLECTUAL & PHYSICAL. No one

246

bought any of the books, and they made faces at the idea of mixing popcorn with fruit juice drinks and granola health bars. Patrons kept asking - "Don't you have any Coke?" Where's the Mars bars?" "Where's the Good and Plenty?" One guy said he had always heard Shakespeare was great, but now having seen an example of his work he didn't know what was so great about him. "It was a stupid movie. Just blah blah blah, and then they all bloody die at the end." Another one said the actors were a bunch of fairies, especially the guy who played Hamlet, those skinny legs! No one had anything good to say, and the dirty looks they gave us made me feel I had personally gypped them.

Shepard wasn't any help. He stayed upstairs in the booth with Mamie and didn't come down until long after the last customer had gone home. I told him how the customers grumbled about the movie and how much they hated the offerings at the concession stand. He didn't care at all.

"Poof, poof," is all he said.

"That's no way to run a business," I said. "You've got to give the customers what they want. Isn't that the American way? It's how you get prosperity, right?"

"Poof, poof."

And Anna said, "Vut's da madder you, Blubber? You vant to make money or no? You got to help. You got to do sometink. Vut's da madder you?" She stamped her foot at him, like she always did to Soren.

"Poof, poof. These trifles mean nothing in comparison with what is to come. You will understand everything very soon, I promise." He hugged himself and added, "Oh, when this bursts upon the unsuspecting world, it will be stupendous, mercurial, sparkling with Shepard-inspired inspiration. You'll see. Be patient a few more days. Let me work things out, this magic, this glorisishness."

"Huh?"

"Vut?"

Shepard put his finger to his lips. "Shush, shush, we must not spoil it by letting you know too soon. It's a fine secret, ha ha! Worth keeping until I am ready to give it birth - like gorgeous

Aphrodite on her half shell!"

Hamlet wasn't what the people of Temple wanted, so after a few days, Shepard sent it back and started showing A *Streetcar Named Desire*. About twice as many customers came to see it but not enough to make us think we were a success. The next week Shepard got an old film he claimed was a classic, *Major Barbara*. And practically no one came to that one, so we were back where we started. Then he got *On The Waterfront*, and that was a real movie. Our best crowd ever – sixty customers on one night – came to see it. But after that things got slack again because we showed another Shakespeare film, this one called *Richard III*, another Laurence Olivier thing, his legs skinnier than ever, and with a hunched back too and ghastly pageboy hair. But actually I thought on the whole the movie was better than his prissy version of *Hamlet*. At least in this one he was mean as hell and got his comeuppance in the end when he couldn't find his horse and the good guys killed him.

So anyway for the most part the citizens of Temple didn't like our choice of movies, our concession stand, the books for sale, the art for sale on the walls. The totems for their lawns didn't interest them at all. It all added up to zero and I lost heart. Temple just wasn't the place for what Shepard called his underwood, underground, neglected, long-lost, classical, pinnacle of genius, manna for the mind, harmonious, radiant gospels of art. His hall of inspiration was a pretty dreary place. It smelled of dank failure and stale popcorn.

And yet again, he didn't seem to mind. Anna and I were running the place by ourselves mostly, and all Shepard did was get the movies and stay with Mamie in the projection booth. I started figuring he was a lazy clod and taking advantage of us. He kept putting us off about this thing he said was a big secret. And Mamie herself was no help. I was getting suspicious. She gave practically every minute of her time to Powers, to showing the movies over and over and maintaining the projector in tip-top condition. The machine was beautiful. It glistened. The obsession that she had with it reminded me of the down cow time, the crippled Jewel that Mamie had brought back to full health. For days and nights on end I hardly saw her at all. Sometimes she came in late to take a shower and put on clean clothes.

But not once from the time she had fallen in love with Powers did we sleep together and do the no-rain. She didn't want me touching her that way anymore. I would try and she would give me that froggy smile and pull away, pat my head or kiss my cheek, but nothing more. It was frustrating. Depressing. I had gotten used to the no-rain and felt like I needed it – at least once in a little while, anyway.

Instead, I spent most of my time lying around reading or going over to watch television with Soren. At night Anna and I would take care of whatever customers showed up. Never very many. And our hearts were no longer into Shepard's dream of combining art and life. We even got to complaining right along with everyone else about the movies we were showing. They were lousy. After the customers would leave and Anna and I went home, Shepard would lock up and turn off the lights and he and Mamie would stay and do whatever they were doing.

I was - to say the least - pretty damn aggravated with the whole thing.

After a month of it, I decided I had had enough. I wrote my folks to tell them what was happening between Shepard and Mamie, and I asked them if it was okay for me to come home now. To hell with Mamie, let her take care of herself. All I wanted was *out*.

Pa Surprises Me

One morning I looked out the window, and there at the curb was our Ford pickup. Pa sitting inside smoking his pipe. I could see he was wearing his winter hat, the one with the earflaps and the ties hanging loose and the brim pushed down to shade his eyes from the low winter sun. The pipe curved over his chin. Smoke poured from the bowl like a miniature chimney. I opened the door and ran off the porch yelling, "Pa! What you doing here?"

He grinned at me and got out and said, "What you think I'm doing here, prodigal child? I come to see you."

I was glad to see him and told him so. We shook hands. His grip was rough with calluses and strong and confident and made me feel a security I hadn't felt since the last time I saw him. My pa was here. Nothing bad could happen to me. He told me that he had left around two in the morning so he wouldn't have to worry about John Beaver following him.

"So he hasn't calmed down," I said. "Still after us, huh?"

"Seems so. But I'll tell you what. He's enjoying the aggrieved father role a mite too much for it to be real. He's like some spoiled brat eating up all the attention we give him. He's an entertainer I'll give him that. Roaring and raving like a big ole bear lumbering back and forth at the bottom of the driveway. Gets me to chuckling sometimes like I'm watching a comedy on TV."

My heart was sinking. It was clear that Pa hadn't come to collect me. He pulled on his pipe, the chicory smell of the burning tobacco taking me back to times we sat on the porch and Pa created a talkative storm.

Looking up and down the street, he said, "Sun's almost open for business, where is everybody?"

"City folks stay up late Fridays and honky-tonk and stuff," I told him. "I stay up late too, but I can't sleep in like them. I guess I'm still a farmer, Pa."

He gave me a wink and said, "Well, I don't know about that. It's a switch from what I recall. Seems to me you always slept in pretty good at home and come dragging ass for chores."

"I'm different now. You wouldn't have to holler so much to get me up now. And I'd be a lot more help, I promise."

"Yeah? Well, maybe so. You do look more growed up. Your face a tad older somehow. Those faint lines on your forehead will deepen as you age. Those are called character lines. They show that you've had some hard times, but the hard times ain't hardened your heart. I mean *hasn't* hardened your heart. So farming's not so bad now?"

"Farming is heaven, Pa."

He chuckled a little and said, "I never thought I'd hear you say that. Let's not push the truth too far, son. Farming is a living. But heaven? I don't think so." He looked again at the houses and stores, the theater. "But heaven isn't this neither, I've got to admit." Nodding toward the Artlife he added, "So that's the place you wrote about? Sure looks old. This whole town is pretty ancient. Kind of like what they call being in a Puritan time warp, ey? If I remember correctly this town was the one full of fiery evangelicals trying to take over the schools. It was in the papers and on TV. No separation of church and state is what they wanted."

"I watched them burning books."

"Yeah, I read that too. They want to go back to censorship when a certain kind of book or attitude could get you arrested."

"Lots of old folks set in their ways," I said. "And they don't much like the movies we show. They want westerns and war films mostly. They think Willie S. is for perverts and sissies."

"Well, more fool them. A person who don't like Willie S. probably ain't got an ounce of culture in him, anyway. No feel for the art of words."

"I saw your favorite play, Pa."

"You saw *Hamlet?*"

"Bigger than life, yep, right there on the screen all those

speeches. To be and not to be and there's more to life than dreaming about philosophy."

"Dreamt of in your philosophy," he corrected. "So they made a movie of it? I didn't know that. The whole thing?"

"I think so, yeah. Maybe not everything, but most of it for sure. Yorick's skull was in it and to thy own self be true, and if you are true you can't be false to any man, the conscience of the king, the play's the thing. The end when everybody gets stabbed and drink poison and all of them, good or bad, are sprawled out dead as doornails."

"Well, I sure would have liked to seen it."

"Maybe it will show up in Superior or Duluth and you and Mama can take a day off and go."

"All because a fella couldn't make up his mind," said Pa. He scratched his chin, the whiskers rasping. "You know what I'm wondering though? Is who the hell is smart enough in this backwater to care for Shakespeare? Don't your friend know that he's going down a deadend road with that kind of stuff? Wasting money and energy."

"He thinks they'll come around. But you're right as rain. People said they couldn't understand half of what Hamlet was saying. Some called him a fairy."

"That's because you got to use your ears and wits when you listen to those speeches. He won't let you slip your clutch, you see what I'm saying. You've got to pay attention and interpret what you're hearing. That kind of concentration hurts your brain, especially if you're stupid." Pa spit in the snow. He scratched a match on his pant leg and relit his pipe. "It's a shame," he continued. "I mean it's all right there for the taking – Willie S. and the Bible got all the foolishness and wisdom there is in the world. Both of them is well worth knowing. Make you larger. Increase the size of your soul. So who played Hamlet? What did he look like?"

"A blond guy with skinny legs. His last name was Oliver."

"Oliver?"

"Yeah, Laurence Oliver."

"Like an Oliver tractor? Never heard of no Oliver actor. I'd

252

pick Errol Flynn for that role. He speaks slow. He enunciates. You can understand every word he says."

"Some fellow said Oliver moved kind of swishy."

"That's why you need a good actor. Shakespeare can be tough if you don't have an actor who knows what he's doing. It's too bad they didn't get Flynn. But then again maybe he's too old now. I haven't seen him in a movie since he played Robin Hood. That was – hell, I don't know – a long time ago. Years and years. So what other movies you show?"

I told him the list and he said he wished he could have seen them all.

"Makes me kind of jealous," he said. "Next time you write, you write about the movies you see. Tell me everything. By the way, you write real good, son. We sure like getting those letters. Even the boys like them." He chuckled. Then said, "Can you imagine what a mess they'd have made if they was in your shoes? Any one of them. Can you see them selling tickets to a show and all that dealing with the public you have to do? Disaster, that's what it would be. Disaster. Shit, they'd scare everybody away."

"Well, it don't matter much. Hardly anybody comes anyway," I said.

Pa put his finger on his nose and cleared it, first one nostril and then the other into the snow. I knew it was a commentary on what I'd told him. "I'll tell you what I think, son. This love of words came to me when I was your age and just trying to figure things out. I had this teacher. Her name was Mrs. Cima and she would read William Shakespeare to us. A little bit of it everyday. It was because of her that I got interested in him. She kept saying he was the greatest writer who ever lived and I wanted to know why she thought that. The kids in my class had a fit about Mrs. Cima forcing those verses down our hopeless ears. They would make faces and pretend to throw up. But not me. I loved it. And that's why you've had a steady diet of it since you were knee-high to a heifer."

"I'm grateful for that, Pa."

"I wasn't gonna allow you to waste your brain. You're the only brainy kid I got. Except Mary Magdalen is pretty smart too. But here's what I'm saying. People can be as dumb as cows when it comes to cultured stuff that would do them good. In fact, some folks make a virtue of being stupid about it. They make fun of you if you're the least bit intellectual. Stupid folks make fun of smart folks because that's all they've got to offer – stupidity – and they know it. You have to teach them what is good and what *isn't*. Because they don't have it naturally in them to do much more than put one foot in front of the other. Thank the Deity for creating teachers, that's what I say."

Pa got his pipe going strong again. He was leaning against the pickup's fender, settling into a rhythm of words flowing from him like ear candy. "Now, most of these turnip heads will take a stab at the Bible and get a phrase or two memorized and stop there, pretending they got all the knowledge they need. And they'll listen to a preacher, and the more ignorant he is the better they like him. I've told plenty of the walking wrathful that they don't know bullshit from mashed potatoes when it comes to interpreting the two gods found in the Bible. And they train their children that it's the only book they need in order to know what life is all about. Tell me that ain't crazy. I tell them there's more in heaven and earth than is dreamed of in their goddamn literal interpretation theology. And they tell me if it ain't in the Bible, then it's not worth knowing. Go over to Egypt and they'll tell you exactly the same thing about the Koran. Every religion has got its book that's got the truth. And so that's what you and Shepard are dealing with here. You're going to need to be patient as Job hisself if you want to teach an ox to be an eagle. You see what I'm saying? They ain't got the wings to get their bloated self-righteousness off the ground. Dumb bastards all of them."

Pa had worked his pipe into puffing out headsized billows of smoke and talking through it like God talking from a cloud. His eyes were bright. His face glowed with the love of speechifying.

"I sure have missed the sound of your voice," I told him.

"And haven't I missed you, you think? Nobody to talk to since you been gone. You're the only one listens and appreciates. Them nosepickers put on hangdog faces like I'm cussing them out when I talk philosophically. That slowness comes from your mother's side of the family. Not mine."

"It always made me feel important that you talked to me," I said. "Made me feel special."

"You are special. The brain's a glutton, son. You've got to feed it reason and common sense to make it healthy. It can't get enough of the rational world. But damn if folks don't damp it down and bank it like a low-burning fire. Ninety percent of the time it's us that makes ourselves stupid. Maybe ten percent got wrecked in the hamper or some accident later on. But most is to blame their selves, making their selves stupid just to fit in with all the other stupids they know." Pa gestured in a circle to indicate the town of Temple. But I knew he also meant the world.

He caressed his jaw and let his pipe go out again. The talking was what he came for. He had stored it up for me. "Yep, it takes time to make a philosophy you can live by. Takes time to make it you. To fill your soul with it and make yourself larger. But one day finally it's there for you and it is what you are. Mark what I say. I'm not just a farmer with cowshit on his boots, like the idea in some folks' heads. Nope. I read Willie S. and can quote him too. I'm a philosopher who knows about Emerson and the Deity. *I* did that. Nobody else in my family was that way exactly, though your grandpa sure had the Bible down chapter and verse. But I switched off that stuff. I got beyond Grandpa's Old Testament fierceness. It is just plain natural for a Foggy to grow in the direction of the spirit, and I saw that direction as the direction to take and that you, too, would follow it. Sort of like the man who gets a degree and that sets the bar for his son and the son has to get beyond his father. You'll go further in life than me. You'll probably be the first Foggy to go to college. Just remember that it's good to know your Bible for the general information it gives and some pretty fine psalms and its tough-minded Ecclesiastes telling you to make the best of this life because there is no other life like this one. But never let that book dictate to you. It can make you a fanatic, and fanatics have warped minds and cause most of the trouble in the world. You don't need someone else's personal vision of religion or a church. Nobody does but idiots who ain't got minds of their own. You don't need all that groveling prayer stuff that just proves you got a disease of the will in the same way that politics proves you got a disease of the intellect. The proper study of mankind is man. That's what a fella named Pope said. Not the Pope in Rome. Some other Pope. Whoever he was he spoke the truth, and there's no better way to study mankind than studying Shakespeare. Nothing that he didn't know about what being human means. For telling us how men think about themselves and their god, who was created in the image of their brutal, nasty selves and then did a little evolution thing by becoming all-loving in his second phase when men thought they'd had enough of being Job-sport for Satan. Someday maybe your mama and sister are going to realize it too and stop rolling those silly beads to convert me and you boys. What I got is more than they can dream of, or Horatio either – a clear-eyed conception of Earth. Wouldn't give that up for a string of beads from here to Africa or the moon."

Taking the pipe from his mouth he tapped the ashes from it and said his feet were getting cold. He wanted to go into the house. I said I had to tell him something before he met Shepard. "I lied to him about me and Mamie, Pa. Said we were cousins and orphans."

"Don't worry about that," he said. "Anybody with an ounce of brains would understand why you lied. All you need do is tell him the truth about that goddamn Beaver chasing you."

We went inside and found Shepard at the table drinking coffee. He looked at Pa. And then at me. And back to Pa. "You look related," he said.

"This is Jacob Foggy," I said. "He's my pa."

"Your pa? Ah ha, I knew it! Prevaricator caught in the tangled web you've been weaving. The orphaned Crystal. I never believed it. It's impossible to fool me, you know."

"I know."

"Yes, well welcome Pa of Crystal Foggy. Welcome. Sit down. A cup of coffee would not be scorned on this cold morning, I'm sure."

"I'd be grateful," said Pa.

Shepard went to the stove. Poured cups of coffee for us. Pa

looked him up and down. "You said he was big, Christian. But this is *big*."

"Four hundred pounds of cuddly love and towering intellect," said Shepard grinning.

"I'd say you and Goliath could see eye to eye."

"I am a most recalcitrant philistinian optimist, yum yum. But otherwise unrelated."

Pa guffawed at that. And said, "A regular cartoon come to life. Yum-yumming and everything. A philistinian optimist? What's that?"

"Philistinian optimist – one who embodies the character of our country. One who lives by the god of materialism and greed. Recalcitrant – refusing to obey custom, stubbornly defiant! Tee hee."

"I like it," said Pa. "Got a nice philosophical ring to it, a fulsome feel in the mouth. Philistinian optimist. The recalcitrant kind." He looked at me and winked. "He's everything you said he was, son. I'm liking his talk already. Yum yum."

"That's because my words have the flavor of truth, Jacob. I divine that you are a truth seeker with an expanded mental capacity beyond the norm."

"Why you think that? Because I like your lingo?"

"Exactly! Tee hee. Thee who likes my lingo can only like it because thee are a superior breed. On the other hand, not as superior as myself, but superior enough. Now, what about Mamie? Do you know why she is superior also?"

"Mamie?" said Pa. "Maybe because she's too dumb to lie?"

Shepard bellowed, "That's what you think! You'll be flabbergasted beyond recovery when you know what I know about that hulk of cinematic film art walking. Wait till I tell you what gifts she has. Tee hee. The ninety-ninth wonder of the world." His finger shot up. "But wait! If she's not an orphan, then who is she? Is she free? Please tell me that nobody owns her."

"Well, not exactly free. Such as he is she's got a father."

"And he – we don't like him, do we? She ran away from him because he beat her?"

Pa nodded. "Close enough. He's a vicious fellow all right. Got fists on him like a pair of Chicago hams."

"An abusive tyrant! Yes, I see it clearly now. He's done *things* to her."

"Probably."

"Intimate things?"

"He's a varmint, a liar, and a rabid dog."

"So! Now it makes sense. She's a victim of trauma. The stammer, the stutter. Her gifts were always there, stifled, buried under the vulgarity of her father's abusive wrath. I knew I could clear up the wonder of the mystery."

"Yeah, you better hope he don't find out she's here. He's a dangerous desperado. Half man, half grizzly. Mind of a cunning coyote. He finds out she's here, I wouldn't give two cents for your chances."

"My chances? Why me? What did I do? I took her in, a poor, starving pseudo-orphan, and fed her and clothed her and kept a roof over her head throughout this bitter winter. And now, what's more, I've taught her a trade. I should get encomiums and kisses and bronze statues for all that I've done, don't you think?"

"He'll put a knife in your ribs for all that, that's what I think. He don't want her knowing nothing but farming. Hope you're as tough as you are tall. Guy your size might make him work for it."

Baring his walrus mouth menacingly, his mustache bristling, Shepard said, "If my wrath is provoked I can be a torrent of devastation, a reincarnation of Tyrannosaurus Rex! I can be Mr. Beaver's worst nightmare, that's what."

"Well, it would be a match I'd pay to see," said Pa. "Yep, I wouldn't mind seeing it at all, not if you could make him work for it. Some tough shits in the bars have tried, but none of them made him work more than a few seconds. He's hardly human. More like . . . he's like a myth of the days when monsters like Grendel roamed the earth."

"Ah ha! Beowulf tore off Grendel's arm. Call me Beowulf."

"And that's about what you would have to do to stop John Beaver if he ever come sniffing for blood. Are you as strong as you are big, Don?"

"Strong as Hercules. Be he Otus or Ephialtes I'll grind his

bones to make my bread." Shepard puffed up his chest, but it was no match for his belly. "Bring the noodle on. He'll know he's messed with Donald Leonardo Shepard before I'm through with him. Grrr!"

"I like your attitude," said Pa.

Mamie came in and stood at the edge of the kitchen, yawning, rubbing her sleepy face. She looked squinty-eyed at Pa. "F-foggy?" she said.

"It's me, Mamie. How you been?"

"F-fine."

"Your hair's a lot longer now, I see."

She turned around and showed him a braid that ran to the middle of her back.

"Looks good," he said.

"Looks good to the world," added Shepard.

Then he said he had an announcement to make. At noon in the Artlife we would see Mamie display her wondrous art. It was a secret. He couldn't say anything more to us than that. "But! This day ye shall behold an apotheosis, a glorification of my own devising of how best to unveil Mamie's genius. I discovered the hidden springs of brilliance coiled inside her, and I have developed what will come gushing forth yumity yum before the world's astonished eyes. In truth very soon. The largess of her *anima mundi* – her world soul – will one day rank her in name-recognition with the likes of Einstein or Lincoln or Elvis Presley. Her traumatized stammering silence has been metamorphosed into a pristine category of fine art. You'll see! You'll see what I'm saying. Be patient, you'll see and seeing is believing. On the other hand, I, oh, *I* - I brought her back from the abyss of extinction. I will be famous for it. Go down in history. Together we will astonish the world. I'm telling you *astonish* is not too strong a word. These great souls 'yearning in desire to follow knowledge like a sinking star, beyond the utmost bounds of human thought.' We! I and Mamie. And I, oh I found the hidden springs. Tee hee."

Mamie reached over and pet Shepard's nose. He sighed with pleasure.

"Sounds pretty good," said Pa. "Did you make that up?"

"I make nothing up, Jacob. Everything I say is true and original. Now, ahem, append this coda. At noon today we shall gather in the Artlife. Crystal will you tell Anna and Soren to come? I will say no more for now. Shhh." He fluttered his fingers like a magician over a crystal ball. Then he shook hands with Pa and blessed him for coming and clearing the cobwebs of Mamie's past away. He told Mamie to come to the Artlife for rehearsals as soon as she had something to eat. Another flourish of his hands and he waddled grandly out of the kitchen.

Pa leaned over and said, "A gargantuan word-wonder, son."

"He's a genius," I explained.

"Maybe so."

"He and Mamie have been keeping a secret."

"Stares at her like she's wearing seven veils. That man's in love. What a match that would be."

I felt a little pang in my heart at his thinking Mamie might match up with Shepard. "I don't know if he's for her, Pa," I said. "He's big, but I think he's all blubber and bluster."

"Yeah, maybe so. Got a belly like a pregnant cow, don't he?" He glanced at Mamie. She was eating a loaf of pumpernickel smeared with butter and grape jelly. "So you like him, Mamie? You think he might marry you?"

"Nup," she said. "P-powers lufs me so."

"Who's he?"

"Powers is a movie projector, Pa. Mamie thinks he loves her. She kisses him and gets graphite all over her face."

"Kisses him? A projector?"

"He lufs me so," she said.

Pa's eyes were a tangle of puzzled wrinkles. "What you loving that for?" he said. "Mechanical made by the hand of man. Might as well love a watch."

Mamie studied his question. Then she said, "Powers teached me st-stuff."

"What she talking about?"

I told him I didn't know. I had given up trying to figure her out.

"Crazy," said Pa, raising an eyebrow skeptically.

"Maybe not exactly crazy. I mean, maybe there's more to her thing with Powers than bats in the belfry. She's been changing almost minute by minute since we got here and she started running that projector. She doesn't stare with saucer-eyed wonder anymore, not the way she used to. Her eyes seem to know things now. Her body even moves different. Like the women in the movies we watched. Almost slinky sometimes. Maybe she's creating herself like you did, Pa."

"Maybe she's creating herself?" Pa bit on his pipe stem awhile. "Could be," he said. " Not a damnation bone in her body, I'll give her that. Never knew her to be evil like her father. Never gave her credit for enough brains to sin. Now what do we think, ey? There's a darkness on the earth causes all our troubles. Is what we see happening here the darkness or the light? The darkness is made of Will, the force that makes the flower grow and makes a man grow and also makes him restless and makes him throw out tentacles of evil when he gets bored. Creating yourself, Mamie, are you? Mamie and Powers. Mamie and evil. Mamie and the darkness. Mamie and the light. The light is reason shining in the darkness and the darkness sometimes knows it not. Maybe so. And what a shame that each of us is such an entire world packed in such a small sack that we can't see into the heart of the other worlds around us – that they're made up of the same dust as our own and we all have to fight our individual selves to come up with the least tidbit of truth. A crying shame. It's the reason for finding comfort in gathering knowledge like a combine gathering wheat for storage. A little knowledge may be a dangerous thing, but a lot of it can let you know the truth about the thickness of your own skull and make you humble and open to learning. It can tell you that the worst human perversion is the way some people cling to the lies that drown out any horse sense they ever got from experience. The widest river in any part of creating yourself is the big lie, the easy way. The widest river pouring into the Will, choking an unfolding flower so it can't swim the river of truth, can't go so far as Washington's silver dollar across the Potomac. And so the soul gets smaller then. And the mind gets darker. But the ember burns. And there is a white dot of hope living in the pit of your belly. And Mamie is having a love affair with a movie projector. Powers. I'm glad I came here today. This is getting more and more promising. Are you listening, son?"

And on and on he went, the dam bursting with words he couldn't hold back. Every few minutes pausing to ask me - "Are you listening? Are you listening?"

The Wonder of the Mystery

At noon I went over to the Gulbrensons and told them that Shepard wanted all of us to meet him at the Artlife. When we got there Pa paused to admire the way we had set up the books and paintings and totem sculptures to sell in the lobby. He said Shepard was doing the smart thing in diversifying. It was diversification that kept some businesses from going under in hard times. "Which is especially true of farming," he added. He gazed a long time at the totem poles and said he wouldn't mind having one of them for himself. Maybe he would buy one and haul it home in the pickup and set it up at the head of the driveway. He said he didn't think you had to be an Indian for the totems to bring good luck and spiritual vibrations. He looked over the books and bought *Walden* and *The Grapes of Wrath*. Which he said every American who hated corporate tyranny and believed in humanity and love of the land should read.

Shepard came down from the projection booth and told us to go into the hall and take a seat. As the lights went down, Anna said she hoped Shepard wasn't going to embarrass us with something stupid. The lamp from the projector cast a beam on the stage. Shepard walked into the beam and told us it was his pleasure at last to present the wonder of the mystery of Mamie Beaver. As he backed away, his hand beckoned her to come forth. Dressed in a black robe, her hair pulled back in a winding braid, like a target on the back of her head, she stood in the shaft of light and looked around. Her face was dusted with white powder, maybe flour? Whatever it was it made me think at first that she was going to mime something. Her eyes were dark and unreal, black smudges pasted onto her stark white face. Her mouth hung

263

loose like the mouth of a puppet. Was she drugged? Hypnotized? Had Shepard worked an enchantment on her? Black magic? The sight of Mamie gave me goosebumps. I was feeling creepy. I wanted to see her froggy smile, so that at least one thing about her appearance would seem normal.

Shepard, still standing out of the light, said to her in a falsetto voice, "Now, Mamie, 'If it be, why seems it so particular with thee?'"

The stupid, hinged-jaw look on Mamie's face disappeared instantly. Her body took on the moves of Laurence Olivier in the Shakespeare movie. And she said, "'Seems, madam? Nay, it is; I know not seems. Tis not alone my inky cloak, good mother, nor customary suits of solemn black, nor windy suspiration of forced breath, no, nor the fruitful river in the eye—'"

"Now, Mamie," interrupted Shepard.

She quit quoting and listened to him. Again her mouth hung. Again her eyes became smudges on a face of mime white.

"'Mark me,'" he said.

"'I will,'" she said.

"'My hour is almost come, when I to sulfurous and tormenting flame must render up my self.'"

"'Alas, poor ghost!'"

"'Pity me not, but lend thy serious hearing to what I shall unfold.'"

"'Speak. I am bound to hear.'"

Shepard came to the edge of the stage and looked down at us. His voice quavering with giddiness. "Are you listening to this?" he asked.

"We're listening," said Pa. "Can she do anything else?"

"She's doing Oliver, Pa," I said.

"That's what I figured. I'm all to hell impressed, Donald."

"Jacob, she plays all the parts. Every single one of them right down to that waterfly Osric." He turned to Mamie. "'Put your bonnet to his right use; tis for the head.'"

"'I thank your lordship, it is very hot.'"

"'No, believe me, tis very cold; the wind is northerly.'"

"'It is indifferent cold, my lord, indeed.'"

"'But yet methinks it is very sultry and hot for my complexion.'"

"'Exceedingly, my lord; it is very sultry—as 'twere—I cannot tell how.'"

Shepard did a little hippopotamus twirl of joy, crying out, "And who knows the interpretation of a thing? How is this possible? It's not. But it is! More. You want more? She can do this all day."

"We're listening," said Pa.

"'Propose the oath, my lord.'"

"'Never to speak of this that you have seen, swear by my sword!'" said Mamie, her voice a ventriloquist version of Hamlet himself, what he said to Horatio and the other wonderstruck men who had seen the ghost of Hamlet's father.

Then he went into one of Ophelia's speeches, and Mamie became Ophelia, saying the lines in the sweet voice of the actress who went crazy in the movie. Shepard led her into the king's roll. Then the queen. And on to Polonius, Laertes, and Horatio summing things up when he said "His purse is empty already; all's golden words are spent."

Shepard bowed to us. He wiped his teary eyes on his sleeve, saying, "You are the first witnesses to what I've created. And we don't do only *Hamlet*. Nay, any movie she's seen lives inside her head. She has the same gift that I have – total recall at will."

To show us what he meant he put her through her paces some more and we heard bits from *A Streetcar Named Desire* – "Whoever you are, I have always depended on the kindness of strangers; *Major Barbara* – "Yes, through the raising of hell to heaven and of man to God, through the unveiling of an eternal light in the Valley of the Shadow; *On The Waterfront* – "You should have looked out for me a little bit, Charlie."

Next to me I could hear Anna breathing heavily. Muttering. Sometimes gasping. Finally she spoke up. She said, "Vut twick is dat, mista?"

"You like it, Anna?" Shepard asked.

"Pwetty goot, ya. But how you make Mamie doink dat?"

He pointed to Mamie in the light, her mouth open and waiting again for more words to be poured into her ears. "It's just who she is, Anna," said Shepard. "It's been her all along, buried within her since birth, no doubt. And I've exhumed it as if from a grave, and created her thusly, this phenomenon you see before you. Think what people will pay to see this! She's worth a fortune! TV. Radio. Documentaries. Interviews in magazines and newspapers. We'll be flown to New York. And Hollywood. Researchers at Harvard and Stanford will want to study her. They'll find that this is beyond anything Freud or Jung ever defined. It's in her wiring. They'll find a name for her condition like they did autism and idiot savant syndrome."

"This ain't natural," said Soren, his voice grumpy. "It's a disease. Probably a virus. Maybe cancer or a brain tumor."

"Disease? Cancer? Tumor? Soren, Soren! Mamie's as natural as nature itself. Nature created her mind to have a certain chemistry that allows her to retain and regurgitate lines from the art she sees on film. Don't call it unnatural. It's . . it's . . . Never mind. It's too complicated to explain if you're not a chemist or biologist or neurologist or a great thinker such as myself who always sees into the heart of the heart of things. She is comprehensible only in the distillery of a vastly superior brain such as my own. I can't expect normal people to understand any of it. Not really."

"But what does it mean?" I cried. "I don't get it. Nature. Chemistry. The heart of the heart of things?"

Quietly Shepard explained that *meaning* had no particular place in interpretations of Mamie's gifts. "Like nature, she simply is and means nothing beyond that indisputable fact, Crystal. Push it farther than that and you'll be overwhelmed. Sensory overload lies that way. Nothing about you is equipped to decipher what you're seeing. You would need to be Spinoza able to break psychological concepts into mathematical formulas."

"Oh, I don't know," said Pa. "It ain't too overwhelming. I recall something like it a long time ago, when she was little - if you can believe she ever was little. Her mother used to take her to movies and tell how she would act them out afterwards, down to the last detail." He turned to me. "I think I told you about this before, haven't I, son?"

"Yeah, you did, Pa. Tell them about her being Charlie Chaplin."

"That's right. They went to a silent movie festival one time and afterwards I saw her do Charlie Chaplin when she couldn't

266

have been more than four or five years old. She had him down pat, the walk, the cane, the derby hat, the charcoal mustache. It was pint-size Charlie to a T. Listen, I'm not by and large superstitious, but I do believe there are things in heaven and earth that are not dreamed of in our philosophies, and this Mamie act is one of them. It's like the Bible says, 'Open you mouth wide, and I will fill it.' Shepard here was the catalyst that allowed it to happen. But this here witness is the completion of what she promised and none of us understood."

"It's unnatural," said Soren again. "It'll lead to trouble. Mark me."

"'I will,'" said Mamie, suddenly Hamlet again.

"Not now," Shepard told her.

"Look, folks," said Pa, "people are born everyday with gifts that we won't ever understand."

"Exactly!" said Shepard. "That's what I'm saying."

"Yep, I'll tell you what," said Pa, "I know a fellow right here in Wisconsin who plays Beethoven and Mozart like a maestro on the piano, but he's never had a lesson in his life. What's more he can't add two plus two or hardly walk or talk or button his own shirt. Can't even tie his shoes. So what's he got going for him? Nothing but some uncanny musical gift. Shepard says it's a certain chemistry. Probably that's right. But it is also the arrangement of that chemistry by the Deity, he, she, or it who has arranged the world and all the life on it. Whatever that process is it produced this girl and also that idiot who can play a piano."

"I don't believe it," said Soren. "Someone had to teach that fella to play."

"Nope, nobody. I'm told that he heard Beethoven on TV, a pianist playing some concerto, and that night he sat down at the keyboard and played the piece exactly like he had heard it earlier that day. It's a true story. The noise woke his parents up and scared them half to death. They thought it was a ghost come to haunt them, but there he was, their little idiot playing like an angel. And he *was* an angel, sort of. Don't you think?"

"A piece of Jesus," I said. "A guy name Robbie Peevy told me we were all connected by being pieces of Jesus."

"That's as good as any way of putting it," said Pa. "It's like a miracle but not a miracle, though it does have the feel of being something holy. A slobbering idiot playing Beethoven. A Mamie Beaver playing Marlon Brando."

"And Laurence Olivier!" said Shepard.

"Yeah, him too," said Pa. "Mamie, come out of the light for now. The show's over. Why you put that kind of makeup on her, Donald? She looks like Halloween up there."

Mamie came to the edge of the stage and sat down. Shepard sat next to her. She looked much better out of the light, not so much like a ghost, though she really needed to wipe off the powder and that black mascara from her eyes.

I told Shepard I agreed with Pa. "Why did you put that junk on her face? She's got a pretty face in my opinion."

"It's symbolic," said Shepard. "I don't expect you to catch the particular trope at work here."

"I think I get it," said Pa. "Mimes mimic and that's what you've got her doing. Mimicking. Mamie disappears behind the mimic's mask and out comes the part you prompt her to play. Right?"

"An astute observation. I underestimated you, Jacob."

"That's okay. I've been underestimated plenty. It ain't painful." He looked at Mamie and smiled thoughtfully. "I wonder if you can remember it, girl. That time I came over to borrow your father's hay wagon and caught you out there in the yard walking round like a duck and twirling that stick. And you had some old Derby on your head. Baggy pants. Oversized shoes. And there you are and I'm thinking you look like Charlie Chaplin and I says to your mother, 'Mary, she looks like Charlie Chaplin.' And she says to me, 'We been to the silent film festival over Duluth with my sister and her kids, and they showed *The Gold Rush* and a slew of others with Charlie Chaplin.' I just shook my head at the wonder of you. Your Chaplin was perfect. You made a big impression on me that day. There was another time, too, that I recall Mary telling me that she had heard you quoting lines from something the two of you saw. So this sort of thing has been in the works for a long while. If your mother hadn't died and you had kept going to movies with her who knows what might have happened? It was her favorite

268

thing to do, you know, take you to the shows. And then she up and burst her heart dragging a calf out of a cow. And then your papa put an end to all your movie mimicking. That's when he got meaner than just mean and started being a recluse and keeping you from going to school or anywhere else. You became his mule and took on that vacant stare like there was nothing but midnight in your head. Yeah, I bet you remember."

Real soft Mamie said, "Yaay, J-Jacob, I mmmember."

And softly Pa said, "'And he has sent out his maid to call from the highest places in the town.' What will you do now, Mamie, now that you got your gift back?"

"She'll get rich and famous," said Shepard. "There is a bottomless well of wealth to be exploited and a lost time to make up for, and I'm the entrepreneur who can pull all of it together and give this girl everything she deserves. Trust me and you'll see."

"Maybe so," said Pa.

"It's unnatural," said Soren. "It won't turn out the way anyone thinks it will."

"Maybe so," said Pa.

"This is as natural as poverty in the richest country in the world," said Shepard. "If you're willing to work you can have it all. It is for her that I bring my genius to bear in a particular direction. Not for myself. I have already given her the gift of an occupation, a vocation. But now beyond her wildest dreams I'm going to give her a profession!"

"Maybe so," said Pa.

"If she's so smart, why can't she read?" I said. "I've tried to teach her."

"The gift is only the gift of mimicry," said Shepard. "Brilliant elocution. 'With these celestial wisdom calms the mind, and makes the happiness she does not find.' She doesn't need to read. Who will resist her? She who speaks the purest verse and prose in the purest ghostly voices of the Silver Screen? Humph, would you quibble about small deformities when her general power is so colossal? Nay, quibble not!"

"You should poot her on telewision," said Anna.

"Television poof, poof. The world will be hardly large enough to contain us."

Pa stood up and stretched. "That's all well and good," he said. "But it's getting late for heading back to Cloverland if I'm gonna make it before chores. What say we get a bite to eat? Then I'll be on my way."

"My treat," said Shepard. "What a day! What a wonderful way of the world has opened up for us."

We went next door to Charlie Friendly's bar, minus Anna and Soren who went home. We took a table near the back. Shepard ordered hamburgers and a pitcher of beer. Charlie threw burgers on the grill. He poured beer. He wanted to know how things were coming along at the Artlife. He had heard that Shepard was broke and close to closing the theater.

"Pure fabrication and sour grapes," Shepard told him. "Those who practice such calumny will be flogged with their own words once my enterprises get going in high gear. We are on the cusp of breaking out, Charlie. We are about to soar on the wings of eagles into the rarefied atmosphere of fortune and fame. Look at my Valkyrie, Charlie. Look at her and say yum yum. Tomorrow's headlines: 'Mamie Beaver Soars Among the Stars!' Going under? Poof, poof, Charlie, wait until I unveil my protégé on the Artlife stage."

"Uh-huh, okay," said Charlie. He set the pitcher of beer on the table. Soon we were eating our hamburgers and listening some more to Shepard who kept telling Charlie what a wonder he was going to see pretty soon and how the whole town would wake up to find two great geniuses in its midst and itself no longer just a dot on a map.

Charlie nodded slowly to everything Shepard said, but he didn't seem much impressed. Shepard called for a second round of burgers and another pitcher of beer. Pa said no more for him. He had to get going. I walked him to the pickup and we stood awhile and talked. He told me Sugar had taken Minna's place as supercow of the barn. She was doing ninety pounds of milk a day and 4.8 butterfat.

"That's my Sugar," I said. I had raised her and shamelessly pampered her. You pamper a cow and mostly she'll pay off in higher milk and butterfat yields.

"You were definitely right about her," said Pa. "You're a good judge of heifers. Maybe even better than me now. When you come back, after this Beaver thing is settled, I'm gonna turn more of the breeding over to you. Send you to breeders school. Now there's a future for you. Everybody is going artificial."

"Artificial breeding is the way to go for sure, Pa."

"We'll do it right and get to be big farmers with a reputation for milking first-rate quality cows. That's what I'm thinking. Nobody will have to go off to the city for a job, if they don't want to. Can't imagine any of my boys but maybe you in the city. I mean if you go on to college and make something more of yourself. But can you imagine any of my other boys making a living without the farm?"

"Can't imagine it," I said, feeling a little bit like I was betraying my brothers. But the truth is the truth.

"That's why we've got to get bigger and diversify ourselves. Run some beefers. Put in a pig barn. Make a cash crop of sweet corn. I've got a lot of ideas." He went on to tell me that Cush got his toes frostbit and lost the toenails on his right foot. Said he just didn't feel the cold coming in. "Your brothers need a keeper," he continued. "The shenanigan they pulled the other day was a beaut. They got this idea that they were gonna trap John Beaver – in a bear trap, mind you. They couldn't tell me what they were gonna do with him once they caught him, but they were gonna catch him whatever. Thank the Deity they didn't use the one with the sawteeth. That would have made a hell of a mess. Instead they used the smooth jawed one. They set it up between those two big poplars at the edge of the driveway and covered it with snow. But they didn't put a marker on it. They didn't even chain it to one of the trees – just put it near where Beaver paces when he comes over and yells for Mamie."

"Did they catch him? Did they break his leg?" I asked.

"Well, not exactly. You see, Beaver didn't show up. I seen them boys sneaking round all morning, hiding behind the house and staring at the road and snickering and pinching each other. And of course I knew something was up with those goofballs. Finally I said, 'What the hell you doing, boys?' 'Oh, nuthin, Pa, we're juss spyin for Beaver to come.' I run them off to the barn to muck out the calf pens and clean the chips off the cows. While they were doing that Duane came to pick up the milk. He didn't look so good. Too much bending the elbow, ey? Gotten bloated he has. I told him he looked hung over and he said, 'Jacob, half this county is drunk by noon everyday, so why not me? What else is there to do when you live in a shit-eating world on the edge of hell?' I told him things ain't so bad if a man stays sober and does his work and teaches himself to take life as it comes. He wasn't hearing none of it. He kept saying we wasn't in hell but we could see it from where we was standing. I give up on him. You know all that old boy does is bitch about something. Might as well shoot yourself if all you're gonna do is bitch your way through life."

"Duane always drinks too much, Pa. I don't see how he keeps his job."

"Yeah, neither do I. So anyway, while I'm talking to him I can hear the boys in the barn fighting about something. I go inside to yell at them and there's two of them wrestling in the shit in the calf pen. Can you guess who?"

"Cush and Cutham?"

"You know those twins well enough. I was ready to kill them. I made them go to the milkhouse and hose down. I told them I was gonna run their asses down to the Brule and break the ice with their heads and dump them in. Sometimes I am sorely tempted. So I get the shit off them and send them to the house to change their wet clothes. So of course, the other three have to start whining that Cush and Cutham are getting out of chores. My patience is wore out. They try me every day, you know?"

"Yeah, I know, Pa."

"Yeah, I suppose you've gotten whacked a few times just cause I was wore out from them."

"You never really hit hard," I told him. And he never did put his heart into a beating, not like a John Beaver would.

"Yeah? Well, sometimes the way you boys yell when I smack

you it's like you're dying." He chuckled awhile. Took out his pipe and filled it. Gently he said, "Sure have missed you, son. Did I tell you that? Your mama misses you too. Turns on the waterworks whenever you send a letter. She's an old sweety, your mama. Loves her boys."

In my mind I saw her with her thick hair in a bun, almost all gray now, but with bits of blond still showing. I saw her kind eyes and the fine wrinkles on her forehead and down her cheeks. I missed her awfully.

Pa lit his pipe and puffed hard. "I got to finish my story," he said. "That bear trap, the night after they set it, we got a good snow fall and the trap got covered pretty good. Not a trace of it. So the next day I seen them standing down by the trees and arguing like gophers. I asked what they were fighting about now and they give me that 'Oh, nothing Pa.' I told them if I didn't get the truth I was gonna send their souls to God and make sausages of their asses. I pointed my crooked finger at Cash and said I was starting with him. He caved in right away and pointed at Calvin. 'Calvin's the one did it!' he says. 'Did what?' I say. And he gives me the whole story of how they were gonna trap John Beaver in the bear trap. And of course I want to know where they set it and Cash says he doesn't know. None of them know except its somewhere in between the two poplars. I tell them not to go anywhere near the spot. I went back up the hill to fetch a shovel so I could poke around with it and see if I could find that damn trap. I got about as far as the machine shed when I heard this blood-curdling howl – worse than the time that cat got caught in the baler, poor thing. So I run back down the hill and there's that stupid brother of yours, that stupid Calvin with his arm in the trap. If it had been the sawtooth he wouldn't have an arm I can tell you that. The other boys was just gawking at him like they was watching a scary movie. I jumped in and pulled the jaws apart and drove him to the clinic in Superior. 'What kind of shit for brains would stick his arm in a trap that way?' I asked him. And he says he thought he'd feel around carefully under the snow and find the edge of that trap and yank it out of there. He said he thought he knew just about where it was. 'I should have took a stick and poked for it, huh?' he says. Jesus, what can you do with a kid like that? It's a miracle those boys have lived this long. You and Don Shepard think Mamie is a wonder and a mystery. Yeah, she is, but so are those boys. I swear they'll be the death of me one of these days."

Phoebe Bumpus

There were days when it seemed that leaving Mamie wouldn't be hard. She was having her love affair with Powers and ignoring me anyway, so why not leave? Why not go home and take my chances? But other days I'd get to thinking about all we'd been through together, from thumping John Beaver and stealing his truck to learning the no-rain next to the pond in the woods, to settling Mike Quart's hash so cleverly that he didn't even know what was happening to him, to losing control of the book burning at the Temple High School, followed by the death of Amoss and breaking Robbie out of jail. And there were the mean-spirited deeds of Teddy Snowdy and the (accidental?) shooting of his father, the good country people who fed us, and the return to Temple to the wild ambitions of Shepard – everything crammed into less than a year now. And when I'd think of all those shared experiences, I would know that leaving Mamie was impossible. Not in this life anyway. And I'd know she was in my blood and brain forever. She was in the air I breathed. She was the focus of my heart. She was a hot spot in my soul that nothing could cool. Leave Mamie? Nup, nup, nup.

Her getting so close to Shepard and Powers bothered me, of course, and made me restless – made me realize how much I wanted to be the center of her attention like before. She spent nearly all her time in the booth fussing with the projector and watching movies. When I asked her if she just wanted to be with Powers and watch movies for the rest of her life, she said, "Yaay, Kritch'n!"

"Because Powers loves you so?" I said.

She hugged herself and nodded her head.

"Well, I'm not happy," I said. "You're gonna get bored, you'll

275

see. And maybe I won't be around to play with anymore. Maybe I'll just move on in the spring."

Her eyes furrowed sadly. She hugged me and made a whiny sound in my ear. I shook her off and said, "Don't be giving me any pity, Mamie. I won't stand for it!" I felt an impulse to take her hand and lead her to the shower. I wanted us to soap each other and do the no-rain. But I didn't do anything except spin on my heel and stomp away like a toddler having a tantrum.

Shepard was in the process of preparing things for Mamie's grand debut in front of a live audience. He had been advertising her all over the city as a miracle and a phenomenon. He had a hundred handbills printed and tacked up on telephone poles and stuffed in mailboxes. The handbills said:

MAMIE BEAVER OPENING SATURDAY MARCH 9
SEE THE IDIOT PHENOMENON OF THE CENTURY
A MORON QUOTING SHAKESPEARE
HOW DOES SHE DO IT?
NOBODY KNOWS!
DOCTORS ARE BAFFLED!
SOME CALL HER A MIRACLE!
COME TO DON SHEPARD'S ARTLIFE THEATER
 - 3 ARBOR ST. -
TO WITNESS A PHENOMENON EXTRAORDINAIRE.
MAMIE BEAVER PLAYING ALL THE ROLES FROM
HAMLET.
 IT WILL BOGGLE YOUR MIND!

By opening night, we were pretty excited. Which was a waste of energy. Mamie bombed. Twelve customers showed up and sat through about twenty or thirty minutes of Mamie's act before they started leaving.

"What's the big deal?" I heard one of them say.

"It's a gyp," said another. "Not gonna sucker me again like this, that Don Shepard - phooey."

"He's a charlatan. He's a phony."

A nice lady said, "Yes, but it was certainly something the way Mamie had memorized all those words. How could she do it?"

"It's a gimmick," said the man beside her. "Shepard's behind it all. He's a ventriloquist, you know."

"He is?"

"Yep."

A stoop-shouldered fellow with a red face and angry eyes stopped me and said, "You sure got nerve charging a dollar for this *phenomenon of the century*. Bah!"

I pulled a dollar from my pocket and gave it to him. He snatched it and hurried away.

So the whole thing went bust. Anna blamed it on *Hamlet*. Too wordy. Too boring. No way to understand half of what he was saying. Shepard said it was the wrong time and the wrong place – "A city of abysmal and appalling arrogant ignorance, humph! Poof, poof!" He wondered if he shouldn't order cheap B-grade movies and show double features and forget the books and paintings and give them what they wanted, give them Coke and candy and action films, shoot-em-up stuff.

Standing around the lobby, we were all pretty pessimistic and glum. Especially after having thought that we were on the road to something big.

Small potatoes now. No sale.

That night Mamie went upstairs to the booth and didn't come down even for beer and burgers at Charlie's. I didn't know if her feelings were hurt or what, but she had already hauled up some blankets and a pillow, and from then on she slept in the booth with Powers. She would come to the house to shower and eat and there would be that greasy graphite on her hands and face and I would know that she had been making love to that idiot projector again. Things got worse and worse, like it was forever just the two of them and Shepard and I didn't count anymore. I wanted to take a sledgehammer and beat that damn machine to death. I would have done it except I was afraid Mamie would hate me.

A couple of weeks went by with very little talking between any of us. Shepard spent most of his time at Charlie's drinking beer and moaning about the lack of culture in Temple. I mostly read books and walked around town and sometimes visited Amoss' grave, where things were quiet and I always felt a sense of peace. I told myself that the Bible was right – all was vanity and vexation of spirit. Mamie spent her days and nights with a cold hunk of steel full of little wheels and little gears that whirled.

So one morning before noon I was sitting on the porch taking in the sun. The snow had melted, except for patches here and there in shady spots. Tiny tongues of grass were shooting up from the lawn. Baby buds were forming on the live part of the giant elm in the front yard. As I sat there mulling things over, I heard a woman's voice saying, "Is this where I can find the phenomenon extraordinaire?"

I shaded my eyes and saw a woman not young, but not old, maybe thirty. She had jug ears that stuck out through her hair. She was tall and thin, breasts the size of small oranges poking against her tight pullover sweater. She looked almost hipless in tight Levi jeans. Hanging by a strap over her shoulder was a camera.

"I'm Phoebe Bumpus from the *Temple Daily Star*," she said. She showed me her card. "Is this the place?" she asked.

Unfolding one of our advertisements, she read excerpts:

IDIOT PHENOMENON OF THE CENTURY.
A MIRACLE.
DON SHEPARD'S ARTLIFE THEATER.
MAMIE BEAVER.
IT WILL BOGGLE YOUR MIND!

"The show was a couple weeks ago," I said. "It bombed."

"Yes, I know. Is the phenomenon still here? Can I meet her? I'd like to do a story for the paper, maybe." She glanced over at the Artlife, her bottom lip pouting up and down, like she was shrugging it. The lip. The Artlife looked shabby I had to admit. Old and winter glazed, the marquee thrusting over the wide-walk needing to be buffed, the dingy black letters saying MAMIE BEAVER MAGIC MEDLEY OF CLASSIC FILMS.

"I might write something that would stir people up. I mean, if this is true," said the woman called Phoebe Bumpus. She waved the handbill at me.

"That thing doesn't say the half of it," I told her. "Mamie is like nothing you've ever seen. I couldn't even begin to explain her. You'd think I was lying."

She wanted to know my name and my connection to Shepard and Mamie and the Artlife.

"I'm Christian and I'm in charge of tickets. I help do lots of things. Mamie is my . . . um . . . Mamie is my—"

"Yes?"

"Mamie is my friend."

"And what makes your friend so extraordinary?"

"She memorizes thousands of words from movies and stands on a stage quoting every character perfectly. Shepard calls it total recall at will. He has it too."

"This piece of paper says she's an idiot. A moron."

"Well, I don't know, maybe she is. Opinions about her run from mentally retarded to autistic to idiot savant to remarkable genius to—" I shrugged my shoulders.

"Has she ever been evaluated by any doctors?"

"They're the ones put the tags on her."

"Where is she? I want to meet her."

Phoebe Bumpus looked past me towards the house. "She's not in there," I said. "About noon or so she comes out of the projection booth and goes to that bar there and gets a snootful and then goes back to the booth."

"A snootful?"

"Mamie likes booze. Especially splow. She likes it like you and I like lemonade on the Fourth of July."

"She's an alcoholic?"

"Maybe. Who can say? She can drink gallons of the stuff without stopping."

"Gallons? Nobody drinks gallons of splow. They'd die of alcoholic poisoning." She looked doubtful. Suspicious. "You trying to do a number on me, Christian?"

"Not me. I'm not trying to do a number. I tell you I ain't got the words to explain her. Nobody does. Not even Shepard."

"How come you're not in school? Are you playing hooky?"

"I'm an orphan," I told her. "I'm all alone in the world and need to earn a living. Shepard give me a job, God bless him."

"Really now, an orphan?"

"Yep."

"How long have you been an orphan?"

"Oh, not long," I told her. "Last winter my pa got shot dead by a hunter. At least we think it was a hunter. Maybe it was murder."

Phoebe's hand covered her mouth. "Oh, I'm so sorry," she said. "So there's no one left to care for you?"

"Well, there's Mama, but she's got to feed my five little brothers."

"A mother and five little brothers. Then you're not truly an orphan."

"Well, technically no. But I can't go home. I can't burden my mother with another mouth to feed. I'm on my own since Pa died."

"Did they catch who shot him?"

"Some hunter is all we guess. No, never caught him."

"A hunter," she repeated, her tone full of disgust for the breed. I swear I can't understand why men think they have to hunt. Every year they go out and shoot helpless animals and end up killing someone like your dad. It's a crying shame."

"Yeah, he was shot nine times," I said.

"Oh, come on!"

"Yeah, nine in the gut and chest. Pretty much made hamburger of poor Papa. He coughed up lots of blood and died."

Eyeing me closely, I could tell she wasn't sure what to make of it all. Neither was I. The lying words came into my mouth and without thinking much about it I just said them.

"Where did this all happen? What county?"

"Oh, long way off in, um . . . in Alaska."

"Alaska? You lived in Alaska? Your father was shot to death up there? And your mother lives in that frozen land with five children to raise?"

"It's affected my mind, I think."

"Well, I don't wonder."

I thought about adding more stuff, like telling her how the pieces of flesh squirted from Pa when the bullets hit him, and how the snow was all slashes of red melting. The pictures of it were crowding my mind, and I realized I was seeing Ben and the dead doe, and I got to wondering if I could describe things graphic enough to make Phoebe cry. And then I wondered if I could make her like me. She had a pretty face if you didn't mind those jug ears sticking out. I liked her for how sad she seemed at the moment about all my troubles. I didn't get a chance to lie to her further because Anna came bustling over and wanted to know who I was talking to.

"This is Phoebe Bumpus from the *Temple Daily Star*. Come to write about the idiot phenomenon."

Anna turned around and shouted across the street to Soren sitting in his wheelchair on the porch. "A witer, a witer on the news!"

"TV?" Soren asked.

"Newspaper," I told him.

"Newspaper, phooey!"

Chee Chee was barking and Soren yelled at her to "Shut up, you damn mouse!"

"You don't know fo shit!" said Anna. She took off for Charlie's place, skipping along on her little legs like a spooked quail.

"What was that?" said Phoebe.

I explained about Anna and Soren, that Soren had broken his back for hurry-up money and that his friend Neil had died and Soren hated everything except TV, which Anna hated like TV was the devil because Soren refused to leave it for more than a few minutes and get on with his life.

Phoebe kept shaking her head. "Such tragic lives," she said.

Down the street Shepard came banging out of Charlie's. He thundered up the walk with Anna right behind taking four steps to his one. He came at Phoebe with his humongous hand thrusting out, introducing himself before he got to her – "Don Shepard of Artlife fame. Temple's resident genius." He was slightly unsteady, weaving a little, like a man standing in a boat on the water rocking. When Phoebe took his hand he sneezed, blowing strands of her hair backward.

"*Pardonnez-moi, madam - scusi!* It's the sun in my face. Spring is seeding the April air with allergies. Or is it March? Who cares? You're here at last." Vigorously he wiped his nose on his sleeve.

Phoebe looked over her shoulder at me, her eyes bulging with astonishment.

"Happy to accommodate the press," he continued. "One minute, forgive me, sensitive olfactories – *Aaa-chooo! Eee-aaa-chooo!* – Gad-dammee this empathetic depuration of the *Marques de Nez*." He patted his nose sympathetically. Out came his hanky, followed by two vigorous honks into it. A final wipe and with a flourish he put it back in his pocket and produced his whiskery walrus grin. She was inching back towards me. I could see she was alarmed and on the verge of sprinting for her car at the curb.

"Ahh, there then, that should purify this envy of Arabia," he said, tapping the flushed cauliflower tip of his nose. "Now down to business. What pray tell can I do for the press?" He grasped her hand again and shook it like he was jerking on a bellrope.

"I c-came because of th-this," said Phoebe, holding out the handbill.

"Ahh, my advertisement, of course. And not the least bit exaggerated, miss, miss, ah?"

"Bumpus. Phoebe Bumpus."

"Bumpus? Onomatopoeic – bump, bump – a good omen doubtless."

"I'm from the *Temple Daily Star* and I thought it might make a good story, if it's all true, I mean. The idiot phenomenon."

"All true?" said Shepard, curling his upper lips, his gums and fangs almost menacing. "Why, Miss Bumpus, Mamie is a walking, talking *miracle*. A story about her could easily make you famous. And me too, of course." His arm scythed through the space between them. "All of us and instant fame in fact!"

"You newer knewed sooch a stowy," said Anna, stamping her feet with excitement.

Once again Phoebe glanced at me, half-terrified, half-amazed, nervous legs and hands jittery. I winked at her and did my best to smile sanely.

Shepard was talking fast, telling her that he had at his command, for her delectation, "a phenomenon extraordinaire, a phenomenon that defies all boundaries of expert hypocrites and scientific quackery of explanation. No borders bind this girl. Like the secrets of the cosmos there is no getting to the bottom of it. One can only gaze in wonder and feel overwhelming admiration for what blessed nature has fashioned of our adorable Mamie Beaver. She cannot be defined or categorized by any of the five senses given to us. You need the sixth sense to grasp that she is none other than the great Platonic ideal of forms."

"Ideal of forms?" breathed Phoebe.

"Of forms," he said, raising his hand in the gesture of giving an oath. Or maybe a judo chop. Phoebe flinched. She took hold of my arm. I patted her hand. Shepard rapidly explained what he meant by ideal forms. "My Mamie is the reincarnation of the universal thing-in-itself, the absolute, the eternal form first imagined by the mind of creation when it gave birth to the idea of woman full-blown from the final mixture of the primeval soups that gave juice to the materializations of all living creatures. Here we stand as imperfect descendents of the first Earth-Goddess as Woman. Mamie is her daughter. Her sidekick. Her clone. Mamie is her glory!"

"I s-see," said Phoebe.

"She is – ub ub – what else is she, Crystal?" He squeezed his head between his hands, trying to squeeze forth what more Mamie might be.

"Strong as a Morgan horse," I offered.

"A Clydesdale!" shouted Shepard. "Immense power! Truly legendary. A female Samson. A visitor from Krypton. Superman's daughter if he had a daughter. A descendent of Plato's meditation on perfection before mankind fell from heaven past gold and silver to bronze and iron. And now man's poor intellect is sealed inside something pewter and petrified. His leaden ass in the gutter, versus Mamie's mind in the stars - a blaze of light, a comet with a tail of utterance reaching outward to eternity! Which would you rather choose, the noble qualities of physical and mental heroism residing in my phenomenon extraordinaire, or a continuation of a polemic species, all these true believers strangling us, they whose lives are so perniciously *small*? Answer me! Answer me instantly!"

"Eeep," squeaked Phoebe.

"Precisely," said Shepard. "At least you are keeping an open mind. And soon you will see that from Mamie's oversized head right down to her scrumptious sloth-envied toes, she is evolution accelerated. From her loins will come *das Ubermensch, das Uberfraulein!*"

Phoebe couldn't stop shivering. I patted her bum to calm her down. She rolled her eyes at me as if she were about to have a seizure.

"It always calms our heifers," I told her, caressing her bum again. It was a very firm gluteus to the max.

She closed her eyes and rubbed round and round her temples and whispered. "Let me think. Let me think."

"Nothing to think about," said Shepard. "Let's get Mamie and let her perform."

Phoebe took out a small pad of paper and a pen and started writing - "Idiot, moron, genius, evolution accelerated and - what else, the ideal form of Earth-Goddess as Woman? Did I catch that right?"

"Close enough," said Shepard. "Listen, my dear, judged by our common standards, we could call her a moron or an idiot. Yes, no denying the similarities. But we might say the same of a Martian were we *unable* to comprehend the Martian's intellectual level. Mamie is like that. On an ordinary level, few but geniuses such as *moi* can absorb what she is. Does she contradict herself? Of course she does, she is large, she contains multitudes! It is her cross to bear that she must lower herself to communicate with us in the idiom of Shakespeare, or Shaw, or a sweaty snotnose genius like Tennessee Williams, humph!"

"Lower herself to Shakespeare?" Phoebe burst into laughter. "Oh dear, I'm feeling a little giddy."

"Tee hee hee," laughed Shepard. Which made Phoebe laugh even harder.

"I think I'm getting hysterical. Stop it now, Phoebe. So unprofessional. Ah, shit! Ah-haw-haw-haw! I'm gonna wet my pants, goddammit!" She squeezed her thighs together and squirmed.

Anna was doing her happy dance. Shepard had his hands on his knees and was bellowing "Oh ho ho ho!" Phoebe wobbled as she leaned into me and held her belly and howled with laughter.

"Gone off the deep end a little, haven't you?" I asked her.

Finally she lowered her head and put her hands over her ears so she couldn't see or hear Shepard. After a few seconds she settled down and I let her go.

"I'm so embarrassed," she said. "I hardly ever lose my cool like that, but oh it was like I've fallen down a rabbit hole. Those little fangs of yours. That nose. And this kid patting my ass. And Anna doing that – what kind of dance was that? I'm sorry. Please don't take me wrong. I'm sure you're all normal. And you, Mr. Shepard, I'm sure you're an intelligent man. But oh gee, I can't explain – never mind, never mind."

" I am a work of art, a genius," said Shepard carefully, like he didn't want to set her off again. "And I understand the ironic humor implicit in Mamie's situation. I laugh about it myself, so don't feel badly, Miss Bumpus. A lesser man than I might take umbrage, but never one who sees the comic levels of life's caprices."

"You are being very nice," said Phoebe, her voice full of butter now. "In fact, there's something rather original about you, something refreshing. I'm glad I came." She cleared her throat. Coughed. "So when can I meet your phenomenon?"

"Yes, you must meet Mamie. She's with Powers in the booth. Let's catch her before the boozing hour is here. Will you please follow me, Miss Bumpus?" He swept his hand in the direction of the Artlife.

We all tromped over there and up the stairs, where we found Mamie polishing Powers with 3-in-1 oil, he glistening like a monstrous jewel, one of those bodybuilders posing on a stage. Shepard introduced Phoebe and for a moment the two women stared at each other without saying anything.

Then –

"What's that on her mouth? A morbid lipstick?"

"It's graphite," I explained. "Mamie sometimes kisses the projector in places where the graphite clings."

"Of course she does," said Phoebe. "It fits."

I told Phoebe that Mamie loved Powers as her teacher. "She

can never learn much from us, but anything from Powers sticks like honey pouring over her brain."

"It's chemistry," said Shepard.

Phoebe said to Mamie, "Does Powers kiss you back?"

"He lufs me so," she answered.

"Oh dear, she does sound . . . slow," said Phoebe. "Nasal-like, like a partially deaf person does."

"Until she turns her genius on," said Shepard. "Often it is difficult to recognize a species of superiority when filtering it through a plebeian mind. I've often had to struggle myself to make others understand *me*."

"I'm sorry for saying that," said Phoebe.

"No apology, no apology. The mundane mind is something I'm used to. It has never been able to appreciate me. Mamie knows what I'm saying. We have great deformability of the brain. Which is a perfect definition of genius – it sees the world anew and gives it an innovative twist."

Phoebe kept studying Mamie hard, smiling at her and Mamie smiling back. "I've never seen anything like you, Mamie." Phoebe turned her eyes on us, blinking kindly. Still smiling. "I can see why you might love her. She glows with health and what would you call it – strength and decency. Where on earth did you find her, Mr. Shepard?"

"She appeared one day from another dimension, in a blaze of light merging from a crack in the universe. An immaculate inception from a fracture in time."

"Whatever you say," said Phoebe. "But you may be onto something as extraordinaire as your handbill says. There is an aura about her like a movie star. Or maybe an angel?"

"What you see is what you get," I told her.

"Uh-huh." Phoebe was biting her lip, her eyes narrowing in on Mamie. "So you say here that doctors are baffled. How so? What do they say?"

Shepard focused his attention on Mamie. "Now, Mamie. 'There is something in this more than natural, if philosophy could find it out.'"

Mamie fired right back: "'I am but mad north-northwest.

When the wind is southerly, I know a hawk from a handsaw.'"

"How did she do that?" asked Phoebe.

"Precisely what doctors are asking," said Shepard. "And that is a mere nibble of what to expect."

"She gave me goose bumps," said Phoebe. "My dear, you are very, very talented." She paused, her eyes puzzling. Then added, "I think."

"You appreciate that this genetic aberration must not go unrequited, Miss Bumpus?"

"Everybody round here thinks she's a gyp and a faker," I said.

"Dey tink she fool dem," said Anna.

"Say something else, Mamie," said Phoebe.

"Ahem, Miss Bumpus. She cannot do it without *moi*. I exhumed her talent from the tomb. I disinterred it from the traumatized regions littered with her abused soul. Without Don Shepard, she produces no evidence of extraordinary thespianism."

"Please continue," said Phoebe.

So Shepard got her going, and Mamie did some big chunks from *Hamlet*, line after line rolling from her like lines of thunder announcing a storm. And all the while, Phoebe stared and gawked and shivered. When it was over, she told us she was goosebumps from head to toe, and that this Mamieism was an amazing story that would have her readers in thrall. She wanted to see her entire act, whatever it was, however long it took.

And Mamie did it. We got her into her robe and (minus the mime mask) Shepard put her through her paces. Shakespeare, Shaw, all those writers she knew by heart came trippingly from her tongue. Phoebe took lots of pictures with her camera. She was crazy for the act. Wild about Mamie. She said she was going to stand Temple on its ignorant ear. Going to wake up all these clods and teach them the possibilities of the human spirit. Make them see the complexities of the brain – Mamie's brain that had such power to recreate what it saw and heard on the movie screen, like the screen of life itself to her. Yes, and everything was yum yum to Shepard. I'd never seen him so happy. By the end of Phoebe's speech, he was sobbing into his hanky.

"My goodness, you're an emotional man," she said.

"He's very sensitive," I told her.

When finally Shepard had pulled himself together, we went over to the house to have a drink and celebrate. Shepard laid out beer with splow chasers, and we all toasted Phoebe Bumpus our savior, who was going to bring the power of the pen to the legend of Mamie. Shepard had to weep a bit more over the whole idea.

"What *is* wrong with that man?" Phoebe whispered to me.

"Don't mind me," he told her. "It is my, ub, ub, my curse to have the soul of a poet. I was thinking now how hard I've struggled and how my dear old friend Amoss struggled with me. He's gone and cannot enjoy the coming triumph – ooh boo-hoo-hoo, cruel fate. Please don't make fun of me. It is that all my feelings are at my fingertips today. My heart is on my sleeve. It is a mixed blessing being me. For this poetic soul of mine fires my genius and makes me want to blaze like a shooting star across the sky, bringing the light of knowledge to all the wanton ignorance I see around me. Ignorance looking through a glass darkly. And yet I know I sometimes look like a fool. Mixed blessing - genius."

Looking at Mamie over the top of his dripping hanky he said, "Mamie, I love you truly. Will you marry me?"

She snorted "Phoo! Nup nup!"

Her abrupt rejection of him brought on another crying jag. It seemed as if he was having a pretty good time. I think all of us enjoyed it too.

So, the five of us spent the day together, drinking and talking, mostly talking about how dense everybody was in Temple. We learned that Phoebe was a college graduate from some little college in Minnesota named St. Scholastica, and that she had worked on the *Minneapolis Star* and this was her first job in Wisconsin. She had been hired as a senior reporter. She wanted to write *big* stories and make a name for herself. End up in Chicago or New York or L.A.

The more she drank, the friendlier she became. She wanted us to know she really liked us, that it usually took her a while to warm up to people, but she had definitely taken to us now. We were different and *viva le difference*. Our honesty. Our unpretentious authenticity. She hoped we liked her as well. Of course we did. We'd have given her anything she wanted right then. She was a petite, totally wonderful, big-hearted woman who appreciated Mamie's talent as much as anyone, and that's all we needed to know. As the day wore on Phoebe got more wonderful. By early evening I was sure I was in love with her.

We ate some toasted cheese sandwiches, with potato chips and pickles and pork rinds, washed down with beer and splow. I was good and drunk and had never felt better about life. We played the radio and sang the songs that came on, whether we knew the words or not, sang into each other's faces, our breaths kissing, sang solos and duets – some sounded so beautiful they made us cry. Anna seemed to get more and more lovey as the songs came and went. She plopped herself on Shepard's lap and sang to him, kissing his nose in between taking deep breaths. She told him if it wasn't for Soren she would let him look up her dress. Shepard blinked slowly as if trying to process the information. Anna on his lap. Anna's dress. Up look it. Up it look. Look up it. After a while I saw his hand petting her ankle. Next thing it was lost inside her skirt, petting something that made her squirm and call him a naughty man.

Mamie got to feeling no-rainy, and she plucked me off my chair, where I had been leaning close to Phoebe, trying to tell her how much I loved her teeth and that I didn't care a sot how her ears stuck out and that the feel of her bottom was still on my palm. My seductions were interrupted in what I thought was a rude way. Mamie dropping me on her lap like I was back to being her plaything. I heard mystery words crooned in my ear. Pretty Phoebe came over and kissed me wetly. She kept saying how much she wished I were older. Her eyes were bloodshot. Her voice steamy. Now and then I'd catch sight of her running her hand over her oranges and looking at what Shepard and Anna were doing.

At a pause in the action, Shepard asked her how long she thought it would be before her story came out. Phoebe looked at him as if he had said something sour.

"Don't bug me," she said. Reaching down she started pinching my legs, saying, "Tut-tut, did I hurt the little boy? Did I hurt his precious? Did I? Tell me, little boy, are you little?"

I was so numb I hardly felt the pinches. I wanted to say it was okay, but about all I could manage was a grin that made my mouth feel crooked and toothy.

"Roll Out The Barrel" blasted from the radio. Mamie wanted to dance. She dumped me on the floor and got up and soon she was kicking her legs and whirling. Anna joined her. The two of them hooted and crashed across the room. The rest of us joined in hooting and calling for more. Faster! Faster!

The polka ended. Followed by a waltz. Phoebe pulled me to her and we danced in a slow circle. Anna and Shepard waltzed too. Sort of. She was standing on his feet and he was moving back and forth. She looked strange, so tiny a thing holding on to him, trying to see his face over his belly. Finally, he lifted her into his arms, locking his hands under her bottom. They shuffled.

Mamie was eyeing me and Phoebe. We were hardly dancing at all, just rocking our hips. Phoebe kept kissing me, sticking her tongue in my ear too. Given another time (and sober) I suppose I would have been embarrassed being now sixteen and sort of making love to an older woman, but I felt a grudge against Mamie for the way she had cut me off and given herself to Powers, his cold ticking, whirring song in her ears more important than no-raining me. The hell with him and her. I kissed Phoebe back and tried to push her down on the couch. She bit my chin. Pushed me away and pulled her sweater over her head and tossed it somewhere. She unhooked her brassiere and there they were – those oranges. Pale handfuls. Pinkish brownish nipples rigid. Amazing what splow will do to a woman's inhibitions. And her conscience.

She was on me and I didn't know what to do. But all of a sudden I wasn't feeling very well. Burping pork rinds, booze churning hotly in my belly. I started thinking about what happened to Amoss. Maybe I would bust open like him and need a blood transfusion. Or maybe I would be dead before a doctor could get the blood in me. And Phoebe kept grinding against me, wanting me, kissing my neck, lifting my shirt and rubbing her bosoms over my bosoms. When she pushed my head down to her nipples it was too much. I broke away and ran for the toilet.

Wrapped myself around it and heaved.

After a minute or so I rested my cheek on the cool bowl, feeling miserable, a poor excuse for a man. Phoebe came in and caught me by the hair, lifting my head back so I had to look up at her face, her blurry lips moving, saying, "I want you!" Her ears seemed to be flapping like little pink moth wings.

"You can have me," I said. She let go of my hair and my head rolled back into the toilet. There was nothing I could do about it. Nothing.

Night. Very late. Quiet house. Christian Peter Foggy wrapped around the toilet like a porcelain lover. I let go and staggered to my feet, weaved into the living room. Phoebe lay snoring on the couch, a blanket over her. Shepard sat in the easy chair, head thrown back, eyes closed. Anna was in Shepard's bedroom sprawled like the cross of Christ on his bed. Her dress pulled up. Her underpants shining like a v-shaped moonstreak. Mamie wasn't in the other room. I figured she had gone back to the projection booth to be with Powers. I didn't care. I went to the kitchen sink and turned on the faucet and drank water until my belly sloshed. Splow. Horrible stuff. Never again, Christian. To hell with splow. To hell with booze. You've learned your lesson.

Stumbling to the couch, I wavered over Phoebe. Finally I bent down and kissed her forehead and said, "Phoebe, wake up, honey. I'm okay now. You can have me."

She opened her eyes, glared at me and snarled, "Touch me and I'll knock your teeth out, buddy. You better believe it."

Speaking in Tongues

A few days later, Phoebe Bumpus's story was on the Entertainment and Life page of the paper:

IDIOT OR GENIUS YOU DECIDE

Don Shepard said he had a Phenomenon Extraordinaire waiting for us at the Artlife Theatre. And you know what? He wasn't lying. The phenomenon is a girl named Mamie Beaver. Remember that name, Mamie Beaver. She is an uncannily talented young lady, eighteen to twenty years old (she doesn't actually know her age) whom I predict will be famous some day.

What is so exciting about Miss Beaver? I'll tell you. She has an unexplainable ability to memorize lines of spoken script from any film she has seen, and I mean memorize them perfectly. All the roles are stored in her head somehow – *everything*. It is not just a talent I am talking about. It is a phenomenon bordering on the metaphysical. Let me try to explain more.

I sat dumbfounded while I watched her play role after role from certain movies that have been shown at the Artlife. First she was Hamlet, then she was Horatio, then Ophelia, the king, the queen, the garrulous Polonius. And she was Major Barbara from Shaw's brilliant play *Major Barbara*, filmed in 1941. Mamie was also Blanche Dubois from *A Streetcar Named Desire* by Tennessee Williams. She was even Stanley Kowalski yelling "Stella! Stella!" And, of course, she was Stella herself. Mamie opened her mouth and out they came, all those actors, their enthralling words. Which I doubt Mamie even understood – not this bumpkin who seems to have arrived on Earth from a crack in space, a behemoth whom

292

doctors have classified as retarded, or perhaps an idiot savant, or an as yet indefinable mental defective of some sort. What do doctors know? Not Mamie Beaver that's for sure. Can I explain her fully? Not a chance. All I can do is repeat what Don Shepard said by way of clarification: "Chemistry." There are those who would sneer piously at the idea of such a practical, scientific-based explanation and say her gifts are obviously supernatural. They will get no argument from me.

Please understand this. Mamie Beaver cannot even hold a normal conversation with you. She stutters and stammers so badly that she must keep her sentences extremely short in order to say anything at all. She cannot read or write, not a word! She knows no mathematics, not even that two and two are four. Time and again she has been called an idiot, but not by those who really take the time to know her. Perhaps you think I have been taken in by a trick. I assure you I have not. Mamie Beaver is just what the advertisement says she is: a Phenomenon Extraordinaire. Onstage all her defects disappear. The depthless blue of her eyes becomes filled with understanding and intelligence and focused awareness. The bulky awkwardness of her body (she must be six foot three and well over two hundred pounds) evaporates like mist in a warming sun. And there you have her – a compelling and graceful figure endowed with the qualities of a chameleon.

Can this be genius as Don Shepard calls it? What else can it be? Unless you want to believe in the supernatural and that some holy spirit has descended upon her. Both sides, I am sure, will have their advocates. But for me the only question is, can genius reside side by side in the mind of a moron? An Idiot? Well, perhaps to our limited senses and understanding, she seems to be a moron or an idiot. Seems, I say, but only seems. Maybe we see her as such because you and I are the brain-damaged ones. Don Shepard calls her Evolution Accelerated. If he is right, then our opinions of her have to be wrong. So perhaps she is, indeed, the future chemistry of a goddess living a thousand years from now, when all mankind will be interchameleon. Anyone out there working on a doctorate in physiology or psychology might want to study the wonder of Mamie Beaver and tell us if she is from some future time warp, a crack in space, another dimension, or just a freak out of sync with contemporary times. Tis a mystery.

In the meantime, treat yourself to a performance that will leave you filled with a baffling admiration for what can only be called, for lack of something more precise, a colorful aberration of great art – a change in the position of a flaming heavenly body. Go see Mamie Beaver. You won't regret it. Now playing at Don Shepard's Artlife Theatre. Call for show times.

Phoebe Bumpus showed up with a camera crew and filmed Mamie's act and put edited bits of it on TV local news. What we saw was pretty exciting, and we believed that Mamie was truly on her way to making a big breakthrough. For a few days she was famous in Temple. People came and paid a dollar to see her perform. They filled the Artlife. They even bought books and a painting or two or a totem. No one said anything about double features or war movies or cowboys and Indians. The people came, sat, watched and listened with interest. Clapped politely when the show was over. And when they left through the lobby, you could hear them talking to one another about what a phenomenon they had seen and repeating some of Phoebe's phrases from the article: "Her big body does just evaporate like mist in a warming sun." "Oh, yes, and isn't she compelling and graceful?" "It borders on the metaphysical." "Dumbfounded. I'm just dumbfounded." Stuff like that. Some even came back for another performance, letting their friends know that they had seen Mamie twice or three times, and wasn't she just too amazing for words?

So at first we all thought we were right there on the edge of something fabulous. Shepard, Anna, Phoebe and I were full of anticipation, waiting for the big papers and magazines to find us. Shepard predicted that soon we would need a bigger theater. We might even need a press agent, said Phoebe. Get ready, she said, because when things got hot, we would have to move fast. We were ready for the hot things to happen. We waited for the signs of the big time on our doorstep: newsmen from Milwaukee, television reporters, major magazines hounding us for interviews - Hello, Hollywood calling, New York calling. Ed Sullivan wanting us on his show! We waited.

We waited.

And none of it happened like we thought it would. The crowds began to thin out again, and within three weeks or so we were almost where we had started. When the crowds dropped off, Phoebe had a fit. She cursed the fate that had planted her in such a backward town as Temple. She even wrote another article about Mamie, telling the people that they were too ignorant to know what was in their midst. But the paper wouldn't publish the article and she almost got fired. She was crying about it when she told us. She asked us to forgive her for leading us into thinking that the power of the pen had the power to make silk purses out of sows' ears. She promised that she would find a way yet to make Mamie famous, even if she had to write a book about her and self-publish it and handsell it to bookstores all over the country. She went away that day vowing she would never give up.

The roller coaster ride we were on finally leveled off after a few weeks. We were into late spring, mid-May, and the countryside was blooming. Trees in the town were lush with leaves. Flowers grew in clay pots and window boxes. Gardens in backyards sprouted vegetables. Bees and butterflies did their thing. The abundance of nature itself seemed supernatural. And there was Mamie every Saturday afternoon and evening performing her act in front of a small but loyal group of followers, about thirty of them – men, women, and children. A few of them I recognized from the book-burning, the old followers of Robbie Peevy. They riveted their attention on Mamie while she did her parts, as if by focusing hard enough they could figure her out. If the kids acted up, the parents would order them to sit still and witness the signs of God's Holy Spirit infusing the holy figure on the stage. They would get caught up in her act. A man here or a woman there might shout, "Yes, Lord!" "I hear you!" "Jeee-sus is talking!" That kind of thing. It really got Mamie going, really made those words roll off her tongue. Sometimes so fast that Shepard would lose his place and couldn't keep up. But that worked too, after a while, because the people had memorized the words themselves, and so they would shout

out the next line for Mamie. As the weeks wore on, the people began to drown out Shepard altogether, taking over his role, making it them and Mamie. She liked it. He got mad about it. Spluttered and twitched and scowled, but it did no good. They weren't afraid of him. Mamie was the ventriloquized voice of the Lord. What did Shepard matter? The people became a multitude that grew and grew.

And once they had it all their way, the people got more selective about what they wanted. They would call out those lines that would bring the right words from Mamie. She would get excited and hurry back and forth across the stage and point to one section or another, and the people in that section would shout out a line like:

"'Thou know'st tis common –"

"All that lives must die –" she would say.

"Passing through nature to eternity,'" would come the answer.

And she would reply, "'Aye, madam, it is common.'"

The crowd liked doing those lines a lot.

Another set they liked to share was Hamlet talking about suicide.

"'Or that the Everlasting had not fixed—'"

"'His canon 'gainst self-slaughter! Oh, God! God!—'"

"'How weary, stale, flat, and unprofitable—'"

"'Seem to me all the uses of this world.'"

It was pretty neat. A sort of sing-song thing, but not monotonous. It would end with a bunch of them bellowing, "Yes, Jee-sus! Hear him now! Hear the words of the Lord!" Loud hallelujahs, incoherent cries, squeaks and squeals. Lots of babbling. It was a really good time they were having.

And so it went for a while, from one play to the next, characters flowing from Mamie's mouth like a river over its banks flooding the people with holy water. They swam together in the waters of inspiration, their voices rising – a heavenly chorus, a sacred echo that bounced off the walls, going from Mamie to them and back again. Words floating everywhere. I had never seen people so alive and on fire as Mamie's followers. I had never seen her so fired up either, except at the book burning months ago. But this was different. This stage-thing with the crowd below and her above making the sparks fly between them - it was out of this world. She, burning like a little sun in the shaft of Power's burning bright lens. The multitude in reflection palely lit like a worshipping moon. That's how Saturdays were spent. The same people came and the same kind of ritual took place. And it got more and more perfect.

May passed into June and it seemed that with the growing warmth came a growing number of followers. The theater got so full on Saturdays that we had to give two shows. And then we were opening on Sundays for two more. We were making money, more money by a long shot than when Shepard had stuck to his ideas about what art was, giving the customers what *he* wanted them to have. Instead of what they wanted.

He had done some soul-searching, he told us, and had come to conclusions about what had gone wrong. "I gave them too much credit," he said. "I forgot that no homo sapiens of the plebian cast of mind, such as these Christers who plague us, are willing to use their brains, not if they can contrive any way at all to let that wrinkled lump of gray matter rest in a dogmatic well. This leads to a phenomenon of the worst kind, where men who suddenly acquire a rage to say something profound have nothing but platitudes and clichés in their pointy little heads. So they spout meaningless dribble to make themselves feel like an important part of an important group. Humph! The people despise all intellectual labor. It hurts them sorely. And even if thinking were easy, they would be content to be ignorant, rather than trouble their minds with genuine thought. But my penetrating intellect and insights will prevail, I promise you. I have a perfect plan, so perfect it might as well be a formula in algebra or geometry, or a universal law like the second law of thermodynamics. Namely entropy. Let me continue," he said, his forefinger upright pontifical.

"I have decided to create the First Church of Art! These Christers wish to pull art down to the mediocre level of themselves, brass crosses and wooden altars, stained glass windows, pious slogans hung on a marquee in front of a steepled church, bells beckoning.

Their own pastel clothing imaging their pastel souls. They cannot bear the mental effort of rising up to art that is actually – well, er - *art*. And what is that, my friends? Let me tell you. First of all art improves on nature. It compensates for the inadequacies of reality. It transfigures. Found in the immortal musings of the Irish architect of *A Portrait of the Artist as a Young Man*, is the knowledge that true art holds you in *aesthetic arrest*. It does not move you towards it or away from it. *You* do not possess *it*. *It* possesses *you*. Without such attributes, it is not art - it is pornography! Yes! So be it. I have spoken."

Lifting his eyes toward the ceiling, Shepard closed them and his breath shuddered.

Obviously pleased with himself he kept speaking, laying out his plan to circumvent the Christers and—

"Indoctrinate their minds and saturate their souls in the language of true art. How do I do that? Listen to me. What is genius for, if it can't outthink these bloody fools? I will give them art as simply as the church gives them dogmas, by which they wander thoughtlessly through their pointless lives. If that's how it must be, then why not learn a litany from the great writers of the ages, rather than from some tired old tome like the Bible that needs to catch up with the twentieth century? That litany is what they are learning already, only they don't know it, and we shall encourage it. We shall keep it up. And slowly but surely, the people will be fed more and more, until it becomes their Eucharist. Do you understand me? They are naturally stupid and dull, but it will soak into them by and by - as I say, through osmosis. It will ultimately saturate them to the core. And the day will come when they will cry out not 'Praise Jesus,' or 'Hear the words of the Lord,' but 'Praise Shakespeare, praise Herman Melville!' Melville is next, dear friends, the Shakespeare of the nineteenth century. I have the movie *Moby Dick* and Mamie is learning it. Gradually shall she add it to the litany, feed it to them like mouth-watering pieces of candy. Bonbons for the soul! I'm so crafty it scares me sometimes. How these Christers have underestimated me! The fools. As if I would ever let them push me aside. Poof, poof! Without even knowing it, they will become my minions, my followers, my little worshippers of art! Their minds will evolve eventually against the inspissations of a pornographic Christ, the embodiment of kitsch, he who would evaporate every cell of individuality in all of us! A titanic battle is about to begin! Art versus pornography! Art versus kitsch! Art versus the mediocre ilk of this mediocre age we live in!"

By now he was shouting and sweating and trembling and holding his arms out as if he were about to embrace the invisible essence of Art itself - add its volume to his already obese body – or perhaps embrace pornography, kitsch, the mediocre age we live in and crush them against his massive belly.

"I have found my destiny, my dears - I the founder of the First Church of Art! Noble Donald Leonardo Shepard – he took men away from worshipping the irrational blood of suffering and gave them the *anima mundi* of true art, the great collective memory of the world that sings 'To lords and ladies of Byzantium of what is past, or passing, or to come'! All was chaos and mob mentality, until Shepard came to save the world and set things right. Don't call it megalomania because it's not. *I am that I am!* I will show all of you that man himself makes miracles of art, 'Monuments of unaging intellect,' as Mr. Yeats puts it. So bless my memory with a tabernacle and raise my monument ten feet high and put a beacon on top of it to guide the multitudes. This precious scheme came to me in the night and told me I shall be raised to stupendous heights! Would any of you deny it?"

Nope, none of us would.

So after telling us how he had it figured out, Shepard slipped *Moby Dick* lines into the act. He also reasserted his total control by having Mamie react to him *before* she reacted to the audience. And I didn't take a dollar at the ticket booth anymore. Instead, between the time Mamie had finished with *Moby Dick* and was getting ready to do *Hamlet*, we had an intermission and I passed a collection plate, just like in church. And the people piously, even gratefully, filled the plate up.

Phoebe showed up with her crew and filmed the revised act, which became more and more refined. Everything but *Moby Dick* and *Hamlet* had been dropped from Mamie's sermon, which Shepard now formed around certain scenes just the way he wanted. Like when he had her do Melville's words, he slipped them in so smoothly the people hardly noticed a change of beat. Mamie would softly say, "Call me Ishmael." And while the camera rolled, she would give the speech about deep November in the soul and needing desperately to get to sea. The speech had the same searching tones as the Hamlet speeches we used ("How all occasions do inform against me . . . What is a man if his chief good and market of his time be but to sleep and feed? A beast no more"), and the congregation would lean forward to listen in a sort of rapture. Mamie spoke the lines so beautifully I was choked up half the time, seeing myself as an outcast Ishmael searching for the sea of enlightenment. And when it was over everyone gave a grateful sigh and a soft-toned amen. And some of them even praised the power of the words to inspire them and make them feel "fully holy."

So, *Moby Dick* started things out and became an important part of the litany, and in no time at all the followers were alternating the lines with Mamie that Shepard wanted. Also, he would hold her back before each service while he gave an introductory sermon. He would come into the light and say, like a preacher or a prophet:

"Behold a miracle of our time. Behold the art of Mamie Beaver. Behold the incarnation of the Supreme Creator's beneficence and pleasure, for she is an idiot whom he has made to speak in tongues. Let this be a sign to those who believe, '*They will speak in tongues!*' Behold, ye people in search of holiness, Mamie speaks in the tongues of the greatest artists of all time. It is the pleasure of the Great Creator to give us the zenith of art from the lips of a moron. Through her we have received a litany that combines the best of his message for the indoctrination of all humanity. Yea, even to those poor players strutting and fretting for an hour upon the stage of this oscillating world. From this time let the word go forth that the First Church of Art is open for worship. And now I give you the symbol and the crown, the witness and the prophet – here she is, what you've been waiting for –

Mamie Beaver!"

I've got to admit it stirred me up every time I heard his speech. And then out she would come in her shining glory, black-robbed stepping into the bright light, but minus the makeup. No more mime props. Shepard let her beautiful face express what she was saying.

"'Oh, ye damned whale! Oh, ye damned whale!'" echoing off the ceiling and into our hearts. Her voice made a wave of words in which the people seemed to swim in ecstasy. And there was Shepard in the middle of it, standing onstage with Mamie, holding his hands out over the masses and looking like a fat pope giving them a blessing. It was spectacular. And it was everything I could do *not* to fall on my knees and pray to him and Mamie too.

It wasn't long till so many people were coming that we had to add more services. People stood in the aisles. The collection plates overflowed. I lived for the multitudes and Mamie and Shepard creating what seemed to me a perfect triangle of verbal art. It was beyond exciting or inspiring – it was *thrilling* – the services themselves, the money pouring in, the happy worshippers taking part in the give and take pattern orchestrated by Shepard, the connections, the rhythms, the voices raised on high. It was the best time of my life. But nothing good lasts forever. What is good, in fact, has no more staying power than a dream.

Wrestlings

During the week things at the Artlife were pretty dull. Monday through Friday we would show whatever cheap movie we had on hand, and a few people might come, and we might break even three or four nights out of five. But it didn't matter, because we had plenty of money from the collection plates to spend. We ate good. We bought new clothes. New shoes. Got regular haircuts. I even went to the dentist and got a cavity filled and my teeth cleaned. Shepard got his gums measured for a set of new front teeth. For a low down payment he bought a fancy-finned Cadillac painted gold. He wore shiny suits and shirts and gold chains and lots of other jewelry. A ring on his left pinky had a blue stone as big as an eyeball. He bought a watch that told the hour and what day and what month you were dealing with. It would even wake you up in the morning if you wanted it to. He drank his splow from a champagne glass now. He smoked cigars smuggled in from Cuba. He hired Anna to cook and clean for him. Life had never been better, he said. He was on a roll. He had more plans for the future. Big things were coming.

One night we showed a movie that no one came to see. It was called *Battleground*, a story about the Battle of the Bulge in World War II. There was lots of freezing cold and snow in the movie. One soldier froze to death hiding under a jeep. Another got shot because he had taken his boots off to sleep and couldn't put them on fast enough when the fighting started. I decided there was no way they would ever get me to go fight in the army. Hitting John Beaver over the head proved I had a bag of mean inside me somewhere, but I felt it wasn't big enough to make me ever want to take a gun and shoot somebody.

When the theater stayed empty, Shepard stopped the movie and we closed up shop and went over to Charlie Friendly's Bar & Grill. Mongoose Jim and Kiss of Death Cody were there playing pool. They were no longer men of the trains like Amoss, since they had been laid off for some months. They were drinking beer and they both looked bored. Kiss of Death Cody was short and thick, with sloping shoulders and heavy arms. He had a fat face and a scruffy beard and a beer belly lipping over his belt. Deep-set eyes. A cigar stuck in his mouth. It kept jerking as he chewed it. He whispered something to Mongoose Jim and looked in our direction. Mongoose Jim didn't look like a mongoose. He looked like an egret - big beak, long neck, chinless. His tiny head dipping as he listened to Kiss of Death Cody. A lot of mumbling went on between them for a while. They kept glancing over, giving Mamie the evil eye. Which surprised me because they had always been nice to her before. Kiss of Death Cody had even taught her how to play pool. That was some weeks ago and she was better than him now.

"Thorn's scorn," I heard him say at one point, the two of them sniggering.

Anna Gulbrenson came in slamming the door and huffing and puffing about Soren, saying she had finally done it, finally broke his television. She ordered a shot of splow to celebrate, but Charlie was out of splow – said he had ordered a case from Bob Thorn and it should be coming in later. So Anna sat with us drinking beer.

"I bweak dat gottdamn telewision," she told us again and again. "I smash it goot. He don't vach no mo. I tell to him he is noot a hoosband and I sick of it. Juss a big baby feeling sowwy fo hisself. To hell with dat. He says, 'Dey bweak my back and tell me go die now. I noot goot for nuttink.' 'Not if you don't wanna be,' tell I to him. I sick of it! I vant a man! I bweak dat telewision and tell to him he don't luf Anna and so he can go to hell!" Her face screwed up and she started bawling. Grabbing a tuft of skirt she sobbed into it.

When the blubbering was over she said, "Bah, he vas sooch a stwong man. All gone, all gone. Now he be a ghoost hisself seeing dat ghoost of Neil. Ghoost coming ewery night ven he sleepink, so he don't sleep. He vach telewision."

Personally, I felt sorry for Soren. If he was seeing ghosts, and maybe TV was his way of coping with them, well, let him watch the damn thing. Shepard sat there as mute as the rest of us for a time before he came up with something to say.

"Anna, darling, I have some tremendous news for you. In fact everyone must hear this. Gather round. You too, Kiss of Death. You too, Mongoose." They put their cues down and came over. Shepard continued, "I've decided that we have outgrown the Artlife. We are bulging at the seams and funds are pouring in at a precipitous rate. On the other hand, such affairs should not vex us. Indeed, as I have observed before, an idea whose time has come is more powerful than any whim of physicality that might try to resist it. The idea devours, absorbs and destroys all degenerate opposition." He leaned in and lowered his voice as if there might be spies trying to overhear him. "My First Church of Art has the potential of being a tyranny over everyone's thought processes, tee hee-hee, more tyrannous and absolute than any Christer sect that ever was or ever will be invented. Once the worship of art takes hold of our little town, adoration of what we are offering will explode across the state. Then the nation. Then the world. We are proselytizing in the name of the greatest achievements ever put into printed words. Once such a notion gets a grip it will dominate the cerebral life of every thinking being on this poor, put-upon planet. And it will save us from the destructive lust for damnation feeding the fires of corrupt religions worshipping death and a fiery Lord. All of them are bad for your spirit, bad for your soul, bad for your digestion. But now we teeter at the cusp of an infinite expansion of sensitivity, empathy, kindness and caring. Brotherly love. We are the forefront, the leading light of a movement that is sure to conquer the world. I mean, look at how easily I manipulated those Christers into worshipping Shakespeare and Melville. Easy, simple. Nothing to it."

Leaning even closer, the pits in his nose looking like the craters of a blood-red moon, he said, "Tee hee hee, guess who's going to preside over the construction of a New Artlife, a greater more capacious edifice to the religion of art. Hmm? Want to guess? All right, I'll tell you. Tis *moi!* Yours truly, the one and only. The Shepard himself looking out for his flock. I've been negotiating in private with several Elders of the church, and also with the filthy rich Cunninghams of Cunningham Chevrolet and Farm Implements. They who own half of this town. With all of them backing me, I have purchased the twenty acres of woods next door. Construction begins in two weeks. The design that we've approved will make the Mormon Tabernacle look like a pup tent. Tee hee hee."

"Geez," I said.

"Wow," said Mongoose Jim.

"You gonna let us in on the action, Don?" said Kiss of Death Cody.

"Precisely," said Shepard. "I've got important jobs for both of you."

"Vee get wich as sin," said Anna.

"For the cause," said Shepard. "All for the cause."

"Do you think I'll make enough to buy a Chevy from the Cunninghams?" I asked.

"Poof poof, we're going to purchase a fleet of Cadillacs, my boy. Long black ones with shark fins and white wall tires."

"Geez."

"Wow."

"I'll be your chauffer," said Kiss of Death Cody.

"Yes, and you'll both be my and Mamie's bodyguards."

"Just let anybody fuck with you, I'll show them."

"Me too," said Mongoose Jim. "Do we get uniforms?"

Anna got up and forced herself into Shepard's lap. She kissed his nose. She told him that if he played his cards right, she would get rid of Soren and marry him. He cuddled her like a child cuddling a teddy bear.

"You bring out the beast in me," he said.

I saw they were going to start messing around with each other again, so I went outside where I wouldn't have to witness it. I was curious about what Soren was doing, since he had no TV to watch and he was all by himself, except for Chee Chee, who he didn't even like. I went over there and looked in the window. I could see him sitting in his wheelchair, staring at a black hole jagged at the edges. His workman's hands draped helplessly over the arms of the chair. While I stood there, Mamie came up and looked in the window with me.

"He sure looks sad," I said. And then I said, "Anna's mean."

When Mamie went inside, I followed her. There was the ozone smell of fried electrical wires floating in the air. Chee Chee came out of a room, her tail wagging, but when she saw it wasn't Anna, she bopped up and down on all fours and yapped at us.

"Shut up, you damn mouse!" said Soren.

The yapping continued until he threw a cushion at her.

"Sure a mess," I said, indicating the TV.

"Anna did it," he said. "She hates me."

"She's over to Charlie Friendly's," I said.

"Good for her. Let her stay. She's right, I'm not the kind of man for her no more. She needs somebody that cares. I've stopped caring. I'm already dead." He looked at his palms as if their emptiness explained everything.

Mamie put her hands on Soren's shoulders and massaged them.

"I've been seeing my friend's ghost," he said. "If I sleep he comes to me."

"Does he say anything?" I asked.

"He says he's cold and he hates it. They buried him in a slick green coffin, but the poor bastard wanted to be cremated. That's what I want too. You can't be cold under the ground if you're cremated. I should dig him up and cremate him. If I was a good friend, that's what I would do. But I'm not a good friend. I'm just a sorry old puke."

"Well, that ain't fair," I said. "If the guy wanted to be cremated, that's what they should have done."

Soren laughed cynically. And he said, "Yeah, that's what they should have done. You're right. But right has nothing to do with ritual. His family buried him the way they thought he should be buried, with a priest and mumbo jumbo and the weeping widow and mourners throwing dirt on the coffin. All that crap that people do to make themselves feel better."

"And now he's cold and hates it."

Soren had a look on his face as if he was sorry for me. "You don't believe he really knows it, do you?"

"Sure I do."

"You're dumber than a box of rocks. Look, kid, its just dreams I'm having. And what's in a dream?"

Mamie had bent down and was petting Chee Chee. She looked at me and said, "Kritch'n. Anna st-stupid, yaay?"

"What do you mean, Mamie?"

"Oh, Kritch'n." Her tone was full of disappointment.

"What?"

She stood up and took hold of Soren's wheelchair and pushed him out the door and down the stairs. Chee Chee was yapping her head off again and following us.

"What you doing?" Soren was saying. "Where we going? Let go of me, goddammit, Mamie! Let me go!"

"Nup, nup."

And off we went toward Charlie's. Chee Chee barking all the way and Soren saying over and over, "Sic her, Chee Chee! Sic her!"

When I opened Charlie's door, Chee Chee saw Anna and gave a yelp and jumped into her lap. "Vut you do to my Chee Chee?" said Anna. "My poor baby-vun. Kiss you mama." The dog squirmed happily and licked Anna's face. Mamie rolled Soren up next to Anna, but he turned his wheelchair sideways, so he wouldn't have to look at her.

Shepard was standing at the pool table with a cue in his hands. He told Mamie to grab a stick and be his partner and help him beat Mongoose and Kiss of Death.

"I'm Kiss of Death Cody!" said Kiss of Death Cody. "I never showed no mercy to no pool player with a stick in his hands. Look out for me. I'm a kiss of death quicker than a rattlesnake. My stick is poison."

"Yeah, and I'm quicker than a rattlesnake too. I'm quick as a mongoose," said Mongoose Jim.

"Your ass," said Kiss of Death Cody. "I eat mongooses for breakfast. No one is quicker or deadlier than I am."

"I'm the mongoose. Mongooses are quicker'n snakes and everybody knows it. I saw a picture where a mongoose killed a cobra. I ain't lying."

"You ain't no goddamn mongoose. You get any slower, you'll be backing into yesterday."

"Naw, bullshit. You're an idiot."

"Don't call me no idiot. You're the idiot.

"I ain't not neither."

While they argued about it, Mamie racked the balls and ran the table. When Kiss of Death Cody and Mongoose Jim caught on to what she had done, they punched each other in the shoulder.

"Pay attention to the game," said Kiss of Death Cody.

"You pay attention."

"You."

"You."

It went on for a while, the guys watching as Mamie hit sixty in the pocket without a miss. Kiss of Death Cody got really steamed. He chewed his cigar to a nub and rubbed the chalk round and round the tip of his cue till the chalk turned to powder in his hand.

"That's it!" he said at last, when Mamie ran the table again. Throwing his cue on the table he stomped off to the bar and ordered another pitcher of beer. "I oughta break her nose," he said to Charlie.

"Should never have taught her to play pool," Charlie told him.

"You punch her nose, she'd kill you in a minute," said Mongoose Jim. "Don't forget what she did to Thorn, man."

"Look here, Mamie," said Kiss of Death Cody, "what you're doing is cheating. None of those balls count, see? You didn't let us lag for break. That's no fair." His eyes lit on Soren, who had a look on his face like he had swallowed something rotten raw. "What the hell you looking at?"

With a cold, level voice Soren said, "Not much that's for sure."

Mongoose Jim chuckled.

"What did he say?" said Kiss of Death Cody.

"He said you ain't much."

Kiss of Death Cody swung off the stool and scuttled to the table, walking sideways, like he was going to give Soren a karate kick. "You lucky you in a wheelchair, Soren, that's all I got to say. But don't push me. You think I won't crack you just cuz you're in a wheelchair? I might - you make me mad enough."

"Fuck you, punk," said Soren.

"I'm Kiss of Death."

"No, you're not. You're Kiss Your Own Ass Cody."

Kiss of Death Cody took the cigar out of his mouth and stabbed it at Soren, not touching him, just stabbing the air in front of his face. Chee Chee leaped off Anna's lap and snatched the cigar and shook it like she had caught a rat, and everybody started laughing.

"It ain't funny," said Kiss of Death Cody.

"I think it's funny as hell," said Mongoose Jim.

"I oughta squish that goddamn dog. Oughta squish it and this old cripple too. Would if he wasn't a cripple. You think you're privileged, don't you, Soren? You think you can act like a wiseass and nobody'll break your nose cuz you're sitting in that chair. I don't give a shit about that, man!"

"Privileged? Privileged?" said Soren "You stupid little pot-bellied runt."

"Gaa! Don't you call me no runt!"

"Sowen beat you stupid face, you . . . you stubby!"

"Stubby? Runt?" he shouted. "I'll beat the shit out of both of you!"

A pounding noise came from behind us. Charlie had a sawed-off bat and was tapping the bar with it. "Knock it off, Cody," he said. "Leave them alone."

Kiss of Death Cody hesitated. Then he said that Charlie was right. "Ain't no glory in kicking ass on a cripple. Even if he does deserve it. But you better watch your mouth, Soren. I'm in no mood."

"You punk sonofabitch," said Soren.

"Am I suppose to take that, Charlie? You hear what he said?"

Soren rolled himself up so his legs were under the table. He splayed his big hands on the tabletop and said, "I'd give both my nuts to be able to jump out of this chair and kick your ass, but since I can't do that, how about some hand-wrestling? Put up or shut up, Cody."

Kiss of Death Cody had his fists on his hips. "Haw, haw, haw, do you know who you're talking to, Soren? Do you know who I am? I'm called the Tiny Titan of Temple. I'm the best hand-wrestler pound for pound in this entire, stupid town. Look at my fingers. Look at my wrists. Look at these bear claws I got for hands. You mess with me, I'll break your goddamn hands off and slap your face with them."

"You were in your twenties when you won that title," said Mongoose Jim.

"I'm still as good as ever!"

"No, you're not. You're fat now. That's all fat in your fingers, not muscle."

"Shut up!"

"You don't know Sowen," said Anna, patting her husband's back. Her color was bright pinkish, her eyes shiny as sunlit water. "Sowen beats dem all. I seen him do it lots of times, you . . . you stubby."

"Look who keeps calling me stubby. Your legs don't even reach the floor, Anna. Look at this." Kiss of Death Cody grabbed Anna's skirt and threw it up, so we could see that her feet hung about two or three inches above the floor.

"Looking up my dwess!" she shrieked. She kicked Kiss of Death Cody in the belly.

"Oof!" he groaned and dropped to the floor. His mouth was opening and closing like a fish out of water. His face got redder and redder. Until finally air gasped back into his lungs.

"No fair," was the first thing he said.

"You're drunk, Cody," said Charlie. "Maybe you better go home."

"My assessment is that you're fired," said Shepard. "I don't need a chauffer or bodyguard who can't control his drinking or his temper."

"Now see what you done?" said Mongoose Jim. "What about me, Don? Am I still hired? I can drive better than him any day, and I'm very even-tempered. Honest to goodness."

"Everybody's against me," whined Kiss of Death Cody. He was rubbing his belly and wincing.

"I'm still waiting," said Soren.

Kiss of Death Cody rose to his knees, then his feet. He plopped in the chair across from Soren. "All right, old man, put 'em up here," he said.

They clasped hands and started to struggle. Soren's fingers bent backwards quickly. I could see the pulse racing in his temples. Veins bulged on his forehead.

"Looks like your head's gonna shoot right off your shoulders," Kiss of Death Cody told him. "Now, don't nobody make me laugh."

Mamie had watched everything from the other side of the pool table. Now she came over and stood behind Soren and put her hands on his shoulders. Leaning down she whispered something in his ear.

"No fair touching!" said Kiss of Death Cody. "What's she sayin? They're cheatin!"

His hands started inching backward as if his strength was seeping out of some invisible hole. Pretty soon both their hands were vertical again. And then Kiss of Death Cody's fingers were bending backward. "Hey, hey, hey!" he yelled. He jerked his hands away and stood up and pointed at Mamie. "She did something to him! I'm sick of being cheated. She cheats at pool and now this, goddammit!"

"I didn't see her do nothing," said Charlie.

"Yeah, what did she do?" said Mongoose Jim.

"How the hell do I know?"

"You lost fair and square."

"No way!"

"What did she say to you, Soren?" asked Charlie.

"She said the one thing that would get me going. She said, 'Hurry up money.'"

"Everybody knows that one."

"Yeah, well, I didn't know she knew to use it."

"She gives me the creeps," said Kiss of Death Cody. "I'll tell you right now, she did something to him. I could feel it. It was something electric she run through him. I felt it tingling my palms." He was rubbing his fingers, his knuckles.

"Aw bullshit," said Charlie.

"Bullshit yourself. She broke my concentration. I felt all the strength running out of me when she put her hands on his shoulders."

"Yeah, yeah, yeah, we believe that."

"Fuck all you guys." Kiss of Death Cody went back to the pool table and started racking the balls.

Anna had taken Soren's hand. They were murmuring to each other. Making up. Shepard was watching them. Tears glistened in his eyes. "'Tis wonderful," he said. "Conjugal bliss. More profitable than its abstinence, that's for sure. Love is the wisdom of fools. It needs no excuses. It just is. How melancholy to think of you without one another – in misery's darkest platonic cavern. Be good to each other, my dears."

The back door opened and Bob Thorn entered carrying a case of splow. He set it on the bar and said, "I got two cases if you want them, Charlie."

"I'll take them," said Charlie. "I got a gal here can drink a case all by herself." He pointed at Mamie.

Bob Thorn did a double take. "You!" he said. "Well, Jesus Christ!"

Mamie frog-smiled him and waved.

Kiss of Death Cody came over cackling and pointing and saying, "Yeah, remember this one, Bob? We call her Thorn's scorn. She whipped your ass in front of the whole town. Yuck, yuck."

"Not the whole damn town."

"Damn near."

"Fuck off."

"Okay, okay. I'm just sayin—"

"Where'd she come from?" asked Bob Thorn.

"You don't know about her? She's the pheenom everyone talks about. She's Don's parrot up on stage."

"This is her?" Bob looked at Shepard. "I thought you said she was working for Snowdy."

"She was. But Teddy threatened to kill her. Don't you know he shot Ben?"

"Is he dead?"

"No, he survived by the thinnest of the thinnest of feline whiskers," said Shepard. "And now Theodore is an inmate in Camelot."

" Right where he belongs," said Charlie.

"Let's get back on the subject, Bob," said Kiss of Death Cody. "Which is *her*, this Two Ton Tessie whose ass you said you were going to kick if you ever saw her again."

"Cody, if you don't shut up, it's your ass I'm gonna kick," said Bob.

"Well, it's what you said, goddammit!"

"Yeah? Well, I'll tell you what, you're so anxious to see a brawl, you kick her ass. You're always acting so tough. There she is. Kick her ass. Let's see you try it."

"Hey, it ain't my fuck'n fight. She never done nothin to me, man."

"Then shut the fuck up."

"Why's everybody so damn sore at me tonight?"

Bob grabbed Kiss of Death Cody by the shirt, drew him close, and said, "You don't know nothing, asshole. That broad ain't human hardly. Fucker could whip Rocky Marciano and that ain't no lie." He shook him a bit and let him go.

"Sure pick on me," said Kiss of Death Cody.

Bob tore open the case on the bar. He took a jar out and opened it and drank deep. Slamming the jar down, he turned towards Mamie.

"Don't do it," said Charlie.

"My reputation," said Bob.

"Oh, give it up, man. She don't mean anything by it. Everything is play to her."

"It's her or me."

Mamie bent into a monkey crouch, ready to wrestle.

"Whoa," said Bob. "You see that? She wants to wrestle me

again."

Charlie had put the bat on the bar and was rolling it under one hand. Bob snatched it away and turned to face Mamie. "No!" shouted Charlie. "Goddammit, I mean it!"

"Come on, hippo. You're messing with the real Bob Thorn now." He waved the bat in a tight circle over his head.

Shepard stepped between Mamie and Bob. His hands pushing out in a pleading gesture, a sort of surrender. "Please, Bobby boy, put the bat down. She doesn't mean any harm. She's as innocent as a child. She doesn't know hardly anything. She's retarded."

"I don't care," said Bob.

Kiss of Death Cody said, "I hope she eats you, you sonofabitch. Sic him, Mamie. I'm with you."

Mamie came around the table in her wrestler's crouch. She shuffled back and forth in front of Bob.

"Gawd, look at her," he said. "She ain't afraid of me at all."

"Mop the floor with him!" said Kiss of Death Cody.

Bob turned and swung at Kiss of Death Cody, who jumped backwards into Mongoose Jim. They both sprawled on the floor in a tangle or arms and legs. "I'm staying right here till it's over," said Mongoose Jim.

Soren was yelling at Bob, telling him to fight her fair. Anna was yelling too. "Sic him, Chee Chee!" she said.

Chee Chee went for Bob's ankles. "Ow! You little bitch!" he yelled. As soon as his eyes swung to Chee Chee, Mamie reached in and twisted the bat out of his hand and threw it to Charlie. Bob stood there slack-jawed, his eyes bursting with anger. And a dollop of fear.

Catching him by the wrist, Mamie jerked him toward the door.

"What's she gonna do to him?" said Charlie.

"I gotta see this," said Kiss of Death Cody.

We all hurried outside to see what Mamie was up to. She had hauled him to the lawn in front of Shepard's house and the two of them were wrestling. Bob didn't have a chance. She took him down a couple of times and made him get up and try again.

"This ain't no match," said Mongoose Jim. "He's child's play to her."

Bob was making a kind of wild sound, a high-pitched whinny. Down he went again.

And again.

"Oh, just pin him, Mamie," I said. "Before you really hurt him."

So she did and I counted him out, "One, two, three!"

When she helped him up, he was grinning and panting and he said, "If you can't beat 'em, then goddammit you better join 'em. Gawd almighty, ain't she something else? Honey, you and me should be friends. How about it?" He stuck out his hand and she took it. "You got a power in you that's supernatural, baby. I've never felt anything like it in my life. I wish I could buy you and keep you. Hell, I wish you wanted to buy me and keep me!"

He turned to us and said his heart was smitten. He kept praising her, calling her Wonder Woman and stronger than Tarzan and definitely as much of a marvel as Shepard said she was. Even Mongoose Jim and Kiss of Death Cody were taken in by what they had seen and the way Bob Thorn carried on about her. They reached out almost shyly to stroke her, to pet her hair and squeeze her massive arms. And she let them. Standing there in the light of the porch, a Wonder Woman stronger than Tarzan was beaming as if our adoration were exactly what it should be – nothing more or less than what a phenomenon extraordinaire was due.

Carnival and the Girl without Eyes

If you can't beat 'em, join 'em. After he fell in love with Mamie's great strength, Bob Thorn tried to be a part of everything she did. Times when I was in the bar with them, and other guys would come in, Bob would always work the conversation to his night of wrestling Mamie and how she could have turned him into a pretzel if she had wanted to. He dared any man to try her, but no one would. He bragged about how she had defeated him at the book-burning too. Threw him into the bushes. It was more proof of her wondrousness – that she could throw him, one hundred ninety pounds of the most perilous player in the history of Temple High football, toss him like a feather, like he was a toy. He was that proud of her. And especially he was proud to be a close part of her life now that Shepard had hired him as her personal bodyguard, because, according to both Shepard and Bob, powerful as she was, she didn't have any instinct for danger or really know how to take care of herself in this dog-eat-dog of a world. Bob said to put out the word to lowlife sonsabitches that Big Bob Thorn was Mamie Beaver's badass bodyguard, and God help the imbecile who touched a hair on her head she didn't want touched.

"Better a train wreck," he said, "than getting between me and my Mamie with hurt on your mind."

He was there every weekend for her sermons, standing guard in the wings, while she did her act, watching her and watching the people, the Mamieites he called them, ready to knock sense into any of them who might get over-rambunctious and want to come onstage with Mamie, just to hug her or pet her or act one-on-one with her. Which happened sometimes and always spoiled things a bit. Shepard had always talked those self-exhibiters into sitting down eventually. He had been mild in handling the situation (gently shooing them off) compared to Bob Thorn, who grabbed them by the collar and hauled them away, their heels dragging across the floor. After a few times of seeing that, the Mamieites quit getting so stage-struck and calling attention to themselves, like some folks do who want to be seen chummy with a celebrity.

It was a Saturday, after her last service near dusk, when Bob came over to the house with us, saying he had a present for Mamie. Phoebe Bumpus was there too. She had come to take Mamie and me to a carnival that had set up a mile out of town. When Bob heard what we were doing, he said he was coming along to keep an eye out for Mamie. A lot of lowlife sonsabitches hung out at carnivals, he said.

In his hands was a box from Montgomery Ward. He shoved the box at Mamie. "Here," he said. "This is something you could wear if you want to."

Mamie tore the box open and a dress tumbled out. She held it up. It was as yellow as marsh marigolds and had puffy sleeves like gauzy clouds and a low neckline with a thin, lacy border. Mamie held it up against her body, her face pink with pleasure. I still had never seen her in a dress and could hardly imagine it.

Phoebe was excited about the prospects. "Come on, Mamie," she said. "Let's do something with you. Let's fix you up." Phoebe told me to go down by the ditch bordering the woods and pick some of those wild flowers she had seen there.

"Pick some flowers?" I said.

"Just do it, will you? I've got an idea."

So I did it. I went out and grabbed some purple alfalfa and some white clover buds and some yellow dandelions. Mamie and Phoebe were in the bedroom when I got back. Phoebe took the flowers from me and told me to wait in the living room. After about twenty minutes or so, she came out and said: "Gentlemen, I present the butterfly out of her cocoon. I give you Mamie Beaver - ta da!"

Mamie came out, trembling at her own beauty. We all gasped to see her looking like that. She was something an artist might paint and call it "The Spirit of Spring," or "Colors of the Country Girl," or maybe simply "The Milkmaid." Barefoot she was, with the dress just covering her knees and showing off her strong ankles and curvy calves. The skirt of the dress was full and had a white border for a hem. The waist pulled in tight, showing the flair of Mamie's hips and the healthy little roll in her tummy. The top of the dress gave room for her bosoms and let just the crease at the top of her breasts show, along with her smooth neck and collar bones, her skin a rich blondish color like the cream that Jersey cows give. Her orange-red hair was crowned with a wreath of the flowers I had picked – green stems weaving through purple and white and yellow and reminding me of Mamie in the meadow at the Brule, when she had woven dandelions and timothy through her hair. I was speechless with wonderment, but the others weren't.

"A divine metamorphosis," Shepard said. Taking out his hanky, he dabbed at his eyes. "That I should live to see her this day is pleasure beyond belief. Move over Hollywood, all you simpering, starving, ethereal symbols of pulchritude. Not two of you would make one of her. Behold – the new woman is born! *Voila, das Uberfraulein!*"

"She looks like she should have angel wings," said Bob Thorn.

"No, Shepard is right, she looks like a movie star," said Phoebe. "All that beauty has just been waiting for the right context."

I shifted into gear and added that Mamie looked like "something from the deep forest, maybe a water nymph, a redheaded one with fair skin and freckles."

So there we were. She was the nth degree of earthly and spiritual beauty -Hollywood coupled with nature's *Uberfraulein* produced by a million years of God's tinkering with the human species. *Voila!*

The only thing I would have changed was the makeup on her face. She didn't need it, not a drop as far as I was concerned. Get rid of the lipstick, the fake lashes, the rouge on her cheeks, that's what I wanted to say. But I didn't.

"What do you think about it, Mamie?" Phoebe asked.

Of course, she was pleased. She nodded her head shyly up and down and did a pirouette, the skirt twirling showing off her knees.

Bob Thorn made a bow and said, "Mamie, I'd be honored if you'd go to the carnival with me and let me show you off."

She held out her hand and he took it gently in his own hand and gave it a kiss, like some Marquis de François or Earl de Englisher.

It was a hot, humid evening and the grounds were crowded with people, kids running by, racing from one ride to another. There were the hammer, the rocket, the Ferris wheel, pony rides, the merry-go-round, the whip, the earthquake. Other rides that whushed and rumbled, causing girls to scream, boys roaring to cover up their fear. Everywhere you walked along the fairway there were all kinds of odors being carried on the breeze - deep-fried foods, corndogs, fried chicken, french fries, followed by sugary sweet smells of cotton candy, perfume mixtures and hair spray. Cigarettes and cigars and pipe smoke merged with human perspiration and the dew of beer – all of it like a sort of invisible skin in the air. Accordion and banjo music puffing from speakers mounted on poles. Dazzling lights ringing the Ferris wheel. Neon rainbows everywhere.

We paired off – Phoebe and I together; Mamie with Bob Thorn – and strolled along looking at things. Shepard had stayed behind to attend to some business he had with Duke Cunningham and the church Elders about building the new Church of Art.

"She's so pretty, Christian," said Phoebe as we passed a booth with a sign overhead: SOUVENIERS - CURIOS - ANTIQUES.

I thought Phoebe meant Mamie, but she was pointing at a small statue of some naked, marbledust goddess sitting on a shelf surrounded by stuffed animals and ash trays with different states painted on them, and straw hats stacked up with CARNIVAL TIME IS TIME TO LET GO banded on the brims. There was plastic stuff – pink, breakable things that my mother would call doodads or knickknacks. Phoebe picked up the little statue and said she wanted to buy it.

"This is Aphrodite, the goddess of love," she said.

"Venus," I said.

"Same thing, different country. Aphrodite in Greece. Venus in Rome."

There were some statuettes of the Virgin Mary wearing a blue robe. I thought I might buy one of them. "People pray to her, you know," I told Phoebe.

"They pray to her too," she said, indicating Aphrodite.

"Not anymore."

"Yes, they do."

"Those gods are dead."

"And yours aren't?"

I didn't know what to say. I put the Virgin Mary back on the shelf. Next to her, Phoebe put back the Aphrodite. Except for the clothes, they looked a lot alike. Their faces were identical. "Let's go," she said.

A tall, angular, long-nosed man pushed by us and said to the girl in the booth, "Gimmee one a them straw hats, missy."

"They cost two dollars," she told him.

"Gimmee one ennaway," he said. He pulled some bills from his pocket and paid the girl. He carefully adjusted the hat on his head so that the words CARNIVAL TIME faced forward. The hat pushed the tips of his ears outward and made him look like a hick. Phoebe burst out laughing and the man's eyes darted toward her. He looked her up and down, dipping his head like a vulture sizing up where the softest spot might be to poke her with his beak. Phoebe got behind me and snickered into my shoulder.

"Funny, missy? Funny?" said the man.

Phoebe controlled herself and apologized. "Your ears," she said. "I'm sorry."

The man felt his ears and said, "Yeah, I guess they look funny stickin out that-away, but, missy, you shouldn't talk."

Phoebe's little moth wings were poking through her hair. The man was grinning at her with crooked caramel-colored teeth. I felt Phoebe shudder. "Let's get out of here," she said. As we were walking away she said, "Goddamn me and my stupid giggles. Did you see that guy's face? Those eyes? Those dirty eyes. You could see filthy dirty thoughts nesting in those eyes."

We stopped at the freak show and stared at the weirdoes. On a day bed reclining was a fat lady who, according to the sign above her, weighed 850 pounds.

"Why always a fat lady?" I said. "Why not a fat man? Shepard might qualify and get paid for just kicking back and eating ice cream."

"It's misogyny," said Phoebe.

"Miss who?"

"Men who hate women. Look - almost all the freaks are women."

There was the bearded lady with a dwarf lady on her lap; and a girl who could look at you with her legs folded up behind her neck. Another one they called the Alligator Lady. She came onstage and stood beside a long, rectangular box next to a couple of sawhorses. She wore a purple robe with a hood, so that all we could see was a pale nose and a dark eye peeking out at the audience. The carny barker explained that she was the offspring of a woman who was raped in Florida by an alligator. Phoebe and I chuckled about that notion, but some people seemed to think he was telling the truth. At least, their faces didn't register any disbelief. An alligator and a human woman? Sure, why not? Didn't bulls and horses and swans make babies with women once upon a time? Didn't the Holy Spirit in the form of a dove make love with Mary to make Jesus?

"And now what you will see," the carny barker told us, "is a throwback to those ancient times when our ancestors still lived on both land and sea, and they had the skin of fish and snakes and alligators. This is a once in a lifetime chance to see evolution in reverse, my friends. Backwards in time we go. It probably won't come again like her, just like the tail you grow in your mother's womb grows and disappears, so will the Alligator Lady, folks. So step up on stage, folks, and for one little quarter come look at the wonder and the mystery of prehistory. The Alligator Lady. One quarter to see the child created when an alligator lusted for a beautiful woman and caught her sleeping on the beach – and jumped her suddenly! Had his way with her and then indifferently let her go. It's the way of alligators. Worse than bull bunnies.

Wham, bam, thank you, ma'am. No sense of responsibility after they've had their way. One quarter is all it will cost you to see a sight that has bamboozled the world!" He turned to the woman in the robe. "Lay down inside the box, Alligator Lady," he said. "And take your clothes off, so the people can see you naked as the day you were born and get a load of that alligator skin from head to toe."

The Alligator Lady stepped into the box. It looked like a slightly oversized coffin. Two men assistants lifted the box onto the pair of sawhorses. The carny man reached inside and out came her robe. "There she is," he said. "The Alligator Lady looking like an alligator sunning itself on shore. Step right up and see this fabulous phenomenon. Pull out your quarters. That's it. Don't be shy. Come on up and take a peek. It's natural to be curious. She wants you to see her, friend. Give me that quarter. Thank you. And you come too, mister. Ma'am, it's all right. God wants you to see all the possibilities. Thank you. Come on don't miss the sight of a lifetime. You too! Get up here! Come one - come one come all!"

I had to admit I wanted to see what was naked in that coffin box sitting on the sawhorses. Phoebe said she wanted to see it too. She took my hand and we went up the steps and gave the man our quarters and stood in line inching forward. The men and a couple of women going by and looking into the box were quiet and respectful. They shook their heads sadly and made small noises, tsk, tsk, like they felt nothing but pity for the Alligator Lady. When Phoebe and I finally got to look inside, I was more than just a little disappointed. I was disgusted. With myself and the whole stupid show. The Alligator Lady was nothing more than a woman with some skin disease, badly dried up skin full of scaly splotches with flaky borders. She reminded me more of a giraffe, with its patterns of white and brown – sure didn't look like no alligator. And she wasn't even naked either. She wore a two-piece swimsuit, white with cherries printed on it.

"It's a gyp," I whispered to Phoebe.

The woman opened her eyes and looked at me. Real venom in her eyes, reddish pupils, like bull's-eyes imprinted on a pair of yellow orbs. No eyelashes at all. Painted on slashes took the place of eyebrows. The blond hair on her head was obviously a wig. I hurried away, Phoebe following.

"Poor thing," she said, "it's some kind of infection."

As we walked along the fairway, I glanced at the Ferris wheel going round. There in a seat were Mamie and Bob. Like a bright marigold next to a brownish, clump of milkweed. I waved at them, but they didn't see me.

Phoebe pulled me to another stage, where THE WORLDS STRONGAST MAN was picking up a weight that had 500 LBS written on it. His muscles looked like knotted ropes as he lifted the weight to his waist and set it down. Then he posed, curling his arms and showing off his biceps and turning so we could see the muscles crawling all over his back. Phoebe liked him.

"Ooo, he's gorgeous. Look at those muscles. What a man." She sighed and blinked her eyes rapidly and said, "What about you, Christian? How big?" She gave my pipe stem biceps a squeeze.

"Not big," I said. "I'm still growing."

"But very hard," she said. "Hard as a rock."

"Yeah?"

"I bet for your size you're really strong. Hey, you wouldn't want to look like him, anyway. Really, he doesn't look real. He's like a comic book hero. Superman in tights."

"Lumpy. Too lumpy. Kind of ugly. All those greased up muscles and them wormy veins sticking out. And he's awkward, all stiff the way he moves. I betcha anything Mamie's as strong as him. I bet she could wrestle him down."

"I bet she could too."

"Her strength comes from God, I think. Like Samson's did."

"Well." Phoebe hesitated. "Well, maybe, who knows? Just don't let anyone cut her hair." She laughed that loud-laugh that was kind of embarrassing. People going by jerking their heads towards her. She paid them no mind. And she said, "You know, Mamie is damn lucky to have found you. I wonder if she knows it? With a bit of bad luck she might have ended up in a place like this, like him hoisting weights to show how strong he is. Gathering up quarters for it."

"Being a freak?"

"Maybe."

"That would be too bad."

"Bad? It would be a tragedy. You're a good kid, Christian."

"I am? Well, I don't know. I'm no angel."

"That night we all got drunk, you sure weren't no angel."

"I'm sorry about that, Phoebe."

"Eh, forget it. Booze can make anyone act like an idiot. Including me."

"The dancing part was fun. It was all fun until all of a sudden my head was in the toilet," I said.

Phoebe guffawed again. And she said, "And there I was trying to rob the cradle."

We stared into each other's eyes, and I felt like something was going to happen. I was determined to stay sober this time. She took my hand. We strolled along the fairway some more.

"There's a girl here, a dancer," she said. "I've heard she looks like Marilyn Monroe. Let's go find her, and then I'll tell you a secret."

So that's what we did. We found a tent advertising THE SULTAN'S HAREM. Inside were the most beautiful women of Arabia. In front of the tent were three cartoony-type portraits of long-haired, big-breasted women all smiling and sexy. Their names were written in sequins at the top of each portrait: Dew, Dawn, and Venus. The paintings were chipped and sun-bleached but the nametags looked new.

"This must be it," said Phoebe.

The carny barker was standing at the entrance, persuading the crowd that a quarter would buy them a million dollar's worth of beauty.

"One quawta! A fowth of a dollah to entah the Sultan's Harem and see the prize possessions of Arabee, citizens. They walk, they wiggle. They dance the hoochy-coo. And the ancient dances of the desert, where the heat makes the women go around mostly nekked. Woo-woo. You will be amazed and astonished at what you see, citizens." His brows wiggled. He leered at us and laughed,

"Heh heh heh."

"Heh heh heh," we answered.

"All of it fo one-fowth of a dollah. So step up fast, the show's about to begin. I can hear the music startin." Cupping his hand round his ear, he made as if he heard the music. "Yep, it's startin, and once they get to dancin, these girls get really wicked."

Then we could hear it too, a steady beat of drums, the sound filtering through the canvas wall – *dum, ta ta dum, ta ta dum.*

"And here comes the goddess of love herself to find out what's keepin you all."

He pointed to the entrance and there was a surge of people forward as a woman in a black teddy appeared. She probably wasn't from Arabee. She looked more like a Wisconsin Swede. She was wearing a black veil over her face, but you could see she had a broad-browed forehead. Swept-back boy-style hair, blond as Guernsey butter. Shapely figure. The black teddy was dotted strategically with sparkling sequins. She had long, slim legs as well. Bare feet. All eyes were staring up at her as if she really was a goddess.

"God, if I looked like her—" whispered Phoebe. "That body."

Venus stood awhile, not looking at us. The lights sparking off her sequined teddy were dazzling. All of her was dazzling.

"Don't she look like she descended from Mount Olympus?" said the carny man. "But nope, she escaped from the Sultan's Harem, as did Dew and Dawn, all of them smuggled out at the port of Alexandria by sympathetic American sailors. They paid for their passage by dancing. You want to see more of this gorgeous creature?"

A few folks clapped.

"Well, do you!"

More of us clapped.

"I can't hear you!"

We clapped louder.

When Venus turned on her heel and vanished inside the tent, we all followed her, quarters in hand. Inside, it was warm and crowded and smelled like dust and canvas and stale perfume and human sweat gone sour. In front of us was a neck-high stage. It was about twelve feet long and curtained by two red shower curtains hanging on a pole that sagged in the middle.

"Bring on them dancers! Bring 'em on!" yelled someone behind us.

"Yeah," bellowed another. "Bring on the babes!"

"I wanna see Arabee cunt," said a man whose voice was low and nasty and not loud enough for the whole audience to hear, but Phoebe heard him and she winced and clutched my arm so hard it hurt.

"Maybe we shouldn't be here," I said.

"It's okay. I wanna see," she said.

When the carny man appeared, he paced up and down the stage in white pants and a white shirt with rolled-up sleeves. He had milky forearms thickly coated with black hair. His fingers wriggled like fat, loose worms. As he bent toward us, the crowd hushed. He licked his lips and grinned. His face seemed to be saying what a bunch of idiots these people are. I wondered how many like me, like us, had stood before the carny man night after night, waiting to see the harem, him knowing that it didn't matter if the girls were from Arabia or not – or even who they were. Maybe they could have been machines, just so they had the right parts. And he knew it. He gazed at us, sizing us up – small city people looking for a kick, farmers wanting to see a behind that wasn't cow, miners and lumberjacks wanting to see something beside dim-lit tunnels and forests being stripped; and there were all kinds of white-collar workers, no doubt, and kids from the college and factory workers. It was a tent full of variety - a stew of whatever Wisconsin had to offer.

As he finished his introduction with a wave of his hand and a side step offstage, the carny barker shouted, "And here they are, ladies and gentlemen! First, for your delectation and delight, welcome Dawn and Dew! Bring 'em on! Bring 'em on!"

And he did. We clapped, whistled and shouted as the girls scurried from behind the curtain and the *dum, ta ta dum* of the drums starting up again. Dawn and Dew wore only underpants and brassieres. Their loose bellies bounced; their hips gyrated. Around their ankles were tiny bells tinkling in time with their movements. Hoots and whistles, lots of them! Oh, baby, oh, baby! Above their skimpy costumes were faces with oval mouths and dim teeth showing. Deep-set eyes ringed in mascara. They were not smiling, just breathing hard, like they were scared or already out of breath. They passed back and forth above us, parading their boobs, flaring their hips, dancing with each other, bumping butts, while men in the audience howled. Some brayed like donkeys – *hee haw!*

The guy behind me said, "Now, that's what you call well-worn pussy. Look how broke down they are. Those baggy tummies."

"Probably got a pile of kids," said another.

A guy standing to my left half-turned his head and told both men to shut the fuck up. They were breaking his concentration. His head came back around and I saw that he was staring at Dawn and Dew with open lust. Both hands were in his pockets working away.

The carny man started coaxing us to clap, "C'mon, citizens, you got to wahm these girls up if they're gonna really get into it. You got to show some appreciation. C'mon, citizens, let's give 'em a hand. Whaddya say!" He clapped and we joined in. There were a few whistles, a couple of rebel yells.

"Citizens! You can do better than that. Got to do better if you're gonna wake up these gals and get 'em to put a little more hoochy in their coochy. The louder the noise, the better they dance and the more you'll see. Let's hear it for Dawn and Dew!"

Again we clapped and whistled and yelled, but it didn't sound to me as if our hearts were in it. Either Dawn or Dew (who knew who was who?) bent over and waved at us from between her legs. Someone howled like a mournful coyote. Others clapped, whistled, wailed.

"That's the way!" coaxed the carny.

As long as we made noise and showed we were having the time of our lives, the girls bent and dipped and wriggled. But after a bit, it got monotonous, and no matter how the carny urged and the dancers strutted and kicked, fewer and fewer of us clapped as loud as the carny wanted. Seeing it wasn't working, he stopped the music and the dancers slumped behind the curtain.

"Don't leave, citizens!" the carny man shouted. "No, no, have you forgotten Venus? Now, let me tell you something. Venus ain't shy like Dawn and Dew. Venus will show you a whole lot more of what you're looking for. I guarantee it! Now, who's gonna stay and see the goddess of love? She's only fifty cents more, citizens, but she's worth a million. Who's gonna stay, huh? Juss go out that way and give the man standing there fifty cents and he'll give you a ticket to let you go around to the front and come back in. Juss follow that man right there." The carny pointed to the side flap opening, a man going through. We followed him. Some folks left, but most of them gave the extra fifty cents and went back through the front flap and back to the front of the stage. Me? I bought another ticket. I felt like I was hypnotized, sort of. Looking at Phoebe, I saw that her eyes were glassy. She wanted to see Venus doing whatever she did. And she wanted to tell me the secret about Venus too, but not yet, she said. She wondered if I could figure it out for myself. I had watched Phoebe while Dawn and Dew did their stuff, and it seemed to me, she was enjoying it as much as any of the men there. I thought she had been staring hard at those spots the men were looking for. And her face was flushed and sweaty. She kept licking her lips a lot.

Venus came out. We worked our way forward and got close enough that we might have touched her if she had come to the edge of the stage. She had taken off her black teddy and was wearing a thin black halter and black thong. That was all. Not even any jewelry. When she walked out, there was a roar from the crowd, and I felt myself getting squeezed against the rim of the stage. My heart was pounding in my throat. I never wanted to touch a woman so much as I wanted to touch Venus, goddess of love. I gasped and moaned and stared with all my eyes up at her, her legs swaying in front of me, her rotating pelvis in its thin wisp of silken string moving to the beat. A spot of moisture right where you'd think it would be.

But as I stared, I became aware of a flaw in Venus. There was a scar on her belly, a slice running up from the thong patch to her belly button, a trail of old pain that proved she was merely human after all and had suffered something that goddesses don't have to go through. The scar was so out of place in my fantasies about her that I felt like I had woken from a dream that might have gone all the way if allowed to. But not now. The thing was, she was too real and I didn't want to look at the patch or the scar on her belly. I looked upward, trying to find her eyes. I couldn't find them. I saw black shadows beneath black brows and long, fake lashes curling from eyeless sockets, little slits of ink.

I grabbed Phoebe and whispered, "Her eyes, Phoebe!"

"She's blind, Christian. Totally blind."

Venus's head rolled downward for a second. Then back up. But I caught the dull flash of cream-colored balls of blindness, purely blind, no pupils, no iris, as if her eyes were turned backward.

The carny man was getting on us to clap louder again, saying that Venus's feelings would be hurt if we didn't show how much we loved her. I looked behind me and it seemed that most of the men were in some kind of a trance, staring at the blind girl with eyes that were blind to everything else but her. There was something almost desperate about the way the men looked, as if they wanted her but knew in their hearts that nothing even remotely like her would ever come their way – only in dreams, maybe. There she was, within eye-reach, but not an inch more, a beautiful blond girl glistening. Just a shimmer and she would be gone, leaving nothing except a memory to make them dissatisfied with anything they might have waiting for them at home. Or elsewhere.

When the music stopped and she went behind the curtain, the crowd roared. They shouted "Encore!" "More!"

"Ain't she the most beautiful thing you've seen on two legs walkin?" asked the carny man.

We shrieked and hooted and whistled.

"You telling me you want her to come back?"

We shrieked and hooted and whistled some more.

"She'll come back if you want her to, and she'll show you a whole lot more of what you're looking for. She ain't shy. You want that?"

Yes, we did.

"Venus don't like to wear no clothes a'tall. She don't feel right with 'em on, even them bits of string she's wearin. You know what I mean? She thinks they cover up her best features."

We all laughed leeringly at that.

"But the law don't allow her to dance up here like she'd like to, citizens."

We booed the law.

"But don't despair, good citizens. Stick with me, and I guarantee you'll see all you want of little Venus. She's got her ways. And the law can go to hell!"

We cheered him like he was our favored politician.

The carny man leaned over the stage, his eyes scanning us. "What about it, citizens? Is she worth a dollah? Will you ever see anything like her again in your natural life? Not a chance. One dollah. One dollah is all. Follow the man."

Like lemmings we followed the man out the side flap once more, got our third ticket and came back in.

This time she wore a yellow skirt that came down just midway on her thighs. She had yellow pasties over her nipples. Her breasts looked hard. They scarcely bounced at all as she walked onstage. Shuffling forward to within three feet of the edge, she stopped. The drumbeat began and she began to kick with her right leg, low kicks at first that sent the skirt riding upward. The people pressed forward crushing each other to get their add-a-dollar peek.

"Eeeee-haaa!" yelled a raspy voice, sounding like its owner was halfway strangling. I looked back and saw the man in the carnival-time straw hat, his head thrusting on his long neck, his adam's apple bulging, his nose pecking at Venus. He was glaring at her as if the heat of his eyes could make pudding of her body and he could slurp her down his gullet. She was kicking above us, kicking higher and higher, the skimpy skirt flapping.

"Come on, baby, let me see that hole!" the carnival-time man hollered.

Her leg faltered, lost the beat. Then got going again, this time faster and harder and higher, so we could all finally see what a dollar more had bought. Phoebe was looking like she didn't have one of her own and whatever was under that skirt was all new to her. Her mouth was open, her tongue licking the air, her eyes reaching under to search out Venus's not so secret places. Looking up I saw a bluish rip and a line of slick pink framed in blondish hair. So there it was and in a second it was over. The leg quit kicking, quit trying to do vertical splits while standing on a stage. Venus turned away and left us standing there staring at the curtain shivering.

This time the show was really over. The carny man had no more to offer. He threw back the exit flap and walked away. We filed out. To one side I saw the carnival-time man catching up to the carny man, trying to hand him a roll of bills and pointing toward the back of the tent. I heard the carny man say, "Get outta here, you fuck'n vulture!"

Phoebe and I hurried away from the Sultan's tent. We didn't talk for a while, just went on some rides and then got some corn dogs with mustard to eat, drank some giant-sized cups of Coke. It was on the merry-go-round, sitting side by side on wooden horses, that Phoebe told me more about Venus.

"Her real name is Mickey Baker," she said. "She's been blind since birth. A colleague of mine knew her parents. He was raised on the same block in Iron Springs. Mickey was always easy, he said. Ever since she was just a little kid, all the boys came around to do her when her parents weren't home. At thirteen she got pregnant. When her father found out, he went nuts and chased her down the street with a butcher knife. She ran into a tree and it knocked her out, and that bastard gave her a C-section right there on the sidewalk. Ripped the fetus right out of her belly. And then somebody came out and shot him. What a story, huh? Fathers and daughters, you can't predict what goes on there, you know what I mean?"

"Did the father—? Was he—?"

"Who knows?" said Phoebe. "My colleague said the dad was a quiet guy. Kept to himself most of the time. Except on Halloween, which he made a big fuss over, setting up carved pumpkins and cardboard witches on broomsticks and scary sounds. Stuff like that. He'd sit on the porch and hand out candy to the kids. You'd never think he would go crazy like he did. It's the quirky ones you've got to watch, you know."

"Poor Mickey," I said.

"People do what they are going to do and there's no stopping it. Might as well try to hold back the tide, that's what I say."

"I saw the scar," I said.

"Yeah. She must feel it everyday, every single day, and know she drove her father crazy enough to do that and get himself killed."

"Not really her fault."

"A heavy burden anyway, Christian."

"Think of her running down the street and can't see nothing and running into that tree. I'd hate to be blind and running from a guy with a knife who says he's going to kill me. What could be scarier than that, Phoebe?"

She shrugged her shoulders and looked away. The merry-go-round stopped and we got off and walked out past some tents to the edge of the floodlights, where a couple were sitting on a blanket near a fenced pasture, talking softly and drinking beer and eating sandwiches. In the distance were silhouetted Holsteins grazing and cud-chewing and sleeping. A clear moon behind them. The moon's dark eyes and dark oval mouth looking surprised to see us. We sat on pasture grass. Soft and smelling like sweet candy for the cows. I kept seeing Mickey Baker running blindly from her daddy and getting knocked out and her tummy ripped open. I thought about the fetus pulled from the womb in such a rude, untimely way. Who could do such a thing? What happens to the brain to make it possible? Not only one human being to another - but a father doing it to his daughter.

"I suppose the baby died," I said.

"What? Oh, that. Yes, it died pretty quickly, I imagine. But it's just as well it did. That thing was a monster. I've actually seen it. It's in a jar of alcohol in the research unit of the Ashland hospital. The thing looks like something from another world. It's about six inches long." Phoebe held her hands out measuring. "And looks like a snaky piece of gristle, long and wavy with a big round knuckle for a head. You can tell it was going to come out female. But it would have had no kind of life. Its head was knobby, not smooth.

And it had no eyes, Christian. There was just skin, a sheet of skin covering where its eyes should have been. It would have walked through life as blind as its mother. Probably been an idiot. It was ghastly." She paused. "It was pitiful." Her breathing was angry. "It was cruel. It was nature being pitiless and cruel. God, I'm sure in a bad mood now." Phoebe put her hands up and fingered her ears. Brushed her hair over them. When the hair shivered and settled, the ears popped out impishly, as if saying, "Nyah, nyah!"

I chewed a sprig of grass and gazed at the cows minding their own business. The moon moved to a pair of hand-spans above the horizon - to get a better look at the shenanigans on planet Earth, no doubt.

Later, we went back to the fairway and found Mamie and Bob Thorn. They were at a beer stand, next to the outdoor dance floor. The band was warming up.

"Some shit-kicking music coming," said Bob. "You wanna stay?"

We decided we would. The colored lights came on over the dance floor. The band started with some slow music, a western song about a bluebird and a broken heart. Phoebe pulled me to the floor and we danced, rocking slowly in a circle like we had done the night at Shepard's when we all got drunk and made fools of ourselves. Seemed like a thousand nights ago, so much had happened since then.

When Mamie and Bob danced too, I felt twinges of jealousy. Mamie was caught up in her sudden beauty and the attention he was giving her. The distance was growing between us. First Powers, now Bob Thorn. But I had to admit the two of them made a couple that looked more natural than she and I had.

The band played a polka and got everyone stirred up, bouncing round and round the floor, the floor heaving like an earthquake. Mamie and Bob stole the show. People saw them coming, whirling like tornados, whooping like locomotives coming through, get out of the way! Which was a wise thing to do. Mamie's yellow skirt flaring and her legs showing off their power. And Bob hanging on, spinning with her so hard that a touch of either of them would have sent even a big man flying.

All the dancers finally stepped aside and started egging Bob and Mamie on. The band picking up the tempo and boom boom boom went Mamie and Bob, the length and width of the floor, sending little shocks up our feet every time they hit the boards. The people clapping, whistling and hooting for all they were worth. It reminded me of the Sultan's tent and how the crowd carried on so for Venus, coaxing her to lift her leg higher and higher, so we could see that place where babies come from. Where her baby had *not* come from. The faint white scar the only reminder.

"Go, baby, go!" "Faster, honey, faster!" "Look at 'em whirl!" "Faster, faster, yeow!" "Look at them legs!" "A pair of pythons!" "Eeee-haaa!" "Waaa-whoo!" And showers of clap-clap-clapping in time to the beat.

Phoebe was coming out of her broody mood, and so was I. She was leaning against me and bumping me with her hip, keeping time with the throbbing rhythms, the pounding in our ears.

When the polka was over, the audience gave Mamie and Bob a big hand and some of them said it was the best polka they had ever seen and they wished they could dance like that.

"It's easy," said Bob. "Carnival time is the time to let go!"

Some of the people reached out to touch Mamie. It was something I had noticed a lot by now – how people loved touching her. The glow coming off of her was more than the moon shining over her skin. It was a kind of dew of life rising from her, a shimmering halo of energy that came from inside and made you want some of it. Racehorses in full stride have it. Cows full of alfalfa and grain, udders heavy with milk have it. Dogs going full tilt with their lugs back have it. Eagles diving have it. Mamie Beaver: big, strong, sexy, pretty, fresh, loving, awesome, holy and good had it. Touch her and maybe some of it will rub off on your palm. Put your palm over your mouth and nose and breathe her. Put her into your bloodstream. And maybe you'll be healed.

It was midnight when we got home. Bob had been kissing on Mamie in the back seat of the car. Saying he wanted to marry her. Saying he had never been so much in love. Saying he would die for her. She was giggling about it but not saying, "Nup nup," like

I expected her to. When Phoebe pulled the car to the curb, they got out and walked arm in arm toward the Artlife. Phoebe said they made a perfect couple and they would make marvelous babies – giants in the earth.

When we went inside the house I grabbed a jar of splow and took a long drink. Phoebe snatched it away and said, "You don't need that tonight, honey. You've got something better here than drinking your liver to death. Don't you? I mean me. Let's finish what we started."

We went into the bedroom. The moonlight through the window made Phoebe's skin look lavender, her lips purple. She pushed up against me and did a grind with her hips and said she didn't really understand herself anymore, because every day I was on her mind making her want to rob the cradle. She pressed me and pawed me, sucking my fingers and lips and licking my neck. I wanted badly to take a shower and soap up with her. But when I mentioned it, she said, "Are you kidding? The odor is an aphrodisiac. We don't want to wash it off." She opened my shirt and sniffed me. "Yummy," she sighed, "you smell so sexy and young. So young and sexy. You're making me feel all oily. I'm being naughty. But you're the naughty baby, aren't you."

"Naughty baby," I agreed.

"Naughty, come touch me. Touch me here. And here." She was braless.

Her blouse came off and she rolled it and tied it around her head, blindfolding herself.

"Why you doing that for?" I asked.

"Shush, don't talk. Don't say anything. Breathe. Let me hear you breathing."

It wasn't hard to hear me breathing.

"Nurse me," she said.

"Okay," I said. Her nipples were hard as the tips of my thumbs rubbing them.

After I nursed her awhile, she shimmied out of her jeans and pushed my head down there and said it again, "Nurse me." I didn't want to, but some part of me did, some part of me went for that odor that scent and I did what she wanted. Reached out with my tongue, my whole mouth. I no longer wanted to take a shower. The dew seeped into me, sweet and faintly salty too. I glued myself to her for what seemed like an entire whirl of the world. And then she pulled me to my feet and helped me tear my clothes off. When we hopped on the bed she wanted to be on top. I lay on my back and let her do whatever. My eyes were closed and I wasn't touching her with my hands. Just taking in the feeling. It could have been Mamie up there for all I knew.

When we were done and she flopped beside me panting, I could smell her on my face, and I felt weird, like I didn't belong to the body that had done that thing with its mouth. The questions turned over and over in my mind - is that what grownups do? Or is it a sick thing just for perverts? It came to me that I had learned something important about women, maybe - that they played a game with sex, played at the borders and over the borders - of normal: Mamie with her no-rain. Mickey, the girl without eyes. Phoebe robbing the cradle. There was a feeling of slipping toward Camelot. And I wondered if it was good or bad that I had learned so young the power of a woman in heat and the things a fellow would do to please her and himself, his will turned to water no matter how much he believed in God. Or Jesus and the Virgin Mary. Doing things that even my pa didn't know, I was sure. Things that maybe most guys didn't know, not my age, anyway. Things that wet the mind down worse than any proof of splow. Things about the odor and taste of a woman and their bodies becoming fantasy worlds. When God made all that did he call it *good*?

Phoebe took off her blindfold and smiled gently. "Little boys in bedrooms making love to older women. If we would only admit it, it's a thought that turns all of us on. Call us nasty, if that's what we are. Kiss me again, Christian. Let me show you something else you'll get into and want more of."

Rioting

The construction of the First Church of Art was going good. Three acres of the woods had been bulldozed, the trees sold off. Backhoes had come in and made trenches for the foundation. The workers were laying pipe and pouring cement. Soon the walls would go up. And the roof. And Shepard would have his dream come true – a huge brick building with two thousand seats in it and a stage and a screen and a projection booth to beat anything Temple had ever seen. It would be a major church-theater. The only one of its kind in all of Wisconsin, according to Shepard.

Once the construction had started, he spent as much time as he could supervising the men working. Rubbing his nose happily, he gave them orders, do this, do that, put that over here, put this over there. Mostly they ignored him, but he didn't seem to notice. If any of us came around, he would chatter about his church-theater to be, the great center of culture and humanity, the spiritual heart of a people, a beacon of hope in a world full of tiny-minded ideologists incubated by circumstances and mediocrity. He would offer them a stimulation they could not resist – the stimulation of his own creations and farsighted genius - with Mamie Beaver as the central symbol of who he was and what his destiny had to be. While he told us of these visions, his hands would clap for himself and he would hug his chest. Lovingly stroke his nose. His fingers would poke the air, sometimes slashing it, making rectangles and triangles and squares, as if forming from space itself the thing he called the center and the beacon and the monument, the invisible temple where the religion of art would fly forth and gobble up the world. Change it for the better by far. Converts would go out and capture more multitudes for Mamie to mesmerize. The church coffers would overflow. And with money would come fame, television, books, radio, film – all the things necessary to carry the litany of art across the country. There were no limits, he swore. It was all going to happen just like he said it would. He knew.

Shepard knew.

But then came a Sunday in June when the familiar service at the Artlife slipped into a different gear. Things changed that day. As usual, the first service was crowded, but there was something odd about the multitudes, about the way they looked and the way they acted. On the west side of the aisle were lots of faces I had seen enough times to know they were the tried-and-true Mamieites. All of them had come around to seeing the litany Shepard's way – filled with *Hamlet* and *Moby Dick*. Most of the hardcore book burner types had abandoned the Artlife weeks ago, after it became clear to them what Shepard was up to – trying to get them to worship the literary texts that great men and women writers had created, rather than the text of Almighty God. So the majority of the worshippers now were Mamietes and not connected with those who caused the rioting and burning of books at the high school library. According to Shepard, the Mamieites had come to a place where art dwelled continually in their hearts, the place of wholeness, harmony, and radiance, and their souls were part of the larger soul of Mamie Beaver.

On the east side of the aisle was this other bunch, different from the Mamieites. I recognized some of them. These were the book burners returning from wherever they had disappeared to. I was worried when I saw them. The fierceness of their faces frightened me. Most of them were carrying bibles, holding the bibles in their hands folded up against their chests, like tiny shields. I caught up with Shepard before he went on stage and pointed out what was happening in the audience. He gave the east-siders a down-the-nose look and decided he knew all about them.

"Poof, poof, they're dyed in the wool hardcore Christers," he said. "Christers on the verge of conversion by the look of things, on the verge of sliding over the cusp into the life of the mind.

Why else would they be here? Temptation. Testing their faith. The bibles are their armor against Mamie's message, they think. Poof, poof, it isn't going to work. Once they've sat through the service and listened to Mamie and her Mamieite echoes, any of them with an IQ one jot above moron will know the Bible is a text loaded with ancient vapor and subterfuge and the dankest nonsense. It will hit them like a rock between the eyes that art is the living symbol of the soul and the aegis to protect them from their own abysmal ignorance – the aegis to protect them from abysmal ignorance, I say!" Running his hand over his mouth, he sucked his fingertips one at a time, like he was getting the last bit of flavor from the words he had used. Then he said, "We will call down fire to light our altar to prove we are the one and only living god. Fire will bring them into the fold." He hurried off to get Mamie ready. I could hear him saying, "Fire! Fire!"

But in my belly was an uneasy feeling about those Christers on the east side. For one thing, they weren't being nice and polite to everyone like the Mamieites always were. They were telling certain persons here and there to get out of their section, that they had it reserved. Which wasn't true. It had always been first-come first-served, just as in any church. The unwelcome ones were always civilized about it and apologized for being on the wrong side. They would go find themselves seats in the other section. While all this was going on, the west-siders were looking puzzled, scratching their heads and talking to each other. Saying, "What's up with them?"

I walked up the center aisle to the main doors and stood there feeling prickly. In a minute both doors swung open and a woman came in, along with someone dressed in a monk robe, hood up hiding the face. The figure walked like a man - long-strides, arms swinging, shoulders rolling. The woman I recognized to be Lulu, the one who had burned *Samson Agonistes* and had told the others to burn Shakespeare because he was so depressing. She escorted the robed figure down the aisle and parked both of them in the front row.

The lights dimmed. And into Powers' eye strode Shepard to give the introduction to Mamie. Both sides listened to him intently.

When he brought Mamie out, she was wearing that yellow dress Bob Thorn had given her. She had fresh flowers in her hair. Behind her in the shadows was Bob watching over everything. She opened her mouth to say - "'Call me Ishmael,'" but a guy on my left, on the east side, cut her off, shouting, "'Before my God, I might not this believe without the sensible and true avouch of mine eyes.'"

"Heh?"

"What?"

"Is that from *Moby Dick*?" asked a woman. She was asking Mamie.

It was *Hamlet* and Mamie replied with the following line - "'Is it not like the king?'"

There were some seconds of grumbling and people wondering what that "avouch of mine eyes" stuff was. I recognized it as the part where Horatio first sees the ghost of Hamlet's father. We had done that scene a long time ago. Then dropped it.

Mamie stared at the east side, waiting for the next line. It didn't come, so she said, "'Call me Ishmael.'"

The Mamieites sighed with relief and settled into the give-and-take of the words about having no money and wanting to see the watery part of the world. The other side said nothing, sat there narrow-eyed and stiff, as if they were waiting for something to happen. Some signal, maybe.

Mamie took up her next response, "'Whenever it is a damp, drizzly November in my soul . . .'"

And again, when it was time for the Mamieites to reply, only the west side said what they were supposed to. They went back and forth, talking about paths to the sea and the magic of the water, where the water is a mirror where every man sees himself. It was soothing and spiritual, the way they chanted it to each other. For a while things went along fine. I was glad the Christers stayed shut-mouthed. But I had a feeling they wouldn't stay that way forever.

When Mamie hit the part where Stubb tells Ishmael, "'If God ever wanted to be a fish, he'd be a whale!'" the Christers mumbled and grumbled and made faces. "Liar," I heard someone say. Some of them held their bibles up towards Mamie, like they wanted the bibles to see what a liar she was to say God would have chosen to be a whale.

One of the Mamieites, a man named Arnold, told the Christers to shut up, and then he cut to the next scene himself, shouting out what Ishmael says about Queequeq – "Better a sober cannibal than a drunken Christian!"

The Christers really erupted then. A lot of growling and huffing and name-calling. Arnold was branded an infidel and a *humanist* (spitting the humanist word out like it was rat poison), and Mamie had to raise her voice to get the next line heard—

"'And God created a great fish to swallow Jonah.'" The line calmed the Christers down. And even got approval from both sides when she said, "'To preach the truth in the face of falsehood.'"

And so it went, like walking a tightrope of words back and forth. The Mamieites holding to the normal litany. The Christers liking some things, but trying to interrupt what they hated. I had a feeling we would never get to the second half, to *Hamlet*. The two sides were giving each other dirty looks, their faces contorting in anger. Everyone looked ugly. The pressure kept building until the part came where Mamie was Captain Ahab saying, "'God hunt us all, if we do not hunt Moby Dick to his death!'"

"'Death to Moby Dick! Death to Moby Dick!'" the Mamieites hollered.

And following them came a familiar voice crying out, "Sweet Jee-sus Christ, I've heard enough of this! I will not hear more! Stand up if ye be for God!"

It was the man in the monk robe. It was Robbie. Out of the robe he came. He leaped onto the stage. His long hair and beard flashing like tinsel in Powers' powerful light. His hands reaching beseechingly. His eyes burning like beacons.

"Robbie Peevy back from the dead," someone said.

"Oh no," said someone else.

"Robbie! Robbie! Robbie!" the Christers started shouting.

He was himself all right, oozing with righteousness and wallowing in the love of his followers. "Jeee-sus called me back to you," he said. "Jeee-sus sent a message to me, told me that ye were in trouble and needed me. Told me there was blaspheming and apostasy tearing up Temple!"

"Amen!" the Christers answered.

"Told me that some of ye were headed for hellfire and brimstone."

"Amen! Amen!"

"Told me, 'Robbie, go ye back in the name of the Lord and seek ye my lost sheep and bring ye them back into the fold, for I am their true shepherd, and their eyes are blinded by an evil *Shepard*, a *humanist* carrying the flare of hell's infernal night to swallow my precious people!"

"Tell 'em, Robbie! Tell 'em like it is!"

"Amen! Amen!"

"Oh, sweet Jesus!"

"God is my subject, God is my object!"

Robbie crossed the stage to where he could look down on the Church of Art members, the Mamieites. His face was long on sadness for them, how sorry he was that they had been taken in by the evil shepherd. "And so I am here for you," he said, sweeping his hand through the air to show he meant all of them, left and right. "I am here for you – yes, Jeee-sus! – here at the request of your one and only savior. Jeee-sus is the demanding voice speaking through my mouth today!"

"Hooray!"

"Yay!"

"Holy and wholly right you are, Robbie!"

"The way! The way!"

"Tell 'em, Robbie! Give 'em the fiery word of God! Give them thunderbolts!"

"Kill 'em, burn 'em."

"If only we were rid of them, the world would be blessed and everyone saved!"

"Peace on Earth, good will towards men!"

"Sic the heathen, Robbie! Sic 'em for Jesus!"

Robbie put his arm around Mamie frozen in the beam of light, her eyes staring up to where Powers was, like she was waiting for him to tell her what to say.

Squeezing her, Robbie told the people that Jesus had a special love for Mamie. "She is his Holy Fool! His Holy Fool led astray and misused and sorely abused by the false prophet preaching the divinity and omnipotence of the creations of *man*."

"Man! Phooey!"

"Man, ugh!"

"Down with man!"

Robbie's lips were pressed together and curled, as if the phrase, *preaching the divinity and omnipotence of the creations of man* was the most disgusting thing he had ever said in his life. He was going to puke. When he continued, he said, "This precious child of Jesus, this Mamie Beaver, has been made into Satan's pawn, made to do the devil's work. God forgive the corrupters of such a sweet soul. God forgive them, for I cannot! Down with them all!"

"Kill the false shepherd! Kill the evil one! Kill for Jesus!" yelled someone.

"Shut up, you fuck'n moron!" yelled someone else.

Shepard had moved over to Mamie's other side and was looking at Robbie like he was polluted swamp water come to life. "Thou are the evil one, not me," he said. "In your immeasurable stupidity is a boundless evil, a boundless suffering for all suffering humanity throughout the world! It is contemptible that a mind of my magnitude must needs lower itself to even speak to you at all. Poof, poof." With his mouth he made a farting noise and stuck his tongue out at Robbie as he jerked at Mamie's arm, trying to pull her away. But Robbie held on tight to her other arm. She was in between, getting tugged both ways.

"This . . . thing!" said Shepard. "This crazy thing can't even tell you what it was he heard just now, that's how infinitely imbecilic he is! Tell us, zany man, what does it mean – the phrase that had you protesting so vociferously – 'Death to Moby Dick'?"

"I can tell you what it means, infidel. Just substitue the name Moby Dick for the name Jesus Christ. That's what it means – it's saying death to Jeee-sus! It's the same thing as calling out to Satan to come on and snatch your soul. Death to Jeee-sus! That's what it says. I'm not crazy."

"Do you know a hawk from a handsaw?"

"What?"

"That's what I thought." Shepard raised a finger to heaven. "That's what I would expect from an evangelical cretin – a superficial interpretation. Death to Moby Dick is death to evil, death to the malevolent spirit pervading this miserable world. This pusillanimous moron with all his amens and Jesus-is-the-way simplicity aids and abets that evil spirit, my friends. Its name is *ignorance*! Ignorance is the only evil! Without ignorance, evil wouldn't exist!"

"Ignorance of God and God's law leads to evil. Everybody knows that," said Robbie.

Shepard rubbed his nose viciously and glared as he shouted, "God is dead! We killed him! Just as the ancient gods ceased to exist the moment we no longer believed in them, so the death of our belief in God has killed that gruesome tyrant *beast*! No more shackles! No more chains! We're free! Man is free. Free to accept responsibility for every evil thing he does, and every good thing too. That's the way it should have been all along. Take responsibility, you fools. Don't put your sins onto a nonexistent father who punishes you! How is it that in the twentieth century there can still be this many minds so locked up and childish?"

"You're the evil one," said Robbie.

His followers as one voice bellowed in agreement, "Evil! Evil! Evil!"

Bob Thorn jerked Robbie away from Mamie and said, "Keep your hands off her, motherfucker." And he threw Robbie off the stage into the arms of the Mamieites, who didn't want him and tossed him over to the other side. The worshippers were screaming at each other, throwing words as if they were throwing punches. Some of the Christers were chanting again, "Robbie, Robbie," while those on the other side were saying, "Mamie, Mamie." Mamie herself stood like a bird caged in light, its head jerking side-to-side watching the words flying back and forth in mortal combat.

Pulling himself back on stage, Robbie went after Mamie again. But Bob Thorn came after him, chasing him round and round, from one side to the other, and finally catching him and knocking him down. Picked him up by his collar and the seat of his pants and threw him off the stage again. He landed in the aisle and rolled himself into a ball. Some Christers tried to pick him up, but when he cried out in pain they let him lay where he was. Someone yelled, "He's hurt! He says his ribs are broken!"

"Monsters!" they yelled at Bob Thorn and Shepard.

"Sinners!"

"Kill them!"

"Kill the evil shepherd!"

"The false prophet!"

"The hoo-man-nist bastuds!"

Voices rose from the other side saying, "Kill the Christers!"

"Kill those knuckleheads!"

"Kill them imbeciles!"

And so it went – louder and louder, until it blended together and you couldn't tell what was being said. It was just *noise*.

Bob came to the edge of the stage and was spitting on the Christers. Some of them went after him, trampling over Robbie, who was still keeping himself in a ball and protecting his head with his hands and his ribs with his elbow. More Christers followed, rushing the stage, where Bob waited in a tackler's pose. The first ones up got smacked down. But more came, cursing and clawing their way over each other towards him. He kicked them and punched them and tossed them, but there were too many and they finally bulldozed him under. He was buried in a mass of writhing bodies and I figured no doubt they would kill him. Shepard got chased too. He got only a few feet before he fainted dead away right there on the stage.

When the Christers rioted, the Mamieites came unglued and in mass pounced on their enemies. Women kicked and punched each other, same as the men. Men punched men and men punched women. Women punched men back. Little kids got whacked by other little kids and some of them ran around biting adult legs and ankles and whatever bottoms were within reach. Everybody wrestled and pulled hair and tore at each other's clothing. A furious buzzing cussing punctuated the air like invisible chisels – "Bastard!" "Bitch!" "Cocksucker!" "Cuntlicker!" "Sonofabitch!"

The woman named Lulu ran past me, crying out, "Jesus is

love! Jesus is love!"

A woman with patches of hair torn out and a bloody nose told me to call the police. Behind her a woman with a split lip and a dress torn open down the front grabbed her by the hair and pulled her screaming back into the crowd of battlers. I saw a man on the floor getting bitten on one leg by a little kid and being kicked in the stomach by a man who was grinning savagely. A woman was being chased down the back rows by a man with a belt. He was calling her a fat twat. He caught her at the door and whipped her, while she screamed, "Goddamn you, Howard, we're suppose to be on the same side!" Another woman crawled out from a swarm of thrashing legs and made her way towards me. Her clothes were gone except for her shredded nylons and a polka dot collar clinging to her neck. What looked like bite marks ran from her shoulder to her buttocks.

The war raged on for what seemed hours, but was probably only a few minutes. I saw Bob slumped in front of Mamie (who hadn't moved an inch) bleeding from his nose and mouth. Shepard lay like the carcass of a dead seal near the exit - stage right.

At last the riot wound down. The people had worn themselves out. Gasping and crying they sank into chairs or onto the floor, their chests heaving. They were a mess of bloody rags and busted faces. A voice rose up from somewhere, a man saying, "What the hell happened?"

A lot of moaning, groaning and whining answered him.

Bob staggered to his feet and took Mamie's hand and led her offstage past Shepard, who woke up, sat up, and checked the condition of his nose. The naked lady in front of me said, "Where am I?" A man crawled past her and said she ought to get some clothes on. People crawled on all fours toward the exits. On their hands and knees like that, there was no way to tell which were the Christers and which were the Mamieites.

I helped Robbie over to the house. He said he was sure some of his ribs were broken. As we mounted the porch, Shepard caught up with us and said, "What on earth are you doing, Crystal?"

"He's hurt real bad."

"Let him go to his own kind."

"He's my friend, Don." ̄

"Friend," he snorted. "Some friend."

But he let me bring Robbie into the house and lay him on my bed.

"I don't want that fanatic under my roof any longer than it takes an ambulance to get here and pick him up. Did you see what he did to my disciples? He destroyed them. Someone should knock this factious dog on the head with a hammer."

"You're the fanatic," said Robbie. "Not me."

"You," said Shepard.

"You," said Robbie.

Back and forth it went accusingly, ten or fifteen yous before they finally quit.

"Some ribs are broken, maybe" I said. "Look at his face. You can tell he's in pain."

"Serves him right, the scoundrel," said Shepard. He chewed on a corner of his mustache and stared narrowly at Robbie. Robbie was pitifully moaning and holding his side. I felt sorry for him and said so. And Shepard said, "Oh, all right. There's a roll of tape in the medicine cabinet. Bring it to me and I'll wrap his stupid ribs. Let me look at you, Peevy." Shepard sat on the edge of the bed and opened Robbie's shirt and tenderly fingered his ribs.

"Ouch!" Robbie kept saying. "Ouch, ouch."

"I don't think anything is broken," said Shepard. "Maybe ligament damage. Maybe a fine-line crack. You'll live."

I got the tape and Shepard wrapped up Robbie's ribcage and told me to give him a couple of shots of splow. Which I did. I brought the whole jar, actually, and propped Robbie's head on a pillow. Sipping the splow, then bolting it, he was soon feeling better.

"No pain," he said. "Gimmee."

Shepard had left the room and Robbie and I passed the jar back and forth, while he told me that he had gone to California. And he said, "It's full of gargoyles and demons. I saw them everywhere. I even felt them in the air, which is rusty brown and tastes like sulfur. That should tell you something. Just stay away

347

from that state, especially L. A. that's all I can tell you. Those people are freaking crazy. I wouldn't put it past them to come after me. Maybe they're sniffing me out right now. Jesus, save me. I *feels* it, I *feels* it. They want my soul, they're coming."

"Your safe here," I said. "No demons want to mess with Mamie and Bob Thorn."

"I don't know about that," he said. "You had to have been there to know what I went through. California disaster, Christian. I threw my best scripture at their empty heads. All my inspiration. All my love of Christ, the only living god. No effect. I might as well have preached to a pack of screeching seagulls. I'm not kidding. Everybody talks, but nobody listens to nobody. Everybody's got an opinion and even if it's only an opinion, a lot of those freaks will kill you for it. Kill you for an opinion. Does that make sense?" He was quiet for some seconds, his eyes full of puzzles.

"California sounds like Wisconsin," I said.

"What? Well, maybe," he said. "Yes, I suppose that's true. What happened in that theater was pure California style. I never meant it to happen. And it wouldn't if the people had only listened to me. Nobody listens to me anymore. I wonder if God has forsaken me. Have I lost my charisma?"

"I don't know," I told him.

"Everywhere I go chaos follows."

His eyes filled with tears that ran over and hid in his beard. Pale as a ghost he was. Skin and bones. His glittering eyes bulging in feverish sockets.

"What did you come back for?" I asked.

"Lulu wrote and told me what was going on. She said too many souls were being lost to humanism. When I heard that I knew my mission. Humanism is a cancer. I have to stop its growth. It denies you have a soul, you know. Man and materialism is all there is. Don't listen to it, Christian."

"But nobody listens, Robbie."

"Nobody listens, you're right."

"We'll get you fixed up and get you on your way."

"I can't go," he said. "I can't run off now. Got to save some souls. Then maybe God will quit forsaking me. I need him now more than ever. So do the people. They can't make it in this terrible world without him. It's Jesus who makes them behave, makes them follow the precious path that is Jesus' way. Without the Lord life is hopeless, nothing to live for, nothing but despair everywhere. Everything is just an ugly joke. Jesus gives us the reason and purpose of our suffering. Because of Jesus, I know the pain in my ribs has a purpose. And I know that nothing in my life happens by chance. Think of living in a world that is nothing but chance. Random actions. The brick falls on your head and kills you, not because God wanted it to, but because you just happened to be walking under the spot where the brick was falling. Bam, you're dead. What killed him? Chance and a brick. Brick and a chance. That's not for me, honey." He held his head and moaned. Then he said, "I wonder if maybe I am zany like Don Shepard says. A little bit cracked, I wonder. Do you think so, Christian?"

"A little cracked? Everyone's a little cracked, Robbie, but right now you're hurt and tired. You need to get some sleep."

"Tell me something," he said. "What has Shepard got to offer that can compare with Jesus?"

"I don't know. Get him to explain it. He says that great art soothes the savage beast in us. It makes men sane, he says. The gospel of art, he calls it. And he says it makes men understand they've got a soul much grander than the old simple soul of a peasant groveling at the feet of his master. Which is what Christers do. Shepard blames all the wars on the fact that no one knows how great their soul is. Don't ask me to explain it. I can't. I'm just a simple farm boy. He's a genius."

"Great art, my silly aunt's fanny. What is that? It ain't nothing but what some smartass so-called *expert* critic says it is, all written up in some book for him. You know what art gives people? Gives them nothing but a headache and a feeling of being inferior. Because they don't know what's so great about it. If Shepard is a genius, why can't he see how empty art is for the vast majority of us? You can't pray to art and get an answer. But Jesus is another matter. Pray to him and you'll feel his love showering all over you like flakes of gold. And you know what else art don't give?"

I didn't know.

"It don't give hope. Show me a world that can live without that. Shepard's the crazy, imbecilic moron, not me, if he thinks it can."

Mamie came in, looking pink-cheeked as if she had just taken a Sunday stroll in the fresh air. Bending over Robbie, she brushed his hair back with the palm of her hand and felt his forehead.

"Blessed girl," he said. Taking her hand, he kissed it. "I am so glad to see you again. I thought about you everyday when I was gone." They stared at each other awhile - for some reason I pictured a sunflower staring at a lily.

"God wants to warn you, honey," said Robbie. "I'm sent to tell you to beware of the anti-Christ."

"Anti-Christ," she repeated.

"That's it, my girl. Listen, I'm going to teach you Bible. Then we'll show 'em. I'll teach you chapter and verse, and then I'll take you to the big cities and you'll stand tall and open your mouth and quote the words of God. You'll be a living, breathing bible, a miracle. Mamie the idiot quotes scripture. What do you think of that?"

She giggled and poked Robbie in the rib with her finger. He cried out in pain.

"Oh!" she said, jerking her hand away.

"It's okay." Robbie took her hand again. "You didn't know."

"You didn't know," she repeated. She straightened up, stretched and yawned.

"Where you going?" he said. "Don't leave me. Stay here with me. I need you. Listen, I got this feeling. I got to tell you about it. The voice has come and told me if I fail with you, my time here is through. You and me, Mamie, chapter and verse. Let's begin in the beginning. Repeat after me: 'In the beginning God created the heavens and the earth. The earth was without form and void, and darkness was—'"

"Nup, nup," she said. Turning away she went into the bathroom and closed the door.

Wide-eyed Robbie looked at me. "What's with her?"

"She only wants to memorize what's on the screen now. I really doubt she'll go along with memorizing the Bible. Unless maybe you put the thing on film."

Robbie thought about it, his brows crunching, his big eyes getting smaller and smaller.

"Some deep-thinking going on," I said.

"Then I'm already too late," said Robbie. "I've lost her. And that means I'm done for. I'm just a ghost-in-waiting. Might as well close my eyes and die right here. Too bad that rib didn't break in half and pierce my heart."

"Quit talking stupid," I said.

His eyes looked desperate now. "Ghost-in-waiting Robbie Peevy. Listen, you're my friend. Don't let 'em roll me in a ditch and – don't let the ants eat me. Don't let 'em do things to my body – cut me up, look at my brain to see why I am the way I am. Don't let 'em cut me up for science. Oh Jesus, not that! Don't let them!"

"I won't, I won't. Geez, settle down. Don't worry, I'll bury you in a nice place."

"Where?"

"I don't know. How about next to the Brule River? How'd you like that? The river rushing by and all."

"River? Yeah, that would be nice. The river of time. Okay, that's what I want. Do you promise?"

"Sure, you bet."

He stared at the ceiling, his eyes far away, maybe seeing the river. "Robbie shushing," he whispered. "Robbie gone to water. Robbie carried to the sea."

"Well, it would be heading for Lake Superior, actually. The Brule I mean."

He said he wanted some water, said he was hot. I touched his forehead, and it was burning up. I got him some water and put a cold cloth on his forehead. He mumbled awhile about becoming water in the watery sea and how cool he would be. He wished he could go there now.

When I left Robbie had fallen asleep, and Mamie was still in the bathroom. I put my ear to the door and couldn't hear anything. "You fall in, Mamie?" I said. No answer. "What you doing?" I said, opening the door and peeking. She was standing in front of the mirror making faces. Smiling at herself and batting her eyes and looking at her left profile and her right profile, fluffing up her hair, pulling it back, shoving it forward, making bangs. Doing things with her mouth, making it look like she was surprised. Then pouting. Then mad. Then moony. Then kissing the air. I had seen Mary Magdalen do those kinds of girly things, but I never thought I'd see Mamie doing them. Like acting various parts. Putting on various masks. Testing what a face can do. Which made a lot of sense, actually. Given the fact that an actress is what she had become - in real life. If there is such a thing, I mean.

Armageddon

It was sunset on a Wednesday, three days after the riot. Robbie was still sick in bed. Mamie, Bob Thorn and I were in the house, listening to Shepard complain about the nefarious ways of the world. He said he wondered if the Artlife experiment was over. Not because he wanted it to be over, but because not enough people wanted to keep it going as the Church of Art. After the riot, some Christers and Mamieites had gotten together and called a truce. They had joined forces and were pushing the Cunninghams and the Elders to form a new congregation under a "modern title that will appeal to Temple's youth": *Church of J. C. Our Savior.* These people wanted to buy Shepard out and go on with the building next door. He growled about how he should have known better than to believe he could break the time-honored hold of mysticism and ignorance on the hearts of men and women - that which had enslaved them since the first bare-forked creatures stood on two legs and walked about. And he should have known the Rock of Ages had always been (and always would be) stronger than the Rock of Reason. Things were going from bad to worse, he said. I could hear the workmen next door. A cement mixer churning. The brick walls rising.

There was a knock at the door. When I opened the door, what I saw made my stomach queasy, my scalp prickly, my heart fluttery. "Oh, my god," I said. Standing there in his farmeralls and chore jacket, a red baseball cap on his head, a wad of chew in his bulging cheek – was John Beaver.

"Close yer mouth, soggybuns. You're attractin flies." He was grinning at me with those same stained teeth and smeary brown

353

lips that I had already seen too often in my life. The odor of salivated tobacco hung around him like an invisible net.

I tried to say hi Mr. Beaver, but all that came out was, "Ai-yi-yi."

"Ai-yi-yi is right," he said. "Now shet yer face." He shoved me aside and entered the house and spotted Mamie. "Goddammit, don't you look like Missy Sunshine. Get over here, girl. Papa is takin you home where you belong."

"Booshit," she said.

"Now, Mamie," he growled. "You know I been real patient with you and this little turd here. I been patience itself, far more than I'm used to. Even let you crack my head open, didn't I? Yep, got myself permanent scarred from that little incident. But, girl, I have to tell you I done run outta patience now. Patience and me had a parting of the ways." His face was getting redder, his shoulders swelling, his fingers opening and closing. "So get that big ass a yers off that couch cuz I got tickets for a bus ride home." He turned his attention to me. "Had to come by bus," he said. "Know why? Cuz a you, you little wormy nightcrawler. Never did get my truck back in any kind of decent shape after what you did to it. It run awhile then give up the ghost. A bucket of rust in my driveway now. A hole in the block big as my fist. You started it on the downhill, overheating it like you did, you little dick-licker."

"I'm real sorry, Mr. Beaver. I thought it was running all right. I never meant to—"

"Never runned all right after you fucked with it! Dumb fuck'n kid. I outta stomp you like a bug. Yer fault, fluffyfuck, you fuck'n punkin-headed-piss-ant curse of my life."

"Yessir."

"Damn right. Stay outta arm's reach. I'll make confetti of you."

"Yessir." I stepped farther away, all the way to the edge of the kitchen.

Beaver crooked his finger at Mamie. "Let's go."

"Nup!"

"You don't tell me no. Don't make me drag you outta here."

Shepard stood up. He tried to suck in his belly, but the effort was too much. "So!" he said.

Beaver looked at him. "So?"

"So you are the proud father of this prodigy. I have taken your daughter under my wing, sir. I have uncovered her hidden talents. Pleased to meet you. My name is Donald Leonardo Shepard." He held out his hand.

"Fuck you," said Beaver. He spit on the floor and smeared it with his boot sole.

"I'm the owner of the theater next door, sir. I'm a business man."

"I don't give a fuck if yer the mayor of Milwaukee."

"I want to make you a business proposition."

"About what?"

"About your brilliant daughter."

"Brilliant! Jesus Christ. What is this, a nuthouse? Listen, buddy, you don't fool me. I know all about you, about yer using my little girl here. I read the whole bisness in the papers. Puttin her on stage. Making a spectacle!"

"I taught her to run a movie projector. I gave her a profession."

"Big fuck'n deal. I taught her farmin. She don't know nuthin of farmin and cows without I tech her. Movie projectors and shit. What the hell is that? No goddamn good for nuthin. What else you tech her, fatso? Tech her to ride yer pud!"

"Shame on you!" Shepard's nose flushed like a sun-softened tomato. "How dare you! I've been her mentor, sir. To me she came, a waif, a pitiful and homeless orphan, and I took her in out of the goodness of my heart. You . . . you hooligan, you should thank me."

Beaver laid his head back, laughter bellowing, spit flying to the ceiling and pattering it with brown spots looking like fly tracks. Stopping suddenly he squinted viciously at Shepard and said, "You know what, chubby, you got a nose looks like an infected wart. Makes me want to squash it."

Shepard's hands flew to his nose. "Don't you dare threaten this noble proboscis, sir!"

"Noble what? Never mind. Folks round here tell me yer the brains a this sorry-assed outfit. Yer makin a mint off her they tell me. I say yer exploitin my dotter, you wartnosed tub of lard. Makin a real freak show of her, a reg'lar carnival."

"Lies! Contemptible lies!"

Beaver twirled a finger in his ear. "Did this fatass just call me a liar, Foggy?"

"No sir."

"Am I a liar, puppybutt?"

"I'd never call you one, sir."

"But yer one, ain't you."

"If you say so, sir."

"Got big plans for you, fluffybum."

He had the wild-eyed look of an axe-murderer. Light slanting through the window slashing along one side of his face, revealing all its creases, making them look like scars. I had already figured he had plans for me. My bowels were loose from so much knowing.

Trying to keep up a brave tone, Shepard, belly quivering, said, "Sir, I never taught her to ride my pud, as you so delicately put it. I've been like a father only having her best interests in my soft and charitable heart."

Bob Thorn, who had been sizing up John Beaver all the while, finally stood up and threw out his chest and flexed his shoulders, his torso swaggering. "You a troublemaker?" he said. He wasn't scared! Bob Thorn wasn't scared of John Beaver! It was a wonderful revelation. I felt my own courage rushing back into my lungs. I wanted to say, "Sic him, Bob!" But of course I didn't.

Beaver smiled crookedly at him. "Yep, I'm trouble. More trouble'n you want, gorillaneck."

"I'm a gorilla?" said Bob. "You ever look in the mirror, man?"

Shepard made the point that the law would say Mamie was old enough to decide for herself where she wanted to live. "You cannot force her to go with you," he added.

"I'm the law for her," said Beaver.

"Mamie, you wanna go live with your father?" asked Bob.

"Ba-booshit," she said.

"There's your answer, troublemaker. Now, why don't you get your ass out of here before something bad happens to you?"

"Booshit," said John Beaver.

And Shepard said, "The law—"

"I don't give a fuck about the law! I'm tellin you to shet your hole, you blubber-bellied ton of lard!"

Shepard's tongue worked over his new teeth, but no words came out. I saw tears welling in his eyes, and I wanted to say, *Not now, for Christ's sake!*

"Blud of my blud," Beaver said to Mamie. "Yer mine and I'll kill any motherfucker tries to keep you from me. Anyone here wanna die fer her?"

Bob's voice came through clenched teeth. "You don't own shit round here, asshole. You try to fuck'n take her, I'll bust your jaw."

"Had nuff of you," said Beaver. His fist flew out so fast I barely saw it, and down went Bob Thorn. It was like a bullet had got him between the eyes. He was flat on his back. His feet quivering.

Shepard scurried behind the big chair and held it between him and Beaver. "O wrath of the father, don't hit me like that. I have a delicate brain!" he cried.

Looking at him with surprise at first, Beaver broke out howling with laughter. Slapping his leg and pointing at Shepard he said, "Delicate brain! Delicate brain!"

If things hadn't been so serious, I would have had to laugh at Shepard myself. His bulky exterior looking the opposite of his timid-hearted behavior – a corpulent galoot, plum-nosed, mustached, raggedy-headed giant with brand new bunny-sized teeth protruding like a warning that he was about to bite somebody. Not a chance. To be so big and so scared wasn't really funny, but the way he looked and the way he said "Delicate brain" made it slapstick, like Laurel saying it to Hardy, or Jerry Lewis to Dean Martin. An hysterical giggle rose in my throat. Beaver roared himself half-sick, getting so carried away he ended up bent over and coughing and choking and having to spit out his entire wad of tobacco splattering like a loose cow turd over the wooden floor.

At last he caught his breath and straightened up, wiping tears away. "Blubberbuns," he said, "nobody give me such a good time since Roy Shift got a butt full of buckshot for stealin turkeys. Weee! I tell you what, you tryin to get me to laugh myself to death?"

Shepard looked at Mamie and told her to throw the

sonofabitch out the door. Beaver quit smiling then. He told Shepard that Mamie was trained to have respect for the papa. "The Bible say honor thee father, don't it?"

Mamie got in her wrestling stance, ready to fight him.

And I said, "Mr. Beaver, I tried to tell you once before that Mamie is the one who knocked you out at the river, not me. I think you're about to see I wasn't lying."

"Shet yer hole, fartface!" Looking at her he said, "You the one break my head that day, Mamie?"

"Yaay, Papa."

He thought it over. Then he said, "Well, I always wondered how a runt like Foggy could hit hard nuff to knock me out. It took a Beaver to down a Beaver. But I'll forgive you if you honor me now like the Bible tells you."

"Nup, nup."

They were of a size, but she was slimmer. He probably outweighed her by twenty or thirty pounds. Seconds passed as they stared into each other's eyes, Mamie still in her wrestling stance, Beaver standing up straight with both fists clenched and a ferocious twist distorting his mouth.

And then he threw a quick right cross but not quick enough for Mamie's panther reflexes. She feinted left just enough to make Beaver miss. The whiff of his fist spun him halfway around and Mamie was on him, spinning him farther and catching him from behind, her arms encircling his chest, lifting him so that his legs swung out in front - and bang! Down he came on his back walloping. Bob, lying next to the table, got knocked on the head by Beaver's head. Bob groaned and opened his eyes. His eyes were crossed, staring at some point at the end of his nose. Beaver's mouth stayed open, his whole face saying he couldn't believe what had just happened to him.

Not missing a beat, Mamie grabbed his legs and hauled him out the door and off the porch, his head hammering like a rolling bowling ball down a stairway. And then she was dragging him up the walkway, dragging him clear to the street, letting go of him when she reached the gutter at last. By then he was growling and cussing again. He tried to get away on his hands and knees, but she kept after him, kicking his backside, knocking him on his face and chest each time he tried to rise.

Shepard and I were outside yelling, telling Mamie to pulverize that bastard. Robbie came limping out, holding his ribs and asking "Will she kill him?" We hoped so.

Across the street, Anna and Soren came out the door, Chee Chee behind them, barking and taking off after John Beaver, worrying his ankles plenty, while Mamie kept him falling forward and he kept moving along inchworm style. Butt up. Then down. On one of his forward thrusts he managed to get a backward kick into Chee Chee's head. She yelped and rolled over, little legs churning as if trying to walk on air. Anna rushed over and grabbed her, and Mamie got distracted by that. It was all Beaver needed to get away. Taking off in a half-running, gimpy limping - pausing just long enough to snatch his red cap and jam it on his head - it wasn't ten seconds and he was half a block away, hobbling backwards, shaking his fist at us and threatening to come back and kill "every damn one a you!" At the corner he disappeared and there was a sudden quiet. All I could hear were people panting. We stood together for a long time staring at the space where Beaver had vanished.

"What thing was that?" asked Soren.

"Vas dat man wobbing you?" Anna wanted to know. Brave Chee Chee was in her arms whimpering softly.

"That was the living breathing nadir of humanity," said Shepard. "A walking, talking, merciless Attila. An incarnated Mars. A murder machine on two legs. The Spencerian-Darwinian survival of the fittest thing in itself. Neanderthal-tainted chromosomes come to life. A thing of infinite evil. A savage Goliath. A—"

"It was Mamie's father," I said. "He punched out Bob Thorn in there."

"A stupendous punch!" said Shepard. "The power of Thor's hammer."

"A tough-looking critter," said Soren. "Being his enemy would make me nervous as hell."

"Poof, poof," said Shepard.

"I know him. He's the devil," said Robbie.

"She make da dewil vit him," Anna said, patting Mamie.

We went back to the house to see how Bob was doing. We found him sitting on the couch, a swelling lump covering the left side of his face. We gave him sympathy, tsk, tsk, but he was having none of us. He glared at us like it was all our faults, like we had done it to him.

"Don't talk to me!" he said.

"He sure caught you a good one," I said. "A sucker punch. You gonna be all right, Bob?"

"You damn right I am. Because I'll tell you something. I've had enough of Beavers to last the rest of my life. I'm through with Beavers. Fuck'n killers. Law ought to lock 'em up! Shoot the fuck'n savages." Standing up, he staggered past us and out the door. On the porch he turned and said, "None of you people is human. Bunch of friggin freaks. You all belong in Camelot!"

"Booby," called Mamie softly.

"Don't Booby me, Mamie. You been the fuck'n baddest luck I ever had in my life. You been more misery than you're worth. You beat me up. Your old man beat me up. Goddammit, I ain't been beat up but twice in my life, and Beavers done it both times. I stay round here, I'll get killed for sure." Tenderly he touched the lump on his face and winced. "Ouch, shit, this sucker's gonna be sore for a week. I got some loose teeth too, goddammit."

After he left, Mamie stood at the screen whispering, "Booby, Booby."

"It's okay," I told her. "Kritch'n is still here, Mamie."

"Kritch'n lufs me so," she murmured.

"Do you still love me?" I asked her.

"Uh-huh."

"Then how come we aren't together like before?" I said. "We don't no-rain or nothing. What's so important about Powers that all you got is time for him, but not me? What gives with that, Mamie?"

She thought it over. Then she said, "P-powers t-teached mmm-ee."

"You told me that already and so what? I teach you."

"N-not like P-powers."

And I knew what she meant. Powers gave her a world one film at a time, and her brain absorbed it instantly. All I could do is slowly read to her, like the passage I had read from *Blythe Spirit* that day at the train station when we had met Amoss Potter. But she didn't want anymore of that. A machine did what she needed better and faster. Words without actions on a screen meant nothing to her now. And I knew that my lot from then on was to be only a part of the whole of Mamie Beaver. Never again would I be the center of her life the way I had been before we had come to Temple. I decided to just go with it - take whatever you can get, and no more whining, Christian.

Wednesday went by. And Thursday. Then Friday came, and I was hoping against hope that Beaver had finally got it through his thick skull that the Mamie time of his life was over. Daughter or no daughter, blud or no blud, she was never going back to him. Surely he saw it. Surely he saw that he was beating a dead horse.

As a precaution Shepard hired Kiss of Death Cody and Mongoose Jim to act as bodyguards for Mamie. Mongoose Jim showed me a pair of brass knuckles he was going to use if Beaver came spoiling for a fight. Kiss of Death Cody said he was born to kick a bad Beaver's ass. "Kiss of Death Cody ain't scared of nobody," he kept saying. It made me feel safer when he talked tough like that, but the most safe I felt was when I was with Mamie herself. Who I knew could kick a bad Beaver's ass.

After the fright with John Beaver, I had taken my blankets and pillow into the booth with Mamie and slept by her side. I would wake in the night and see the outline of Powers standing over us like a palace guard, and I would snuggle up to Mamie and feel that maybe everything was going to be all right after all. Those were good nights for me, Mamie hugging me closely, cuddling me in her big arms, wearing me out with the no-rain. I no longer wondered if I might love Phoebe Bumpus. It was only Mamie I loved. It had always been only Mamie.

So Friday afternoon arrived, and Shepard had come back from the post office with a movie he said would get the people back to the Artlife again and get them wanting to play roles with Mamie.

He was talking about *Gone with the Wind*. I, along with Soren and Anna, and Kiss of Death Cody, and Mongoose Jim gathered inside the hall to watch the movie Shepard had chosen. Mamie was in the booth readying the projector. Robbie Peevy had managed to shuffle up the stairs to the booth to be with her.

Shepard had to give us a speech first, of course. He decided that he was an irrepressible optimist, yum yum. He had been way down in the dumps about the riot, and the people giving up on the Church of Art. But the Rock of Ages supposed triumph was only a temporary setback. The film he had chosen would retrieve those poor souls shackled within the confines of Paulist doctrine, bitter, conservative hardheaded boob of mystified antiquity, who had looked in a mirror darkly and found no optimism, only inevitable death and damnation for those who did not *list* to his song. Shepard would get them headed once more in the right direction – the direction of the universal truths of - *Creativity-is-God-is-Art*. Would you be like God? Would you be close to him? Would you touch him, imitate him? Then create something – it's as god-like as you can get given your mortal limitations. Bouncing with confidence, he said he would give us the special preview in a moment. But first, one more thing – terribly important for us to hear this: "No matter how unheroic our species might often be, our hearts are usually in the right place, even if our backbones aren't. We would always be brave and noble. If we could. We would always do the right thing. If we could. We would always be heroic on a grand scale like Mamie! Visions of greatness dance before my eyes when I imagine the future for her. I see the mighty oak she will become. The beauty of Scarlett O'Hara, the strength and courage of a hundred Rhett Butlers. And when she unfolds her wings at the epiphany of metamorphosis, and stands before the world, resplendent as Psyche from regions of the Holy Land, I say, when that butterflication occurs, Christ himself will step aside in awe, and the true deity of humanism will burst forth – and recognize Mamie as the future! Mamie Beaver – Messiah!"

Up there on the stage, Shepard's face was a shadowy shade of purple, his lips and cheeks vibrating, his eyes popping as if he were undergoing shock treatments.

"I've had a vision!" he cried, plastic bunny-teeth grinning. "I've had the vision of all visions since the beginning of our lack of belief in the reality of Time. When genius has that kind of vision, you better listen. It's the Second Coming that I'm talking about! Oh ho! Yum yum! Ey?"

For a few seconds his voice trailed off and we could hear him mumbling. And Anna said, "That man is cwackas."

"It's been a strain," said Soren. "We've all got our breaking points."

Shepard raised his arms and stared at the booth and shouted. "And now, on with the show! And imagine, if you can, if your minds will let you soar one-tenth of the way to Mamie, what this place will be like when she does *Gone with the Wind* – yummy!"

The lights went off and the movie started, the music full of violins, their haunting melodies, and GONE WITH THE WIND came on the screen, the effect of wind blowing through the letters as if trying to blow them away. And then the words went wobbly, badly blurred, needing adjustment upstairs. Mamie at the projector was not responding as the picture jumped from one edge of the stage to the other.

"Steady on, Mamie! Steady on!" yelled Shepard.

Yelling didn't work. All hell broke loose. The movie went dancing off the screen and darting over the curtains from one side to the other before winking out, plunging us in darkness and noise – a crash, lots of yelling, the sound of the walls shaking.

"Vut's dis? Vut's dis?"

"What's going on?"

"There he is! There he is!"

"He's here."

I ran up the aisle, across the lobby, and up the stairs to the booth. The door hung on its side, cracked in two. John Beaver was killing the fallen projector, stomping up and down on it. Mamie was getting up from the floor behind him. Robbie was using the wall to help himself rise. He was holding his ribs, blood streaming from his nose and from a gash in his forehead. Beaver turned, and in his hand was a cylinder that filled his palm and stuck out about two inches above his thumb and forefinger. It was Powers' eye, the steel tube holding the lens. Mamie dove at John Beaver and he used the lens like a little club to pound her back. She fell down again. Shaking her head, trying to get her bearings. He stomped on Powers some more, ripping pieces off, tossing them into the wall. Robbie was on his feet and staggering towards the door. Mongoose Jim came up behind me and said, "Where's Kiss of Death Cody? Where'd that chicken shit bastard run off to?"

Mamie was up again and charging John Beaver. She knocked him over, smashing him into a wall so hard the drywall cracked in a dozen places. Some of it crumbling into tiny white pebbles raining. Plaster shooting out and white dust falling over both of them, making their faces ghostly. He cussing and growling, picking himself out of the wall. Mamie should have followed up, tied him in a knot or something, but she didn't. Turning her back on him, she stared brokenhearted at the ruined Powers, while Beaver got his feet under him and came roaring back at her. They wrestled like two grizzlies gone mad, tearing at each other with everything they had. At one point he knocked her to her knees, but she came up under him, her head between his legs and lifting and flipping him over her shoulders. He fell onto the pile of broken pieces. Mamie staggering, leaning against the wall, her gaze shifting toward me, eyes looking like an explosion of blue poppies bursting through powdery snow.

I kicked Mongoose Jim and told him to get some help. He took off out the door yelling, "Call the cops! Call the coppers! Oh gawd, where's Cody?"

When Beaver rose again, he still had the lens in his hand. He came after Mamie, lunging, and at the same time Robbie intervened, throwing his body in front of Mamie. It didn't work. Beaver clubbed Robbie on the head, making a sound like a stick snapping in half, and came rushing on at Mamie. He swung and caught her on the left side of her head, dropping her to her knees. I leaped onto his back and banged my fist on his ear and tried to choke him. Reaching back, he plucked me off, tossing me away like a dishrag. The next thing I knew he was dragging me around by one leg, whipping my body into a wall and into pieces of Powers.

"Mamie!" I cried. "Mamie, he's killing me!" Somehow she pulled herself up for another run, caught him belly-high and rammed him into the wall again. They both hit the floor. Both of them gasping.

At that moment Shepard came in and took one look at Mamie's bloody head and his eyes rolled up and over he went, hitting the floor with such force the boards around him dimpled. Mamie was on her feet and going sideways dizzily, bumping the wall and trying to stay on upright, but she couldn't. She collapsed next to Robbie.

Beaver was standing up, weaving drunkenly, the lens still hanging in his hand ready to hammer Mamie some more. "Please don't hit her anymore," I pleaded. "For the love of Christ don't! You've killed her!" Crawling to Mamie I hugged her head to my chest and covered it with my arms. "I wish I had a gun, you sonofabitch," I said. "I'd blow your mink-carving brains to kingdom come."

Far off I could hear sirens. He heard them too. With one hand on the wall he steadied himself, listening, his eyes blinking as if unable to believe what he was seeing - the pile of rubbish that used to be Powers, Robbie splayed out and apparently not breathing, Mamie in my arms bleeding all over, her breath raspy as if she had blood in her lungs. And Shepard sleeping peacefully.

"You done it now," I said.

"Not me," he said. "You and her, if you'd only listened."

The sirens got closer.

"Juss like a rat in a trap," he said. The murder had left his eyes and he looked scared and confused at the same time.

"Coming to get you, John Beaver," I said. "Coming to put you in prison where you belong, you fucking monster!"

"Shet yer puky face," he told me. "Let her go. I ain't gonna hit her no more."

I put Mamie's head on the floor and scooted back. She wasn't moving. Her eyes were partially open but seemed to be staring at nothing. The powder plaster had sifted down and made a little outline of her head on the floor. Blood dripped on it, red polka dots on white.

"You hurt her real bad this time," I said.

Then he did a funny thing, funny for him, I mean, like the time he called the butterfly in Mamie's meadow *pretty*. He tore off the tail of his shirt and tried wiping the blood from her face. "Beavers can take it," he said gently. "Can't we, honey? Ah, look what you made me do. Mamie, you know I love you." He shook her arm, but there was no response. The sound of the sirens was almost on top of us.

"You're a killer now, John Beaver. Even if Mamie ain't dead, he is." I pointed at Robbie.

"Damn fool. Who is he?"

He's a holyman who said a demon was coming to kill him. He was our friend. He was a preacher preaching the gospel."

"A preacher? Shit, you might know it. But look here, the dumb bastard jumped in hisself where he had no bisness. What the fuck kinda pa would I be if I didn't fight for my dotter? I never cared for nothing but her, Foggy. But you think anybody's gonna give a good goddamn about my feelings?" Hefting the lens in his hand, he looked at it closely. Then jammed it into his chore jacket pocket. "What the hell is goin on anyway? I've kilt everthing I ever loved. It don't make sense. None of life makes a lick of sense." He stumbled past me and out the door. I heard him banging down the stairs. I heard Anna and Soren shouting and the sirens at the curb winding down.

Anna came up and gasped when she saw what had happened. "Did dat dewil kill dem all?" she asked.

"Did he get away?"

"Out da back. Dey chase him. I hope dey shoot him." Bending over Shepard, she slapped his cheeks and said, "Look at dis blubber! Call dis a man? Vake up, you! Vake up!" She sat on his belly and he broke wind. "Ach! Listen to dis! Vut can you do vit sooch a one!"

The police came in and soon there was an ambulance and medics. One medic pronounced Robbie dead at the scene. He moved to Mamie and examined the side of her head. "Skull fracture," he said. "Let's get her strapped in. Let's go. Let's get her out of here pronto!"

When he looked at Shepard he said, "What's wrong with him? How the hell we supposed to carry such an atrocity? Look at the size of this guy."

Putting a tiny bottle of ammonia under Shepard's nose and waving it, the medic woke him up and the first thing he said was, "Where's Caliban?"

"Being chased through the woods," I said. "By the cops."

There was no room in the ambulance for me, so I had to run all the way to the hospital. By the time I reached there, Mamie was in the operating room and Robbie was in the morgue below. Anna and Shepard showed up and sat with me in the waiting room. After an hour or so a cop came by and wanted to know about John Beaver. I told him the whole story, starting with finding Mamie at the Brule and ending with the fight in the booth. It took a long time to tell all that I remembered. When I got to the part about Robbie jumping in front of Mamie to save her, Shepard interrupted to say he had never liked Robbie.

Softly he said, "Camelot-bound, a nut, you know, a latter-day Savonarola. But noble nevertheless, noble – as even nuts can be. Nuts like poor Robbie Peevy."

I finished my story with the warning that John Beaver still had the lens in his pocket and wouldn't think twice about breaking another head with it. After that the cop questioned Anna and Shepard. Both of them nearly talking his arm off. They were jabbering away when the doctor came in and said the operation was over. He didn't know yet how Mamie would make out – the first twenty-four hours would be the key. "She could die or perhaps become a vegetable or maybe fully recover, it's hard to say. We've got brain waves now, but they're not normal. At this stage nothing is predictable. It will help if the swelling comes down. I'll feel more optimistic if that happens."

I was allowed to go to her. I sat by her bed as she hung on to life in a little white room, in a white bed that was too small for her. Her head was dressed turban-like in rolled bandages. A bag of clear liquid hanging on a chrome tree dripped something into the vein on her left arm at the elbow. A tube was up one nostril and a brownish tube came out from beneath her bottom running into a container sitting on the floor, both tubes gurgling. And a machine behind her was wheezing, making breathing noises. And steadily beeping. A greenish line on a screen jaggedly going up and down. Numbers flashing beside the line. Now and then a nurse came in to change the bag of liquid and check Mamie's numbers and write them on a chart.

My mind couldn't fully grasp what was happening, but I had this idea that if I stood by Mamie and massaged her the way she had massaged Jewel the cow, I could work the same miracle on her as she had worked on Jewel's leg. So that's what I did, I massaged her arms and her breasts and belly and legs and her feet. Hoping that I had the healing touch that she had. Her eyes were swollen shut. Such big eyes and now so swollen, the lids popping from her head like black bubbles about to burst. Her mouth slightly open, her breathing harsh like a wood file was running up and down her tongue. Foul, acidic breath, as if her lungs were filled with bile.

A doctor came in later that night and examined her and said she was holding her own. In the morning a new doctor came and listened a long time to her heart. He nodded his head at me and he said, "Most anyone of us would be dead by now. This woman's got the heart of a lion." I was very encouraged to hear him say that. I went on massaging. Only slipping out to the cafeteria to catch a quick bite to eat and some coffee to bring back with me to keep me awake. I told myself that if I stayed awake, Mamie would stay alive.

That day passed and night came again. I was in a daze, moving on automatic, up and down Mamie, forcing myself to keep my hands on her. Laying on of the hands, you might call it. Isn't that how Jesus worked most of his miracles? Isn't that what the saints and prophets do? Lay on the hands. In the hands lies the power of the will.

Sunday morning I woke up hearing singing coming through the window. I was under the bed, curled into a ball. "Oh no," I moaned. "How could you fall asleep, you idiot?" Pulling myself up, I saw that Mamie was still alive, tubes still gurgling, machine beeping quietly and wheezing. I looked out the window and beheld a multitude gathered below. Shepard was there, and Anna, and Soren in his wheelchair, Kiss of Death Cody, Mongoose Jim and Charlie Friendly. Bob Thorn was there. Dozens of people, all the Mamieites and the Christers mixing with each other in the parking lot in front of the hospital. Phoebe Bumpus waved to me and blew a kiss. Lulu was holding a sign that said PRAY FOR MAMIE. Some of the multitude singing "Go tell it on the mountain—" Some shouting out, "Call me Ishamel!" And others were quoting verses from *Hamlet*. The people weren't getting in each other's way, plenty of room for everyone their bodies seemed to say. And what they were singing and saying didn't clash either, like you might think it would. It sounded sort of like one of those roundelays like we used to sing in school - *frere Jacques, frere Jacques, dormez vous, dormez vous*. Or one huge prayer made out of two types of praying. Two kinds of scripture made into one. It made me think about my pa and how all my life he had been quoting Shakespeare and the Bible and Emerson, and it had always seemed that he was quoting just one book. Right then I knew that Pa was what I wanted to be, a man who could balance all the forms of the infinite forms of truth.

The multitudes stayed outside until that evening, singing and quoting whatever came to mind, celebrating what I could only think of as *The Book of Mamie*, each in his or her own way, each in a way that meant there was a lot of collective love down there for Mamie Beaver. If love alone could do it, she would stay alive and get well.

When the sun went down and the full moon rose, the congregation broke up and went away, leaving the world quiet again, the only sound behind me the wheezing, beeping and gurgling and slow breathing of the fight for life. I went back to Mamie and put my hands on her and massaged her madly, my fingers searching for the chemic heart that would wake her from her coma. Her skin was clammy cold.

That night she died.

Raising the Dead

The night Mamie died, I went back to the Artlife and up to the booth, where I gathered all the pieces of Powers around me and laid myself in the middle, the gear cover for a pillow. In the dark I saw myself like a soldier in a foxhole, arms and legs sprawled over mounds of shrapnel. My thoughts were a plague of Mamie and Robbie and Amoss going from being alive one moment to dead the next. Over and over I kept seeing them smiling or preaching or quoting something. And then I'd see the utter stillness of their bodies, the otherworldly rigor mortis turning them into human-shaped blocks of wood. Cigar-store Indians.

I cursed God and Jesus and called them phony balonies. "There ain't no heaven. There ain't no hell," I said. "Ain't nothing but nothing." A black-hearted ogre slithered through my stomach and ran its tentacles up my arms and legs, swimming inside my veins like sluggish acid, taking over the beat of my heart – my pulse whispering deaaath . . . deaaath . . . deaaath. It reminded me again that I was going to die one of these days, just like everybody else. I was going to die. My parents, my brothers and sister, all my friends – everything living was going to die. What a system! No getting out of it. It would come and you'd have no say in the matter. It would pour into you and put you to sleep *forever*. Stars and planets and the sun would go on shining without you. You wouldn't be there to see them.

"Me too," I whispered. "Christian Peter Foggy. Just like you, Mamie. And Robbie. And Amoss. Nothing will warm them up ever again. Not in a million years."

Her skin had been so cold it had made my hands cold massaging her. That is death, the endless cold, exactly like the ghost of Soren's friend had told him, the repellant feeling of cold skin. It was hard on me thinking such morbidities, but I couldn't help it. Death was more real than the so-called reality of life. Death was no illusion or dream. Life was nothing but illusion and dream - and kidding yourself. Death was like an octopus inside me, its suckers sucking on my oblivious organs and warning them not to count on anything, not to waste a second of my life, because even if I lived for a century, it was nothing - a hundred years would be too soon to die. It also said that I was alone essentially. And would die alone. That's what it said. Nobody did it for you. You had to be there when it happened. My hands didn't keep it from Mamie. If Mamie could die, I knew for sure anybody could die, even Superman or Wonder Woman or Tarzan and of course, Samson. I started crying a real gusher full of sobs and moans, worse than any crying I could ever remember doing. It practically choked me, but I couldn't stop. I felt like a tiny boy in a dark dungeon, left there like in a grave and nobody coming to the rescue, no Mamie to save the day.

"My heart is broke," I said. Then louder, "My heart is broke!" It made no difference. My words went out into the dark, and came back as silence sitting on the ruins of the battered metal, the pieces of Powers shattered like Humpty Dumpty all around me.

In the morning I woke with a plan to do better than all the king's horses and all the king's men. I would put Powers back together again. I laid him out like a giant puzzle and moved the pieces here and there to get an idea of what fit where. I could see that the gears and wheels had no serious injuries. Mainly, it was the big-sheeted stuff, all dented and bent, that would need some torch-warming and water and a ballpeen hammer to straighten them out. I started with Powers' foot and set it back on its rollers. Then I fit the leg back on, only it was cockeyed and wobbly and had a split seam that would need some welding. I switched my attention to the main box housing the motor and traced the course where the film snaked through it. I could see how it was supposed to be, and little by little I fit bushings and gears and wheels back on the pegs where they belonged. I spent hours at it and came to believe in what I was doing. I was bringing Powers back from the dead. But I would need some tools, some delicate screwdrivers and long-nosed pliers and slim wrenches, open-ended – three-eighths and five-sixteenths, for sure – and cotter pins, screws, washers, and nuts. With those bits and pieces and a little luck I knew I could make Powers operate like he used to. Or at least nearly so.

In the afternoon, I went over to Shepard's house and ate a sandwich, drank a glass of milk and took a shower. I scrubbed myself raw, especially my hands, coated with graphite and grease and Mamie's death. When I had finished, I put on clean clothes and walked over to Charlie's. All the gang was there, including Bob Thorn crying in his beer.

First thing Charlie said was, "Your old man is on his way to fetch you. He called and said to tell you to sit tight."

"He knows about Mamie and John Beaver?" I asked.

"Everybody knows. There's a statewide manhunt on."

"It's shoot to kill!" said Kiss of Death Cody. "Take no prisoners. Sonofabitch is lucky I wasn't there. He'd be dead already."

"I went looking for you," said Mongoose Jim. "You skeedadaled."

"Nature called. I was in the john. I had no idea what was going on."

"Funeral's today," said Charlie.

"Already?" I asked.

He told me that Duke Cunningham and the Christers had taken over everything and were going to bury Mamie and Robbie together marking the entrance to the new *Church of J. C. Our Savior*. Shepard raised his head from his glass and moaned about the Christers making themselves a shrine for worshippers, the worst kind of infantilism. Everybody agreed it was a typical religious notion – to make Mamie and Robbie into martyrs and give the faithful a place of pilgrimage where they could kneel and pray and find solace of some kind.

"Ancestor worship," said Shepard, his mouth sour, his false

teeth missing, his lips caving inward so much they nearly disappeared. "Next thing they'll be working miracles and making those two into bona vide saints."

I recalled what I had told Robbie when he got injured at the riot – that I would bury him at the Brule. But getting made into a shrine seemed like a better idea, one he might appreciate more than sleeping forever between our pasture and the river. Or would he? What would he actually have wanted? *Robbie shushing by, Robbie gone to water.* I had kind of promised him that - hadn't I? And what about Mamie? Enshrined in front of the *Church of J.C. Our Savior?* She didn't belong there. She belonged back home, next to her mother. Of that I was sure.

"Who do these folks think they are?" I said. "Mamie don't want to be buried in a concrete crypt in front of no church. How come nobody asked me about it?"

"They didn't need to ask you," said Charlie. "No kin to claim Mamie, so the church claimed her. It's either the shrine or up on the hill next to Amoss. Which would you rather have?"

"Neither. She should be buried next to her mother by the Brule River."

"You'd have to fight the Cunninghams and the Christers. They pretty much run this town, you know."

"They'll turn her into a cult," said Shepard.

"Hey," said Kiss of Death Cody, "a Robbie-Mamie shrine is worth a million bucks to this city."

"It'll be the Lourdes of the North," added Shepard.

Bob Thorn was still crying in his beer.

After lunch we went to the funeral, over to the site where what had been beautiful woods was now a monstrous brick building, the walls almost finished. The roof and the window glass needed to be installed yet. And a tower with a bell to call the faithful. Twenty yards in front of the church were a pair of holes in the ground - the graves. The coffins were there, the congregation gathered around them. The coffins were stainless steel – a metallic gray color, like cold ashes. Each had a ring of yellow chrysanthemums arranged on top. At the edge of the flock was an architect fellow standing next to me and Shepard and the others from Charlie Friendly's Bar. The architect showed us a sketch he was making that had a pointed archway overhead, under which the worshippers would walk, passing between the graves on either side, the graves being covered with raised slabs of pink granite with the names and dates of the deceased carved on them.

Shepard scorned the design. "Like the resurrection of medieval gothic," he said. The architect sniffed, his eyes full of contempt for Shepard's opinion.

"Get lost," said Kiss of Death Cody, "before we put a match to it."

The man hurried away to the other side of the crowd. Duke Cunningham, thin, storky-looking, Adam's apple dueling with the knot in his tie, stood at the head of the graves sermonizing the people, telling them how brave and holy Mamie and Robbie were in life, and how lucky they were to die for what they believed in. "There is no better death we could ask of God than being a soldier battling to make the Lord's holy words heard throughout the world. God has given his faithful servants a priceless gift. He has given them martyrdom!"

The flock nodded their heads in agreement. Some of them saying, "Yes, Lord."

And Shepard said to me, "See, what did I tell you!"

Cunningham continued, his voice at a-preacher-in-the-pulpit level. "And a boy once lost – I'm talking about Robbie Peevy - given over to Camelot as certifiably crazy, and yet he was made to speak in tongues and to witness and to save souls. If that's crazy, then we're all crazy, brethren and sistern. And a magnificent species of Girl as pure as driven snow, born a certifiable idiot, given the power of Christ descending upon her, and she too bore witness by speaking in tongues for the enlightenment of the faithful. How good is God! How mysterious his ways, brethren and sistern!"

"Amen!"

"Hallelujah!"

And so on and so forth.

There was Lord is My Shepherd chanting going on. Worshippers holding up their hands to the sky, weeping and moaning. Lots of hugging. A fat woman threw herself on Mamie's coffin and sobbed and shook uncontrollably. The sling underneath slipped up toward the head of the coffin, and down slid the footside and the weeping woman with it, tumbling into the grave at an angle, like riding on a child's slide. She really wailed then. Another woman close by fainted and had to be carried to the outer edge for air. Two men held her, one by the armpits, the other by her ankles. And alongside came a little boy in a blue suit, hanging onto the overcome woman's skirt and saying, "Whatcha doin that for, Ma? Whatcha doin that for?" The fat lady in the grave got dragged out. She looked very frazzled, her eyes shimmering, staring over her shoulder at where she had just been – a place which someday, and in similar rectangular proportions, she would find herself again. Her personal grave. Her name on a headstone. That's what her face said. Her face said she had had a trial run. A man held her, rocking her while she wept. It was infectious. One after another the women started shrieking and weeping. Some of them fainting. At least half a dozen had to be carried away. A man with a familiar voice cried out, "Before God I might not believe this without the true avalanche of my bleeding eyes!" Which was a bit off what Horatio actually said, but it didn't matter. People caught the man's drift and started shouting, "Oh ye damn whale! Oh ye damn whale!" and other fragments of the Artlife litany.

Shepard said he was leaving before the people made him regurgitate his lunch. We followed him back to Charlie's

Inside the bar, we sat glumly drinking splow with beer chasers. Everybody kept saying it was a sad and stupid day. We could hear the congregation down the block going on and on, making a commotion for better than an hour before they finally buried Robbie and Mamie and went on their way. Time for supper by the time the last shovel of dirt was piled on. Time for time out. By that time I was feeling vaguely drunk and ready to weep or to cut loose with a rebel yell.

Phoebe wanted to play some music and dance. "Let's dance for Mamie," she told me.

So I did. The music played and we danced and she rubbed on

me, but I was too full of numbness down there to care. Last thing I wanted was to do the no-rain. It would have felt like I was betraying Mamie fresh in her grave. When I didn't respond to Phoebe she got bored with me and turned her attention to Kiss of Death Cody. He was glad to waltz her over the floor. The look on his face said she knows a living man when she sees one. Get lost, punk. So I did. I sat next to Shepard and Bob Thorn and we shared a pitcher of Grain Belt beer.

A little past dark, Pa showed up. I gave him a big hug and kissed his cheek. I didn't want to let go of him. "Don't get mushy on me now," he said, roughing my hair. He sat with us and told how the whole North was out hunting for Beaver. So far the wily bastard had given the posse the slip. But by and by they would catch him, Pa was sure.

"I wisht I could've got my hands on him," said Mongoose Jim.

"Go on," said Kiss of Death Cody. "You had your chance to be a hero and blew it big time." He was twirling Phoebe around, making her hair fly, her ears catching flickers of the overhead lighting, turning them into teapot handles. The jukebox played boogie-woogie. Go, girl go.

"Well, " said Pa, "he's wanted for double murder now. It's the kind of thing you'd expect if you live the way he did. Hard justice eventually has its way with you. It's in the Over-Soul's scheme of things."

"I hope they blow him to pieces!" Shepard blurted out savagely. "A sacrilege, a desecration, a profanation. Goddamn that man! Oh, Mamie! Oh, Mamie!" Laying his head on his arms, he cried for a while, his shoulders heaving.

'It won't be easy to catch him," Pa told us. "He got to Oulu in a stolen car and slipped off into the woods there. Those are thick woods to squeeze through, you know, pillars of birch so close in places you have to slip through sideways. Lots of alder brush too. A regular jungle. They've got an army after him, though, and dogs and helicopters. Still, it won't be easy. Beaver's an animal. He knows what to do in the wild."

"They'll get him, though, won't they Pa?"

"Oh yeah, they'll get him eventually."

Kiss of Death Cody and Phoebe sat down, and Kiss of Death Cody said he was going to go out there and track the sonofabitch himself. Bob Thorn, who had finally quit crying in his beer, said he was ready to go whenever anyone else was. Mongoose Jim said he was ready too. They passed the splow and drank to the hunt.

"He was there in the booth," said Kiss of Death Cody, sneering at Mongoose Jim.

"It would've taken ever goddamn man here to stop him," Mongoose Jim said. He shook his fist at Kiss of Death Cody. "Get off my back, you little, pot-bellied rat!"

"Hadn't been for nature calling, I would've stopped him!" Kiss of Death Cody showed us his knuckles, holding them up to Phoebe's jaw. "Pow, right in the kisser!"

Phoebe glanced at me and rolled her eyes. Kiss of Death Cody wasn't the one for her. I could have told her that.

Holding my glass up, I gave a toast, "To Mamie and Robbie. R.I.P."

"The warp and the weft of all that is good in humanity," Shepard added.

The splow was making a burning whirlpool in my belly. It scalded the octopus of death, its tentacles evaporating and leaving me with a sort of nauseous glow in my mouth, and I told myself that this time I would keep the booze down and keep up with the rest of them, I'm a man. Pa didn't say anything about my drinking. On his face was a small, sympathetic smile. In his eyes were kindness and understanding and a touch of curiosity.

Round and round the splow and beer went, everybody joining in. Even Chee Chee got her own ashtray full to drink from, she liking splow better than beer, lapping it up as fast as Anna would pour it in. It wasn't long before Chee Chee was sideways on the floor, eyes glazed, tongue hanging happily. In fact we were all feeling more optimistic by then. Anna was on Soren's bony lap. Phoebe had switched to dancing with Bob Thorn, a better fit, while Kiss of Death Cody and Mongoose Jim were matching each other drink for drink and saying what friends to the death they were. Pa and I talked, and I filled him in on what had happened in the booth – the battle Mamie put up, the bravery of Robbie and all that.

Shepard said it was - the war of the Titans, colossal and awe-inspiring.

"They've become particles of the Deity now," said Pa. "And they're probably better off than we are."

The music stopped.

I put my head between my hands and snuffled. Shepard joined me. Then Anna and Phoebe were crying. Bob Thorn did it silently. Chee Chee woke up and started whining and the dark mood of pessimism and failure returned in a flash.

Mongoose Jim said, "I should'a tried. I could'a tried."

"Me too," said Kiss of Death Cody. "But I was stuck in the john. Nature called. It was nature's fault. I didn't know what was goin on up there in that booth, I swear."

Bob Thorn said, "I shouldn't have run out just cause that bastard kicked my ass. But it was hoomiliating! Ah gawd, I'll never get over it. Mamie, forgive me for abandoning you to your fate. I'm a no good bum."

'Now, now," soothed Phoebe.

Pa was filling his pipe, that sympathetic smile plastered to his face was sort of annoying.

"How would you like to be me?" Bob continued. "I was the number one bodyguard and that fuck'n Beaver flattened me like a toothpick. How would you like that on your ego for the rest of your life?"

"No, thank you," said Kiss of Death Cody.

"I'm used to being a hero. Now I'm a low-down skunk."

"You think you got it rough," said Mongoose Jim. "At least you stood up to him and took his Sunday punch. I was in the booth. I was on duty and had brass knuckles. Try livin with that!"

"Try livin in this shit for brains town," said Kiss of Death Cody. "Try raisin a family without a job and no trains runnin. Try livin on unemployment. You can't do it. And does anybody care? Nobody cares."

"Live with ghosts and your back broke for hurry-up money," said Soren. "And no goddamn TV because your wife threw a hammer through it."

"Vut a vurld!"

"Woe, woe . . ."

Listening to them complaining made me realize how stupid it all sounded. I quit my blubbering then. And an idea came to me. "Well, let's do something about it," I said. "We don't have to take their Christer shit."

"What you talking bout?"

"Talkin bout those Christers taking over, burying Mamie and Robbie like they owned them. Nobody consulted me. Nobody consulted any of us. Is that fair?"

"What you want to do about it, son?"

"I want to dig them up and take them home, Pa. Back to the Brule."

Everything was quiet. My friends looked at me like I was either out of my mind or a flaming genius. Seconds ticked by. I told them how I had promised Robbie a place by the Brule and how Mamie belonged there too, next to her mama.

"No doubt about it," I added.

"We could do it," said Kiss of Death Cody.

"It's an idea," said Bob Thorn.

"Gee, I don't know, fellas," said Mongoose Jim, his egret head jerking toward the green sign that said EXIT.

Shepard was rubbing his hands like he was rubbing away his grieving. "Think of the multitude praying to empty concrete crypts covered by pink granite slabs. Get the picture? Ha, ha!"

"We could watch 'em from here right out the window," said Kiss of Death Cody.

"Splow has made you all goofy," said Charlie. He was chuckling.

"Yeah, somewhat," said Pa. "But there's a feeling of righteousness warming my heart right now. I mean, Mamie does belong with her mother, not in this city with those silly people making a spectacle out of her and—"

"Better than having her become a relic!" said Shepard. "It'll be Canterbury Mamie, I tell you. Dunces coming for miles to walk on their bleeding knees around her grave. Metaphysics for mystics. Atavism. Dark labyrinthian rites of passage and unevolved reason. They'll dig them up one day, mark me, and steal their bones and worship the tatters of their clothes and hair and sell

379

their snot-rags as relics. They'll bronze their boots and set them up as shrines. It is the nature of the beast to want rabbits' feet, clovers, horns, icons, dice, pebbles, beads, Ave Marias, potions, feathers, and crosses – or Mamie Beaver's thighbone hanging over the altar."

"I like Christian's idea," said Phoebe.

Bob pounded the table. "I'm for digging them up and letting the Foggys take them back to the farm. Let's see a show of hands."

Every hand went up. We were all pretty cheerful again.

Phoebe told a story of a woman from Racine, a rich one who wanted her Thunderbird buried with her when she died. They buried her sitting at the wheel, as if on judgment day she would drive up and offer Jesus a ride.

"It's paying your last respects when you do what the dead wanted done," said Phoebe.

We toasted last respects, and Anna told us her last request was to have Chee Chee buried with her when she died. We toasted her last request. Anna put Chee Chee on the table and we all shouted, "To Chee Chee!" We bolted our drinks. The dog was so drunk she couldn't hold her hindend up. It kept flopping over.

"That mutt can't hold its liquor," said Kiss of Death Cody.

Chee Chee quit fighting it. Her head joined her hind parts and she went to sleep.

We toasted the sleeping Chee Chee. We toasted one-by-one everybody in the bar. "And a toast to my legs!" said Anna, jumping up, lifting her skirt and doing a little jig. "Vut legs I had vunce!" She danced a can-can, showing her fat, little legs and underpants, while we shouted and clapped and pounded on the table.

It was just around the fifth or sixth toast to Anna's legs that I realized I was floating. The floating feeling making me snort and snigger. I felt my lips playing over my teeth like ticklish rubberbands. Pulling on my lips, I tried to straighten them, but they kept bouncing into a grinning, off-kilter angle that made my words slurry: "Toos Wanna's eggsss." I put my hand over my mouth and sniggered.

"That boy has a snootful," I heard Pa say. "Don't drink no more."

The splow had hit my brain so abruptly I couldn't keep up with the company. Lowering my head into my arms I thought I might catch about one or two winks and start over when I woke up again. Lots of laughing. People talking about what? I didn't care. Chee Chee had the right idea.

The next thing I understood was that I was being dragged through the night air, Bob Thorn on one side of me, Pa on the other. "Walk it off, Walk it off," Pa kept saying. I saw that everyone was walking with us. I saw shovels, and when we got to the graves, soft dirt started flying. In about fifteen minutes or so, Robbie was uncovered. A rope was snaked around one end of the coffin and up the end came. Bob Thorn slid down the coffin, into the grave and pushed, while others pulled and in a moment, Robbie was on the ground outside. Next thirty minutes or so, up came Mamie. Then Pa backed the pickup to the curb and the coffins were loaded onto the bed. It wasn't quite wide enough, so we had to tilt them on their sides a little, forming a V with their edges together. Kiss of Death Cody and Bob Thorn went over to the workmen's gangboxes next to the church and carried two big ones over, dropping one each into the graves. Then hurriedly dirt was piled on them.

"Hail to thee, holy gangboxes. To thee we pray," said Shepard.

"I'm coming to services every Sunday," said Soren.

"I'll pray from afar," said Charlie. He started walking back to his bar.

I asked Shepard if I could have the pieces of Powers to take with me back to the farm. He said I was welcome to take them. So Pa pulled up to the Artlife and we went inside and got Powers and loaded him into the V of the coffins. Pa brought out some rope and tied everything down.

"Hope no cop stops us," he said. "This'll be a mite hard to explain."

Phoebe had gone to her car, and she came back with a canister of film for me. "Here, take this," she said. "Whatever comfort it is, she's here big as life. Bigger than life, in fact. I want you to have it. None of it's any use to me anymore."

When I started saying goodbye to everyone, Shepard threw his arms around me and had a little weeping jag. "First Amoss and then Mamie, and now you're going away," he said. "No one will know how dearly I've suffered. Take her gently, sweet prince. And may flights of angels sing my Mamie to her rest. Tend her with love. And think of me alone, a hollow, tortured genius, farsighted, unique, an eccentric who should have been showered with wealth and fame, and would have been had it not been for the desiccated fiery furnace of old-time religion. With Mamie I had a chance once upon a time of creating a new mythology. But that was then and this is now. Think of me as a comet that had a brief moment of oneness with the universe, my message written across the fiery sky. Across the fiery sky, I say, and then poof – gone to cold slag upon the rock of time. Think of me with a jar of splow in my hand and the memory of what could have been breaking my heart daily. The quotidian of my life from these sad events forward into the eternity of slumber waiting for me will be the sad lament of Mamie, Mamie, Mamie. Think of me, Crystal. Ub ub ub, don't forget old and brokenhearted Donald Leonardo Shepard. For I, on the other hand—"

Bob and Kiss of Death Cody pulled him away from me and told me to get going. As we headed down the road, I looked back and saw my friends standing in the middle of the street looking after us, silhouetted at the edge of the haloing streetlight. Behind them was the great wall of the unfinished church, the two burial mounds at its entrance shining beneath a pumpkin moon - a Mamie face, her crater eyes watching over the site evermore, unwearyingly.

Resurrecting Powers

It was milking time when we drove into the yard. The lights were on in the house, and I knew my brothers were dawdling at the table, having their toast and coffee with cream and sugar. Mama would be shuffling back and forth in her robe and slippers, holding the pot and telling the boys to drink up, it's time for chores. They would be yawning and rubbing their faces. Mary Magdalen would be coming out of the bathroom all set to tell the boys how worthless they were and what a wonder it was that they even knew which end of the cow to milk. They would hiss and grumble at her, and she would bully them until they would hurry with their coffee just to get away from her. And I thought about how when tomorrow morning came, I would be sitting with them, everything like it was long before I went away with Mamie. The dream would be over, the tiresome older dream returning to take its place.

When they came bursting out the door, five inkblots flowing toward the pickup through the ground fog, Pa said, "Hang on to your nerves. Here they come and they got us cornered." My brothers surrounded us and started howling, "They're here! They're here!" The first rays of dawn hit the inkblots and they lit up with arms waving and heels kicking up like a herd of calves showing off.

The door opened on my side and someone hauled me out and shook me back and forth, like I was an apple tree ready to drop my apples. The rest of my brothers started punching and pinching me and yelling "Christian! Christian!" Calvin pulled my nose and Cash wiggled my ears. Cutham yanked my arm, while Cush seemed to want to tear my other arm off and wave it around.

Calah had a hold of my hair, pulling my head back so he could scream in my face, "Christian, it's us!" The only way I could get them to stop was to kick them in the shins and use my elbows to hammer heads and chests. I finally broke through and got away from them, running for the porch, where Mama and Mary Magdalen stood watching the mayhem.

"Look who's here! Look who's here!" my brothers kept shouting.

When I got to the porch, Mama threw her arms around me. Naturally she was weeping. "Oh, son, oh son," she said, "don't ever go away like that again. I like worried to death about you and near to wore out my Rosary beads praying."

Mary Magdalen got in on the hugging and said she was glad to have me back, the only sane brother she had, the only one that was recognizably human. My brothers shouted at her, saying that Mary Magdalen herself wasn't human. She was the Thing from outer space. She was the Blob.

"Oh, shut up, you boys!" said Pa. "Give a body a rest, will you?"

No way.

Cush jumped up on the coffins and stomped around on them and kicked Powers and said, "What's this here junk?"

Cutham banged a coffin with his fist and said, "It's hard as iron!"

Calvin called the twins a pair of insufferable morons and told them they didn't know coffins from mailboxes. The twins looked at each other and said "Coffins!" simultaneously. Then they got solemn, both pulling their lower lips inside out and staring at the coffins in awe. I told them Robbie was in one and Mamie in the other.

"Dead?" they both said in unison.

"Oh, for pity's sake!" said Mary Magdalen.

Calah asked why we had brought them to the farm.

"To bury them," said Pa, "in a dignified and peaceable place. That gravesite down by the Brule where we found Mary Beaver. I'm gonna fence it off and make it the family plot."

They nodded their heads like everything made perfect sense now. Cush was fingering the remains of Powers and asking, "So what's this, Pa?"

Pa told him it was a Powers Electrical Chicago movie projector that Mamie Beaver had been in love with.

"I'm putting it back together," I said. "I'm gonna make it run again." That made perfect sense to my brothers too.

"A fer-sure projector?" said Cash. "Can we watch movies?"

"You gonna show us movies?" said Calvin.

I said I was going to show them a film that a reporter had made of Mamie doing her act on stage.

"Hot dog!"

"Neat!"

"We like you, Christian!"

My brothers untied the rope and hauled Powers off to the machine shed. When they came back, they wanted to know if they could see inside the coffins.

"We never did get to see this Robbie fella," said Calvin.

"We want to say goodbye to Mamie," said Cash.

Pa thought about it. "Okay," he said. "But you be composed and respectful. No shenanigans, you here?"

"No shenanigans, Pa. We'll behave."

The coffins came off the pickup and were lowered to the ground. We unscrewed the lids and lifted them off. There lay Mamie and Robbie, each in a cocoon of winding sheet. Pa pulled the sheets off their heads, and we could see their peaceful faces. All the swelling was gone from Mamie's head. And except that she was skim-milk pale, she looked pretty much the same as she had when she was alive. On her face was a partial smile, like she was dreaming something just slightly funny. And Robbie didn't look half-bad either. Except he had a blue ridge across his forehead, where Beaver had crushed it. Otherwise Robbie seemed tranquil, his blond beard and hair fanning out and starting to catch the first rays of the sun just peeking over the garage.

And it was at that point in time when the sun's rays created something strange. Wisps of ground fog were rising around the coffins, forming a ghostly prism through which the shooting beams created a hazy rainbow hovering briefly, before transforming itself into a golden cascade glittering over the bodies and the winding sheets so intensely that the light was almost blinding.

Mama cried out, "Holy Mary Mother of God," and dropped to her knees. Mary Magdalen answering, "Pray for us sinners now and at the hour of our death." The whole thing, the light, the blazing bodies the chanting prayer gave me goose bumps on the goose bumps I already had.

"Gawww," said my brothers, one after the other, "Gawww," "Gawww," "Gawww," "Gawww."

Pa's sense of poetry kicked into gear: "Like a glory," he said, "turning them into pure energy, a jillion molecule stars raising up the particles of their souls. A regular filigree of sun-spangled atoms heading toward the Deity. Who's gonna fear the afterlife now?"

"Gawww," continued my brothers.

Then it was over. The fog shimmered away and the light fell in normally. And the glory faded.

After a few seconds Calvin said, "Can we bury 'em now, Pa, you think?"

"After chores," said Pa. "Get the lids back on and take care of the cows."

There was no messing around. The lids were screwed back on, and the coffins loaded into the pickup again. We went to the barn and did the milking and cleaning as fast as we could.

Afterwards, we drove with shovels and picks to the gravesite. We used the front-end loader to make a hole large enough to hold two coffins side by side. We finished the hole off neatly with the shovels and pickaxes and laid the coffins in, Robbie on Mamie's right-hand side, her mother Mary on the left.

Opening his Bible, Pa read the part about the Son of Man coming with his angels to repay all sinners for the bad they had done in this life – mainly I knew Pa meant God was coming to get that daughter-killing Beaver. Closing the Bible, Pa said, "Let me now talk extemporarily from the heart. The Deity sits in the bosom of Nature and is the Lord Over-Soul of all visible and invisible phenomenons. In every spirit he dwells and connects that spirit with its father-earth and mother-sea, and the salt of the sea is in its veins, and the minerals of the earth is in its blood, flowing from the beginning and endlessly rocking in the cradle of time throughout the world, the union of brotherhood and sisterhood ubiquitous as stars in the sky. Return then, Reverend Robbie Peevy and Miss Mamie Beaver, to the bosom of creation whence you came, and one day we will all join you there in the infinitude of endless exchanging of souls for bodies and bodies for souls. It won't be no calamity at all, no more than the settling and rising of drops of dew. Amen, I say, and now let's bury these two."

We said amen and stared proudly at him, proud that he could say such wonderful things just off the top of his head like that. He nodded at us and his smile was small, his face very modest-looking yet satisfied. Mama leaned her cheek against his shoulder and made the sign of the cross. On top of Mamie's coffin, Mary Magdalen dropped a rosary knotted in a lace hanky. It made a snapping noise as it hit the lid and slid off.

"That was some preachin, Pa," said Calvin. "Wish I could do it that way."

"Start reading and get something in your head other than moths and feathers and you will," said Pa.

There was no more to do for Robbie and Mamie but to bury them. So there you go, that's what we did.

Some gray and drizzly days came on, just the kind of weather a farmer needs to get caught up on machine and barn repairs. It was also the kind of weather to quicken the pasture and the hayfields, add that extra lushness to their multi-colored green. It was during these days that I got to spend time with Powers. Piece by piece, gear and cog and belt and wheel, I got him back together again. Pa did the wiring for me and helped braze all the split seams and tighten with torch and water the wrinkled metal covers. He went into Duluth for supplies one day, bringing back a light bulb that fit the one Beaver had shattered. We put the leg back on the foot, screwed it down, and mounted the main box on top and the arms for the reels, for which we had had to invent some spring-loaded belts made of old inner tubes. They worked pretty well, actually. When I flipped the switch the hum of Powers' motor filled the room, all the segments of his transmission turning in the right directions and the lamp glowing inside casting a huge white square of bright light against the machine shed's whitewashed wall.

"We gonna have to order us a lens," said Pa. "We'll get this thing figured out yet and see what you got on that reel of film."

Powers stood there, somewhat the worse for wear but looking like he could still do the job, given an eye to find his way.

A few days later it stopped raining and we were able to get out in the fields. Pa wanted us to move the pasture fence, so the cows could get at the sweet brome and trefoil mixture on the other side. We headed out with posthole diggers and shovels and picks. On the way over, Pa told me to check on the graves. He was sure the rain had made them sink a bit and they would need some filling in.

It was when I got close to the graves that I saw something wasn't quite the way we had left it. Something had been added - a tube sticking out about six inches from the middle point of the sunken double-grave mound. I knew before I got there what it was. When I saw I was right, I spun around and yelled at Pa and my brothers, "John Beaver! John Beaver!"

They came running. In Calah's hands was the sixteen-pound sledgehammer. The rest carried shovels and picks and posthole diggers. "Where is he? Where is he?" they shouted.

I told them he was in the woods. Probably watching us right now.

They all stared intensely at the woods on the other side of the whispering Brule. "How you know it's him?" said Calvin.

I pointed to the lens in the ground. "That's Powers' eye," I said. "That's what John Beaver used to pound Mamie and Robbie to death."

"Gawww, no," they said.

"The murder weapon itself," said Cash, bending down, fingering the lens.

Calah hugged the big hammer. "Don't you worry none, Christian. We'll fight for you." And he shouted towards the woods, daring John Beaver to come out.

They called him names. "Scaredy-cat!" "Stinking rat!" "Dirty old murderer!"

"I got traps in there!" shouted Calvin. "Bear traps, John Beaver! Cut your legs off!"

"Boys, boys," said Pa. "Calm down. Take it easy, boys. Make a guard line here and keep your eyes peeled." They formed a line between the river and the graves and marched back and forth with their weapons on their shoulders. Pa told Cash to run quick and call the sheriff and bring the twelve-gauge shotgun back.

I went up to the partially sunken mound and pulled the tube out of the red earth, took it down to the Brule and washed it in the water. Dried it on my shirttail. Looked through it and saw that for all the banging it had taken, it wasn't broken. It magnified the trees, making them fuzzy and I thought about John Beaver in there, in that fuzzy world at the edge of what passed for civilization. Where had he gone? Was he in there looking at us right now?

But then it struck me that I had lucked out. I had the very thing I needed, the last part - the eye to see through to see Mamie once more on the stage. Mamie as Hamlet, Mamie as Ahab. And so on and so forth. I tossed Power's eye into the air and watched it cartwheel, catching the sun and flashing quarter-size dots of light at my face and over the graves, Powers coming down like fire into my hands.

"Pa," I said, "can I go see if this thing still works?"

"Yeah, we'll hold the fort," he said.

I took off running for the machine shed.

Inside the shed, Powers looked like some great icon standing there, facing the white wall, while waiting for me to finish the restoration I had begun so many days ago, when I had made it my mission to resurrect him. I slipped the lens into its socket and took the film from the canister and threaded it through the wheels and pulleys. When I flipped the switch the motor started and the beam of light was thrown onto the wall. In a moment there was a blurry image of Mamie. I messed with the lens until I had focused the image. And there she was. I turned on the sound and she said

"Call me Ishmael."

And Shepard off-screen answering –

"Whenever I find myself growing grim about the mouth."

And then Mamie again –

"Whenever it is a damp, drizzly November in my soul."

The gears turned, making ticking noises like a thousand tiny clocks. The voices faded in and out, as I stood watching and remembering it all –

"It is a mild, mild wind and a mild looking sky. On such a mild, mild day, very much such a sweetness as this –"

And on she went.

On and on.

It was Mamie, a little fuzzy, a little scratchy-voiced but not hard to understand –

"Staggering under the piled centuries since paradise . . . Let me look into a human eye." And she looked at me, and I answered her –

"It is better than to gaze into sea or sky—"

"Yee are tied to me. This act was immutably decreed. It was rehearsed by ye and me a billion years before this ocean rolled."

And I following—

"Oh, my captain! My captain, noble soul, grand old heart!" I moved toward her image on the wall and raised my hand and put it over Mamie's hand. Palm to palm.

"Yes, it's a fine, fine day," she said, "fine day to be home, it's a fine, fine day, a mild blue day, a mild looking sky—"

I stood there satisfied and remembering what Pa had once told me - *Mamie is in you and you in Mamie, and both of you are limbs of the organ of life and the organ is the Over-Soul, the Deity under your feet and over your head and in every breath.*

And it was all of that, and more. The two of us touching, that face smiling kindly down on me as it had before - that face that would be with me so long as film and the projector's power would bring her forth. Forever? Well, at least until the day, somewhere waiting in the future, when I would finally join her at the Brule.

DUFF BRENNA is the author of *The Book of Mamie*, which won the prestigious AWP Award for Best Novel; *The Holy Book of the Beard*; *Too Cool*, a New York Times Notable Book; *The Altar of the Body*, which won the Editors Prize Favorite Book of the Year Award given by the South Florida Sun-Sentinel and also received the San Diego Writers Prize in 2002. He is the recipient of an NEA grant, Milwaukee Magazine's Fiction Award, and a Pushcart Prize Honorable Mention for the publication of a chapter from *The Altar of the Body*. His fifth novel, *The Willow Man*, was launched in October 2005. The first trade paper edition of *Mamie* is being published by Wordcraft of Oregon in March 2006. A Minnesota native and onetime Wisconsin dairy farmer, Duff Brenna is now a freelance writer and Professor Emeritus of English literature and creative writing at California State University, San Marcos.

FROM OUR BACKLIST

Contagion and Other Stories, Brian Evenson, 1-877655-34-1, $11. Includes the 1998 O'Henry Award winning story, "Two Brothers," and O'Henry runnerup, "The Language of Polygamy."
"*Contagion* remains one of the most strange and poweful books of the new millenium." – Bob Ehrenreich, The Believer #2, May 2003

Smoking Mirror Blues, novel, Ernest Hogan, 1-877655-37-6, $12.
"One of 2001's best sf novels." – Claude Lalumière, sfsite.com

Realism & Other Illusions: Essays on the Craft of Fiction, Thomas E. Kennedy, 1-877655-38-4, $12.
One of ePublisher's Weekly's best fifteen nonfiction books of 2002.

Red Spider White Web, novel, Misha Nogha, 1-877655-29-5, the first U.S. trade edition of 1990 finalist for the Arthur C. Clarke Award.
"Misha Nogha's *Red Spider White Web* is arguably the definitive feminist cyberpunk text, a searing work that crashes upon the reader like a catastrophe." – Alan DeNiro , Rain Taxi On-Line Edition, Fall 2003

Molecular Jam, poems, Dan Raphael, 1-877655-21-X, (out of print), which included the 1995 Rhysling Award winning poem, "Skin of Glass."
"There is a new way to write and a new way to read the world in all its stupefying beauty and Dan Raphael is leading the way in." – Charles Potts

West of Paradise, poems, George Venn, 1-877655-31-7, $12, finalist for the 2000 Oregon Book Award for Poetry.
"This is poetry of big love, great heart. George Venn's scale is immense and inclusive...The only other poet I know whose work has such range is Tom McGrath, who, like George Venn, told the stories of his region in such a way as to make them magical, luminous and permanent..." – James Bertolino

I Am Madagascar: On Moving West from New England, poems, Ellen Waterston, 1-877655-41-4, $10 (second edition), winner of the 2005 Willa Award for Poetry.
"This slim, plain-clothes volume attests to poetry's power to distill experiences down to their emotional essence." – Karen McCowen, The Register-Guard (Eugene)

Check out other titles at:
www.wordcraftoforegon.com